THE MAS
INNOCENTS

The continuing voyages of HMS SURPRISE

ALAN LAWRENCE

Huzza! Hodgson, we are going,
Our embargo's off at last;
Favourable breezes blowing
Bend the canvass oer the mast.
From aloft the signal's streaming,
Hark! the farewell gun is fired;
Women screeching, tars blaspheming,
Tell us that our time's expired.
Here's a rascal
Come to task all,
Prying from the custom-house;
Trunks unpacking
Cases cracking,
Not a corner for a mouse
'Scapes unsearch'd amid the racket,
Ere we sail on board the Packet.

Now at length we're off for Turkey,
Lord knows when we shall come back!
Breezes foul and tempests murky
May unship us in a crack.
But, since life at most a jest is,
As philosophers allow,
Still to laugh by far the best is,
Then laugh on—as I do now.
Laugh at all things,
Great and small things,
Sick or well, at sea or shore;
While we're quaffing,
Let's have laughing—
Who the devil cares for more?—
Some good wine! and who would lack it,
Ev'n on board the Lisbon Packet?

Lines to Mr. Hodgson
Lord Byron: on leaving Falmouth in 1809.

THE MASSACRE OF INNOCENTS
The continuing voyages of HMS SURPRISE

The isles of Greece, the Isles of Greece!
Where burning Sappho loved and sung,
Where grew the arts of war and peace,
Where Delos rose, and Phoebus sprung!
Eternal summer gilds them yet,
But all, except their sun, is set.

Lord Byron
1788-1824

A tale of the struggle for Greek independence by
ALAN LAWRENCE

Mainsail Voyages Press Ltd, Publishers,
Hartland Forest, Devonshire

www.mainsailvoyagespress.com

THE MASSACRE OF INNOCENTS

The continuing voyages of HMS SURPRISE

This *second* edition is copyright (c) Alan Lawrence 2014 and 2017. Published by Mainsail Voyages Press Ltd, Hartland Forest, Bideford, Devon, EX39 5RA. Alan Lawrence asserts the right to be identified as the author of this work in accordance with the Copyright, Designs and Patents Act 1988. The reader may note that this book is written by Alan Lawrence. It is not authorised, licensed or endorsed by Patrick O'Brian's family, agent or publishers. There is no association with any of those parties.

ISBN-13   978-0-9576698-3-3

Story text typeset in Times New Roman 11 point.

Printed and bound by CPI Group (UK) Ltd, Croydon, CR0 4YY

Cover painting by Ivan Aivazovsky:

'The Battle of Chesme at night',

Photograph courtesy of www.russianpaintings.net;

Cover comment by David Taylor, Cheshire;

The Reef Knot graphic in this book is courtesy of and copyright (c) United States Power Squadrons 2006

**The continuing voyages of HMS SURPRISE,
the series**

The Massacre of Innocents   *(first edition 2014,
second edition 2017)*

Freedom or Death   *(2017)*

*was originally published split within the lengthy first
editions of the preceding and succeeding titles, both of
which have been abridged for the second editions*

The Fireships of Gerontas   *(first edition 2016,
second edition 2017)*

The Aftermath of Devastation   *(2017)*

THE MASSACRE OF INNOCENTS

The continuing voyages of HMS SURPRISE

A FOREWORD BY THE AUTHOR

This historical novel is founded upon the continuing voyages of *HMS Surprise* – not the 28-gun ship of 1796 in Patrick O'Brian's marvellous fictional series (a ship design based on the captured French ship *Unité*) but the later 38-gun, Leda-class frigate of 1812 (also a design based on another captured French frigate, *Hebé*). This latter *Surprise*, though a relatively young ship, lay at Plymouth Dock in 1822, about to be reduced to a prison hulk. In this story her fate takes its fictional turn for the better. To our good fortune her sister ships, *Trincomalee* and *Unicorn,* remain preserved in Hartlepool and Dundee respectively.

I fondly imagined for years that the many fans of Patrick O'Brian's seafaring tales of Jack Aubrey and Stephen Maturin sorely lamented, as did I, the end of his wonderful, utterly exceptional stories and hugely missed those two warm and intensely fascinating individuals, characters always of the most engaging interest while possessed of the most human of personalities, for that surely was O'Brian's gift: Jack Aubrey and Stephen Maturin never resembled superheroes; rather, in their warmth and fallibility, they endeared themselves to us as any current personality might well do, and the gulf of two hundred years between their (fictional) lives and ours simply faded away. With no prospect (sadly) of any further historical novels from Patrick O'Brian and missing his characters so much myself, I decided I must write a sequel so as to bring them back, to enjoy their company all over again. After writing the first draft and by then in a dialogue with his estate, I was made aware of Patrick O'Brian's wish that no sequel to his series should be published, and hence a different course was subsequently plotted, the finished result being no longer a faithful reproduction of his ingredients but a book with different characters, though one which still draws its inspiration of form and flavour from his genius.

For any novelist the writing of historical seafaring tales set in the early 19th century is to follow in the footsteps of and to strive for the literary heights reached by the author so appropriately described as *"the greatest historical novelist of all time"*. It most certainly represents a challenge of the very first order. Who would honestly conceive that there could be two writers of his ilk? Certainly not I, and so this book could never have become one that reads as if written by the master himself. I make no claim of attaining his glorious pinnacle; it would plainly be an unrealistic aspiration. Consequently, the reader must be content with a historically detailed, seafaring tale of adventure, a story of battle and fascinating exchanges between all aboard ship, a tale which chronologically follows the enthralling Aubrey & Maturin novels and hence a story which might well have been conceived by O'Brian had he been blessed with more time to continue his wonders.

The officers of the early nineteenth-century Royal Navy were drawn from every part of England, Scotland, Wales and Ireland (including the present Republic). It has been estimated that one in eight officers were Irish (though Catholics, if they had neither renounced nor concealed their faith, were not accepted) and that Scots represented a higher per capita ratio of officers to population origin than the Irish. The author therefore feels perfectly justified in enlisting a Scot as first lieutenant to serve alongside his Irish captain. Scots too were well represented as ships' surgeons in those times, and another has come aboard for this story.

This tale, a detailed and interwoven fabric of history and fiction, is set in the early nineteenth-century war of Greek independence. From the historical detail herein I hope that the reader may find his or her own interest in the history of that period stimulated to find out more, as I did. The subject matter of this novel, generally the war fought for the independence of Greece and the story of the Philhellenes, is seldom taught (except in Greece) and hence appears to be little known in any great detail outside the most narrow of academic interest. Yet it presents a most suitable subject for a work of historical naval fiction.

The conflict was a long one but this story must necessarily restrict itself to a very few of the significant and the minor naval engagements, detailed references to many of which are singularly few and hard to find even in these days of the facility of the web. Conversely, there are numerous contemporary books and reports from the Philhellenes themselves, the ones by Gordon and by Finlay being remarkably detailed. Two more modern accounts are well worth reading: *That Greece Might be Free* (1972) by William St. Clair, an excellent book and one which recounts the exploits of the Philhellenes of all nationalities; and the more general 2011 book by David Brewer, *The Greek War of Independence*. For an authentic description of life at sea in the early nineteenth century and battle in all its gruesome detail, it would be hard to surpass Roy Adkins' superb book, *Trafalgar*.

Adding to the treasure trove of actual events that the historical novelist is blessed with are the real people of those times, many of whom grace this book. It is particularly pleasing to develop this rich *mother lode* into brief but colourful appearances within the story, the places and timing of which, if not the actualité, accord with the known detail of their lives. Lord Byron is one such person, and the author has taken the liberty of including a few words of simple yet sublime prose which Byron himself wrote within his journal for the 17th October 1823 describing his quietude in Cephalonia some weeks before he departed for his final destiny in Missolonghi.

A selected verse of Byron's famous poem (within a poem) *The Isles of Greece* (within Canto III of *Don Juan)* precedes each chapter, the first verse being on the front title page. Lord Milton's stirring address to the formative London Greek Committee on 3rd May 1823 is similarly reproduced verbatim. The reader may also perceive the influence of that engaging wit Mark Twain gracing a few of these pages.

Notwithstanding that this is a work of fiction, the author has strived for the inclusion of many real historical events throughout the story. It is little realised, for example, that the phrase *'truth is stranger than fiction',* now in commonplace use, actually originated from Lord Byron. The capture of Byron's companion, Count Gamba, by the Turks (which is described in this book) was a real event, and there surely cannot be anything stranger in fiction than the true tale of the Turk captain fortunately recognising his Greek captive counterpart, his own former rescuer, after an interval of fully fifteen years.

The historical researcher's task is made more difficult by the many and varied names which almost all the Greek, Turkish and other locations referred to within this story have possessed, not only since the early nineteenth century when these events occurred, but from centuries beforehand when these lands and islands were within the grasp of a succession of colonial overlords, including Genoese, Venetians and Ottomans. For contemporary veracity many Greek places are referred to in this story principally by their then still widely used Venetian names, their Greek names generally only being used when mentioned by Greeks. These include, with today's name following:

Candia / Crete
Cape San Maria / Cape Mycale (Turkey)
Cerigo / Cythera
Cephalonia / Kefalonia
Colones / Pythagoras (Samos)
Leghorn / Livorno (Italy)
Modon / Methoni
The Morea / The Peloponnese
Nauplia / Nafplio
Scala Nova / Kusadasi (Turkey)
Thira / Santorini

The author would like to thank the following people, all experts of the first rate on their subjects, for their courteous and helpful assistance: Hugh Ferguson on Paganini, Peter Cochran on Lord Byron, the immensely helpful and enthusiastic Elaine Vallianou on all aspects of Kefalonia. Thanks are also due to Edward Gaskell for encouragement in the early days, Don Fiander for consent to use the Reef Knot graphic, Ivan Gorshkov for the cover photograph, Paul Jones and Geoff Fisher for much help with the cover, Jackie Taft for editing help; Anna Ravano, Anthony Gary Brown and Larry Finch for valuable comments on the emerging book; Don Seltzer and Mark Myers - both invaluable - for considerable ship- and sail-handling guidance; a very helpful David Lilley, HMS Trincomalee shipwright; Margaret Muir, David Hayes (webmaster at *www.historicnavalfiction.com*), my brother Geoff who long ago introduced me to the inspiring O'Brian novels, my son Alastair who managed to prise me away from prevarication disguised as continuing research for this book with a wholly appropriate "Just get on with it!" and last but far from least: heartfelt thanks are due to my love and greatest supporter, Sally.

With just a very little of artist's license, the first and third verses of the song in chapter four are the author's modest adaptation of the traditional song *Mary of Dungloe*, an Irish song originally penned in 1936 by a Donegal stonemason, Pádraig Mac Cumhaill. The second verse is from *The Setting*, a marvellous song from Ralph McTell. The two songs are customarily performed melded together by that musical treasure of the south-west of England, *Show of Hands*.

The beautiful poem in chapter six was written by Sally's mother, the late, much loved and missed Caroline Byron; bless her.

At the end of the book there is a glossary of contemporary words occurring within the story with which the reader new to the naval historical world may be unfamiliar.

This book is dedicated to all those who have served in the Royal Navy, past and present; to whom - lest we forget - our debt is immeasurable.

Give you joy, shipmate! Come aboard! Voyage with HMS Surprise! Share her crew's reminiscences in familiar old haunts and revel too in their exciting new adventures. Come aboard! Swiftly now, there is not a moment to be lost!

Alan Lawrence   *April 2014*

THE MASSACRE OF INNOCENTS
The continuing voyages of HMS SURPRISE
HISTORICAL NOTE

On the 24th of February 1582, Pope Gregory, by decree, determined that the Catholic world would abandon the Julian Calendar, introduced by Julius Caesar in 45BC, and change to the Gregorian Calendar after October 4th (of the Julian) when the date next day would be October 15th (of the Gregorian), ten days therefore being lost from that year's calendar. The two calendars differ only in the rule for leap years. The Julian has a leap year every fourth year while the Gregorian also has a leap year every fourth year except in century years not exactly divisible by 400. The Julian year therefore averages (over four years) 365 and one quarter days in length while the Gregorian year (averaged over 128 years) is 365 days exactly, and so after every 128 years (after 45BC) the date in the Julian calendar lags one further day behind the Gregorian.

Those regions of the early Americas, including lands now part of the United States and influenced by the colonising Catholic states of France and Spain, changed over in 1582 as per the Pope's edict, but the originally British colonised States changed over when Britain did herself, in 1752, losing eleven days from that year's calendar. Greece, however, not independent until 1829, did not make the change until as late as 1923. The reader of Greek history may therefore be presented with Julian dates differing from dates referred to by other sources using the Gregorian calendar, the same day having two dates twelve days apart. The sea battle off the Greek island of Samos, for example, is sometimes quoted as having happened on 5th/17th August 1824. The battle did not take thirteen days! The Julian (Greek history) date being 5th August and the Gregorian (British history) date being 17th August, which was the date on which the climax of the six-day battle was fought, it having started on the 12th.

1 Flying jib
2 Jib
3 Fore topmast staysail
4 Fore staysail
5 Foresail, or course
6 Fore topsail
7 Fore topgallant
8 Mainstaysail
9 Main topmast staysail
10 Middle staysail
11 Main topgallant staysail

12 Mainsail, or course
13 Maintopsail
14 Main topgallant
15 Mizzen staysail
16 Mizzen topmast staysail
17 Mizzen topgallant staysail
18 Mizzen sail
19 Spanker
20 Mizzen topsail
21 Mizzen topgallant

The sails of a square-rigged ship, hung out to dry in a calm.   *Source: Serres, Liber Nauticus.*

Chapter One

The Scian and the Teian muse,
The hero's harp, the lover's lute,
Have found the fame your shores refuse;
Their place of birth alone is mute
To sounds which echo further west
Than your sires' 'Islands of the Blest'

Thursday 1ˢᵗ May 1823   *Westminster, London*

The public saloon of the Feathers tavern, off the Strand and within the Liberty of Westminster, a very dimly illuminated room even approaching the top of the day, was filled with the drifting smoke from Mrs O'Donnell's faltering efforts to rejuvenate the smouldering logs on the stone flags of the hearth, near to which in a much creased, green leather armchair sat a nondescript man of large stature and indeterminate age, dressed in even less determinate and somewhat crumpled attire, slumbering fitfully, coughing occasionally, but resisting persistently any inclination to fully wake or shift despite the rising clamour and bustle of the growing preparations for the customary midday clientele.

The Feathers tavern being a particularly convenient and welcoming hostelry for visitors to the nearby grand offices of State was also oft frequented by actors and publishers, as well as politicians of several inclinations and generally fewer principles, but the man between sleeping and waking states in the chair was not of that ilk. Lieutenant Duncan Macleod - albeit a relatively seldom visitor, having been in near all the past twenty years more often than not to be found on board one or other of His Majesty's ships – was almost a member of the extended family of genial hosts, headed by Mrs O'Donnell, who served the Feathers clientele so personably, and he was directly responsible for the presence at the Feathers of the two attractive young ladies, Sandra and Emma, his twin nieces from the isle of Lewis, now busily serving the food, the aroma of which appetisingly permeated the room. However, it was the matronly presence of Mrs O'Donnell that tipped the scales in favour of waking, her optimistic if none too careful crashing deposit of a very large log sending the consequent explosion of sparks and crackling embers cascading out from the hearth towards the fireside armchair and its occupant.

'Ah, Mr Macleod; to be sure 'tis yourself, sir. A pleasure to see you this fine morning, indeed it is. Would you care at all for coffee?'

The nondescript figure looked up. 'Thank ye kindly, Mrs O'Donnell. A more welcome and roborative beverage I cannae think of at present. The stronger the better, if ye will... and perhaps a toasted muffin might be forthcoming?'

'Yes, sir; which the pot and butter have been a'waitin' these five minutes past.'

'I confess to a grand hunger.'

'Here you are, sir, and why ain't you a'sleepin' in our best room?' from Mrs O'Donnell with the coffee pot and a huge plate of hot, buttered muffins a few minutes later, fending off the keen interest of Sandra and Emma, neither of whom had previously realised it had been Macleod slumbering in the chair.

'Bless ye, Mrs O'Donnell. It was a long and most exhausting journey these past four days. An uncomfortable crossing on the packet from Stornoway, a horse through the Highlands, a tiring coach journey from Edinburgh, another post down from Nottingham yesterday, and so I am brought here long past midnight. Being so very cold and damp I partook of just a bite of supper... grateful for this fire... with a wee dram of the malt, and then I fell asleep until just now.'

Mrs O'Donnell, who knew the lieutenant well of old, had the shrewd conviction that he had eaten nothing at all for his supper, certainly no breakfast since, and that he had simply fallen asleep in his clothes whilst warming in front of the fire, and likely very soon after his arrival. 'I will send Sandra to air you a room, sir, d'reckly. Come along you two, leave the gentleman to his coffee, and see now to your duties. You can attend him later.'

2

'Thankee again, but I must away at two o'clock for a most important assignation. I will return this evening, and 'tis to be hoped Captain O'Connor will be here to join me. Please prepare supper for eight o'clock, Mrs O'Donnell. His Majesty's captains dinnae care to eat later.' The man in the chair yawned wide, smiled at Mrs O'Donnell and relapsed into a contented doze.

In that awakening state between indistinct haze and sharp focus, his thoughts of hunger banished with some difficulty, a tired Lieutenant Duncan Macleod contemplated the events of the recent few days and the brief letter he had received with uncomprehending astonishment from no less illustrious a person than Lord Melville, First Lord of the Admiralty. It was exceedingly fortunate that the letter had reached him, since for almost two weeks beforehand he had been contemplating leaving his Lewis croft, his half-pay of eighteen pounds fifteen shillings per quarter proving woefully inadequate to eke out even the most parsimonious existence on the windswept, bleak four acres of moor that represented his home on that northernmost Hebridean island.

He had previously determined to accept the offer he had long held in abeyance – command of the tiniest of merchant vessels, a Buckie-built scaffie, plying her trade, fishing, around the outlying Hebridean islands - a position to which was attached the princely pay of seven pounds a month. Her retiring master had long ago submitted his retirement resignation to MacDonald of Stornoway, her long-time owner, and Macleod's departure - so abruptly and unexpectedly presented after his initial and grateful acceptance of employment - had met with the stony faces of men who held long memories in small places. His interests were, he had discovered, more than life on Lewis could offer him. He had concluded during his ruminations through a cold, wet winter, huddled and often shivering in front of a smoky hearth fire for its meagre warmth – his peat stocks being so damp – that his interests lay in a much broader spectrum. Although a keen participant in and a proponent of the traditional folk music of the Western Isles and of Scotland generally and a Gaelic speaker, he held a passionate interest too in the sketching and painting of landscapes; it was a pastime he had been able to indulge himself in during many voyages throughout the Mediterranean and across all the oceans. He now longed so dearly for the company of his shipmates of those long years serving in the Royal Navy during the testing times of struggle against the Corsican tyrant: his very good friends Captain Patrick O'Connor, a Galwayman, and Doctor Simon Ferguson, ship's surgeon, a fellow Scot who hailed from Mull.

For the four years from September 1815, after the end of the interminable strife to counter Napoleon, O'Connor had commanded and the three friends had served aboard *Tenedos*, a Chatham-built, 38-gun frigate of the Leda class. Post-war the Admiralty had designated Falmouth as her home port. After a summer in the Mediterranean in the year 'sixteen, she had patrolled on the South Atlantic station until the year 'nineteen when she had paid off from active service for the final time and gone into ordinary, laid up at Chatham. The next two years Duncan Macleod had spent at O'Connor's fifteen-acre farm on the Atlantic coast near the village of Claddaghduff in Connemara, County Galway.

After that first two years ashore the captain and lieutenant, the closest of companions, had gone their different ways: Macleod had returned to Lewis with his wife, who was also O'Connor's sister-in-law, and his daughter to pick up the pieces of his neglected Hebridean croft, to draw and to paint, the wild and rugged landscapes of Harris and the Uists being his particular fascination. Pat O'Connor had remained on his small farm to try to scratch out a living on half-pay. Their other firm companion, Doctor Simon Ferguson, formerly surgeon aboard *Tenedos* and also a Gaelic speaker, had returned to his adopted Plymouth Dock where employment was assured with a local doctor and fellow of the Royal College of Surgeons, Cornelius Tripe. The two medical men served the seafaring community founded on the Royal Navy base. Very little seafaring was now called for by their Lordships as post-war Admiralty budgets were severely trimmed, numerous ships decommissioned, experienced crews laid off, many captains and even admirals pensioned off.

It was therefore with rising joy and great expectation that Macleod looked forward to meeting again with his close friend and captain of the Napoleonic war years, Melville hinting in his unexpected and mysterious letter that O'Connor would also be summoned by the First Lord. Why, he asked himself, had he - a lowly lieutenant - received such a letter from Lord Melville, requesting his earliest attendance in London and at Melville's home rather than at his office in the Admiralty? He had not the slightest clue to the purpose of the request. Though he had, in parallel with his duties as *Tenedos's* first lieutenant, sent periodic written reports on political developments and sentiments from some of the South Atlantic ports that *Tenedos* had visited to a longstanding friend at the Admiralty, never before had he received a communication from such exalted heights. The message had fortuitously reached him by messenger on the final day of his preparation for departure from his tiny croft. His interest piqued, he had switched his journey to London rather than, as he had planned, assuming command of the forty-two feet, larch on oak-built, herring lugger, *Monica*; long past her prime, but sound enough at least to ply her trade, fishing, during the summer months around the waters of the Hebrides.

The fire in the hearth now blazed vigorously, the smoke had cleared and the hubbub in the room had risen considerably as the number of patrons swelled. It was 2 p.m. and Macleod savoured the last of his coffee and determined to walk the short distance to Melville's house and to gainfully use the blessing of a warm and sunny spring day to contemplate his unexpected summons from professional Royal Navy retirement – as life on half-pay had long seemed. His old uniform had been in his sea-chest in his damp croft for several years and had been lost long ago to the mould, so he consoled himself that, as his invitation was seemingly of an unofficial nature to Lord Melville's private residence and the First Lord not being a commissioned Royal Navy officer, he might be forgiven its absence. Throwing on his old, still damp cape and donning a nondescript and very weather-beaten even older hat Macleod left the Feathers and stepped out purposefully along the Strand towards his mysterious appointment.

What he did not know was that Captain Patrick O'Connor was strolling down the Strand a bare two hundred yards behind him. His friend, a man of modest height and stature with flame-red hair, had arrived in London early that morning and had all the time in the world before his own appointment. He was immersed in pondering his recall from Connemara; summoned by his third cousin, George Canning, the Foreign Secretary; his presence in person also requested by Melville on the morrow. He walked west down the Strand, along the Mall, turned right into Constitution Hill and thence along Brompton Road, down Cromwell Road and so to Gloucester Lodge, a brisk walk of a pleasant hour and a half in the clement Spring weather.

'What's afoot?' O'Connor mused as he knocked twice and waited for the door to open. The formally attired porter responded immediately and, forewarned of his arrival, escorted him into the drawing room.

'Ah, O'Connor; how wonderful to see you again,' said Canning, a distinguished looking, immaculately attired gentleman in his early fifties, offering his outstretched hand.

'And yourself, indeed it is too, sir,' replied O'Connor, smiling.

The distant relatives warmly shook hands and gazed for a few moments at each other. Their long-deceased fathers had been the firmest of friends for many years and second cousins. In but an instant, with just that hint of warm inflection in their voices, they achieved that cordiality customarily requiring of years of friendship – the Irishman from remote Connemara and the respected statesman who considered himself to be an Irishman born in London, his family hailing from County Londonderry.

'Come in, come in,' enthused Canning, and closed the door. 'Come upstairs to the library. Allow me to take your cape and hat. It is a rare day that I find I am here near alone. Mrs Malone is away to her sick daughter... and so there is only Albert the porter to attend us.' Settling into an armchair in front of the coal fire O'Connor was presented with a generous measure of fine old brandy before Canning sat in the other chair, gazing as if in inspection of his cousin, the sight so pleasurable after the long absence. Several minutes passed, both sipping their brandies, until finally he spoke, the warmth in his voice so very evident, 'Welcome, welcome, dear cousin. It is so good to see you again. When was the last time? So long ago, it escapes me. Was it five years, perhaps six or even seven? I hope that you are keeping well.'

'Tolerably so, sir; and yourself? How is Mrs Canning?' O'Connor suppressed his curiosity whilst he keenly awaited Canning's expected revelations.

'Myself? Alas, whilst the mind is as vigorous as ever, one laments that the body is less so with advancing years. But I am still in relatively fine fettle. Mrs Canning is well, thank you.'

'And my cousins?'

'You doubtless collect that George died but three years ago of the consumption. I grieve so much for him still. William is a lieutenant himself now, in His Majesty's service... aboard a frigate, *Venus*. Charles and Harriet are well, thank you. How are Sinéad and the children?'

Thursday 1ˢᵗ May 1823, 3 p.m.　　*Arlington Street, Westminster*

In his office at home an uncomfortable Lord Melville and a nervous Duncan Macleod had made their formal greetings and sat sipping tea, a grandfather clock ticking loudly in the background, each contemplating the other and passing a few moments in that expectant pause that frequently precedes the subject at hand. Eventually, the moment now pressing upon them, Melville, his considerations apparently satisfied, set down his own cup. 'Lieutenant Macleod, how do you do? My apologies for asking your presence here at such short notice. It is exceedingly good of you to come up from the Isles so swiftly. It is a matter of some urgency, my letter prompted by the Board... their Lordships making it plain that immediacy was to be the prime consideration. In fact,' he said in a low, significant voice, 'this is also a matter of interest to the Foreign Secretary who particularly desires that I tell him the results of this interview when we dine this evening.'

Macleod felt overwhelmed by the importance that Melville seemingly attached to his attendance and could say nothing. He began to perspire, just a very little. His back itched unbearably but he did not dare scratch it, and his heartbeat seemed to pulse through his every thought. The First Lord, sensing his visitor's discomfort or perhaps his intimidation, continued in a more conversational, re-assuring tone, 'Doubtless you are wondering my purpose in requesting your presence? I thank you again for your swift attendance; most courteous of you, and such a long journey in but a very few days.' Macleod simply stared at his host, nodding as Melville continued, 'You will collect it was your most commendable report to their Lordships in respect of the Tucumán declaration of the United Provinces in the year 'sixteen which engaged my personal interest in your - will I say-*irregular* services. May I say that your subsequent reports from the South Atlantic on the Falkland Islands' developments were of the greatest of interest to me?' Melville looked closely at his visitor, 'Would you care for more tea?'

Macleod mumbled his acceptance, conscious of but trying hard to avoid the appearance of simply staring at Melville, his mind whirring at he strived to think what conceivable further interest in him Melville might reveal.

'Perhaps, Macleod, we now have need of you again in a similar capacity. I will explain my letter... a most intriguing matter was recently expounded to me, one which only most slowly has His Majesty's Government come to consider as worthy of the wholehearted endeavours of the Royal Navy. It is one for which I can perceive but two individuals suited to such aspirations. The first is Lord Cochrane, who has exhibited the most exemplary success in similar endeavours in the service of Chile... but any decision as to his present suitability must rest in the delicate deliberations of the highest political circles... and I can say no more. You will be acquainted with the second, an individual well known to yourself. I am meeting with him tomorrow afternoon, yet I find myself uncomfortably reticent to postulate said matter to the officer in question in my capacity as First Lord, having only the slightest of personal acquaintance with the gentleman... and that many years ago. I find myself most uncomfortable indeed, and so my letter to you was ...' Melville paused briefly in his halting preamble as the servant entered with the teapot. He leafed through the file of papers on his desk for some minutes. After pouring the tea he pressed on in a somewhat uncertain tone whilst continuing to peruse the file. 'Perhaps I am grasping at straws, but no better person than you yourself could guide me towards how best to broach a somewhat unusual proposition to your friend and brother officer. Yet, perhaps the task and the man may not be suited at the present time? He is a young man still... and it may be too early in the career of ... of your friend to merit consideration... but I am talking in irritating riddles.'

'Not at all, sir; celerity is, I find, nae always the friend of discourse. Pray take your time,' said Macleod cautiously, finding his tongue and successfully concealing his growing curiosity.

Melville looked up from studying the file on his desk, his tone firming, 'I understand from your official service record that you have served for many years with Captain Patrick O'Connor?'

'Why, aye indeed, sir. He is an officer I have been most pleased to serve with; indeed, he is the very finest I have ever found, and in so doing we are now become the firmest of friends. I would most dearly wish to depart to sea with him on the first tide of the morrow, and I believe O'Connor himself would share my feelings about a ship again, my Lord.' Macleod nodded emphatically, as if in reinforcement of his affirmation, his mind striving to find the significance in Melville's words.

'That is indeed warm testimony to your captain... and your service with Captain O'Connor was for fifteen years I note. Your own Royal Navy service record is quite unblemished, your conduct unassailable, your occasional... *covert* service to their Lordships of inestimable value, and I note too that with O'Connor you have represented well their Lordships on more than one occasion when called upon for - will I say - matters more requiring of diplomacy in some of our more far-flung outposts on the Imperial periphery. Indeed, your friend has recommended and requested of their Lordships that your step be granted. I note that *Tenedos*, Captain O'Connor in command and with your good self, peaceably resolved that aggravating little spat five or so years ago with the American sealers on Saunders Island. There's many as have received their promotion for much less. I will therefore add my own recommendation for your step, late as you may consider it to be.'

'Why, thankee... thankee sir; that is most gracious of your Lordship,' a pleased and surprised Macleod exclaimed his thanks, the meeting taking the most unexpected but welcome turn.

'I will confide in you in this matter,' Melville lowered his voice to a whisper and pushed the file on his desk to one side. 'It is one on which I have recently been asked my opinion by the Foreign Secretary. Your colleague, it has been mooted, may be suited to a role which is but recently emerging. You will be familiar with the ... the quite *independent* service of Lord Cochrane several years ago in Chile with the frigate *O'Higgins*. Their Lordships are considering whether such a similar scenario might arise in the near future, *the very near future*, and whether another officer suited to a venture of that nature, a suitable ship too, might be forthcoming. His Majesty's Government has observed the developing deterioration in the Ottoman provinces of Greece; that is our area of interest. Political interest is rising in all the states of Europe, most particularly directly across the Channel. Contingency planning it is, Macleod. Naturally His Majesty's Government cannot condone serving officers entering into such a venture... which would be quite contrary to the Foreign Enlistment Act; however, *retired* officers and other persons *quite outside* His Majesty's Service would be perfectly and properly entitled to serve. Macleod simply stared, speechless, as Melville continued. 'It is plain that their Lordships cannot order any serving officer to such a post were they minded to do so, and hence I find this a most uncomfortable task indeed... and you are therefore to consider our discussion is not of an official nature. Hence before my interview with Captain O'Connor on the morrow, when I intend to ask of his interest, I have asked you here to invite your opinion of his likely inclinations about such a proposal; entirely in confidence of course, and our private conversation, most unorthodox as it is, must never be revealed to any person.'

The First Lord now staring pointedly at him, self-evidently awaiting his response, Macleod, striving to grasp the complex extent of what Melville had asked him and feeling well out of his depth, was sparked to reply, 'Sir, what ye say is of such import and substance that I cannae conceivably offer my own opinion of the likely interest of such a venture to O'Connor.' He continued cautiously, somewhat taken aback by the gravity of what he had just heard, 'From his recent letters, which are of course confidential and from which I cannae quote excepting in only the most innocuous of generalities, I might conclude that life in Connemara with nae sea-going commission these past few years has nae sat well with him. He is a sailor through and through, certainly nae farmer, and so the economies of the fleet lie hard with him. He is surely the most temperate of men in his considerations, none more so, and I have nae doubt that such a proposal would receive the most patient reception.'

'It is pleasing to hear that O'Connor holds you in his confidence, and perhaps therein lies the opportunity to ascertain any likelihood of his interest in a scheme such as this,' said Melville with less than complete conviction, though with his purpose now blindingly clear and his voice as close to plaintive as ever it might be, he pressed on, 'Would it not be too great an imposition to ask you to moot the idea... perhaps in the most cautious of terms... perhaps too to express the search, *the requirement* for a senior naval officer in terms of the third person? Would such allow O'Connor to avoid any answer which might be embarrassing to either of you?' His somewhat awkward request made, Melville relapsed into thoughtful silence, leaning back in his chair. He sipped the last of his tea, now cold, allowed his head to droop as if to leave his visitor a moment to ponder, to collect his thoughts, the mood of the meeting seeming to slip into uncertainty as he glanced surreptitiously towards his visitor, awaiting his response, the significance of his request so very important.

Macleod, having gazed at his hands for several minutes, the clock ticking so slowly but loudly in the background even as his mind raced, looked directly at the First Lord. He so much did not wish to disappoint with his answer. 'I am, fortuitously, taking supper with O'Connor this evening, sir. Perhaps it might be a timely moment to expound upon the subject?' This was said in a tone of some uncertainty, of caution, with as much commitment as he could summon.

Melville brightened, 'Capital, capital, Macleod; that would be most obliging of you. Then there is but one other matter to speak of, and I will be brief if you are to be at your abode ere dusk; it is near five o'clock now. A new body of political interest has been formed, and this *Greek Committee* is meeting on Saturday at noon at an inn in the Liberty of the Savoy... at the Crown and Anchor on the Strand. Should your discussion spark any interest with O'Connor... and failing any immediate arrangement with him whilst you are both here in London, it would seem to be an ideal moment to attend the Committee and gain a grasp of what these gentlemen are about: whether it be practical in substance or mere wind and hot air. Were you also to accompany him to Greece, reports from that place with the proven veracity we came to expect of you from the South Atlantic would be of the utmost value to their Lordships. It would serve them well were you to associate yourself with the emerging Greek authorities, to gain and report some cognisance of their naval officers and capabilities.'

'Sir, I thank ye for your kind words and your pledge to support my step. I will do all I can to help ye. I find myself likely late for supper already... aye... and must away speedily ere the footpads and never do well loiterers in the vicinity are emboldened by the dusk. I thank ye for sharing your confidences with me and,' after a thoughtful pause, 'whilst I cannae speak for O'Connor, I hope I may see him supporting your proposal. I believe I may assure ye that we shall both attend the Committee,' Macleod volunteered, taking his cape and hat from the porter, a degree of normality returning to his thoughts, to the timbre of his voice, the interview coming to its close, his spirits bouyant, indeed soaring; his step now assured - well, almost. In his wildest of dreams he could never have conceived the day this was proving to be.

'I bid you good day and please accept my thanks for your time and your earnest considerations,' said Melville in the most cordial of tone before the porter closed the door.

Macleod set off with a brisk step in order to overtake the approaching gloaming and in hope of reaching the Feathers in the last fading vestiges of daylight, his mind whirling in the most vivid maelstrom of thoughts and emotions.

Thursday 1ˢᵗ May 1823, 4 p.m.   *Gloucester Court, Brompton*

At Gloucester Court George Canning continued his somewhat rambling briefing, 'It seems only yesterday that we were rid of Bonaparte and the prospects for more peaceable times were brightening, yet once again the French have crossed the Bidassoa and the Pyrenees into Spain – *have they no shame?* But even that, cousin, is not the reason for my murmurings as I will seek to reveal. No, much further away than Spain another spark has ignited and appears to be poised to burst into a flame which could have untold consequences for the interests of His Majesty's Government... most likely adverse ones, O'Connor. Such consequences remain unpredictable, the magnitude of them uncertain. The likely celerity of the changes too is unknown... and yet it might have been reasonably foreseen that these changes have been long in coming and were surely destined to come about, notwithstanding the very substantial forces aligned to resist them.'

Patrick O'Connor, knowing his cousin well of old and aware that any interjection would likely not be well received, simply sat and listened as Canning continued in full flow. 'The Ottoman Empire, I have no doubt, is creaking like an old and rusty hinge in need of oil. The Turks are under pressure from the Russians in respect of the Black Sea. Their Egyptian fiefdom is subservient in title but increasingly less so in practical matters of control...

and now their Greek subjects are revolting against the Turk yoke. The Turk economy has not been a success for some years and the Sultan has had recourse to print new money to fund his military apparatus, with the consequent debasement of the piastre, and so his credit is no longer considered sound in London. He can consequently ill afford to lose his Greek provinces. Even the Janissaries have revolted and been put down. As the frictions between Greek and Turk have been rising the Greeks have resorted to outright piracy in the Aegean. Brigands abound in the mountainous terrain of all their territories, and only last year the most severe massacre of innocents... of a substantial part of the island population was perpetrated on behalf of the Sultan on the Greek island of Chios.' Canning sighed deeply, studying his cousin's face, '... reportedly tens of thousands of Christian women and children being taken away to slavery. Subsequently I have received reports of plague and pestilence arising from the unburied bodies of countless victims of both sides. It was not, however, an event that stirred His Majesty's Government to interest let alone action until recently. The Treasury is, as ever, urging restraint in case of the slightest thing arising which might call upon the most severely depleted coffers. Since Bonaparte drained us so very nearly dry the government debt is in consequence now large, very large indeed. No, the government will not be stirred to remonstrate with the Porte, let alone move to anything more - will I say - *militaristic*,' Canning paused, as if in expectation of comment or question.

O'Connor nodded, he had no conceivable comment to offer, the subject so far removed from his interests, his purpose in coming to London that he assumed it was simply his cousin's political conversation, and so he sipped his brandy in silence as Canning resumed. 'Castlereagh, Metternich and even the Tsar have been resolutely opposed to any support for the Greeks. The official French position is unclear, and whilst they do favour some form of intervention this is concurrent with their stated belief in the inviolability of the Sultan's territorial integrity.'

'Sure 'tis a pity they don't have the same opinions about Spain,' murmured O'Connor quietly under his breath,

14

recollecting the long years of blockade in the war, many months on station, tossed about at sea in leaking ships, in all weathers and no prospect of leave.

Canning blinked and continued in full flow, 'Unofficially, it is clear that France aspires to greater influence in any independent Greece as may come about and is covertly behind the scheme promoted by the Knights of Malta, who have offered a loan of ten millions of francs in return for the permanent sovereignty of Rhodes, though His Majesty's Government has recently blocked their loan promotion in London. France is backing both horses in this race and has trained a modern army in Egypt for the Pasha. The Tsar, however, steadfastly ignores the injustices perpetrated against his co-religionists. Yet since the Sultan hanged the Patriarch of Constantinople from his cathedral gates, *poor fellow*, and the shocking massacre on Chios there is a deal of public opinion fomenting against the Turks, with a growing number demanding support of some nature for the Greeks... both here and in many European populaces. Since August last year I have succeeded Castlereagh ...'

'A blackguard that none will miss, may he rot in hell,' thought O'Connor, his concentration drifting. His Irish republican sympathies were now dim but never wholly forgotten, and Castlereagh had been a brutal suppressor of the United Irishmen. His attention returned to Canning's somewhat tedious briefing.

'... as Foreign Secretary, and it is no secret now that I am sympathetic to the Greek cause. As I declared but three weeks ago, *when a whole nation revolts against its conqueror, the nation cannot be considered as piratical but as a nation in a state of war.* His Majesty's Government has since made our friendly relations with the Porte conditional upon a respect for their Christian subjects. Further, I have instructed Maitland, colonial governor in the Ionians, to deprive the Turks of resupply from those islands.'

O'Connor sipped again from his brandy and refrained from comment, perceiving his cousin unlikely to welcome interruption.

'Lately, as well as the Spanish Committee there has been formed a self-styled London *Greek* Committee... with a goodly leavening of Members of the House, perhaps a score or more. For the main comprising of Whigs, Radicals and Liberals, but even some Tories: all postulating strong commitment and support for the Greek rebels, seeking supporters, proposing even to raise a loan for a provisional Greek government; though no doubt the more keenly mercenary proponents will have a vested pecuniary interest... as we will doubtless see in time. This committee also comprises military men and persons of some financial stature; there is even talk of enlisting Lord Byron to promote it.'

Canning paused once more as as if to gather breath, to compose his further thoughts, and O'Connor interjected at last, his brandy exhausted, his patience ebbing like a tide as he politely endured his cousin's blather, for so it seemed, and his curiosity was now insistent, 'It seems a near lifetime that I have spent fighting Boney's tyranny, for the most part afloat upon all the oceans and in His Majesty's ships and service. I abhor tyranny in all its guises, most particularly the slavery which is practised by the most odious of regimes; the Ottoman empire is surely one, oppressing Greece, that precious font of civilisation, but pray, may I enquire why this has brought about your direct approach to myself, sir?'

'Yes, yes, cousin; I will return to that subject in but a moment; please forgive my loquacious ramblings...' Canning for the first time sensed his cousin's impatience, '... which no doubt seem interminable and grow longer as I grow older, but as you will readily grasp and as I will seek to explain... the essence of the matter is twofold: in the first part the Greeks are perceived by many of His Majesty's Government as brigands and pirates, and therefore unlikely to long forestall the Sultan's territorial recovery and consequent unpleasant retribution, at least without the assistance of more professional military officers to the Greeks being readily forthcoming. As to the second part, His Majesty's Government cannot and does not wish to be remarked assisting the Greek rebels.' Canning reached the crux of the official British dilemma.

'In what form then, may I ask, does His Majesty's Government envisage matters developing?' asked a puzzled O'Connor in a low voice, staring at his cousin, his mind dimly beginning to perceive the possibility but groping to establish the nature of some indistinct connection with himself.

'There are already a number of – will I use that rather indelicate term for want of another – *mercenaries* assisting the Greeks, including reputable former British officers. Latterly the Committee has enlisted a veteran fellow officer of yours from the war against Boney, a very able officer, Abney-Hastings, a proponent of some new kind of naval vessel. This *modus operandi* appears to offer the opportunity to His Majesty's Government to encourage limited and yet wholly deniable support... *covert* support. This has found favour with certain members of His Majesty's Government who are also aware – thanks to our Post Office friends in Abchurch Lane who have intercepted and deciphered the letters from several consulates to their governments – that there is an emerging European sympathy for the cause of Greek independence. Old Mr Willes, a capital man, has never been defeated by their ciphers and his son is an expert *par excellence* with the repair of broken seals. But I digress, I now find myself sympathetic to such aspirations, but this is far from the Government's official position, which is one of friendship with our ally the Ottomans. It has been discreetly mooted to myself very recently the possibility of a loan of an able British captain with appropriate experience, were I able to identify such a candidate officer. There is of course Lord Cochrane. The First Lord, when I pressed him, opined that there could be no finer fighting officer for such a venture than Lord Cochrane. However, their Lordships at the Admiralty have expressed certain reservations about his candidacy... which we need not go into.'

'I can only concur with his Lordship in that respect, sir, though I am no more than an occasional acquaintance of Lord Cochrane.' Curiosity now shrieked loud in Pat's mind - where was this leading? 'Sure, we have met in passing... when our ships shared the same port. I collect once enjoying dinner with him in

Portsmouth, long after *Tenedos* had paid off, and later we exchanged the odd letter, one unemployed captain to another. Well, of course, he is in the Brazil now.'

'I believe that you are meeting Melville tomorrow to discuss your prospects of a ship... and that he expects you to attend him in his private house in the afternoon?' Canning resumed, his voice lifting.

'Why, yes, sir, that is the case. I hope that we may discuss my prospects for another command, however trifling they may be. I have long held hopes of a frigate; one of the new twenty-four pounder ships would suit. In my dreams I conceive of a ship-of-the-line, *ha ha,*' Pat joked. 'However, I must refrain from these fanciful notions until I speak with the First Lord on the morrow. Conceivably he may be more minded to speak of the Fencibles... or some receiving hulk. Either would be a bitter blow, to be sure.'

'Dear cousin, some moments ago I mentioned Cochrane as suited to such an unusual venture; however, it would seem to me that there is a further candidate, another fine officer, one whose career I have followed at some distance – when time has permitted – whose occasional letters I have much appreciated, and so I conceive that he is perfectly suited to such a task.'

'Sir?' Pat's heart began to thump as he sensed the very purpose of the meeting was upon him, so loud he felt even his cousin must hear it.

'Why, Captain Patrick O'Connor himself.'

'I am most gratified, most honoured, honoured indeed by your opinion of me, sir,' Pat replied, his voice barely a whisper, sitting bolt upright in his chair in some small state of shock, his brandy glass rattling as it settled on the table.

It was fast approaching seven o'clock and the sunlight beginning to fade when O'Connor reached the Feathers, his thoughts in turmoil.

Macleod had arrived an hour previously, and his mind too was spinning with the momentous matters which Melville had revealed. 'How best to raise such a delicate subject with Pat?

Mercenary indeed! Yet perhaps Lord Cochrane's past Chilean venture was nae so very different?' pondered Macleod, the significance of the First Lord's request still pressing upon his mind.

No such hesitation subdued Pat's warm greeting for his friend. Upon entering the public bar he immediately encountered a pacing Macleod who, smiling broadly, offered his hand even as Pat, with the same delight, disregarded it and seized his friend in a fierce bear hug. 'Duncan! Is it you? Give you joy, dear friend! How are you?' the questions poured from Pat's mind and lips in a swift stream whilst Duncan gasped for breath within his friend's firm embrace. 'I hope Kathleen and Brodie are keeping well.'

'Och, I am glad to see ye too, Pat. I am very well, aye, thankee. Kathleen and Brodie are in fine fettle, though Kathleen has been unwell this past winter. What of Sinéad, what of the bairns?'

Pat could hardly contain his enthusiasm for his old friend and his curiosity for news, 'All are well, thankee, and lamenting still your and Kathleen's departure, Brodie's too. What are you doing here, tell?'

Duncan hesitated for only a moment, putting aside his thoughts of his meeting with Melville for later before replying, 'Let us proceed directly to supper and wet the swab; there is plenty to talk about. Mrs O'Donnell has been a'fussing this past hour... and we are to settle in the snug. Come, let us share a bottle or twae with our news; so much to catch up. How long, tell, are ye here?'

'Why, 'tis but a brief visit; I am summoned by the First Lord. Likely I will be back to Ireland within a day or two. What of you?'

'Och, I have spoken with Melville myself this afternoon. I will doubtless be off to my wee croft on Monday, if nae before,' Duncan spoke as casually as he could, not wishing to raise the burning matter of his meeting with Melville so soon.

Pat was greatly taken aback; indeed, he was astonished that Duncan, a mere lieutenant, would be meeting the First Lord. This most eventful day was proving to be the strangest he could recall, but he did not press his momentarily burning curiosity. He forced his thoughts back to the joyous reunion. 'Oh for you to come back to Connemara, to Claddaghduff with me... at least for a short spell. Sinéad would dearly love to see you, and we so much would enjoy walking the Twelve Bens together; it has been long in the planning,' this said in hearty good spirits.

A little later, in the privacy and quietude of the snug, Pat and Duncan sat together enjoying supper with several of the best bottles from Mrs O'Donnell's cellar, exchanging fond and memorable recollections of their time together aboard *Tenedos* and other vessels in His Majesty's Service: times and adventures which were recounted for several hours, neither man seemingly willing to let the slightest tidbit of bad news cloud their enjoyment of renewing a friendship built so solidly since a first meeting in Portsmouth in the year 'three. Subsequently, whilst serving on the brig-sloop *Starling* together, they had discovered their mutual interest in playing musical instruments. The 'cello and playing of Irish traditional music was a passion of Pat's and the flageolet or pennywhistle, that delightful feature of Gaelic music, was Duncan's personal joy. It was a pastime which had proved so valuable in cementing their so solid comradeship during many difficult voyages and hardships across all the oceans.

Time passed until, food all consumed, wine near gone and reminiscences temporarily exhausted, they remained silent for a few minutes, each contemplating the other. It was Duncan who broke the silence. 'Ye seem happy, brother,' he observed with great satisfaction. 'Doubtless contented and settled ashore after all our long years at sea, I fancy.'

'Oh, a landsman's life is not for me, old friend; such tedium, to be sure. These days I oft collect our time serving together... sixteen long years it was,' Pat sighed, his voice dropping, 'Oh how I ache for a ship again. 'Tis a long time now since we fetched home to Chatham and *Tenedos* paid off.' A shard of melancholy came to his mind before he recalled his own pressing objective for his visit and the perhaps doubtful prospects for it, notwithstanding what his cousin had said, for in truth the significance was unclear to him.

'And is there nae some wee silver lining in that dismal grey cloud, Pat? Time ashore with Sinéad? Time with the bairns perhaps? Have ye nae enjoyed these past four years?' pressed Duncan, striving for encouragement in his voice.

'Eh? Oh, most certainly, and I would never look into the mouth of a gift horse... even if it be long in the tooth. That is, no... that ain't what I meant. These four years past with Sinéad have been the greatest of pleasures... though with the swabs less so; but of late my dreams shift to standing astride a deck; nor even a seventy-four, a tight little frigate with a crack crew would make me the happiest sailor that ever served. Lord, I would be content with one of the horrible, leaky *Forty Thieves*; even the smallest brig would serve. To be at sea again is now my dearest wish.' Pat stopped, his thoughts shifting from his own aspirations. He poured out the last of the wine and gazed at Duncan, the warmth of long years of firm friendship lighting his face, his deep affection exuded in his voice, 'And you, old friend; have you been happy in the Western Isles since you took your leave of us? You know you will always be welcome back. Sinéad misses you all so much.'

Duncan smiled and nodded. 'I grant ye Connemara is splendid and nae so very different from the Isles, but Lewis is my home, Pat.'

'What news of Brodie and Kathleen? What report do you have for Sinéad who is anxious of her sister and niece, 'tis some months since the last letter?' Pat waved to a distant but attentive Mrs O'Donnell.

'Both are well, thankee, and reside with me in my wee croft since leaving Claddaghduff. 'Tis in some disrepair, I grant ye, as a dwelling and lacking a wee tait of comfort, but we have spent there many happy days together. Kathleen, being another of your Irish ilk...' Duncan joked, '... near fresh off the bog... she does nae find my ascetic tastes too disagreeable, and so 'tis a marriage that works tolerably well. We oft stride together over the Harris hills in companionable fashion... and spend hours at the hearth in the most cordial of discourse. We have grown very much closer these past twae years and know each other now so well. Brodie too oft accompanies us on our walks, and we have a brace of Shetlands to carry our dunnage, the easel and paints... in the main a pleasantly docile breed, as ye know. Brodie is now a much more confident wench. She speaks the Gaelic, a wee French too... even she is learning the Latin; such a cannie lassie she is. We have passed many occasions in Edinburgh too - such a splendid city. But now all is up... I nae longer possess of twenty pounds and I must return to sea with what employment that I might find. I had been near accepting MacDonald's offer of his scaffie.'

'There you are, Mrs O'Donnell; a bottle of port if you will,' said Pat pleasantly, smiling at his hostess, his attention swiftly returning to his companion. 'But you will all be most welcome again in Connemara, old friend. The twins have repented their objectionable treatment of Brodie and now lament her leaving. Sinéad so dearly misses Kathleen: Murphy being no companion at all and hardly ever to be found when needed, always frittering away his wages in beer. Like myself, this landsman's life sits ill with him, and I have had occasion to speak sharp these past months about his slacking off. The man is like a fish out of his depth, Duncan; quite unmanageable for Sinéad, yet the twins adore him. He can be both a pearl and a swine, and at the same time. Fergal and Caitlin, the swabs, become ever more a tribulation; sixteen going on twenty-six, spending all their time with the village lads, no efforts made for the household chores; daily routines hold no interest for them. They can cook neither a simple potato nor even burgoo, and what am I to do about it? I can't fathom it at all, 'tis impossible to choose the right course to steer...' This was said with a sigh of deep resignation, Pat's spirits dropping momentarily.

'Och, I am sure of it, dear soul, yet persevere ye must. Kathleen and Brodie are in Minorca at present, in Port Mahon; they have been these past three weeks. Kathleen is an accomplished artist, as ye know, but she has been unwell for much of the past winter, so terribly damp it is in the Isles. I greatly fear that it may be the onset of consumption, and so they are enjoying the Mediterranean warmth, Brodie painting now whilst Kathleen recuperates... for the next few months at least; but what news of Simon these past twae years?'

'Oh, he is still in Plymouth, I believe; though I receive but scarce news from him... perhaps an occasional letter oft lamenting his long absence from his beloved Mull.'

After more enjoyable reminiscences had been shared, the port all consumed and the relatively recent events of the past two years recounted again they settled to enjoy a wonderfully aromatic pot of coffee, being their particular favourite, brought without bidding by Emma.

Pat's mood began to sink a little. 'The fleet is much reduced, so my cousin in Portsmouth reports; even those ships that remain are, in many cases, in such poor shape as could hardly put to sea in a breeze let alone a storm. Many are unfit to sail, much of their timbers devoured by the worm... and there is a want of crew - the Press now long gone. All ship's supplies are short, stores of foodstuffs rotten – if they have not been stolen by some dishonest quartermaster... capperbar is rife you know. Powder is lacking and often damp, anyways always insufficient for practice; ship's officers are frequently away, captains are at Westminster more often than aboard ship, shipyards merely feign their restorations, port admirals fail on their promises... and over all this lamentable debacle their Lordships claim lack of funds to do more. 'Tis a pretty state of affairs. God help us were Boney to come back.'

Pat's reference in passing to the deceased Bonaparte had provided the opening for Duncan to introduce the subject still burning within his mind, Melville's request persisting though the wine and the convivial reminiscing of the long evening. 'Och, I am fully persuaded of it. I dare say 'tis dismaying to ye and but wee consolation that Boney will never come back. But perhaps there is one matter on which I might seek your opinion?' Duncan had been pondering for some time how best to broach such a delicate subject. 'Doubtless ye collect our times in the Aegean waters, pursuing French ships amongst the many isles.'

"'Tis certain they will never be forgotten, never in life,' murmured Pat, staring across the table, a gleam rekindled in his eye despite the fatigue now beginning to settle upon him.

'It seems that troubles are afoot there once again. The Greeks are in rebellion against their Turk masters and great bloodshed is being inflicted throughout the isles and in the Morea... as I imagine ye will have read in the press and, nae doubt, heard of even in the wilds' of Connemara?'

'I have scarcely visited Dublin these past two years and returned to London not at all since we dropped our anchor in Chatham. Save for a very occasional visit to Galway town I have never left Connemara, paid no attention to anything in London or elsewhere... save for my correspondence with their Lordships... and the farm of course,' replied Pat. 'Now that you mention of it, I do recall some talk about a new form of warship for Greece. Yes, it comes back to me now; a steam-driven vessel, by God, and we have one too in service, *Comet*, and a second, *Lightning*, on the stocks. 'Tis sure they are the coming thing. I collect *Savannah* steamed across the Atlantic in the year 'nineteen in but twenty-four days... 'tis most assuredly a signal for what is yet to come.'

'Och, I am nae engineer, Pat; little do I know about this emerging form of motion or the construction of ships – such things are wholly outside my experience – but of one thing I am certain, progress is relentless in all of our activities and certainly therefore as sure for the propulsion of ships.' Duncan was thinking now rather more nimbly as to the line that he might take with this particular subject. 'In fact, now that ye mention such a device, I do collect it was spoken of only this afternoon in a discussion I had with Lord Melville.' He began to feel his way to surer ground, 'His Lordship referred to a most interesting dilemma which had arisen following the succession of Castlereagh by Canning as Foreign Secretary and the emerging interest amongst the Whigs as well as the Radicals for the cause of an independent Greece... free of Turk suzerainty and with a generally Christian society... albeit of the Orthodox persuasion...' Duncan paused, Pat's interest wavering.

24

Pat sighed inwardly, politics held not the least interest for him and he wondered where this was leading. He nodded to Duncan, 'Please... do continue.'

'Apparently, a committee has been established to further this cause, to procure supplies and funds, military provisions too, so as to aid the Greek liberation. That is where I recall mention of this new form of ship; steam-driven, as ye say, and 'tis propounded by a former naval colleague, Abney-Hastings, an officer whom I believe served with Lord Nelson at Trafalgar.'

Pat began to feel an emerging interest in Duncan's explanation and sloughed off his fatigue, his mind recalling the name after but a moment, 'Abney-Hastings was a youngster, a volunteer aboard *Neptune* at Trafalgar, aged but eleven; he later became a lieutenant and master of the survey vessel *Kangaroo* in Jamaica. I collect he left the service after some disagreement with the flag-captain at Port Royal, who bawled him out publicly, for he had overlaid his cable... Captain Parker shouting from his deck that his ship handling was not seamanlike. Did not Abney-Hastings offer him out... and so was dismissed the service, Melville refusing to hear his case? A thoroughly shabby affair.'

Duncan, sensing firmer ground approaching for Melville's proposal, continued, 'I am sure ye are right, but we digress. Those Members of Parliament and others who have declared support for the Greek cause meet in committee at the *Crown and Anchor* on the Strand this Saturday to procure able military and naval officers to further the prospects for the formative Greek government. I have heard mention of Abney-Hastings in that respect... and indeed also Cochrane.'

'Cochrane! Cochrane, the Sea Wolf, the Old Dog!' exclaimed Pat, his voice rising. 'Well I never; his name was mentioned to me only today, this Greek committee too. My cousin, Canning, was sounding out my interest in some rum venture to Greek waters. I cannot fathom it. Certainly Cochrane would be an excellent prize for the committee and the Greeks, but, as I collect, he was still in service for the Brazil when we quit the South Atlantic... and if my memory serves me well... yes... I do believe that he continues in service there.'

Duncan was taken aback to find that Pat had already been introduced, to some degree, to the very same subject which he had been manouevring to broach for several hours, and he gazed with astonishment at his friend. A silent minute or more passed as he summoned with difficulty near-forgotten memories from a patchy recollection of a conversation with Cochrane himself during dinner in South America several years previously, eventually relegating his recollections as irrelevant. 'Doubtless ye are well informed and correct as to his whereabouts as well as his continuing responsibilities, and there can surely be nae certitude that Cochrane would return in response to any call from their Lordships at the Admiralty; indeed, I imagine that the friction with which Cochrane engages still with ministers might well be prejudicial to just such a proposal.'

Pat nodded, 'Of course Cochrane has lobbied hard these past years to secure his pardon and his knighthood restored in the face of the King's unwillingness to entertain his case. 'Tis surely unlikely that he could be persuaded by any pleas originating from anyone associated with His Majesty's Government. No, Cochrane will not do... and a further matter to be minded: any serving British officer, myself included, is forbidden from engagement by the foreigner... which surely narrows the field considerably.'

This latter comment from Pat, being a fresh element in Duncan's exceedingly thin knowledge of the restrictions of the British state for its officers in foreign military servitude, stopped his tentative thoughts dead in their tracks until he recalled that any officer acting for the Greeks could not be a serving British officer in any event, as Melville had explained. The Foreign Secretary would only commit to participate in such an undertaking in support of Greece were the arrangement to have absolutely no overt link to His Majesty's Government whatsoever. Of what arrangement was Melville possibly thinking when he referred to O'Connor? How could he suggest Pat become a participant whilst being a serving captain of the Royal Navy? Deep fatigue began to overtake Duncan, for the continuation of a subject in which he was clearly foundering on the very limit of his experience was rapidly proving beyond him. Time to leave matters until the morrow, he thought. 'I cannae linger with ye longer; my bed beckons.'

Pat too, despite the more intriguing elements of their conversation, was flagging, and mindful of his appointment the next day with Lord Melville he resigned himself to his bed. Their eyes met as they rose from the table and Pat reached for Duncan's hand. 'Good night, brother; 'tis so good to see you. I will surely sleep well tonight.'

'Good night, auld friend,' Duncan nodded, returning Pat's unwavering, fierce grip.

Chapter Two

The mountains look on Marathon —
And Marathon looks on the sea;
And musing there an hour alone,
I dream'd that Greece might still be free;
For standing on the Persians' grave,
I could not deem myself a slave.

Friday 2ⁿᵈ May 1823   *Westminster, London*

At nine o'clock in the morning, Duncan and Pat were back in the
parlour enjoying Mrs O'Donnell's breakfast; both had slept
exceedingly well. It was a meal that Pat particularly favoured
over all others, whether ashore or at sea. In Connemara his
breakfasts were prepared by his steward, Freeman, and were
often just the simple sea-going dishes of burgoo or skillygalee,
which meals were at the very limit of his steward's culinary
abilities. Pat employed two men to serve him: Freeman, an
ebony-black former slave from West Africa, who was his butler
and cook for Pat's simplest of meals, and Murphy, who had been
Pat's servant and valet for as long as he could remember. Hailing
from Galway Town, he had been serving on Pat's first command
in Portsmouth in the year 'three and had miraculously ingrained
himself into Pat's life, the Galway connection perhaps one of the
doubtful reasons he had persisted. Freeman had been liberated
some six years previously when *Tenedos*, passing through the
Caribbean, had stopped and impounded a Bristol slaver running
her cargo of misery long after the prohibition. Freeman and
scores of others had been thrown over her side by her captain.
Freeman had swum to *Tenedos* and hidden away in the for'ard
locker until the slave ship had departed, in fear of being shackled
once again. The *Tenedos* crew, and later the officers, had all
warmed to his gentle nature and good humour, Pat bestowing his
new name upon him and the crew teaching him his limited
English. A reluctant Murphy had been ordered by Pat to take

Freeman under his wing as assistant steward, and in this capacity he had excelled - to the point where Murphy, one of life's inveterate grumblers, had long ago become anxious about his own position. Freeman could not come close to Mrs O'Donnell's finest cooking except for his toad in a hole, the meal that Pat and Duncan generally shared for supper when at sea, the cooking of which had been taught him by Wilkins, Pat's personal cook aboard *Tenedos*.

Duncan, still wondering precisely what Canning might have said to his friend on the matter of service for Greece, determined upon a cautious exploration as he returned to the previous night's subject. 'Pat, ye will forgive me for expounding last night upon political matters of which I know not the least... or at the most just a wee tait, but it crossed my mind that perhaps Melville may have something worthwhile to add to our considerations. Indeed, his Lordship might conceivably offer some suggestions which could be delivered to the Greek Committee on Saturday. Melville suggested ye may care to accompany me... and we will find out what these gentlemen are about?'

'Certainly, it is a matter of some interest to me, and I would be pleased to do so,' Pat lied in agreeable voice, pouring the coffee, the welcome smell of which was so invigorating. 'Though to be sure nothing worth tuppence e'er came out of any committee. Doubtless it will be stuffed with self-important, conceited windbags: parsimonious, niggardly, full of ignorance and hot air, with precious little sense, yet pressing all to endure their ill-considered, pompous blather. I will speak with Melville of the specific difficulty we identified. I am meeting him at his private house at two o'clock,' Conversation passed by pleasantly enough for some hours, much of it a return to the subjects of the prior evening, no conclusions being reached in the prevailing background of fundamental uncertainty in the matter in hand - the potential for a return to sea.

At one o'clock Pat O'Connor departed for his appointment with the First Lord. For Duncan Macleod it was his first opportunity to speak with his twin nieces, Sandra and Emma. Their mother, Macleod's sister, had died giving birth, and their father, a fisherman, had been lost at sea several years ago. Consequently, Macleod had brought them to London where they were assured of a warm abode and a friendly upbringing during his absence at sea. The twins had since become quite beautiful and also the most wonderful of cooks, turning out meals of a quality renowned throughout the Liberties of Westminster and the Savoy.

'Are ye happy my bonnies?' ventured Macleod.

'Yes sir,' chorused the twins.

'Learning well your writing?'

'Yes sir,' trilled their reply.

'And your Gaelic?'

At that only a few giggles came back.

'Bless ye, weans,' said Macleod, delighted to see them happy.

As the St. James's clock struck 2 p.m. Pat O'Connor knocked on Lord Melville's door in Arlington Street. The servant led him into Melville's study where the First Lord, a man in his early fifties but looking older in his rather dour tweed attire, was seated behind his desk. 'Welcome, Captain O'Connor,' said Melville in a loud but cordial voice, rising and extending his hand to Pat with a genuine air of welcome. 'I am most pleased to see you. I hope I see you well. It has been some years, some long years indeed, since we last met.'

'Thank you kindly, my Lord,' Pat murmured; his throat dry in anticipation, he could say no more.

'Please be seated. May I offer you tea?' Lord Melville was indeed particularly pleased to greet his guest, and as his porter disappeared for the tea he bestowed his warmest smile, 'Thank you for your swift passage from far Galway; I am in your debt.'

'Not at all, sir,' Pat gathered his thoughts, swallowed hard and launched directly into his plea. 'I have been ashore these four years past and hence am most solicitous of your interest in myself. To be sure, I had begun to despair of ever going to sea again in His Majesty's service...' his mind began to race but the words, frustratingly, would not come.

Pat's nervousness was plainly apparent to Melville; scores of officers had become tongue-tied in similar circumstances in every prior year in his office. His eyes widened as he immediately smiled and interjected to preclude any embarrassing pause developing, his voice maintaining a low, encouraging tone. 'O'Connor, pray take your time.' The servant returned with a tray. 'Will I pour you some tea?' asked the First Lord.

Pat, encouraged, looked Melville squarely in the face, nodded and resumed, his voice rising with his confidence returning. 'Sir, my only sea time these past four years has been fishing aboard a Galway hooker. The smallest sloop would appeal greatly. I would happily return to the tedium of a blockade, were one in the offing, and even, dare I say it, a Revenue cutter begins to exhibit an appeal. I cannot stay longer on my farm without I forget which is the bow and which the stern. My Lord, if I may? Since I have been recalled from the South Atlantic I have sat cooling my heels in Connemara. It pains me to hear from my cousin in Portsmouth who writes often of ships in fine fettle reduced to store hulks, new ships off the stocks going straight into ordinary... and he reports nine hundred dockyard men laid off last year... *nine hundred*... and five hundred and fifty the year before! It is all very dismaying.' Pat deflated, surprised that Melville had not quickly interrupted his tirade. He pressed on, 'I have sat like a stone these past four years... certainly gathered a great deal of moss... and when is it to end? Have I any prospect of ever returning to sea?'

Melville looked sternly at Pat for a few moments before replying. 'O'Connor, you speak very plainly, and I understand you well, but you must collect the public purse has been exhausted these past ten years or more. Boney did more damage to the Treasury than ever he did to the Fleet. Our resources are much down and tax is higher than ever before, yet we still lack for money; and now ministers are minded to reduce the naval estimates and postulate that the navy will be adequately served with but forty-four ships. It is a quite preposterous notion, O'Connor, when one hundred might conceivably be no more than adequate. Many ships of the fleet are old and rotten with the worm, as I dare say you know; such ships cannot endure much longer and are fit only for scrapping, but new ships are also on the stocks. There is, for example, *Asia*, in build now at Bombay... plentiful timber supplies there... and shipbuilders who do not charge an arm and a leg... and, furthermore, do not put back rotten timbers; there is *Hastings*, was built in Calcutta back in the year nineteen; there is *Unicorn*, in build now at Chatham; there's *Prince Regent* and *Britannia,* launched at Plymouth Dock... both first rates. I venture that these new vessels may not all be known in Galway... or indeed even in Portsmouth, but I do assure you that sound ships we have aplenty. Assuredly and regrettably many fewer ships than previously, and the economies forced upon us by the Treasury have no end in prospect.'

'No doubt, sir. May I beg you to speak of the particulars so far as they relate to me?' Pat asked quietly, his curiosity overcoming his natural reticence in the presence of the First Lord and he not greatly following Melville's train of explanation.

Melville frowned and stared closely at Pat's face, as if considering how best to continue, before resuming. 'I was speaking of economies, sir; *economies*! It is most unlikely that we will see the fleets of Boney's era afloat this year or next, nor for quite some time for that matter.' Pat did not dare to interrupt again; gratefully he sipped his tea. The First Lord rose from his chair and paced towards the window. He looked out for a long minute, as if gathering his thoughts, before turning around to contemplate his visitor. He gazed at Pat for a moment before his stern face at last broke into a slow smile as he resumed, 'O'Connor, I have the conviction that you do prize fortitude and that you will not be shaken by disagreeable news, however bitter it may come.'

'I hope I can bear it, my Lord.'

'You may not know that when I became First Lord there were one hundred and eighty-eight officers appointed admiral, though but few were serving with any squadron. Whilst there still remain nine officers appointed to fleet commands, these appointments have become, in the present lamentable diminution of the fleet... somewhat... *hypothetical*. It is far worse for captains... and as for lieutenants... well, I will say no more. You are to remember that whilst you are made post you are − will I say − with little influence, and so can expect to be ashore these next few years, pending perhaps the unfortunate death of several or even a score or more of your fellow captains.'

'Most dismaying, sir, bitter news indeed,' was all a shocked Pat could mutter, his discomfit starkly plain, his confidence draining away like an ebb tide leaving exposed all its hidden detritus.

Melville resumed, his voice rising, 'I have been in discussion with the Foreign Secretary on a matter requiring of the utmost discretion. He has pressed me to expedite matters, and so I will speak candidly with you. Doubtless you are familiar with the events occurring in the Ottoman Greek provinces, which His Majesty's Government deeply laments, particularly as it represents an opportunity for the advancement of Russian − their Orthodox brethren − or even *French* interests in the region... interests which one might easily conceive as being not necessarily wholly coincidental with our own. A great number of Philhellenes - adventurers for the most part - have left for Greece these two years past from many countries on the continent. These men have been ineffective, fighting and dying on land, and the survivors are now reportedly starving, bereft of any commissary. The Greeks have no regular forces, no artillery and hence no prospect of reducing the Turk fortresses, which are resupplied by sea. Hence, it has become plain to all professional military men that thwarting Turk resupply *by sea* presents the most propitious means of assisting the Greeks...'

Pat nodded, mumbled 'No doubt, sir,' Melville directing a frosty glance at his waning attention.

'I am reliably informed, O'Connor, that substantial funds are being raised in certain circles to purchase proper ships of war for the provisional Greek government. Their Lordships are aware of intentions to procure a small fleet of steam-driven sloops or corvettes... and even heavy frigates: ships which would not disgrace a post-captain, nor any admiral for that matter. For the moment the Greeks have only ships of such small size which can hardly stand against the Turks - were it not for the considerable ineptitude of the Turk officers and crew; yet stand the Greeks do, and they have achieved surprising victories. I am reliably informed that were the Greeks to be assisted by even the most modest of warships with competent officers then substantial success could well be achieved. In fact, even the smallest frigate, well founded and competently manned, would be perfectly capable of dealing heavy blows to the Turk fleet.'

A momentary assessment of a silent Pat's interest and Melville resumed, 'Captain O'Connor, the Foreign Secretary has pressed me to find one or more officers of the measure and experience of such as yourself to join such a venture. However, such officers *cannot* be serving Royal Navy officers. Whilst some subterfuge may be necessary at the present time because of that, any officers on such a secondment - if I might use that term - would be highly regarded by their Lordships, by many Members of the House and indeed by the country at large. Need I say more?'

'Sir, pray tell me... am I to believe that you wish me to resign the Service? Sir ...' Pat, his mind in greater turmoil than he had ever experienced before, his blood pumping, his curiosity searing his every thought, tried vainly to interject, but the First Lord was once more in full flow.

'I wish to speak with you about a prospective command. I do not say that it is one which will suit your interests... that is for your consideration. The Foreign Secretary did, as you doubtless collect, strive to preclude any French interest developing in the new South American states. He is similarly minded to do the same for any new *Greek* state. Canning is therefore inclined to do everything within his power to ensure His Majesty's amity for any emerging Greek government is recognised there by their nascent leaders. But assuredly, at this indeterminate stage of potential developments, we cannot be known to be a participant in the current turmoil. However, His Majesty's Government is not averse to the activities of Members of the House seeking to promote independence for Greece... and notes the emerging activities of the so-called London Greek Committee... its efforts to procure competent military officers in the service of the provisional Greek government. Do you follow my drift O'Connor?' Melville, seeing Pat's self-evident exasperation, paused.

'My Lord, I have not been to sea these four years since fetching home to Chatham,' Pat seized his moment, his voice loud, all care cast aside, his indignation exploding. 'I had thought I am come here to discuss my next ship *or lack of one.* Since arriving in town I find I hear little else but constant mention of the Greek war - *Greece*, the piddling periphery of the Porte's realm - and from all corners... and I confess I am astonished that I find it at the forefront of your own interest too. If I deduce rightly what your Lordship is suggesting, am I now to choose between my rank - with few prospects of active command - or resignation and serving with a country with no navy to speak of – save perhaps for a few fishing smacks... *am I next to command a sardine boat?*' Pat spluttered, almost in disbelief that it was himself uttering such words to the First Lord, a being considered by Royal Navy officers to be higher than God in the celestial firmament.

Melville was taken aback, irked by Pat's candour, 'That is coming it a trifle high...'

'I beg your pardon, sir.' his outburst exhausted Pat sat back, his hand reaching to scratch his head, now drooping with some little embarrassment as his fervour cooled.

The First Lord continued in haste so as not to brook any further interruption, 'You will forgive me for perhaps not explaining matters as best I might. No, it is not suggested that you irrevocably discard your well-earned rank, far from it, and even your worst enemy would hardly deny what a well-earned rank it is, indeed. No, the Foreign Secretary has proposed a rather similar scheme to Cochrane's Chilean adventure, albeit different; actually *rather* different on consideration, if I might explain?'

Pat was speechless and quite unable to interject as the First Lord continued. 'Certain senior persons in the Foreign Office have devised a scheme which, so they believe, would allow His

Majesty's Government to deny any - will I say - *unorthodox* participation in such a venture, as I will seek to describe. You will be aware that we have far more post-captains than ships, and so for the majority of them a life ashore on half-pay is all that they may reasonably contemplate. Some of them are politically well-connected... and have expressed their grievances most candidly, several resigning to take up *foreign* service; Cochrane is a perfect example of such a process, O'Connor; well... perhaps not a *perfect* example, but you will grasp the general notion. Indeed, in your own case, your service in the South Atlantic was considered somewhat unorthodox in certain circles. Yet in such unconventional arrangements... that is to say *when notable success is achieved*... at a convenient later time it would be churlish indeed to refuse reinstatement to post. In similar circumstances to this Greek venture one might easily conceive of such a possibility.'

At this last point of Melville's, Pat, recovering himself and beginning to embrace the attractive prospect of a ship again, thawed very slightly. 'My Lord, I am sorry. I expressed myself badly. I see now that there is something in what you say. If I do not mistake you, your Lordship is suggesting having two bites of the cake and eating the cherry.'

'Exactly, quite so,' replied the First Lord after a momentary pause and concealing well his inability to grasp the precise provenance of O'Connor's phrase. 'I am heartily sorry for your embarrassment. It would be extraordinary, indeed downright incredible were a serving captain of the Royal Navy to enter service with a provisional government and serve in command of no more of a fleet than a frigate and a collection of Greek brigs. His Majesty's Government could hardly expect to credibly deny any allegations of the Porte that such an arrangement was merely a convenient subterfuge to conceal their interest in such a venture. No, such an obvious provocation most certainly cannot be countenanced. *Resignation*, O'Connor, is plainly a necessity. I venture that this is all highly irregular and quite beyond any scheme that their Lordships could conceive of... and could only come from a branch of service more familiar with subterfuge and deception, if you catch my drift. I will add that His Majesty's Government can suffer no record of any such arrangement to be made... *were such a scheme to find favour with you.* Of course, I will assure you of restoration to the List - and with no seniority lost.'

At last, Pat found a moment to speak, but he floundered as the words were still formulating in his mind. 'Sir, you put the matter very well, and perhaps I was in haste earlier. The scheme has merit, no doubt. I am most sensible of this mark of confidence; it is most certainly an honour to be described in such terms and to receive this opportunity... and such a welcome and unexpected prospect. To be sure, I find myself taken aback, without wind in my sails. You spoke of a frigate; what ship will you have me command?'

'Our requirement is for imminence, and so I find I have few choices left to me, the fleet now so much reduced. A frigate would suit our purpose tolerably well. I have considered of *Unicorn*; she is but recently launched at Chatham; though to equip and ready her for service will take several months at best, perhaps a year before she will swim... no, she will not do. Also at Chatham is *Shannon*. I collect you served on her if my memory serves me well. The yard believes it would require of at least four months to bring her out of ordinary, though I am minded she will follow you later. In similar condition at Portsmouth there is *Trincomalee;* she too would require of several more months to bring her to readiness. No, there is but one ship which appears to be eminently suitable, particularly in view of your former command, and which can be spared. Admiral Sir Alexander Cochrane from Plymouth Dock has informed me this past hour by messenger that down there in the south-west, within his province, he has this past month completed the refitting of a fifth rate, a frigate of 38 guns; much the same ship as your former *Tenedos,* eleven hundred tons. She is now seaworthy and awaiting her crew. She had been sent there from Milford Dockyard for hulking to a prison ship, but on inspection the shipwrights were amazed at her condition. She was one of the original class of Leda's and built with the very best of oak... and so has survived both Boney and the worm. She is presently about to come out of ordinary and back to service. Ain't that the most amazing thing?'

'And what ship is she, sir?' Pat racked his brain to recall the whereabouts of all the frigates in service and in ordinary.

'She is *HMS Surprise*, sister of your former *Tenedos*,' Melville announced, gratification plain in his voice - as if announcing some naval victory to his premier.

'My Lord, at the first I am greatly pleased to hear such a proposal,' Pat replied, the mystery resolved, deep satisfaction expressed in his own tone, his relief overflowing his every thought, 'and thankfully she is not one of her rotten, fir-built sisters. A fine ship she is, to be sure. Sir, I doubt I can long further endure the tedium of life ashore, sitting idle on my Connemara farm – these past three years have not been kind for the potato crop – and a return to sea and on a ship such as her is the most welcome of prospects.'

'I have this on the most impeccable authority, I will not enlarge on that: you will be purchasing *HMS Surprise,* for she cannot credibly remain a Royal Navy ship.'

Pat had thus far in the interview experienced a veritable assault on his mind, though he had since rebuilt his equilibrium, yet he reeled with this latest shock, leaving him speechless for a few moments until he spoke, his disbelief plain in his tone, his mental processes recovering, 'Ha ha! You jest, sir! It is a delightful thought, I confess, though I could scarcely buy an Inishturk curragh. *A frigate...* it is far more than I could ever afford.'

Melville smiled in the realisation that he had not explained himself at all well. 'I beg your pardon, O'Connor; I have not made things plain. Whatever may be the cost of this venture, sufficient will be pledged from the secret fund for you to ostensibly pay for her and to bring all restorations about... *and at best speed.* Should you find my proposal of interest I will be most grateful if you could put in hand immediately such arrangements as you think necessary to bring *Surprise* to readiness, and in any yard that you care to choose. If you will be so kind as to do so then I will look forward to hearing from you with such progress reports as you can offer as her readying proceeds. I will await your decision.'

It had been some considerable minutes in which Pat had been striving to grasp the totality of Melville's incredible briefing, and he could not shake off his state of utter astonishment, amazement – nothing like it had he ever heard before. He could barely whisper his reply. 'Perhaps my Lord would allow me to contemplate your proposal for the very briefest of delay before reaching any decision? I find myself, unexpectedly, attending that same Greek Committee on Saturday with Lieutenant Macleod. With your permission, sir, I intend to discuss this with him after the committee meeting and before reaching any conclusion. If your Lordship would graciously allow me a little more than twenty-four hours I will deliver my decision to you in person.'

'That is perfectly proper. I will be at the Admiralty tomorrow and I will expect you at 5 p.m.,' pronounced the First Lord with a degree of relief, rather vaguely indicating the door. 'Thank you kindly and good day; I look forward to seeing you on the morrow,' Melville concluded, rising, shaking Pat's hand as the porter entered to escort Pat out.

'Good day, sir,' was all that a stunned O'Connor could mutter, exiting the study.

The servant showed him out to the street. The walk back to the Feathers was slow, and Pat, wholly engrossed in his ruminations, was almost run over by a carriage and four on the Strand, leaping aside only at the shrill shout of the enraged driver.

It was approaching seven o'clock when a hungry Pat O'Connor arrived back at the Feathers, long after his customary dinner time when at sea, although the thought had not crossed his pre-occupied mind in the slightest until the aromas of the public room restored his attention. 'Duncan, there you are!' Macleod was seated again in his favourite armchair by the fire. 'A glass with you... and perhaps then a bite of mutton, eh?'

'Pat, will ye tell me about your meeting?' asked Duncan, setting his cup down and staring intently at his friend.

'I am all at sea. Yes, I must tell you of my meeting with the First Lord... I am dismasted, rudderless, quite brought by the lee. Where will I begin?' A clearly consternated Pat began to recount his meeting, 'It started well enough, Melville welcoming me. He was pleased to see me, and that ain't happened afore, cordiality generally being in pretty short supply from all the First Lords I ever served. The pleasantries did not linger, and I began to see my prospects swiftly foundering until Melville offered me some rum command... *a privateer, indeed it was*. I could not believe my ears... and in *foreign service!* My heart churned over. The devil to that! Pray ask Mrs O'Donnell for a jug of ale... a man could pass out in here, it is so damn hot. I had hoped, *prayed* he would give me a frigate again, even were it to be in the West Indies... that festering, vile station of yellow pestilence. I would have snatched his hand off; I would have departed on the morning tide, but no, I am asked to resign... *resign*. I have been offered a letter-of-marque... *a privateer*. Brother, tell me; have I ever laid myself athwart his hawse, fouled his cable? What have I done to deserve that? My mind is all ahoo since that moment.'

'Did ye decline his proposal?' The blunt question was asked in some trepidation, Duncan most anxious for the answer.

'Eh? I may seem a whit slow alongside you learned types, but it would never do to turn down the First Lord... to bite the mouth that feeds you; no, no, no, that ain't likely to ever secure you another command. That is a sure way to remain on the beach, half-pay forever, your card marked... there is no doubt... no doubt at all, and I could not countenance that. I said I would consider of his proposal. I am not committed, though to be sure a bird in the hand is surely worth two sitting afar on the fence. I am to meet with him again on Saturday.'

Long before Pat's return to the Feathers a grasp of the likely well-developed and close association between Canning and Melville had dawned on Duncan, mulling matters over, as Canning's careful scheme had become clear. Much of what Pat had recounted therefore came as little surprise. 'A privateer, ye say; in whose service? Would I be far astray in thinking of Greece? They are in revolt against the Turk... have been since the year 'twenty-one.'

'Greece... yes. It has been a long time since we were in those waters. Later, he mentioned a frigate, the sister of our old *Tenedos: HMS Surprise*. A fine ship she is, there is no doubt... and it seems that she is now near restored... to be sold... *sold to me*... am I dreaming, tell?' Pat shook his head, his dolorous face exhibiting his confusion.

'Pat, I see now that Melville is the instrument of Canning, and the scheme has been some time in the making. I consider that, Lord Cochrane aside, there cudnae have been many worthy candidates for such a venture. Yet Cochrane is now serving in the Brazil, is still in bad odour with many at the Admiralty, and so I cannae conceivably imagine why they would consider him undertaking such a scheme? Ye are surely... there cannae be any doubt... the man they seek.'

'Why, to be sure 'tis back to sea. Admittedly in foreign service and in command of some disparate flotilla of small vessels... brigs most likely; anyways likely scarcely bigger than fishing smacks for the most part... *and Greeks too*... but I will be restored to post and seniority at the end. How long is this enterprise likely to last? God's my life, will I be too old on my return to hoist Royal Navy colours ever again? Forgive me, I have yet to hear your considerations on this rum proposal: will you tell me your thoughts?'

'Och, I will nae. I beg your pardon, my capacity in service with ye was as your First. Little understanding of the Admiralty and its workings do I have, let alone the high political circles such that ye now appear to find yourself in. There are days when I flounder with a particular difficulty, a curious predicament perhaps, and I feel as if I am fresh from bonnie Lewis, just off the peat bog, but to be sure my grasp of the politic in this Greek business falls far, far short of offering any opinion worthy of more than a Brummagem farthing. Let us, I venture, attend tomorrow this Greek Committee, and ponder further as we find our course.'

'Mrs O'Donnell!' Pat hailed, 'Can you find us a splendid leg of mutton and perhaps a brace of ducks? 'Tis far past time for my dinner.'

'The mutton to be sure, sir, but we have no ducks. We do have a lovely side of venison, slow roasted with fresh herbs, and we have fresh soda bread, baked this past half hour.'

'Capital, my dear, the venison if you will; and please bring a pair of red, *first rate* bottles of red... burgundy perhaps,' urged Pat, as an emerging inkling of his customary good cheer returned, 'and a fine plum pudding to finish if you will.'

'Yes, sir; d'reckly.' Mrs O'Donnell hastened away.

The boiled leg of mutton was sublime, with hot buttered mashed turnips and carrots, served with caper sauce; the venison came roasted with young red onions and was served with steaming bright yellow rice; and the dinner finished with the sweetest, fruitiest, richest plum pudding Pat had ever eaten, with liberal sprinklings of cinnamon and amidst plentiful hot custard.

'A magnificent dinner, Mrs O'Donnell; thank you kindly, and please be sure to pass these two shillings, one each, to Emma and Sandra,' insisted a now very happy Pat, 'and a bottle of Port, if you will.'

At 10 p.m., another bottle having followed the way of its fellow and two pots of coffee having been finished, Pat peered rather vacantly into the distance with an uncertain gaze and a furrowed brow, and rose to retire to his room. 'Duncan, a ship and a command again is a powerful sauce for a gander,' Pat steadied himself. 'Yet were I to return from Greek service and their Lordships not recall me to post... my goose would be quite roasted to a crisp.'

'Never in life, dear soul, the public clamour for the Greek cause will make a hero of ye, and on your return I have nae doubt that ye would be restored to post,' Duncan ventured, a little more optimistically than he felt. 'Your position would be unassailable.'

Pat, standing now, paused, supporting himself upon the table edge before speaking very softly to his old friend, ''tis the long road we have trod together these past years since Portsmouth. All the world's oceans we have crossed, ships sunk under us and good comrades lost aplenty. I oft think of many of them; in my dreams I speak with some of them still. Through all these years, in those black moments, I have been most sensible of your enduring friendship, most precious it be. Thank you kindly for what you have told me these two days past. I find I must now go directly to my bed.'

'Aye, pray sleep well... and good night ,' mumbled Duncan, his own head drooping.

Saturday 3rd May 1823   *Westminster, London*

'Good morning, my friend,' said Duncan to a still obviously tired Pat as they settled for a late breakfast. 'Ye will forgive my curiosity, a deplorable vice for sure, but have ye considered further Lord Melville's proposal?'

'All night. I have scarcely slept a wink considering the pros and cons. No prospects of hoisting any colours, no ship, Melville making it plain this tedious and thankless time ashore could endure for years. Should I enter into this Greek scheme indefinitely? If I do not, will I miss my tide? Should I leave Sinéad in Connemara alone for some years longer? And, were I to accept, what would she think? I don't speak the Greek. And are good men still to be found for a crew, officers too, to join me on such an enterprise? All my life I have been at sea, since I first put on long trousers. The sea is all I know. Four long years now with no ship. I had always thought of Fergal at sea with me, beginning the long road to become made post. I despair, I do. I collect you are away directly to Stornoway; will you fly off, abandon me? Will you see me depart for Greece without you?'

'Never in life,' replied Duncan, reaching for the bacon. 'Am I nae telling ye for ever that I am always with ye?'

'I am heartily pleased to hear it,' Pat looked at his old friend with glowing affection in his gaze.

'There is, to be sure, a tide in the affairs of men, as the bard said, brother, and will I deduce that ye conceive that yours has been at its ebb these twae years past, yet such a decision must be taken in the round, with an honest acknowledgment of all your circumstances. I allude to your family in that respect. Another

43

egg, if ye would pass that pan please. Is there a wee tint of coffee left?'

'What a capital shipmate you are,' Pat smiled, 'More than anything I have a hankering to return to sea, master of my own ship and with a crack crew. But in Greek service? Is it the sensible thing to stay on the beach these years to come, awaiting a ship and my squadron? I wonder... am I beating about the wrong tree... ' adding after a moment's hesitation, 'barking up the wrong bush?'

'Dinnae suppose I am unaware of your eagerness to set foot aboard ship at the earliest possible moment. As your friend I must also be concerned with Sinéad's happiness. Ye will be a great way off, near twae thousand miles or more... and she is nae longer a young lassie. Your presence at the hearth will doubtless weigh more with the lass than some escapade in foreign service, for that is how she will see things. Ye may therefore consider how to reconcile the twae. D'ye suppose Sinéad might be persuaded... were she to accompany ye to some nearer place, some safe haven, out of peril, but with the prospect of your company more frequently than she has previously found in these past years at sea?'

'You are very good, and I am most sensible of your advice,' replied Pat, grasping at the straw.

'I collect that after the tyrant had finally been defeated the Congress of Vienna established yet more of His Majesty's far realm in that very location. A protectorate of wee isles... if my memory serves me, though precisely where they are I cannae say. Perhaps an abode for your family might be established there, facilitating contact with a frequency we never afore enjoyed?'

'I catch your drift, old friend,' Pat smiled, 'The Ionian isles - *a capital notion* - thankee. I will speak of it with Sinéad.'

As the twins cleared away after breakfast Mrs O'Donnell announced in a whispering voice plainly filled with awe, 'Mr Canning is here to see you, sirs, if you are at leisure.'

George Canning had arrived, in evident good humour. He nodded pleasantly to Duncan and Pat. 'Macleod, it is a great pleasure to see you after all these years. It has been an age...'

'Indeed, since ten years at least. Captain O'Connor's visit to ye in the year 'twelve or perhaps it was 'thirteen. Och, 'thirteen it was - after *Shannon* took *Chesapeake*! How could I forget? 'Tis a pleasure to see ye again, sir,' Duncan proffered his hand with undisguised warmth and cordiality, shaking Canning's hand vigorously.

'And you too,' Canning graciously replied before turning to his cousin. 'O'Connor, I have decided I will accompany Lieutenant Macleod to the Greek Committee this morning, and I will look upon it as a most particular favour were you to join us. It will surely prove most interesting.'

'You are very good, sir, I would like it of all things. Macleod has already suggested I might come along, and I will be most happy to join you. I am particularly interested in hearing of the prospects for new ships of war for the Greeks, which only yesterday were mentioned to me by the First Lord, and also the opportunity, perchance, to meet with one of the proponents of the new steam-driven ships... not vessels with which I have been acquainted at all. One Abney-Hastings has been mentioned, a veteran of Lord Nelson's victory at Trafalgar, and it would be a particular pleasure were I to meet with him today.'

'Well, let us be away; 'tis but a short walk,' said Canning, collecting his stick and hat.

In the growing warmth of another fine spring day, walking east through the bustle that was the Strand, it was just a few minutes to reach the Crown and Anchor, located on the corner of Arundel Street and almost opposite the church of St Clement Danes. At the door the meeting was signed "along the corridor and up the stairs" to the first floor committee room. A hubbub of conversation filled the room from approaching thirty gentlemen including many MPs, largely Whigs, many of whom were known vaguely in passing to Pat from his occasional attendances as an Irish Member in the House.

'Aaahh... O'Connor, welcome to our small gathering,' from a not entirely unfamiliar person, hand proferred to Pat. The rather uncharacteristically friendly greeting from Sir Francis Burdett, an outspoken Whig MP, surprised him. 'Er, thank you kindly.

Burdett, is it? Allow me to introduce Lieutenant Duncan Macleod, my particular friend,' he replied.

'Macleod, my pleasure, sir. Are you a Philhellene?' asked Burdett in a conversational tone.

'I am, sir, a friend of freedom in every sphere,' Duncan replied cautiously.

'O'Connor, Burdett is a supporter of the Papists... as you may know, a particular friend of Cochrane too,' Canning volunteered, sensing Pat and Duncan's confusion, 'though he is also one of those promoters of wild ideas, like Tom Paine: revolutionary ideas, democracy and benevolence for all. Bah! Such puerile notions would doubtless lead us to a pretty state of affairs.'

'Och, he has sound qualities then,' remarked Duncan, the comment prompting raised eyebrows all round.

'What have we come to here, Whigs a'plenty and ne'er a Tory can I see? 'Tis a hotbed of Radicals,' said Canning, smiling.

'I am reliably informed that the Committee has at least one Tory, sir: the Reverend Thomas Hughes. Are you acquainted with the gentleman?' asked Burdett, pursing his lips.

'No sir,' Canning scowled.

'A thoroughly ghastly man; doubtless he has missed his true calling. I understand that he advocates the extermination of all the Turks in Greece... hardly the tolerably benevolent approach which we have come to expect from our - will I say - more enlightened clergy. Let us hope the Radicals might serve Greece better,' the hint of triumph plain in Burdett's voice. Pat and Duncan found their interest wavering, Canning visibly tiring of Burdett.

'Macleod! came a familiar voice from the nearby throng, 'What brings you here, how do you find yourself? Tolerably spry, I hope... so good to see you.' It was a welcome distraction for all. 'You remember of me?'

'Why to be sure, my friend, never forgotten. Pat, allow me to introduce John Lempriere, scholar and long an acquaintance of mine. Lempriere, Captain Patrick O'Connor,' Duncan brightened.

'Your servant, sir,' nodded Pat respectfully.

Duncan was plainly relieved to find an attendee at the meeting who was not a politician, and gladly entered into a discussion with Lempriere about the classical ancient history of Greece. Meanwhile, Canning had disappeared into the far corner of the room and was engrossed in conversation with a trio of distinguished looking gentlemen. Pat had begun to feel a little detached from the gathering, political matters never holding great interest for him, and so he looked around, rather hesitantly as if to search for a fellow military man. Although his gaze fell upon one or two of conceivably military bearing he could not identify any.

Shortly after, nearing 1 p.m., there came a strident shout from the corner, 'Gentlemen, gentlemen; may I bid you all heartily welcome, and the meeting is about to convene. Please be seated, thank you.' The hubbub of conversation died as the assembly sat down and the announcer resumed, 'Thank you for coming today to this meeting of the London Greek Committee. My name is Bowring and I am Secretary of this new body, which was formed only in March, so we are young in our standing and young in our achievements. However, our aspirations are strong, our support is growing and we are determined to effect everything we can to support the worthy cause of freedom for the valiant Greeks, striving to shake off their Turk oppressors.' He paused to assess the murmured reception of his words before continuing. 'Today I have great pleasure in welcoming our esteemed new Chairman and distinguished Member of the House who will give the address. Please welcome, gentlemen, Lord Milton!'

There was a polite ripple of applause and Lord Milton stood up and began to speak, his voice a little stiff and formal, 'Thank you kindly, gentlemen. I am exceedingly honoured and pleased to be here today as Chairman of this most admirable cause, one which is truly worthy of the support of all parties of the House and all outside, as can be vouched today from your attendance.' Whilst looking round the room he continued, his voice very low and serious, 'Through our efforts and those of our valiant soldiers and sailors we have seen off one tyrant, Bonaparte, and it is surely within our collective desire to help liberate Greece from another, the Porte.' There was a general murmur of assent from the room. 'Under the most disheartening circumstances the Greeks strive to achieve the independence they have long aspired to, but they are failing. To all friends of humanity and civilisation this insufferable Turk yoke presents intolerable anxiety. Throughout Europe societies have raised considerable sums to support our holy Christian brethren, yet in England little money thus far has been raised. And so it is to this committee and to all friends of the Greeks – formerly a free and enlightened people – that the obligation falls to make public appeal to provide support and funds for the Greeks to throw off the Ottoman tyranny. The Turks have signally failed to put down the early insurrection... and it is clear that the struggle can now end only with independence. It will doubtless be beneficial to England and the world that the Greeks establish a government in the Morea, and in that we will assist. We must also strive to help prevent further Turk butchery, as has taken place on Chios. This committee will henceforth seek the most effective means to do so. We will be seeking donations. We will be seeking also the assistance of military officers of Christian principle to help the Greeks. Gentlemen, your support is sorely needed. These endeavours will be communicated to the provisional Greek government after our next public meeting on the fifteenth of May. Thank you.' There was warm, vigorous applause for the speech and many shouts of 'Hear! Hear him!' as the formal meeting dissolved into numerous informal and voluble discussions which filled the room, the babble vibrant, busy, enthusiastic.

Canning reappeared at Pat's side. 'O'Connor, I regret I am unable to introduce you to Abney-Hastings. I am informed that he is at present in Hydra, in Greece and in the service of the provisional government there. However, may I introduce, from the shipbuilder's company, Mr Daniel Brent, who will describe his proposed new ship?'

'Very pleased, sir, I have heard but little of this new steam propulsion and greatly aspire to know more,' said Pat, turning and offering a hearty handshake to Brent, warm pleasure in his voice.

'If you please, Captain O'Connor; let us repair to the quietude of the saloon downstairs where we can speak further of it.'

'Most happy,' Pat replied. They left together, engaged already in animated conversation.

'Will he support the idea, Macleod?' Canning asked, the tinge of nervousness, the apprehension and his uncertainty plain in his voice.

'I dare say he is turning over the situation in his mind. We have spoken of it at some length...' Duncan replied, striving to place confidence in his reply, '... and we will probably know on the morrow, sir.'

'Macleod, how did you receive the address?' Burdett had returned and was standing alongside Duncan, leaning on his stick.

'Admirable words and worthy sentiments, sir; 'tis to be hoped that such a campaign can be concluded rather more quickly than it took to put Bonaparte down.'

'Yes, indeed so,' said Burdett sharply, concealing well a sympathy for the early republican aspirations of Bonaparte's regime.

By now, it being after 4 p.m., Pat had cause to make haste in order to fulfil his promise to the First Lord, and he double-timed down the Strand, no carriage for hire to be had at all. His lack of fitness let him down after fifteen minutes, but he struggled on even as he gazed about him for a coach. It was fortunate that he was able to hail a Hackney carriage, and he urged the driver to haste. He was growing anxious as twenty minutes later, as 5 p.m. pealed from the church bells of St. Martin-in-the-Fields, the coach arrived at the Admiralty, to Pat's great relief. He gratefully pressed a half-crown, hastily retrieved from his pocket, into the coachman's hand and hastened over the cobblestones into the Admiralty courtyard and thence to the main waiting-room, at that time quite deserted save for a solitary porter. With a nod he passed through to the tiny room adjacent, termed by visiting captains immemorial "the Bosun's Chair" and reserved for appointments solely with the First Lord. The room was warm despite the high ceiling. Though it was the height of summer the customary fire was lit and exhibited a warming cheer in a room in which generally the occupants sat nervously, awaiting their moment with their ultimate superior; moments which for many had been the make or break of their career. Pat did not sit down, rather he paced slowly up and down the room whilst glancing through the little window from which could be seen the Whitehall Arch. Anxiously he inspected his uniform coat and brushed off two or three specks which caught his roving eye. He smoothed imaginary creases in his sleeves, his gaze then falling upon his shoes, which he briefly considered buffing with his handkerchief. He dismissed the thought and gazed through the window, passers-by under the Arch catching his gaze though not his attention. He mused that he recognised one or two of the officers, though at that distance he could not be sure. His nerves were on edge. Had he come to the right decision? He could not waver with the First Lord. He was staring again through the window and started when the summons came, the porter's tone quiet, neutral but not unfriendly.

'Captain O'Connor, sir, you are expected, and the First Lord will see you now.'

'Thankee, Tom, much obliged,' murmured Pat, his pulse instantly racing. He smiled weakly to a familiar old face of many years service at the Admiralty, a man who he had known since his days as a young lieutenant. With some anxiety he paced the corridor, following the porter, constraining his step behind Old Tom on the stairs, and so to Melville's office.

'Good afternoon, O'Connor; be seated if you please. Can I offer you tea? How has your day been? Did you find the Greek Committee of interest?' said the First Lord, coming straight to the point, a thin smile offered as he shook Pat's hand.

'I thank you most heartily, sir, tea would be very welcome.' The clerk disappeared. 'As to the Committee, they were all more in the political line than anyone I could be comfortable with... not a one a military man at all. I was but a bystander. No, I could never move in political circles, to be sure.'

'Pray, did you consider of my proposal?' Melville pressed, raising an eyebrow at Pat's hesitation, a flurry of it passing fleetingly through a mind made up but in momentary turmoil, anxiety showing plain in his face.

'My Lord,' said Pat, suppressing the nervous anxiety he felt, and speaking with as much authority as he could summon, 'I would give my hearth and home away today for a plum ship, one on any station of His Majesty's realm. It would give me joy to consider of anything which will float; even a receiving hulk begins to exhibit an attraction which I never would have conceived of. I have served their Lordships o'er all the oceans, and so to consider of a ship in... in *foreign* service is something I have never been accustomed to. I have been quite despairing of ever going to sea again. Sir, may I say that I have found these past three days particularly stirring; I have encountered my dearest friend, Lieutenant Macleod, after an absence of near two years; I have attended a committee formulating proposals for a fledgling new fleet; I have heard explained the mechanicals of the new steam propulsion, for ships only just now coming of age; I have reflected on the likelihood of several more years on the beach, which is not something I am sensible of... far from it, as you are aware. My absence from command, I reflect, gives me great concern; I have only this past day considered your Lordship's proposal for a return to sea... in foreign service... and giving up my cherished post.' He paused, searching for the best way to further explain his own turmoil of thoughts.

'Yes, yes, but does this, pray, lead you to any conclusion?' prompted Lord Melville with a hint of impatience.

Pat stared, unblinking, at Melville for a moment, swallowed to clear his throat, uncomfortably dry it seemed, and made his commitment, 'Your Lordship will be pleased to know that I will be most uncommon happy *and I have decided*... to accept your proposal.' The reply was stated with a firm voice, the words coming as if from afar, even to Pat's own ears. He exhaled deeply with the release of tension, the pledge made.

'Well done, excellent! Capital! I am most heartily pleased to hear it,' said Melville, rising to offer his hand.

'I have one question of the first significance, my Lord,' said Pat quickly, sensing that the interview would be short.

'Please to continue, O'Connor.'

'I must necessarily require officers of the very first rate for this enterprise, and so I must be assured of your Lordship's commitment – your *personal* commitment, sir – to restore any that join me to the List when this venture is concluded.'

'Of course, on that you have my word,' Melville replied unhesitatingly and with some relief, shifting quickly to conclude the interview. 'Weel... I have an eight o'clock appointment with the Foreign Secretary himself, so away ye go now, 'til we meet again to make the necessary arrangements... and perhaps Lieutenant Macleod might join us next time? Good evening to you. Thankee.'

As they approached to shake hands Melville rang a little bell whilst edging towards his inner door. Pat, his heart racing still, gulped down the remnant of his lukewarm tea, shook hands firmly with the First Lord, nodding as he replied, 'Your servant, sir.' He was shown out by the longstanding porter, who handed over his hat and coat in the reception room downstairs. He looked hopefully at a not unhappy Pat, who paused in the hall, standing stock still in reflection, the gravity of his commitment coming home to him.

'Something Bristol fashion, sir?' enquired Old Tom gently. He knew almost every officer in the Navy, and by longstanding tradition was perfectly entitled to a tip if something had come up to the satisfaction of the visiting officer.

'Indeed, Tom, thankee,' whispered Pat absently, his mind whirling. He pressed the only coin he could find in his pocket, a long-forgotten two pound gold sovereign, into the porter's hand.

An astonished Old Tom rushed ahead to open the door whilst gabbling on with pronounced gratitude, 'Thank you, thank you most kindly sir; obliged, thankee.'

But Pat was already marching across the cobbles and deep in deliberation now that he was committed, his mind whirring frantically with a myriad of matters to organise, until came the alarming thought which quite stopped him in his tracks, 'On my life, how am I to explain this to Sinéad?'

Monday 5th May 1823   *Truro, Cornwall*

Pat and Duncan arrived by carriage in the late evening at Sinéad's aunt's Truro home, their temporary abode, and settled before the fire, a brace of fine port bestowing relaxing contentment upon them after their dinner. They intended a speedy return to the Feathers and the Admiralty, planning only the briefest of interlude at Truro and allowing for just enough time to alert Murphy to proceed with all haste to raise a crew for *Surprise* from former *Tenedos* crewmen, many of whom lived in Falmouth, and, with luck, for Pat to persuade Sinéad of the merits of the scheme. She had accompanied him from Connemara, her mind filled with trepidation at what she might find the purpose of Pat's invitation to be, her acerbic tongue exhibiting the greatest truculence, shrill and unceasing for the whole of a most uncomfortable journey; at least that was how it seemed to a subdued Pat, the Truro arrival coming not a minute too soon, his nerves at breaking point. After some minutes of reflection, he lifted his gaze from a contemplative stare into the fire's flames and looked across to his longstanding friend. 'Duncan, I dare say Murphy will raise a good many men for *Surprise* in Falmouth these next few days... and doubtless will enjoy his time spending my shillings, *indeed my guineas...* in the taverns, and most likely in doubtful company; but we must go ourselves and recruit the best of our old shipmates. We cannot offer them any prizes since Boney has long gone and our American cousins no longer truckle with our commerce, but Falmouth has been hit hard since so many of our fleet was struck off and so many more laid up in ordinary. With commerce being so down these past few years 'tis sure we will have our pick of the best seamen.'

'There is nae doubt, nae doubt at all, brother,' murmured Duncan, most pleasantly surprised to find a glow of enthusiasm, lost since these four years past, rekindling deep within his heart.

'I must speak of this with Sinéad afore she hears of it from Murphy or anyone else,' this spoken with some slight anxiety.

'Gently, I beg ye; given time to consider of it, doubtless she will come round, though I beseech ye, please dinnae press her.'

Sinéad was no different from any other naval wife, accustomed to the lengthy absences of her husband at sea but dearly enjoying his company during the interludes at home. After the unprecedented near four years of being in Connemara it was all the more an unwelcome shock when Pat broke the news of his aspiration to go to sea again. Her reaction was one of the utmost vexation, followed by many hours of sobs, her contentment and accumulation of peaceful quietude in having her husband at home now proving so fragile and temporary that it was more than she could cope with. She had made the journey from Connemara to Truro most uncomfortable, and now that a new commission seemed imminent her dismay and truculence knew no bounds.

In vain did Duncan too consider how best he might help comfort and convince Sinéad, pleas in support of Pat's career seeming wholly inappropriate given the proposed changes in Pat's circumstances. 'He has been offered a command, he is going to sea. Is such so very disagreeable to ye, my dear?'

Sinéad's withering scowl gave him his answer, her reply scarcely necessary. 'I have endured many long years of his absence. Until the year 'nineteen the twins did not know him. Our farm is now strewn with dross, mounds aplenty across all our fields, no precious metals have we ever found; our potato crop has failed these past three years. Home... *home*, is where we need him.'

'Ye spoke of dross, my dear, of precious metals?' Duncan was puzzled, such had never before been mentioned to him.

'Indeed; vile promoters from Dublin it was. Gold aplenty assured, of that there was no doubt; so they said,' Sinéad's despairing reply.

At that an astonished Duncan, blinking, could find no words at all for some minutes, 'How little I know of commerce,' his eventual and rather inadequate reply.

Later that day, Pat himself tried desperately to convince his wife to accept his looming return to sea. 'My dear Sinéad, for near two years I have fretted ashore, ne'er commanding more than a Galway hooker, my uniform collecting dust, all the officers and crew of *Tenedos* thrown on the beach. The fleet continues to be paid off, my dear friend Duncan will again be afar in Stornoway; my other - Simon Ferguson - I have never seen these four years; the twins become ever more feckless, Murphy is more than ever a mumping nuisance... and even my horse tires of me. 'Tis a chance to be at sea again, with a ship, with Duncan... and Simon too perhaps, Murphy and the crew afloat once more... full pay restored, and I don't ask better than that. It will surely make our life easier. My dear, the Ionian isles are a pleasant enough place for you and the twins to spend a summer.'

It was Pat's last throw, a quite desperate plea to recover a losing position, which was obviously the case as he readily saw; all this to a distinctly frosty Sinéad. 'No, Pat, I will not have this. The twins are in need of your presence, your guidance. The farm is failing; we have ne'er seen a potato crop worth tuppence these three summers gone, and I will not stay there without you for more years, I will not!' With that she dissolved into tears and refused Pat's embrace.

Despite Pat's most persuasive and heartfelt efforts, with Duncan maintaining a most diplomatic silence, it was an unexpected and wholly coincidental letter from Sinéad's sister, Kathleen, written and posted weeks before from Stornoway, that ultimately swayed her. The letter expounded on the prospects for the twins to travel, perhaps to visit her in Stornoway or further. She wrote of an imminent visit to Port Mahon and suggested the twins might gain a little worldly experience, perhaps more rapidly mature in mutually reinforcing new and unfamiliar family surroundings, and yet stay close to and see more of their father were he to accompany them. She urged Sinéad to embrace wider prospects for the twins in comparison with the recent years wholly spent in Connemara. In short, Kathleen had suggested that the twins would, in travel, grow up and out of their adolescence and their petty jealousies of Brodie, and would develop into the young adults that they so nearly had become. Sinéad could not deny these points and at the end, after several days, had quite accepted them as the benevolent advice that she had become accustomed to hearing from her older sister.

After this changed conviction had finally been embraced by Sinéad, preparations for departure were adopted with a bustle and enthusiasm Pat could scarcely have imagined, copious orders being issued by the lady of the household, Sinéad's aunt Nora – a wealthy and greatly excited old woman – with letters to a myriad of local tradesmen: for clothing which he could hardly credit as suitable, but to which he made not a whisper of protest, and for foodstuffs by the wagon, ordered for delivery to Plymouth Dock where *Surprise* was being slowly refitted. All despite Pat's attempted but wholly disregarded protests that a crew was yet to be found and there must be some doubt about how far the caulking had progressed, never mind the restoration of the hull's copper-plating.

'I congratulate ye, brother. Never did I think for a moment that it would be Kathleen that would bring her round,' said Duncan, delighted, satisfaction flowing throughout his very being.

'She had pressed me to consider of command of the old seventy-four, the Plymouth receiving-ship. Full pay assured... to be sure there's a great deal to be said for that... and all my nights ashore ... but 'tis no ship for a proper captain, and I would surely be yellowed in time. To be sure, we have the blessing this day,' murmured Pat quietly, great relief in his voice and coursing through his every fibre.

Chapter Three

And where are they? and where art thou,
My country? On thy voiceless shore
The heroic lay is tuneless now —
The heroic bosom beats no more!
And must thy lyre, so long divine,
Degenerate into hands like mine?

Wednesday 7th May 1823   *Falmouth, Cornwall*

It was with great anticipation mixed with rising joy that Pat and Duncan had mounted their horses early in the morning to ride down to Falmouth on a very fine spring day so as to assess the likely crew numbers to be engaged there. Not more than two hours of gentle riding brought them into the town where they had taken rooms for the night at James Wynn's Royal Hotel; time enough remaining during the day and on the morrow to interview applicants, of which Murphy had gleefully reported to Pat, 'Well, there is plenty enough, even were we a seventy-four.'

The port's population of ship owners and mariners generally had been much concerned in recent years by rumours and fears of unemployment. The near neighbouring and long established port of Plymouth Dock hosted much of the Royal Navy, and hence the town's particular fear had been losing the packet trade entirely to the navy. It had now happened, in April, and the takeover of the service had only served to heighten fears generally within all the Falmouth seafarers and merchants. The end of the French war had meant the loss of any sure and significant opportunities for the few remaining local fishermen, demand from the fleet greatly reduced, leaving many to engage in smuggling. The Revenue watchpost on Pendennis Point was a successful deterrent to this, save when the weather in the Channel was inclement and no shore watcher could see the slightest movement through the fog or discover landings on nearby Maenporth Beach. Even so the economy of the town was not prospering, the pilchard catches being so much down, and many seamen were idle for want of a job.

Pat had posted letters to several of his former officers, and whilst no replies had yet actually reached Falmouth - let alone any of the men - he was determined to press on in the meantime and personally engage the crew. The fame of Pat O'Connor as a fighting captain and *Tenedos* as a lucky ship was well known by all the locals, no crew member had ever returned without a sizeable purse from her cruises in the French war, and so there was no lack of volunteers to the call, which Murphy had spread throughout the popular and well patronised public houses of the town for several days, diligently speaking at length over necessary refreshment, as he saw things, with many ladies of less certain repute he found within them. Pat and Duncan therefore had the greatest difficulty passing through the thick crowd awaiting their arrival. The ostler at the Royal Hotel having taken their mounts, the two old friends walked down to the Fish Strand Quay, cheerfully recognising many familiar faces and greeting with pleasure old hands, veterans of prior voyages, prime seamen by the score presenting themselves; both shaking so many hands that the flesh became sore and the bones ached. At the end of the quay some ten yards away Pat, Duncan and Murphy were astonished to see a most unexpected figure, a man of between forty and fifty, of medium but wiry stature, ill-dressed but radiating an energy, a joie de vivre all about him, exuding a feeling of well-being which was captured and reciprocated by the excited, voluble throng of seamen in whose midst he stood. A gathering of old Tenedos's stood all about Doctor Simon Ferguson, boisterous and loud in their shouted exchanges.

'Simon!' shouted Pat as joy spread throughout his every fibre, not having seen his close friend for four years. He quickened his step and gently pushed through the throng of seamen, accepting the briefest of handshakes from a dozen or more pressing him, the men keen to greet their former captain; all were now laughing and gabbling with great joy at this unexpected reunion. Pat nodded to many more, a very few words exchanged with others.

'Greetings, brother,' Simon smiled broadly and the two embraced, arms thrown about each other, no words of adequacy found in the immediacy and warmth of their reunion.

'Joy be with you, old friend,' said Pat after some moments in great exuberance. 'It makes me so happy to see you.'

'*Ceud mìle fàilte[(i)]*' Duncan pronounced, pumping Simon's hand even before he could extract himself from Pat's embrace.

'*Tapadh leat, ciamar a tha thu?[(ii)]*' was all that Simon could reply before Pat released him from his grip and seized his hand immediately upon Duncan's release of it in his enthusiasm to perpetuate his greeting of his old friend. From inauspicious beginnings when the trio had first met in Portsmouth in the year 'three, a deep and enduring friendship had grown and blossomed over the sixteen years afterwards whilst they served together on His Majesty's ships.

'We will speak the Gaelic then. *Gabh mo leiscéal, Duncan! Ní fhaca mé le fada thu,[(iii)]*' Pat interjected.

'Och, ye have the Gaelic. I would never - in all these years - have thought it,' said Duncan in mild surprise.

'Oh I speak it so little... perhaps with the villagers at Claddaghduff. A very few of them speak no English, and so it lingers there still, in the hamlets of the bog and on the islands. It is so very close to the tongue of the Western Isles, and I imagine that your Hebrideans would understand my neighbours. On *Tenedos* I would hear it occasionally spoken by some of the hands, men of Clare and of Galway, sometimes speaking with our marines who hailed from the Uists - the dialects are tolerably close, and it would always bring a little cheer and remind me of home. We have a ship, a ship again, Simon! Ain't that the wonderful news of the world - eh?'

'Why certainly it is a capital development; there is no doubt, no doubt at all.'

A fleeting anxiety for Pat, 'You *are* with us... eh? Simon?'

[(i)] '*A hundred thousand welcomes*'   [(ii)] '*Thank you. How are you?*'
[(iii)] '*Excuse me, Duncan! Long time no see.*'

'I received your letter only yesterday and I came immediately. I had long ceased to contemplate going to sea again, and so your letter was welcome indeed.' Simon, smiling, pointed to his companion. 'Mr Tizard, ship's carpenter and a native of Falmouth, is here with me. He is a veteran of the old *Surprise*, and so has shifted to this successor ship.'

'My duty and best respects sir, if you please. Stuart Tizard, carpenter, in the old *Surprise*... Captain Aubrey.'

'A pleasure to meet you, Mr Tizard,' said Pat, proffering his hand and shaking the carpenter's vigorously.

'Murphy!' exclaimed Simon, 'How are you keeping? Tolerably well, I hope?' He enthusiastically seized and pumped the steward's hand.

Murphy was revelling in his role bringing about the reunion of so many old shipmates, his gap-toothed smile never absent this day but usually seen only on the rarest of occasions. 'All fine and dandy, sorr; an' you look spry if I may say so. Well, ain't it grand to be goin' back to a barky?' he said with great emphasis, the pleasure so evident in his face and in complete contrast to his customary bearing as a sour curmudgeon.

'Indeed it is, for sure,' replied Simon, the pleasant prospect becoming more real to him by the day.

'Well, the whole town is a'fired up, sorr; no better news 'as been heard these five years past. I ne'er knew so many in Falmouth afore these few days: prime seamen aplenty all pressing me for news, old *Tenedos* lads and many others, wives too. Well, I was ne'er so popular with the ladies, your 'onour.'

'Take no liberties, Murphy,' laughed Simon. 'The ship is a small place to share with any husband with a grudge. I collect you had a wife - in Pompey was it?'

'Well, only in the rovin' kind, sorr, if you know what I mean,' Murphy laughed aloud now, in high good spirits; his old shipmates stared, open-mouthed, for such was an exceedingly rare event.

'And was there one in Mahon too?' this asked quietly with a whiff of suspicion but none of reprobation in Simon's voice.

Murphy laughed again - his shipmates looked shocked, 'Well, I 'ad wives in Wapping Dock an' Plymouth Dock as well, though only when we was in port, like.'

'Browster wives all, Murphy; a crabbit auld laidron ye are,' said Duncan, standing alongside Simon, the exchange catching his ear.

'To be sure, there's a deal of sense outside your head, Murphy,' added Pat, smiling.

'Well, sorr, empty and cold is the house without a woman.'

Amongst the Falmouth seamen, Pat's reputation for his ship handling, his plentiful and profitable victories – tactically so well managed as to be won generally at very little cost to his own men – and his kindly and considerate crew management meant that *Tenedos* had always been filled with willing Falmouth hands, embarking not solely for financial gain but also in a spirit of adventure. The seamen were long accustomed to the often poor standards of food and accommodation aboard a fifth rate, but Pat O'Connor offered a harmonious regime without the starting or hazing customarily found on many Royal Navy vessels, and so, for the old *Tenedos* hands, the self-imposed mutual discipline of professional seamen was a great part of their keen interest in joining up again. As most of the old *Tenedos* crew were well known to them all, Murphy had already, with the aid of a clerk, constituted the prospective crew list for approval, and Pat spent the day meeting many of his former shipmates and others brought along by them, every prospective crew member vouched for by veteran shipmates until, by 8 p.m. when they stopped for supper, over one hundred and fifty had been interviewed – albeit very briefly in the case of those particularly familiar to Pat – and over one hundred and thirty men had been engaged; only the old and infirm being turned away in kindly fashion and with the most gentle words of reluctance. Simon Ferguson, meanwhile, was consulted by several old shipmates with minor ailments and one or two with social diseases, which he was able to treat, having brought with him the basics of his medical chest in anticipation of just such a necessity.

By eight o'clock in the morning there was gathered a further queue of hopeful applicants to complete the crew of *Surprise*, all keen and filling the public room of the Royal Hotel to capacity. Scores more waited outside, for the most part former shipmates from *Tenedos's* years in His Majesty's service, particularly from the more recent voyage to South American waters. More men had gathered than had been present to welcome Pat on the quay the previous day; hence Pat, Simon and Duncan, with Murphy leading, struggled with difficulty through the loud crush at the public bar out again to the street outside, the bar proving wholly inadequate in size for all the boisterous seamen gathered within and without, all of them anxious in every case to know whether they could make the crew roster.

'I will tell you what, we will have no want of shipmates, Duncan, the line since this past hour is a hundred yards if an inch,' remarked Pat.

'There is a deal of prime seamen like myself with nae work since so many ships were paid off.'

'We will have no need of the Press then?' asked Simon.

'There ain't any Press,' Pat smiled, "tis gone these eight years, but with so many men seeking a berth we shall have no need of any scrovies in our crew; we will have no froward troublemakers; we will take none but prime seamen, the pick of Falmouth's tars.'

Murphy, glorying in his role as recruiting sergeant, stepped up on a bench brought out to the quay and, at Pat's nod, commenced calling out the roll of men in the line which had been prepared by the attendant clerk, 'Adams, Bailey, Bartlett, Benson, Bluett, Bolitho, Boscowen ... Bower... Barton, Brompton ...'

'Capital gunners,' said Pat, with a wide smile, recognising many old *Tenedos* hands. 'Welcome Boswell, welcome Brompton.'

'Thankee, sir,' the excited replies came back with huge grins.

Murphy resumed, 'Beer, Belker, Boulderson, Bown, Braithwaite, Browne, Bull, Carne, Clies, Collins, Corker, Courtney, Currie T, Currie W - Tom's younger brother, sorr.'

'Do you vouch for him, Tom?' demanded Pat of one of his oldest *Tenedos* veterans.

'Aye, your honour. He is right masterly on the yards, sir; a grand man to have aloft. He came d'reckly all the way from Pompey as soon as he heard you was recruiting.'

'I will take him. Murphy, enter young Currie as able, topman.'

'Aye, aye, sorr. Daniels...'

'Daniels! Welcome back,' cried Pat to his captain of the maintop of long ago, 'Grand it is to see ye.'

'Thankee, sir,' came the cheerful reply.

'Dalby,' continued Murphy, shouting loud, trying to make himself heard above the general babble.

'There you are, Dalby. Welcome back!' shouted Pat with just a shred more enthusiasm than he felt.

'An honour, sir,' bawled "Clumsy" Dalby: probably Pat's most devoted crew member of many voyages, but a man with a fully deserved nickname. He looked very pleased to be acknowledged by his captain and touched his knuckle to his forehead.

Murphy pressed on, 'Horsey, Jelbert...'

Pat glanced momentarily at a young man who he did not recognise, yet the name was familiar to him: an older Jelbert had been his master gunner on *Tenedos*, an able and valued shipmate.

'James...'

Pat shouted across the throng to several of the old Tenedos's who customarily served two of his great guns. 'Abel James, William Horsey, home again to our new barky. We will be well with our guns now, lads!' His greeting raised a great cheer.

Another veteran, Maclean, pushed forward, 'Douglas Maclean, gunner and topman on our auld *Tenedos*, your honour. I hope I see ye well, sir?'

'For sure 'tis a pleasure to see ye, Maclean; that it is.'

'Marder, Millett, Mould, Mumford,' Murphy battled on, valiantly persevering for a full two hours, his voice cracking, his throat sore despite his plentiful swigs from a quart flagon of ale kept nearby, until the end of his list of more than one hundred and fifty names approached, with Pat greeting many more old shipmates with a kindly word or two until, his throat now sore, he shouted once more over the hubbub, 'Welcome, Mr Wagstaff; shipshape, I trust!'

'Prime, sir, thankee, sir,' came back the enthusiastic reply.

'Ah... Wilkins! Grand to have you back,' said a smiling Pat to his personal cook of *Tenedos* days. 'Praise the Lord, we will not have to count on Murphy for my dinner!' a delighted Wilkins grinned, touched his forehead as Pat laughed loud and long, and Murphy scowled.

'Zabinski... sorr, 'tis the last,' croaked Murphy with considerable relief, his voice beginning to fail him.

'Make your mark, here, Zabinski,' croaked Pat amiably to another *Tenedos* veteran, 'and welcome back.'

'Thankee, sir; a happy day this is, so it is; thankee, thankee.'

'There is no man here happier than me, Zabinski. Deeply pleased I am to see so many old shipmates... men of *Tenedos* aplenty. Will you wait on 'til we are finished here? I have a few words to say to all our lads.'

'Aye sir, for sure I will. We all will. Thankee, sir, thankee.'

The second day had now passed with barely any pause. Early evening was near upon them by the time all one hundred and fifty candidates had been interviewed to select the final hundred and ten or so needed to make up his crew of some two hundred and forty men in all, plus officers and warrant officers. At the end Pat was very satisfied. 'Well done Murphy. Well done indeed; a capital job!' Pat tried to shout across the street but his voice failed him.

'Lads!' Duncan shouted, 'Pipe down!' The hubbub faded.

'Lads,' Pat resumed in a quieter voice, 'We cannot be sure of any prizes on this voyage, Boney long being dead.' A great cheer arose, fading after a minute. 'We will not start in the thick of any war... and our particular circumstances will be for us to discover... but I can assure ye of timely wages...' Another huge cheer rose, '...good commons, safe lying...' Pat, his own throat dry and desperately painful, seized Murphy's flagon and took a deep draught. 'I can... I can assure ye of the companionship of a sound crew, kindly officers and an adventure for sure. What say ye lads?'

The cheering resumed, tumultuous for several minutes, reverberating along the quay, the atmosphere of the gathering jubilant, all standing in the warm evening air, women staring out of all the opened quayside windows, waving, laughing. Very slowly the roar abated as Pat raised his hand in happy acknowledgement, in joy, his face radiating happiness.

From the back of the crowd, from Wright, a very stout former Tenedos and a prime gunner who Pat had been particularly pleased to re-enlist there came a loud shout of 'Off hats.'

The street filled again with resounding cheering, continuing for some moments, blissful to all present, until Pat slowly raised his hand again and waited for the din to subsume. In a low voice, for that was all he could manage, he whispered, 'The bar is open this evening, lads, on my purse for all the crew.'

This brought further cheers from the contented assembly and loud shouts of, 'Hurrah! Hurrah! Hear the captain! Hear him!' interspersed with scores of whistles; all shipmates, for that is what the gathering all now felt themselves to be, vigorously clapping. The cacophony diminished only after several minutes when an obviously tired and emotionally moved Pat raised and waved his hat in salute to them all.

'Does it not lift your spirits mighty high, Simon, our old Tenedos's here again, a prime crew, not a landsman amongst them... almost all rated able... the barky being readied for sea?'

Simon nodded, 'And we will have no hallions; we will have none of the sad gomerels inflicted upon us in *Tenedos* by the Press.'

'Is this not our happiest day for many a year, Duncan?'

'I wholly share your sentiment, brother; nae brighter day ever arose in all my time in the Isles.'

By 6 p.m. a very happy Pat prepared to leave for Truro with Duncan. An extra horse had been procured for Simon. Murphy, being no rider, was to settle the bar account next day and follow on by coach.

'A prime set of lads, Duncan, prime. So many Falmouth men are competent sailors... and many of them navigators too; we will not want for a good crew,' declared Pat with satisfaction as they mounted their horses. The sun was sinking beyond the higher town behind them, quietude beginning to descend over the quay as the gulls settled for the night, the masts and rigging of the smaller ships tied alongside the quay still just illuminated by the sun's fading rays; dark shadows reached out from the walls of the buildings, the vapours now beginning to rise from the water into the cooling evening air, the more distant and larger ships in the Carrick Roads disappearing within the rising mists.

'Never in doubt, my friend,' Duncan replied, pleased to see the deep satisfaction so evident on Pat's face.

Near two hours of wearying, slow riding brought the now deeply fatigued trio back to Truro where they sat in front of the blazing log fire, the later hours of the early spring evenings still cooling quickly. Within a short time they were delighted to enjoy their favourite supper of toad in a hole, prepared by Freeman, washed down with a bottle of excellent madeira from the wonderful vintage of seventy-five, which Pat eked out from his travelling dunnage and brought out from his private cellar only on the most particular of occasions. He explained recent events to Simon: the call from his cousin, Canning; his interview with the First Lord and the offer of *Surprise* for the Greek venture. 'Tomorrow, I must away to Plymouth Dock and see what can be done to speed the refitting. Would you both care to join me?'

'I should like it of all things. Pray, is there much yet to be done, tell?' inquired Simon, who had not heard much about the venture.

Pat set down his glass and recounted the refit progress, the minutiae of it all so clear in his mind. 'The hull caulking and sheathing fixing must be nearly finished by now, the rotten keel bolts may not all be out and replaced yet, new sailcloth has come but recently from Pompey and the yard are making new mainsails and jibs...' Duncan was listening closely, Simon's attention wavering as Pat continued, 'Some cordage is to be replaced... the rats having inflicted grave damage on it whilst she has been lying up, and there remains the decking to be recaulked in some few places; some netting is very old and will need replacing ...'

Duncan interjected, 'Och, 'tis all in good hands at Plymouth Dock, nor any other place would scarcely do better?'

'Oh yes, *Surprise* is in the best possible place, and in very good hands for her refit, dear friend, be assured of it,' Pat replied with an undisguised tremor of growing enthusiasm in his voice. 'On the whole she is not far from being shipshape and all Bristol fashion. She is a prime ship; I dare say she may be the very finest fifth rate afloat. Perhaps another week or two...' Pat paused and smiled.

'I am most heartily glad. What better prospects could we see, auld friend - eh?' said Duncan, sharing his enthusiasm.

Pat resumed, 'The report I have received from the Master Attendant explains her state as she was and as she lies now. The yard in her refitting has installed strong cross bracing within the hull and even new knees... that is, where there has been any doubt of the originals.'

'She has knees then?' asked Simon, his attention recaptured.

Pat paused, as if deliberating on how best to reply to his revered old friend's plainly absurd question. He stared at him with sincere kindness, affection. 'Of course she has knees; have I never explained ships' structure to you afore?'

'Oh, I dare say you may have mentioned it.'

'Not above a score of times.'

Duncan replenished the glasses with whisky, 'Auld Scotland wants nae skinking ware; but, if ye wish her grateful prayer... to our dear *Surprise*, aye!' He raised his glass; Pat and Simon, both looking puzzled, followed. 'A wee tait from Robbie Burns.' Drinks were downed in one and all sat back in utter contentment, the pleasure so much more in all being together for the first time in years.

'I have never doubted the Plymouth men. Though there be many rascallions in that yard, as I have found these four years, there can be no doubt at all of their abilities, none at all,' said Simon, sipping a fresh measure of a gentler madeira, the glow of satisfaction spreading within him.

Saturday 10th May 1823   *Plymouth Dock, Devon*

With the warm and fine spring weather persisting, the trio of friends had set off from Truro after a very early breakfast, all in good cheer, and ridden the Friday to Liskeard, resting there overnight before riding through the bright morning at a gentle pace to reach the Hamoaze at noon the next day. With a rising sense of anticipation they stared across the grand, sheltered river where three seventy-fours and two frigates were anchored, gazing for long minutes in the bright sunshine to take in the satisfying sight of the familiar naval ships, something about them so reassuringly strong and substantial even as they rocked gently on the sparkling waters. They crossed over via the New Horse Ferry from Torpoint and walked the horses through the fort gates, passed by the barracks and on to the Dock gate. They were directed along the length of the rope-houses, past the mast pond and so to the waterside, the yard busy with many men moving all about it. Carefully they picked their way through timbers, ropes and materials of all forms, strolling amidst the aroma of boiling hot tar, staring about them as if to drink in the pleasure of being amongst ships once again. They walked slowly a hundred paces further in their excitement, all the while staring everywhere about them; and so came to *Surprise,* propped majestically on the slip, quite resplendent even though her masts were absent. They stared in silence for some minutes, each in private contemplation, the pleasure so very deep.

'Look, Duncan, Simon. Ain't she the prettiest sight of the world,' exclaimed Pat eventually, the ship so significant, right in front of him, his excited thoughts formulating only slowly into his words.

'Och, there is a sure resemblance to our auld *Tenedos*. She is practically indistinguishable I find,' said Duncan quietly, finding the moment so uplifting, a return to sea after long years now so imminent, so real.

'Magnificent, nothing finer could we behold,' Simon added, finding his own spirits soaring.

'Let us find the Master Shipwright, Edward Churchill. Simon, *mind that yard!*' shouted Pat when they moved off after some minutes towards the ship. 'Step carefully now.'

They went onboard to find Mr Churchill, a grizzled old man approaching seventy; still with a plethora of white hair, wrinkled hands and the florid, wind-burnt face so customary to those engaged in outdoor working. He was inspecting the new deck caulking, and when they asked of the works he pronounced himself delighted with progress, declaring with enthusiasm, 'the ship's hull is as sound as the strongest bell.' Having also expertly assessed the bracing he deemed it 'as firm as the day it was installed.' In the preceding week he had scrutinised the keel on the slip with the utmost care, and so assured Pat that every single keel bolt had been changed so as to hold not the slightest doubt about the hull strength, even all seemingly sound bolts having been pulled out and replaced. 'To be sure, 'tis the iron of the bolts and the copper of the sheathing, and they don't get along. Best change 'em all whilst she is out of the water. She be good for at least another five years now,' he pronounced with unfaltering confidence. 'Her masts are in good order, and my lads will begin to refit them on the morrow. The sails will be ready next week; the new Riga cordage will be here come Monday... and fitted too by Friday - we will have no twice-laid, rotten rubbish. Just you be leaving us to it, Captain O'Connor, sir, and we will see all is finished, timely like, afore Whit.'

'That is very welcome news, Mr Churchill, and I thank you kindly for your progress thus far,' said Pat gratefully, trying hard to keep his face turned towards Churchill, everything about the ship, *his* ship, demanding his eyes. 'Sir, 'tis our intention to be away to sea on the Tuesday after Whit, as doubtless we will find few crew happy to sail on the holiday.'

'No sir, neither will any of my lads be here in this yard 'til the Tuesday,' the Master Shipwright replied.

'Duncan, we must fetch her crew here afore Whit Monday to ready her for the passage to Falmouth, declared Pat, 'and that means at least forty men. We will use *Eleanor;* we can accommodate them aboard *Surprise...* she will be off the slip and in the water by then. It will be no bad thing to have them here by the Friday so as to check and tighten rigging, and to load the casks of salt pork and beef. She will receive her stores from the victuallers here for we have none of significance in Falmouth.'

Satisfied that *Surprise* was in good hands and the refit proceeding admirably, Pat, Duncan and Simon left the yard for dinner, the horses resting and being fed at the yard's own stable. A pleasant stroll past the New Basin and the drydocks brought them to the Steam Packet public house.

'Have I acted in haste, Duncan... this new venture decided upon out of my own frustration, not being at sea these four years past?' asked Pat, pausing from a very welcome steak pie.

'Nae, my friend, I dinnae suppose ye have,' replied Duncan. 'It seems very much akin to Lord Cochrane's voyages for Chile, and ye are to consider we will be accompanied for the most part by our close friends and family. What more could ye ask? Give ye joy with all my heart.'

'I will be very happy. Thank you,' whispered Pat.

Friday 16th May 1823   *Falmouth, Cornwall*

Early on the Friday morning before Whit, the sun emerging, weak and low in the sky, the three friends were once more at Falmouth with their dunnage already loaded aboard *Eleanor,* a Garmouth, Geddie-built, two-masted topsail schooner belonging to Pat. Bought on Duncan's personal recommendation and a fast sailer even when close-hauled, she had served as tender to *Tenedos* in her latter years under Pat's command. With *Eleanor's* small crew were a forty-strong nucleus of old *Tenedos* veterans, many of whom were members of the Wesleyans of Falmouth, an ecclesiastical movement, recent in origin but not the only one in the town, which was also home to many other nonconformist chapels. Men from most of these chapels had been represented in the crew of *Tenedos* on prior voyages.

Whilst the last of *Eleanor's* stores were loading, Simon engaged the master in conversation. He was a cautious and scrupulous man, a Wesleyan elder. They sat on small kegs - water butts for the boats - along the Custom House Quay, 'Mr Prosser, good morning to you. I venture the crew seem to be in prodigious fine spirits this morning, very pleased to be serving again... and with Captain O'Connor.'

Jeremiah Prosser was old in comparison to the average seaman; a veteran of many voyages aboard *Tenedos*, his face and arms were burned brown by long years of exposure to the sun, deep wrinkles covering every visible area of his skin; his hands were large and muscular. From his eyes, still bright blue, shone an energy, a spirit, which radiated confidence to all men aboard the ships in which he served. 'Why to be sure, Doctor, there is no doubt. We have all of us given thanks to Our Lord every day in our chapel since Murphy brought news of the Captain returning and *Surprise* coming out of ordinary at Plymouth to go to sea again. These past four years have brought hard times to this town. After the French were beaten most of us were turned ashore; even our kin working away in Plymouth and far Pompey dockyards have been laid off, precious little work to be had and our families all long since on short commons... little or no fishing left anymore... no privateering these days, no money hardly at all and no brandy smuggling worth a candle this past year since them new Revenue cutters were built in Poole. Very swift indeed they be, Doctor... and then the rumour in the town which all have long feared - that the packets would be handed over to the navy - has come true! No, we all gave praise to Our Lord when we heard that the barky was coming out again, to Falmouth, and the Captain seeking a crew for a year or two; 'tis a chance again for pay and to put some bread on the table.'

'Mr Prosser, did Murphy explain to you and the lads that this was not to be another surveying voyage? *Surprise* is no longer a Royal Navy ship and we are to be privateers, *mercenaries* in the service of the new Greece,' Simon enquired cautiously.

The master's smile stretched all the way from one luxuriant sideburn to the other, unkempt sideburns being common to the

Wesleyan seafarers of Falmouth. 'Oh, yes, sir, 'tis clear, and nobody cared, nobody cared at all. Even were we to be sailing against the French, against the Yankees... or even the Spanish, sir... just as long as we could get back to sea. The same pay as our brothers still serving on His Majesty's ships and the prospect of some prize monies as well... it seemed too good to be true. We thanked Our Lord.' There were nods all round from the hands coiling away *Eleanor's* cords, and Prosser continued. 'We all hurried to make our preparations, to tell our wives, mothers and fathers. Off to sea again... praise Our Lord and be thankful.'

'We are all thankful of that, Mr Prosser,' Simon said warmly.

'When the Captain himself arrived, sir, it was all that many of us had hoped for... and for a very long time... and then *Eleanor* came into the harbour. When she came alongside the quay there were already more than a score of us to help tie her up, and a goodly cheer was raised when the job was done. Young Mr Reeve, her skipper, is a Falmouth lad, sir, born and bred. A grand day it was, indeed. Plentiful ale was drunk in the King's Arms later... and the chapel was full that evening, Doctor, I can tell you.'

'I am sure of it,' Simon replied, heartily pleased to hear of the good spirits pervading Pat's new crew.

At last *Eleanor* was ready and the tide was high, just past slack water; she was set fair for the ebb current. Pat was perfectly at ease leaving master's mate William Reeve to take her out. The lines were cast off, and with just her topsail and jibs to drive her, the schooner's men standing ready to hoist her fore and main sails, with only the faintest of north-westerly zephyr acting upon her, *Eleanor* slipped gracefully away from the quay, moving slowly out from the inner harbour towards the Carrick Roads. The Falmouth men were all waving to their families, a happy multitude still thronging the quay, all of them still waving back to *Eleanor* as she receded a mile distant into the Roads, many anxious hearts and happy faces left far astern in her wake.

The master hovered at Reeve's elbow in a schoolmasterly fashion, not wanting to utter a single word of guidance unless it became absolutely necessary; not that he thought it would be. The Falmouth men, the Surprises, some forty or so now aboard, lined *Eleanor's* sides, as if in a kind of wonder, all striving to savour the realisation, that fleeting moment of joy: they were at sea again - on a respectable venture and departing in the full glare of daylight. Several still gazed back for long, thoughtful minutes to their now distant family and friends; most simply savoured the moment, basking in the pleasure of being aboard a vessel once more. Once *Eleanor* was in mid-channel and Pendennis Castle off her starboard beam, Reeve ordered the fore and main to be hoisted, the Eleanors aided by the Surprises making light work of the sail handling: *Eleanor* was now bearing for Falmouth Bay.

Pat was watching events with the utmost delight from the taffrail, and not a word passed his lips until he spoke to Duncan as they passed the Black Rock to starboard, 'William is a splendid man to have with us. Ne'er a better master could we ever have for *Eleanor.*'

'Nae doubt at all,' said Duncan, pleasantly engrossed with the spectacle of their departure.

'I should take it very kindly if you will join me for dinner, Mr Reeve,' said Pat with a broad smile, 'when she is set fair on her course.'

'Oh, with great pleasure, sir; thank you.'

Both fore and main sails were now full and *Eleanor* swiftly picked up speed. 'Nicely done, Mr Reeve, most uncommon neat indeed,' pronounced Pat as she passed St Anthony Head. With a strengthening north-westerly wind behind her and a very pleasant sea state *Eleanor* made short shrift of the bay crossing to Plymouth. By early afternoon she approached the emerging new breakwater and sailed on past Saint Nicholas's Island, past Devil's Point and so to the shelter of Mutton Cove, tying alongside there: neither Reeve nor the master were greatly familiar with the Hamoaze, and both were anxious not to foul any ship's cables by approaching the anchorage.

It was but a brief walk for the Surprises, a short half mile from *Eleanor's* berth to where *Surprise* had previously been on the slip. She was now anchored within the Hamoaze, still very near the New Basin. The men shuffled along the quay and through the yard, chatting away in prime good humour, every man eager to go aboard the frigate - so nearly identical to *Tenedos* which for most of them had been their home afloat for many a year. Their rising excitement was palpable as they were rowed out to *Surprise* in the yard's boats, revelling in the day; their loud, jocular comments and good-natured banter endemic. Pat could not bring himself to call them to order, feeling precisely the same himself. He was the first to climb aboard. There was no formal, welcoming guard of marines, nor would there be on this *unofficial* voyage, but he cared not a jot. He gazed slowly all about him, subsumed in his happiness, his mind swiftly registering the yard's restorations. Her guns, masts and spars were all restored and half a dozen yard workers were still aboard, making final touches to deck caulking. The Master Shipwright himself, Edward Churchill, was there, keeping a wholly unnecessary eye on his team, of whose workmanship Pat had never seen the equal.

'Upon my word, Mr Churchill, she does look prime!' Pat gazed about him, noting the masts and spars all a-tanto, the rigging restored and the deck all freshly caulked; only in a very few places was it yet to be holystoned to remove the little surfeit of pitch – a task for the Surprises on the morrow. The new sails were for the most part all loosely hung and strapped from the yards – not in any ways that any other than a yard crew would be happy with, but hung nevertheless. The cordage was everywhere new, nicely coiled where it lay on the deck. All the old Tenedos's were immensely gratified to see that the men of the yard – knowing that *Surprise* was bound for Greece as her primary warship, the Royal Navy grapevine being what it was – had hung a long, blue pennant at the mizzen, now fluttering proudly in the strong breeze. It was not a pennant that could be considered official, of course, and it was one that would be swiftly struck down as soon as *Surprise* left the yard, but it was a visible and generous token of the esteem in which Captain O'Connor was held in all the West Country ports, Devonport most particularly.

'I am infinitely obliged to you, Mr Churchill. A finer and faster refit no other yard could have accomplished in the time. Thank you kindly, sir; she is a beautiful sight to behold,' said a delighted Pat.

'The task has been a great pleasure for us all here in the yard, sir. Indeed, my lads all think of her as *their* ship, since she has oft been in and out of this yard in the past. 'Twas my lads, bless 'em, that fitted her new knees, and no other ship has ever given them so much pride in their work,' offered a deeply moved Churchill, so obviously and genuinely pleased to see a ship returned to active service rather than the now far more customary work of his yard of hulking ships – ships that in many cases had many more years of useful life left in them. He was visibly delighted and relieved that *Surprise* was preserved from that particular and ignominious fate, and proud that she had been saved by *his* yard and by *his* lads.

'Allow me to say that she is a credit to you and your men, sir... no doubt, no doubt at all.'

The Surprises, for that is how they all immediately felt themselves to be, were now swarming over the quarterdeck, the gun deck and the rigging. Some were already preparing to shave and holystone the new deck caulking, prominent in its seams. The cook had gone below to light the galley fire; others were checking the water butts, inspecting the bilges, testing the pumps and generally busying themselves in every conceivable task, all to a man delighted to be aboard a ship once more.

It was gratifying to Pat to see all the activity happening, all wholly unbidden. 'Simon, dear friend; ain't it very like a homecoming?' he whispered, feeling quite emotional.

'You are of my way of thinking entirely, soul. I do not believe I had expected this... this deep satisfaction,' Simon seemed genuinely overcome, 'Though Dr Tripe at the Dock is a fascinating man... and a member of the Royal College, I have oft enjoyed the most cordial of hours with him in examination of his collections, his stuffed birds most particularly... and his wife, Mary, is the most kindly treasure... I admit I have long tired of that place.' He gazed all about him at the ship. 'She is remarkably beautiful, for sure. Never afore did I have the same pleasure in simply stepping aboard ship. But is she not now an auld lady?'

'Old?' Pat stared at his friend, mildly affronted, 'Old? She ain't old, Simon. Only a scrub would say such a thing. You must never say that. Sure there are some who would say she may be old-fashioned, long past mark of mouth and too puny to engage with her modern sisters, forty-fours and the like... and that she is too small for the current age. These opinions have credence for the most part in those lubbers who have ne'er found themselves spitting out the salt stream, wipin' their eyes of the powder smoke when the shot is flying... or firing three broadsides in five minutes. She is but thirteen years old... and has been looked after tenderly, like a maiden aunt... handled gently like a risen pudding afore it reaches the table... since ever afore she was laid up for so long. No, she has a long life in her yet, our dear *Surprise*. I am cast down and mortified to hear you say such things; shame on you.'

Simon looked anxiously into Pat's face. 'I am so sorry, brother; I use the term only as an endearment... akin to making the acquaintance of a long lost, auld friend... a dearly beloved friend... one who perhaps had been thought lost and was found again, the pleasure being so much more in the finding. Doubtless you are correct as to her longevity. Forgive me, Pat; I meant no other inference. I find I love the ship as much as you, and there you have my confession, coming from a mind of a generally scientific persuasion... though assuredly our dear *Surprise* now brings the nature of a philosopher to the fore. Give you joy of our homecoming, brother... a precious event it is.'

At that moment Pat, smiling broadly, was distracted by Murphy, struggling by himself to hoist Pat's two bags up from the boat, loud cursing evidencing Murphy's return to his customary form. 'Murphy! Belay that whingeing. Stow 'em away in the cabin, handsomely does it!' He looked round for helpers. 'Hartley! Currie!' he shouted to two of the crew of one of the *Tenedos* aftmost starboard eighteen-pounders, who were engaged already in chipping away peeling black paint from a gun, the equivalent gun to the one on their former *Tenedos;* their gun, as they now considered it to be, and scraping away just a little crusted salt from the carriage woodwork. 'Bear a hand! Bring the Doctor's dunnage aboard. No need to pay any attention to the great guns just yet, lads.' He turned back to his steward, 'Murphy! Pass the word for the cook; plenty of bacon and soft tack for the crew in half an hour, and grog to wash it down. Freeman! Light along there and see about some coffee and kedgeree, if you will.' His orders were expressed rather more politely than his customarily more formal manner with his servants, for nothing would be allowed to intrude upon his enjoyment of this particular day.

'Well, just aboard and no bleedin' peace already,' grumbled Murphy, standing with Freeman to recover from his exertions hauling up the baggage before going to the cabin and awaiting Pat's further rebuke.

''Tis comin', massa!' shouted Freeman.

'Waites! Fisher! See how much water is in the well.' Pat was once again in his natural element.

'She's nicely tight and dry, sir; barely an inch or two,' came back the report within minutes.

'Very good; get yourselves some grog, lads.'

After a further two hours had passed with a myriad checks completed and as the crew were sitting on the deck with their grog and finishing up their bowls of burgoo, Pat, standing amidships on the gun deck and, as was plain to all, marvelling at his good fortune, called them all together. 'Lads, we will be taking on stores tomorrow, we will hold church on Sunday; on Monday we will bring aboard our water and livestock, and load powder and shot from the hoy. We will leave on Tuesday's ebb, over to Falmouth. Let us have no riotous drinking here in Plymouth Dock. Any hand who is drunk will be left ashore. There's ten shillings each for all hands for your needs until we depart on Tuesday. Anderton! Belker! You will keep those lines just fine and dandy.'

'Aye aye, sir,' they acknowledged, grinning happily.

All day preparations continued to take *Surprise* to sea. The forty or so Falmouth seamen - the majority of them Wesleyans - worked from sun up, several of them nursing thick heads from over-indulging in the taverns of Morice Town the prior evening, but not a man missed the early start. Mr Tizard, the veteran ship's carpenter, checked the yard's workmanship with an experienced eye. Deck holystoning wnt on incessantly; the great guns were cleaned and oiled, several men continuing to chip away at their lingering remnants of peeling black paint. Below deck was aired, the deck gratings all lifted away. The galley was cleaned and the fire relit, bilges were freshened with salt water and pumped dry, and so it went on: the crew pausing only for water, grog and the cook's burgoo; a great pot of which was maintained steaming on the galley, repeatedly fed with fresh milk and more oats.

From nine o'clock onwards a constant stream of coaches and wagons arrived on the quay with stores from the Plymouth victuallers, brought onboard by *Surprise's* boats: casks of salt pork, salt beef – every man entitled to six pounds a week, gristled, bony and fat as it was; bread, beer, suet, oatmeal, oil, ship's biscuit, dried peas, flour, salt, onions, carrots, turnips, sugar, cheese, great barrels of lime and lemon juices, and kegs of vinegar and rum. Much baggage had also been sent down by Sinéad from Truro, anticipating *Surprise* being in Falmouth for the very shortest of stays and likely leaving little time to take the family's necessaries, as she deemed them, aboard. There were many and varied outfits of clothing, boots, wet-weather gear, hats of all sorts, woollen gloves, leather gloves, calfskin gloves, belts, crockery, even a silver dinner service. From the local vintners there were cases of good burgundy, fine French brandy, of malt whisky for Pat's Scots companions. Pat's 'cello, Simon's viola, music stands, rugs, blankets, many and varied chests with Sinéad's accoutrements, clothing for Fergal and Caitlin, further clothing for Kathleen and Brodie - all came aboard; and so it went on for many an hour, all Pat's family's chests being manhandled by a disgruntled Murphy.

'Well, I ain't ne'er seen so much bleedin' dunnage afore, and where is it all to be stowed?' declared Murphy to his helper, Clumsy Dalby. 'A dozen o' shirts for the Captain! Well, all will need pressin', an' we ain't ne'er 'ad more'n six aboard afore. We ain't some dandy Indiaman. Dalby, stop your blathering, get your nose and paws out o' that chest, you graspin' sod,' grumbled Murphy in his high-pitched, nasal whine.

'Well, sorr, if you please, now here is your second-best breeches,' said Murphy later in the morning when unpacking clothing in the cabin. Murphy had served with Pat for many years. Never a master mariner but originally a passable foremast hand, his very few abilities and perpetually complaining attitude as the captain's servant left absolutely everything to be desired. Yet with his old-maidish skills for sewing, silver-polishing and pressing Pat's clothes he had inexplicably overcome all rational selection processes to become Pat's valet and servant, performing the same service for Simon. Since he had been apprised of the imminent return to sea aboard *Surprise,* Murphy was a new man – almost; he had taken on the task of rousing out the old *Tenedos* men in Falmouth with an enthusiasm never before seen by Pat or Simon.

Such stores of wine and brandy that had so far come aboard had, inexplicably, not suffered from any accidental breakages. Even his disagreeable, righteous whingeing had gone by the board for the most part: greatly to the astonishment of Pat and Simon. Still, Murphy could not quite rein in his matronly concern for his captain as he stepped up to the busy quarterdeck, distress mixed with anger as he cried, 'Mind your breeches on that 'ot tar! Oh bejabers, your honour has sat on it an' you'se ruined 'em, your best bloody breeches, for shame. Ne'er will it come out nor I spend a week a'washin'. Ain't I for ever tellin' you your sleeve is in the soup, an' that takes a deal o'scrubbin', an' now 'ot tar on your breeches. Ruined, quite ruined they be. Well, I laid out them very old breeches this morning, an' they be still there. Well, what your wife would say - were she here, the Lord only knows …' adding a proper, 'ax pardon, sorr,' after but a moment and a grovelling 'Coffee's up, sorr.'

'Thankee, Murphy. Now cease your blathering and pass the word for the master,' replied Pat patiently, long accustomed to Murphy's irritating idiosyncrasies. The steward left and within moments Prosser appeared with a knock on the door. He had been listening behind it with barely contained pleasure to Pat's exchange with his steward and had strived diligently to avoid laughing aloud. 'Mr Prosser, the lads are working uncommon well these two days. You are familiar with all of 'em and the new lads. You would favour me most deeply by proposing one of them as my cox'n.'

The master paused momentarily, staring for several seconds as if weighing his reply carefully. It seemed to all the onlookers as if wisdom was radiating from his wizened face as he replied, 'Aye, sir; there is but one man I would favour as cox'n.'

'Who is this man, Mr Prosser?'

'He be coming from Pompey on the mail coach today and will be here presently. I took the liberty, sir, of sending for him when we was in Falmouth.'

'Pray send him in directly, as soon as he arrives, and we will ask his mettle,' said Pat, concealing well his curiosity: his deep respect for Prosser, a veteran of many voyages together, bestowed unquestioning confidence in his selection. 'Murphy, where is Doctor Ferguson?' he shouted, wholly unnecessarily as Murphy was in his customary position whenever Pat conducted an interview in the great cabin: behind the door, his ear close to it.

'Below, sorr, in his store,' Murphy's face appeared.

'Perhaps it is a timely moment for an inspection of the lower and orlop decks?' said Pat to himself, and he paced out of the cabin and stepped down the companionway into the gloom of the lower deck. He looked about him: there were no men below, all were working above, and he was about to descend the steps to the orlop when Simon stepped up from below. Both were crouching in the low space afforded them, scarcely more than five and a half feet on the lower deck.

'Ah, Simon, there you are. Will you come up to the cabin and take second breakfast with me?'

'It is a benevolent offer, but not now. I am engrossed at present. I am mixing my stock of Paré's digestive.' Seeing Pat's blank look he continued, 'It is an ointment, a most excellent remedy in the case of gunshot wounds; but I am in need of fresh egg yolks - would you think the cook will spare some?'

'I hope you will leave Wilkins at least a brace to accompany my bacon, it ain't the same without eggs,' Pat laughed. 'The crew have done tolerably well and the ship nears readiness for sea. We will load our powder from the hoy on Monday and be away with the tide for Falmouth on Tuesday for the rest of our men - should we have any room left that is for the crew and family; never did we ever see so much in the way of stores loaded aboard. The master has proposed a cox'n, and I expect him directly; after that we will repair ashore for supper at the Steam Packet. Tell, eggs and ointment aside, are you now prepared with your customary medical supplies for our voyage? Is there anything you lack?'

Before Simon could answer there came a voice from the top of the companionway and Murphy's shrewish visage appeared, but instead of his customary high shrilling nasal whine it was almost a whisper, 'Beg pardon, sorr, your visitor's arrived... Mr Prosser's cox'n be 'ere.'

'Send him down, Murphy. At once, if you please,' Pat's voice boomed out imperiously. He wished for no distractions and remained intent on continuing with at least some small survey of the hold. However, the sight of the man who stepped down from the companionway, in the instant that he turned towards them, stopped Pat and Simon in their thoughts in a flash: the effect was overwhelming, heartbeats were missed, eyes widened, words were left unformed. For the first time ever in his ship, in the moment of the profound shock Pat instinctively straightened bolt upright. He cracked his head on the low deckhead beam, shouted in some pain and fell back into a crouch against the gunroom door, nursing a sore and bleeding head. He gasped in astonished disbelief. He stared for long moments before he could find any words at all, finally uttering, 'By God, 'tis Barton himself here before us,' his voice barely more than a whisper.

Murphy, further words failing even him, scrambled in haste down the steps even as Pat recovered himself and stood staring, open-mouthed, at this so shocking sight. Pat's coxswain of ten long years, Brannan Barton, had been killed alongside him in the year 'thirteen in the boarding of *Chesapeake,* and Pat simply could not believe his eyes, was in total shock. Murphy stood there in dumb show, unable to shift or speak: never before had anything like it happened aboard.

Simon hastened round to Pat's side, wiping the blood trail away from above Pat's eye on his shirt sleeve, all the while staring at this apparition and whispering to himself, 'Oh, my Lord.'

Before them the unassuming seaman spoke up. 'Barton, sir, it is. George Barton, cousin of Brannan Barton. Mr Prosser sent for me.'

'Barton! 'Pon my word, ne'er did two peas more resemble the same pod,' whispered Pat, struggling to find suitable words and trying unsuccessfully to come to terms with the sight of a man so utterly indistinguishable from his former coxswain.

Barton bravely resumed, 'Well, sir, Brannan Barton was my twin, but I was placed with my aunt when aged one on account of my mum having no breadwinner, our father having died afore I was born. She could not afford the upbringing of both of us, and so I have always been called cousin, even as we grew up not half a league apart in Falmouth.' Seeing that Pat was still agape, Barton pressed on with the details of his naval career, 'I started at sea in the time of his Lordship, Admiral Jervis, in the year 'ninety-seven, sir. I was a powder monkey for him at Cape St. Vincent on *Victory.* I was promoted able when serving on *Royal Sovereign* at Trafalgar. I was standing alongside Admiral Collingwood when *Santa Ana* struck to her, sir. The next year I was promoted to captain's barge crew. I served with the Admiral until the year 'ten when his Lordship passed. I was tie mate with Bill Mindham, gun captain on *Shannon,* in the year 'thirteen when we captured *Chesapeake.* Bill opened the firing on *Chesapeake* that day, sir, and we boarded her together, Brannan alongside o' me.

'Most admirable indeed,' murmured Pat, fascinated.

'My brother was serving on *Tenedos* when Captain Broke sent her away, and she left 'im and a score of others aboard *Shannon;* her Second and Third were there too. We was rushing to help the cap'n who was downed when the prisoners broke out. Bill and one of the officers from *Tenedos* saved the cap'n, sir. I ne'er knew who he was. Bill and he reached the cap'n when he went down, one or t'other struck down the Yankee about to kill the cap'n... Bill I think it was, and we stood over him together 'til our marines came. It was a bloody business, sir. When the cap'n led the boarding he was followed by Mr Dunn his clerk and Mr Aldham the purser. Can you believe it, sir? Both were shot down dead behind the cap'n even afore they reached *Chesapeake's* deck. Tom Stevens, the bosun, had his hand hacked right off while 'e was lashing us alongside, though 'e carried on with his other hand 'til he was struck down by a musket ball, bless 'im; I have ne'er seen his like since. Poor Tom lingered for near three weeks, sir, and died in Halifax. I was wounded dragging the cap'n back to *Shannon*, a ball from the tops, two mates and my brother Brannan killed alongside o' me. I spent three weeks laid up afterwards, below in the sick bay and later in the Halifax hospital. I am glad I was able to give old Tom some little comfort there, sir, afore he passed. I was promoted bosun by Lieutenant Wallis on *Shannon* after I recovered, to replace old Tom. After *Shannon* went into ordinary, sir, I joined *Spartan,* and served on her as cox'n until the year 'twenty when she also went into ordinary. I haven't found a berth these past three years, sir. Been working at the Pompey dockyards on ship refitting since,' Barton concluded his truly exceptional record of service.

'Barton, that is the most worthy of records... admirable; indeed, it seems we have already served together,' said Pat, still in a state of some wondrous disbelief, nodding to Duncan. 'Mr Macleod here and I came aboard *Shannon* from *Tenedos* just a day or so afore *Chesapeake* struck to her, your brother Brannan with us. I was Second and Mr Macleod was Third on *Tenedos*. Captain Hyde Parker sent us aboard with twenty men to assist *Shannon* before Broke sent *Tenedos* away. 'Twas I with your gun captain that saved Captain Broke... and you were directly behind us, you say. I have five guineas in my dunnage for you, Barton. Mighty pleased I was to have half a dozen good fellows behind me when I reached Captain Broke; 'twas a desperate moment ... a very bloody business indeed. And you were wounded in the boarding you say? Alas, I never saw you, nor anyone else I would collect after Broke was cut down; 'twas every man for himself for a few minutes there. As you say, we lost your brother Brannan that day; a painful loss to all of us on *Tenedos*, good man that he was. Lieutenant Macleod and I shifted to Halifax after the battle. And you served with Old Jarvie himself! 'Pon my word, that is a prodigious fine record, Barton, a handsome record indeed. The master speaks well of you, I need ask no more. You would favour me most deeply by shifting aboard directly as our new cox'n,' pronounced Pat, seizing and shaking Barton's hand in a vice-like grip. 'Murphy, lend a hand there, trundle Barton's dunnage aboard, cut along now. Take him to the galley for a pint of grog and then show him the barky.'

'Thankee kindly; I will not let you down, sir.' Barton touched his forehead and left in the company of a still dumbstruck Murphy.

'You seem taken aback, brother,' said Simon, who had heard the story with great interest.

'I should scarcely have thought it possible... Barton, standing there in the flesh, and hard to believe 'twas not really him,' Pat heard himself whispering, remaining still in some small state of shock.

'To be sure, the twin's resemblance was assuredly so completely indistinguishable from that of our old shipmate, but it is not as rare as you might think. Perhaps one in three hundred births are identical twins,' replied Simon. 'If I may venture a suggestion, my dear... would it be improper to suggest we get off this vessel and step out for our supper now?'

Chapter Four

'Tis something, in the dearth of fame,
Though link'd among a fetter'd race,
To feel at least a patriot's shame,
Even as I sing, suffuse my face;
For what is left the poet here?
For Greeks a blush — for Greece a tear.

Sunday 18th May 1823   *Plymouth Dock, Devon*

At first light, Pat roused himself, dunked his head in the washbowl, applied just a very little of Number Six cologne, it being Whit Sunday and no work being intended, the perfume being a present which had been given to him many years before by a particularly friendly local young lady in Halifax, Nova Scotia and which had remained unremarked by Sinéad in the intervening years, being in his shipboard dunnage. 'That will have to go to the deep six afore Sinéad comes aboard,' he thought absently. He dressed swiftly, his best coat and breeches having been pressed and left out the night before by Murphy. 'Freeman!' Pat shouted. 'Light along a pot of coffee... and do we have bacon left?'

Freeman appeared immediately, muttering, 'Pot 'im ready this five minutes, massa.'

Some little time later Duncan entered the cabin, sniffing the twin scents of coffee and bacon with undisguised delight.

'There is a whole pile of bacon, eggs too, in that pan, Duncan; Simon has left us a few.'

'A most handsome prospect, for sure; I will gladly share your breakfast with the utmost pleasure.' Duncan settled at Pat's table and swiftly piled his plate with generous helpings.

'Freeman! Bring some more soft tack for Mr Macleod... and pass the word for... for Murphy.' Pat remained still in some disbelief and confusion at Barton's arrival of yesterday, his thinking since oft slipping into small muddle. 'Will you not regret staying in the Hebrides, Duncan?'

Duncan paused from his obvious satisfaction with the fried breakfast and looked up. 'Och, I am sure they have their charms, but how greatly pleased I am that we are back here, aboard our new home, at sea again, aboard the barky, our dear *Surprise*. How agreeably homely it is, there is nae doubt,' the deep conviction so plain in his voice.

'As you say, *there is no doubt*... so long ashore now I had near-forgotten.' Pat looked wistfully into Duncan's face. 'A ship... once again. Oh how I have longed these past three years for this moment to come, my hopes near dashed, and here we are.' Duncan merely smiled and nodded, chewing with great satisfaction, his mouth full. Pat sat down again in his chair and poured himself more coffee. 'Allow me to help you to a few more rashers; would you care for another egg or two?'

'Most certainly, I will finish the last three in the pan, if ye will. Would there be another wee drop of coffee left, at all?'

'Murphy! There you are. Coffee for Mr Macleod... and then we will rig church; I believe we will hoist the church pennant... if it is in the locker? Rouse out all the men, if you will. We are too few to muster to divisions, though it being Sunday I am minded to speak to the lads when we hold church. I fancy I will preach the sermon.'

'What? Ye will preach the sermon?' Duncan could not conceal his astonishment, laughed aloud, slapped his coffee down on the table and clapped three times in merriment, as if in applause.

Pat glared at him. 'We ain't at war these days... and the Articles don't seem right. I have long had a copy of The Good Book in my dunnage all these years, and there are plentiful things in it which will suit when you trouble to look. It was plainly written by some honest fellows, fishermen and the like; doubtless many others were mariners too.'

'Aye and was Jonah one of 'em, Pat? I collect he spent much time asleep. I doubt ye should mention him to the men,' retorted Duncan, followed by his hearty laugh.

Rather than below in the customary lower deck location, church was rigged on the gun deck. With so few crew aboard and no chaplain either - *Surprise* not ostensibly being a Royal Navy ship - and the weather promising to be clemently warm, Pat felt a more informal occasion was called for. The ship's bell struck four bells.

'Murphy! My best scraper if you will.'

Murphy, looking unusually spry himself, was there in an instant. 'Well, 'tis on your table already, sorr.'

On stepping up to his quarterdeck Pat and Duncan were greeted by the Wesleyans, two dozen or more of them all lined up near the wheel, all scrubbed up, pigtails all newly plaited and mystifyingly all garbed in a myriad of shades of red; evidently all prepared and awaiting the service. The other crew members, tailing back to the ship's waist, were all also looking particularly prime.

'What's afoot? Has the fleet adopted a new uniform since we were last at sea... and forgotten to tell us?' joked Pat.

'It is the biblical colour for Pentecost, brother, and the Wesleyans are particular about the auld traditions, as ye may collect.'

'I do not believe I have ever heard it remarked upon before. Very creditable in them, indeed,' said Pat pleasantly, being something of a traditionalist himself. The skeleton crew, barely four dozen men including the Eleanors, assembled in front of a sea-chest over which was draped an ensign to serve as a makeshift lectern. Pat was not a conventionally religious man but he was a pious traditionalist by nature. Lacking deep familiarity with the scriptures, he generally contented himself when required to give the sermon at sea with reading the Articles of War, which had become almost a venerable substitute for an appropriate ecclesiastical script. On this occasion however, *Surprise* not really being - officially at least - in His Majesty's Service, he considered that he should not read the Articles but expound on their particular circumstances before they sang the hymns. Stepping to the sea-chest, Pat paused long to look around, taking a deep draught of the salt air borne on the early morning chill breeze, and he gazed up as if towards the heavens. Finally, he tucked his hat under his arm and began to speak, quite softly as there were so few present. 'Good morning, lads. As we are so very few today and not quite yet in commission, I am minded to speak just a short piece to you. I ain't one for speeches, as you know, but allow me to share a trifle of my private thoughts from these past few days with you. Here we be, aboard our new home... the barky... our dear *Surprise*. It does my heart good to be aboard ship once again ...'

'Hear hear,' the softly spoken murmur from the crew.

'Lads... most of you have been with me through the dam... the gravest of hard times, fighting Boney's ships and others too. We have been round the world together, through storms and the vilest of seas... We have shared hard tack and short commons...' Pat was speaking quite slowly now and with deliberation, as if searching for the right words. 'We have lost some fine shipmates along the way...' He paused for a minute or two, looking round at all his crew, studying each of their faces, remembering most of them from long voyages in years gone by, until his gaze alighted on his new cox'n, standing to the fore, and in that instant his heart moved within him, a huge physical tremor rising from deep down, his throat drying, and his mind painfully flashed back, recalling lost comrades, one of them in particular very much at the forefront of his thoughts at that moment. A long further minute passed before he could speak again. He swallowed hard and forced his mind to focus. Quietly he resumed, 'I am minded of one lost shipmate... Brannan Barton was with me – *with us* – since my very first command, the gun-brig *Starling* in Portsmouth in the year 'three. In the year 'four I will never forget boarding *El Valiente* with him alongside of me, and when I was felled by a pike he saved my life, pistolling the Spaniard ere he could stick me again. Brannan Barton in those years became my friend... *our* friend... and served with us until he was killed in the year 'thirteen. I have oft thought of him these ten years gone.' It was obvious to all the assembly that their captain was struggling, in some considerable difficulty as he resumed; his words, still very quiet, not more than a whisper, wafted across as if borne by the breeze to reach them. His head lifted and he spoke again, the very few words revealing his thoughts with brutal clarity, 'I miss him greatly.' He paused again amidst a soft echoing of accord from the crew. 'Today, as you know, 'tis the day of Pentecost, the day our Lord Jesus returned to us...' Pat faltered once more, his knowledge of the scriptures was a little hazy. With only the familiar, shrilling noise of gulls in the background, the crew, bluff seamen all, their whispered exchanges now brought to silence by his words, he continued, 'And perhaps we too have seen someone come back to us yesterday; 'tis Barton here who reminds us that from our tragedy, out of that ache of our despair... will always come hope afresh.'

Not even the quietest murmur now disturbed the moment, all present listening intently, unaccustomed as they were to words of such poignancy. A long pause, a minute or more followed as Pat again gathered his thoughts and, as if realising that he had been speaking very quietly, he swallowed and continued, raising his voice, 'Afore we venture out again, lads, aboard our new home at sea, our dear *Surprise*... let us welcome aboard *George* Barton... our new shipmate... our cox'n... our *brother.*'

Pat concluded his address to hearty cheering from his men, 'Hurrah! Hurrah! Hear the captain, Hurrah!' As he looked up again and across to his crew, the wind having shifted round to the exposed south-west since the start of church and the sky having become progressively darker, a fine rain began to set in, quickly wetting the faces of the assembly: a minor inconvenience, for which Pat found himself profoundly grateful, and obscuring, or so he thought, the flood of tears now streaming down his cheeks.

All hands had noticed that in the lattermost of Pat's address his voice had taken on a halting, softer tone than was usual on these occasions, one much more so than the very firm tone he customarily adopted for reading the Articles of War, and despite the rain none could miss their captain's tears. Mr Prosser, the master and elder of the Wesleyans, stepped up to the makeshift lectern – quite unbidden but understanding perfectly the moment – and waved the now chattering crew to silence once more. 'We thank you most kindly, sir, for your very 'andsome words.'

'Carry on, Mr Prosser,' said Pat very quietly. After two hymns had been sung and church concluded the bosun piped the hands to dinner and the crew returned to the lower deck for the customary Sunday pork followed by plum duff: the culinary highlight of the week aboard His Majesty's ships. It was a tradition that Pat would never change. Shortly thereafter Dalby beat *Roast Beef of Old England* to signal readiness of the officers' dinner.

Back in the great cabin, Pat awaited his dinner with Duncan and Simon, attended intermittently by Freeman. 'Allow me to fill your glasses, gentlemen. This is rather better than our ordinary, I believe?' Pat offered, pouring from a bottle of his dwindling private stock of the madeira 'seventy-five.

'I am entirely of your way of thinking,' Simon replied, 'an exceptional wine. What are your present thoughts, tell?'

'What butter or whiskey does not cure cannot be cured,' declared Pat rather obliquely, not quite ignoring his friend's question. He paused before adding - twenty minutes having elapsed with nothing to eat in sight - 'I wonder if there *is* any pork left or whether Murphy has eaten it all up?'

Just at that moment Freeman appeared at the cabin door with a large and overburdened silver tray. 'Vittles is up, massa, if you please. Cook sending best underside for dinner, massa; here 'tis.'

'Thankee, Freeman; my compliments to Wilkins, if you will.'

After Freeman had busied himself piling the most generous of portions on silver plates he left the cabin.

'I heartily commend you, Pat; those were very fine words today, most commendable words. None finer have I ever heard uttered afore aboard this or any other vessel, and particularly well received it was indeed,' said Simon. 'Nothing like it have we ever heard before, and... forgive me, brother... I should scarcely have thought it of you. But, allow me to ask... I have a certain... perhaps *unfounded* impression... pray tell, dear soul, is there some uneasiness on your mind?'

'Never in life. Will I help you to some stuffing?' Pat retorted, a little too quickly to pass Simon's notice.

'Excuse me... if I might be permitted an observation... You were tolerably eloquent today, using very fair expressions which I do not generally expect to hear from you.'

'Sure, I never was one for speeches,' replied Pat, smiling a little more broadly now, 'though I can bring something out now and then, given time.' And nothing more could Simon extract from him.

Tuesday 20th May 1823   *Plymouth Dock, Devon*

The fair weather of the weekend had deteriorated into a mid-grey sky with dawn bringing a prevalent westerly, light wind accompanied by soft steady rain, all so typical of the south-west of England at virtually any time of the year, but moderated, as is so often the case in those climes, by a warm temperature. The crew were assured that all was well for the bay crossing to Falmouth, though it would be a difficult task were the wind to strengthen exceptionally with a crew of just four dozen, capable hands though they were. The Admiralty had denied *Surprise* any serving Royal Navy seamen from Plymouth, maintaining their official separation from the covert venture, and so, for the very short voyage, Pat had decided to rely on those few Falmouth volunteers who had come to Plymouth aboard *Eleanor*. As four bells struck, signifying the master's choice of time for departure just after high water, a few of the yard shipwrights were still onboard, though finishing up and removing their tools from about the deck as the Master Shipwright, Edward Churchill, accompanied by the Master Attendant, George Sidley, climbed aboard from the Yard's cutter and stepped up to Pat's quarterdeck to bid their farewells. They shook hands solemnly with both Pat and Duncan before looking about the decks and gazing at the masts and rigging as if in final inspection, and then Churchill spoke up, pride so very evident in his face and voice, 'Just you be very careful with her, sir, and bring her back to us in good time.'

'Never in doubt, Mr Churchill, never in doubt. My thanks to you again, sir,' Pat replied, smiling broadly, his pleasure irrepressible.

'I bid you all safe passage, Captain O'Connor. Goodbye, sir,' said the Master Attendant.

'Thank you, Mr Sidley. Goodbye.'

Pat watched his visitors disembark, and then with the deepest sense of satisfaction he gazed all about his ship. He allowed himself a few minutes to study those faces of his crew nearby, competency and experience so very evident in all of them; he watched the remainder as they busied themselves with final preparations, some glancing occasionally to the quarterdeck in anticipation of the imminent commands for departure.

The shipwrights were now all departed, rowing towards where the yard crew, many scores of men, all lined the quay. From the cutter, Churchill and Sidley gazed back, not wishing to miss any part of the spectacle of *Surprise's* departure. Barton, with two of the Wesleyans, was at the wheel, Mr Prosser, the master, alongside them. Simon stood at Pat's side on the quarterdeck, gazing at the final preparations. Despite witnessing many such departures the nautical nomenclature had never rooted in his mind and the ship handling procedures still left him largely mystified. 'To be sure, we are particularly few, Pat, in comparison of our customary numbers; short-handed, I dare say? Will this present any difficulties for our leave-taking, would you think? I only throw out the remark.'

'Why certainly it will. Be a good fellow for once and lend a hand there on the capstan... and push hard when I give the word, will you?' replied Pat with a suppressed smile. The old hands at the wheel looked at each other, barely concealing their astonishment.

'Certainly, brother; I have oft heard you mention that particular device, but be so good as to remind me: where *is* the capstan? My familiarity is lacking a trifle in these nautical, these *mechanical* devices, as you may have noticed.'

'No, not at all.'

'Pray point it out if you will,' said Simon, falling wholly into Pat's little trap. The helmsmen tittered, stopping only when Barton kicked them. 'I see you practice upon me.'

'You are a hoot,' laughed Pat, his good humour plain.

'I am no mariner.'

Pat gazed with deep affection at his friend. 'Oh, I should never say that. For sure you're an odd one: none finer in the philosophical line, a capital man with the Latin and no doubt the only sight all aboard the barky would pray to see were they ever carried down to the cockpit; yet for all these years at sea you scarcely have any notion of the bow from the stern or your larboard from your starboard. If you will, pray see if that rascal Freeman might find us a pot of tea in about ten minutes.'

'I find you in tolerably better humour this morning, brother,' replied Simon, in good spirits himself.

'I am uncommon happy. Afloat again, a fine ship with a goodly set of hands; Falmouth bound we are, and a prospect of some proper seafaring ahead; 'tis a fine day, none better.'

Simon left the quarterdeck and Pat turned to Duncan and the master, both waiting patiently alongside him. 'Our time is come to depart, Mr Macleod.'

'All hands, prepare to make sail!' shouted Duncan.

'Lay aloft!' shouted Prosser, and the men scrambled up to the yards. 'Rig capstan bars and bring to the messenger,' he bawled, and within a few minutes, 'Man the bars!'

Surprise was anchored larboard side on her best bower, the cable hove short, her starboard side towards the quay as she was beginning to be drawn by the current, the tide beginning its ebb. The wind too seemed ready to assist the frigate's departure, veering to a north-westerly, fine on her larboard bow.

'Breast the capstan,' shouted the master.

'Up anchor!' ordered Pat.

'Up anchor for home!' Prosser echoed, jubilation in his voice.

'Heave and a-weigh!' cried Duncan.

The cable began to be wound in on the capstan, the sounds of a shanty coming from the men, '*Walk her round and round she goes, way oh, way oh.*' It was a vociferous departure from Royal Navy practices and one to which Pat paid no heed, for nothing short of King George himself stepping aboard could possibly impinge on his genial and deep satisfaction this day.

Even the old *Tenedos* veterans had departed from their customary, restrained standard of *two-six, two-six*, all swept up in the enthusiastic fervour. The capstan men, their singing now general, ran the cable in just fast enough for the few tierers present to keep up.

'Up and down!' came the shout from the bow.

'Thick and dry for weighing!' shouted Duncan.

The topmen meanwhile had shifted out on to the yards, had cast off the gaskets, the lines that held the sails tight furled to the yards. They gathered the canvas under their arms and waited. The tierers were coaxing in the remaining cable until all was swiftly stowed, and the best bower appeared, just hauled out of the water.

'Standby aloft, let fall!' ordered Duncan, and with his shout came the howling *peep-peep, peep-peep* whistle from the bosun alone, no mates available whilst so short-handed.

'Let fall! Sheet home, sheet home, hoist away!' the master shouted. The topmen standing ready at her topsails let fall the sails: down they tumbled, unfurling, loosely flapping, the men hauling on the braces. *Surprise's* afteryards were already braced ready for the tack to turn her gently to face downstream in the ebb tide, the headyards abox, headsheets hauled to larboard. She would come round slowly but would be afforded little steerage for the first few minutes.

'Hard a-lee!' Duncan commanded the two helmsmen.

Surprise now backed slowly, stern coming round to larboard as she gained sternway, her bow coming round to starboard, turning faster now without the anchor constraint, her fore topsail pushing her, back, back, the main and mizzen flapping until she came further round and they filled.

'Helm up!' shouted Duncan when her bow faced the yard and she was beginning to be driven forward.

The combined wind and ebb tide were pushing her now with greater momentum, and the rudder was kept hard over until she was fully turned about and facing down the Hamoaze.

'Helm amidships!' The wind and current now combining to give her speed, she swiftly moved away downstream whilst on the quay a hundred men or more waved their farewells. The deck crew heaved the remainder of the cable in and the anchor was quickly catted. Within a very few minutes *Surprise* was well underway in the fairway, the Hamoaze, and all along her sides there creamed a ribbon of white water.

'That was handsomely executed... and with just two score hands. 'Pon my word we have some prime seamen aboard, Barton,' Pat shouted across to the wheel, slipping without thinking into the easy manner of past times with his old cox'n.

'Aye, sir,' Barton shouted back, mightily pleased to hear his captain's compliment.

The master kept *Surprise* firmly in the deepwater channel and well within the half hour she came out through the Narrows, the small crew making good work of the sail handling tasks. *Surprise* came swiftly out into the Sound, making a south-south-westerly course, sailing close-hauled with the westerly wind, passing the emerging breakwater and so to Penlee Point. As Rame Head came up on the starboard beam the ship's bell rang eight bells and half the crew disappeared below for dinner. The rain had ceased and the sun broke through the clouds, bringing welcome warmth and good cheer to the hard-working crew.

Pat turned to his long-serving companion and First, 'At sea again, a frigate of the very first order, our old crew aboard; don't it give you a shiver down your back, Duncan?'

'Aye, for sure it does, there is nae doubt at all,' whispered Duncan with some emotion. 'I dinnae ever collect a bonnier day for many a year. I widnae exchange it for a barrel of gold pieces.'

Later in the great cabin, Pat, Duncan and Simon shared a pot of tea with sizzling-hot white pudding, brought aboard fresh that morning. '*Eleanor* is to follow us tomorrow and William will bring her over to join us in Falmouth with his small crew. We are still short of officers. Even with the fleet so reduced I have no hope of serving officers quitting their commands to join us. No, our best prospects lie with those of our old friends who have been these past years a'fretting on the beach: lieutenants on their paltry half-pay with no prospects of a ship and no hope of being made post. I have hopes that James Mower may join us yet. I have written to him - his family has long lived in Falmouth - and to Tom Pickering; do you collect what a wit that man has? Doubtless the merchant service may have taken one or t'other of 'em. Do you collect them both on our first cruise together? Master's mates they were... on our old *Starling*... my first command, back in the year 'three. Happy times, happy times they were.'

'Aye, I collect the twae, brother, but we were poor, widnae a dollar between us.'

'To be sure, yet I collect that sense of adventure, so long now lacking. Dear God, how good it was to be alive in those years. All of Boney's ships against us and fleets afloat that we shall ne'er see the likes of again.' A nostalgic Pat turned to the other side of his table, 'Do you miss those days, Simon?'

'The sentiments of adventure and, much later, of anticipation of profound political change that came about but which was so sadly snuffed out in Scot... that is to say in *Spain*.' Simon suppressed distressing recollections of Hardie, Baird and Wilson, all hung and beheaded after the failed rising a mere three years previously. 'Those feelings I miss most dearly. Since Agnes's death I have felt only the cold chill of disappointment in my bones and melancholia in my bosom. This new expedition comes with great hopes for me, even a rekindling of purpose. These are aspirations and feelings which I had long thought dead these ten years past. For sure it would also be a pleasure to see our auld shipmates again.'

'All have been laid up ashore for some years since, and with none having any connections they are unlikely to find any berth. It has reached my ears that William Codrington is hiding from his creditors and near bankrupt this past year. I gather that allegations of his severe gambling losses are well founded. He has been losing badly, as so many sailors do when ashore with a pocket full of guineas, and might well relish an absence from home; doubtless some foreign service would be particularly welcome. We are to meet with the First Lord on Friday and sail on Sunday week, come what may,' said Pat.

'I do not like to sound forward, brother,' Simon ventured, 'but might I trouble you and suggest it may be useful to our expedition were we to engage a proficient surgeon's assistant? One would hardly be a supernumerary. Have you, perchance, also considered engaging a member of the cloth?'

Pat looked doubtful, 'I believe there is something in what you say. Our time away is uncertain and our particular efforts may not signify for a long time. Yet there ain't room enough in the gunroom for all these extra fellows... should we find all our officers awaiting us in Falmouth.'

'Allow me to raise the possibility, the very slight possibility, dear, of finding one single person to fit the bill for both these capacities. I have received a letter from Michael Marston... you collect him, an auld shipmate of ours? He has been fretting to find some means of employment these four or more years. Would you consider of him... Pat?' asked Simon a little apprehensively. Marston's presence on board *Tenedos* previously had not been an unqualified success - Pat not greatly taking to Marston in his role as a chaplain aboard ship, and the crew considering it unlucky to have one aboard. He had admitted him only in his capacity as Simon's surgeon's assistant.

'Allow me to mull it over. We will speak further about it at supper,' Pat replied noncommitantly, hedging. Simon was content at that moment to ignore the evasion, plain as it was.

The afternoon passed pleasantly, the sun staying to warm and cheer them as *Surprise* tacked through Whitsand Bay, passed Dodman Point and left Gull Rock in her wake, coming up to the approach to Falmouth. Seven bells struck as Pendennis Point came into sight directly off the bow. The master was back in his home port and carefully brought *Surprise* past the Black Rock to larboard and into the Carrick Roads, the wind now south-westerly, abeam, her double-reefed topsails alone driving her on a north-westerly tack, her courses long since furled before her approach to the inner harbour. Pat had decided to bring her as close as the master thought fit to the town, and the topmen, skilled as they were and needing no bidding, gradually checked her braces to deaden her topsails, so slowing her momentum to a snail's pace; her course shifting closer to westerly, she could not get closer to the wind. Simon stood alongside a silent but plainly pleased Pat on his quarterdeck, Barton at the wheel, as *Surprise* crept closer towards her intended anchorage, passing Killigrew's original Town Quay, the Custom House Quay to larboard, the master ordering her course changed again, to north-westerly once more, the town now abeam and her bow pointing in the direction of Flushing village.

'It is a great while since I saw you so happy, brother,' Simon remarked conversationally. 'In such moments I could wish our voyage would go on for ever, all together in our contentment.'

'Fiddler's Green ain't in it,' whispered Pat, a little overwhelmed himself by the emotions engendered within him during the day.

There was barely a breath of wind, and the sound of her hull through the water - only the smallest ripple at her bow - was plainly audible even on the quarterdeck. Inch by inch, *Surprise* approached the master's intended anchorage, the King's Road, the ship near silent, sliding along, tops'ls all backed, until the Fish Strand Quay lay two cables off her beam, the master declaring further beyond which he would not wish her to lie at low water. *Surprise* slowed as her way began to fall off, the current acting upon her, making a little leeway, slowing... stopped, no longer any forward movement at all upon her.

'Let go!' shouted the master, and the best bower was dropped with the distinctive sound of its splash heard all about the ship and the harbour. Pat looked all about him, then gazed over towards the town; he saw, to his astonishment, lining the Market and Fish Strands, hundreds and hundreds of Falmouth people, recognisable and familiar faces prominent amongst them through his glass even in the distance; many of them former *Tenedos* crew: old hands from prior voyages and new *Surprise* crew members too; for the most part standing together with their wives, sweethearts and numerous excited children. Suddenly the throng were roused as one and broke into wild shouts of greeting, then cheering; all waving exuberantly, clapping and shouting to greet *Surprise, their* ship as they now considered her to be, their menfolk now her crew, come home.

Pat was standing near the wheel, very moved by the spectacle, a deep sense of gratitude for such a welcome swiftly arising within him and a heartwarming feeling of well-being quite overcoming him. 'Welcome home, Barton,' Pat turned to his cox'n, grasped and shook his hand with enthusiastic vigour, 'welcome home.'

Wednesday 21ˢᵗ May 1823   *Falmouth, Cornwall*

After breakfast Pat and Simon remained in the great cabin with a fresh pot of coffee, reviewing the expedition preparations and awaiting the arrival of the mail coach from Truro, both keenly anxious to discover whether at least any letter of reply might be received from Pat's former officers. Duncan was away to the harbourmaster's office, attending to the port formalities. It being high water *Surprise* had been towed by her boats a little nearer to the Custom House Quay to facilitate the loading of her remaining stores and to allow boarding and disembarking for shore-leave of her all-volunteer complement, the Falmouth men making their farewells.

'Art happy, brother?' asked Simon, looking up from his papers. 'Tell me of your contemplations. I have the impression - will I say - of a trifling lack of contentment about your person, a certain anxiety... if I may venture so?'

'I am a little put out, I confess,' Pat seemed to welcome the interruption of his thoughts. 'I have been considering of our prospects, but there is one damn matter I cannot shake.'

'How do we stand without our customary complement of officers if their arrival does not eventuate? Is it that which is oppressing you? Surely they are still to be expected, if a trifle late?'

'I do not like to count all my eggs before they hatch.'

'I suppose not. It would seem we have only Macleod in the basket. If the others do not arrive, would you suppose this will present us with insuperable difficulties, being so short-handed?'

Pat exhaled deeply and nodded. 'Oh, without 'em we can sail the ship, of that there is no doubt; but to fight her... now that is a different barrel of fish... no officers on the gun deck and Lord knows how we will fare. A hundred and eighty men, let us say, to fight the guns, both sides together; forty more to sail her and a dozen aloft with small arms and in the magazines; two hundred men and more but ne'er a one of officers, save for Duncan - *and me* - on the quarterdeck. And if one or t'other of us should be wounded... I will not say knocked on the head - I fancy I will never say anything as unlucky as that, I will not tempt fate - no, we could not fight her, that is plain.'

'I dare say. So if not a one arrives this day on the mail coach, we are to pass a summer here in Falmouth... surely not?'

'You cannot have a ship sailing about without officers, it won't do.'

'I am no great navigator, but that is undeniable, a most commendable observation.'

Pat raised his eyebrows at Simon's jest. 'We will lack midshipmen too, and without officers I fear we will sit idling, knocked back on our heels, festering in some Ionian port; and that won't do... no, that certainly won't do. Why, I don't need no mumbo-jumbo seer, no astrological quack, nor any damn necrom... nec... necrophile to tell me what the Greeks will think.'

'Let us hope not,' Simon suppressed a laugh.

'Damned poltroons and cowards we will look, and what could we say to that? Precious little! Is there a tint of coffee in that pot?'

'There is none. Will I send Murphy for fresh? Perhaps we may enjoy a last glass of stingo while we remain in port, if it is not too early? Let us await the mail at the Marine Hotel, it a commendable tavern on the quay there. Perhaps your concerns will prove unfounded and this principled scheme of yours can still be delivered, the departure of this vessel as intended?'

'The mail is disgracefully late. We will wait a trifle longer, and if our officers ain't on it we will go ashore the moment it arrives.'

The crew, now that they were at full strength and numbering more than two hundred and forty men, busied themselves with the myriad preparations for the imminent voyage, all to a man supremely pleased to be onboard ship once again and with a particular favour for *Surprise*. From all quarters there came the familiar noises of shipboard activity and bustle, so satisfying to Pat - not having been to sea since four years or more. From above him he heard the resounding thump of the 'Bible' holystones on the quarterdeck as they were shifted from place to place; through the door he could hear the hails aloft from the seniors of the crew on deck and the general to-ing and fro-ing of men busying themselves in a myriad of routine tasks, and from below there came the rhythmical noise of the pumps. Even the shrill calls of the gulls were pleasurable and welcome to Pat's ears, the ambience of the whole - aside from his concern for the lack of officers - bringing about a quietude and relaxation within him which had been lacking for a considerable time.

Simon, never the most organised of souls, was similarly pleased to return to contemplation of the emerging and tidy inventory of his medical supplies, at that moment calculating his stocks of portable soup - a glutinous jelly requiring melting before it could be imbibed and a standfast of very doubtful welcome to all occupants of the sick berth. From within the cabin came the mutterings of Murphy, cleaning the windows - the lights as they were termed. And then came a pause, a suspension in the customary shipboard noises; it was replaced by a rising babble of voices, becoming louder and louder, coming from the quarterdeck. Pat, noticing after but a moment, his contentment broken, shouted with some irritation, 'What is that infernal row? What is that din, Murphy? Tell 'em to clap a stopper over it. What's afoot?'

'Well, it's the mail coach arrived, sorr, and some visitors be here,' replied Murphy, looking through Pat's glass, staring intently through the lights and across to the Custom House Quay, his naturally excessive curiosity piqued.

Pat and Simon broke off to go up on deck. The mail coach had disgorged its passengers. Even at the distance of almost two cables, the figures on the quay were recognisable and confirmed with the glass. To Pat's great pleasure two of them were Tom Pickering and James Mower, both former midshipmen with Pat on *Starling*, Pat's first command, and Pickering a lieutenant on *Tenedos* after that. The crew had ceased work and were standing about, animatedly gabbling amongst themselves, pleased to see two more old shipmates, both held in the very highest esteem. Of William Codrington, Pat's third invitee, there was no sign. In high delight to see such welcome arrivals Pat beamed with intense pleasure; he waved with enthusiasm across to the quay. 'Barton, you are to bring them aboard directly.' He turned to Simon, 'Why, ain't it a grand sight?'

'To be sure, a most pleasing event indeed. A more joyous development cannot be imagined,' Simon smiled beatifically.

The barge swiftly brought Pickering and Mower aboard, the two saluting the quarterdeck, as was the old custom, their faces shining with self-evident happiness.

Pat greeted his former lieutenants with vigorous handshakes, his enthusiasm unrestrained, 'Very happy, most exceedingly happy to see you both. Tom, James, come into the cabin. Murphy, bear a hand there, bring Mr Pickering's and Mr Mower's dunnage aboard... and ask Freeman to bring a brace of burgundy too, if you will. Shift along there. Please come in, gentlemen.'

'Well, I ain't got three 'ands', muttered Murphy irritably under his breath; he left in search of his mate, Old Jim Lamb.

'Tom Pickering, by George it is grand to see you!' from Pat, shaking his hand again vigorously as they came into the cabin. 'And James Mower himself! Upon my honour, how do you do? Please be seated. Allow me to press you both to join me for dinner. Freeman! Freeman! Where is that mumping villain? Ah, Freeman, there you are. Tell cook we will be dining a little earlier, and there be five of us eating now. Please to put dinner in hand directly. Pray tell, where's the wine, Murphy?'

'Well, it's just comin' up, ain't it, sorr,' grumbled Murphy, though without the slightest of genuine discontent, as pleased as Pat to see Pickering and Mower come aboard once again. All sat at the cabin table, each gazing amiably at the others, their mutual joy in reunion so very evident, none wishing to disturb the deeply satisfying moment of contemplation with the least intrusive of questions. Murphy returned and poured the wine.

'Mr Pickering... *Tom* - if I may be so forward - pray tell us of your experiences since *Tenedos* was laid up,' coaxed Simon eventually.

Tom Pickering was neither wealthy nor well-connected, and so his recent four years ashore as a half-pay lieutenant did not facilitate his financial obligations to his family life, being with wife and four children; his lack of connections, as Pat had presumed, precluding him from finding another ship. 'Why, Doctor, so very dull years they have been... no prospects for a ship at all, my letters to their Lordships bringing the very briefest of acknowledgements, but sadly no promises. Half-pay at six pounds five shillings a month, just a little work in the Portsmouth dockyards to be had and in the most tedious of tasks; that is to say, negotiating on behalf of the port admiral with the repairers. The sole consolation being time with the family and seeing the children grow up. I oft wonder if prosperity is the surest protector of happiness,' replied Pickering in a downcast tone, the sparkling wit of many years ago seemingly absent. All felt their prior contentment just a very little diminished.

'Tom, let me offer you a glass of this delightful burgundy, if you will,' said Pat jovially, striving to restore the mood. 'James, what of you since *Illustrious*, when you last departed of us in the year 'ten? By God, so long ago... fully thirteen years since we was shipmates!'

'Aye sir, so it is, and in ne'er a one have I not thought of those days aboard *Starling*... and all her crew. Many a poem have I toyed with in my thoughts since, fondly remembering of her,' said Mower nostalgically and with the barest nod. He had left *Starling* when promoted to first lieutenant with *Illustrious* in the year 'ten, voyaging with her to the East Indies where she gained battle honours at Java. 'Well, sir, *Illustrious* returned from Java and the Indies in the year 'thirteen to Portsmouth, and since then she has been in ordinary, the crew for the most part laid off and all the officers on the beach. I came back very sick and stayed ashore for two years with the flux until I joined Captain Mould aboard the brig *Mutine* in the autumn of the year 'fifteen. I served aboard as First on the expedition to Algiers in 'sixteen, alongside *Impregnable* during the bombardment, and was discharged again sick when we came home.' The collective mood was diminished just a little further as all wondered what the implications of long term ill health might be.

Simon, ever the physician first and concerned for all his shipmates in case of anything contagious being introduced so soon before departure, prompted quickly, 'My dear Mower, I am sure you will forgive me for asking, art thou still sick? Please to describe your sickness. Excuse us but for a moment, gentlemen. Mr Mower and I will shift to the gunroom for a more private consultation.' Simon, without hesitation, swept up the lieutenant with a broad grasp of his shoulder and moved swiftly through the cabin door, no murmur of objection being heard from Mower. Their departure left the prior cabin ambience of contentment entirely absent.

'Tom, allow me to fill your glass,' said Pat, striving to recover the mood and smiling encouragingly to Pickering. 'We are sailing on Monday and I have but a single officer, Duncan Macleod as First. We will be accompanied on this voyage by *Eleanor* – you may collect her, my schooner – she will serve only as tender and messenger, and so I should look upon it as a most particular favour was you to join us on *Surprise* as Second. I explained in my letter only the bones of our purpose, which is to return to the Ionian islands, to render assistance to the forming Greek government resisting the Turk. Mind, 'tis not a mission for their Lordships, 'tis quite unofficial. Our status will be as a letter-of-marque for the Greeks. 'Tis akin to how Cochrane operated for Chile and now the Brazil. We will be away for a year or two. We can offer full pay and but the slenderest prospect of prizes. What say ye?'

'I am most heartily glad of your offer, sir... and grateful to you for remembering of me, and would dearly wish to join you again, and on *Surprise* too, *Tenedos's* sister ship; doubly pleased, sir. If this crew is not the finest of company, where will I ever find it?'

'Capital, Tom! I am most heartily thankful to hear it, and welcome back, old friend, welcome back. Murphy will stow your dunnage in the gunroom, and after dinner we will take a tour of the barky. Murphy! Murphy! Trundle along to see cook and ask after our dinner, if you will.' Murphy was pleased to see Pat still in exceptional good humour, albeit for much of the interview his ear had scarcely shifted from the door.

In the gunroom Simon and Mower were conversing in near whispers, there being no place on a ship the size of *Surprise* for assured privacy of communication. 'You will forgive me, Mr Mower ... *James,* for pressing you to explain your sickness. Whilst I naturally rejoice to see you again, I must be sure there can be nothing of any contagious nature introduced to this vessel. Particularly not just before we sail, and what I am minded to know is whether your long-lasting illness might persevere still and what may yet be done or be necessary... and – if anything – what help I may provide. Tell me of the very nature of your sickness.'

'You are very good, Doctor, and thankee for your kind interest for me. In the Indies I was struck down with the most severe flux, persisting for week after week until I was so ill I could hardly rise from my cot in the sick bay. I was in fear of my life, but the surgeon, good man that he was, could do nought to help me. I was bled four ounces every other day. For six weeks I was given no food save for onions, lemon juice, fresh fish and ship's biscuit aplenty. I recovered slightly afore we left Java and became a little stronger during the voyage home, but the dysentery was so bad that the captain took pity on me and allowed me to shift into the great cabin, where I spent more time in his quarter-gallery on the seat of ease than ever on deck. The Second was obliged to assume my duties, the Third his... and so forth. When we arrived back in Portsmouth I was discharged sick. My wife, good lady that she is - *bless her* - nursed me back to health, but it was a full two years afore my strength returned such that I could beg a place on *Mutine*. But three months later, at sea again, and my flux was back,' Mower recounted the sorry tale, his voice full of worry, and he was clearly ill at ease even speaking of his illness.

'Pray, how are you at present?' asked Simon tentatively.

'All a-tanto, Doctor; my wife has again nursed me back to good health.' Mower tried hard to smile, but his determination could not quite overcome his anxiety, plain in his voice, betraying a concern, a fear that he might not be believed and so would be left ashore.

'Console yourself, dear James,' Simon's voice carried the conviction of kindness and friendship. 'The flux and dysentery are present on all His Majesty's vessels, more prevalent on some. Disease on His Majesty's ships has struck down many more men than Boney's sailors ever managed. You appear to have been singularly unfortunate, being stricken and incapacitated for so long and so very severely. You will subsist only on a light diet, the basis being that which my colleague specified for you in the Indies: onions being an excellent antiscorbutic, lemon juice, oranges when we can find them and fresh fish, which is excellent for the fibres. We will allow you neither salt pork nor any salt beef. Vegetables you may eat aplenty but no butter or fats. No water unless it be of the very freshest, only small beer for you should there be any doubt of its provenance... and I venture we will keep you in fine fettle. A glass of wine or brandy will do you no harm; it will doubtless rectify the humours,' Simon concluded his reassuring prescription.

'You do me the greatest kindness, Doctor, thankee,' Mower replied, brightening with the realisation that he was not to be tossed ashore, his acute anxiety dispelled with the greatest of relief and greatly heartened to find himself under the care of Doctor Ferguson, an infallible legend amongst his shipmates and well regarded in much wider circles: it being well known that he had been consulted by the First Lord.

When they returned to the great cabin Pat was pleased to find that Simon had not discharged Mower and insisted he take another glass of burgundy, to which Simon nodded near imperceptibly to Pat. 'You would do me the most essential service, Mr Mower, were you minded to accept the duties of my Third, Mr Pickering here having joined us as Second,' said Pat, considerably relieved by Simon's verdict and finding his satisfaction in securing another of his old officers now preserved.

'Gladly, sir; it would give me the utmost pleasure to serve again with you,' came the unhesitating reply from Mower, his relief evident for all to see. At that moment Freeman and Old Jim Lamb arrived, carrying the dinner, steaming on Pat's silver plate. They set it down to delighted looks all round and hastened away for more burgundy, the first two bottles being quite empty.

A little later, the main course having been eaten, a brace of bottles of fine port also consumed and with all about the table settled in the most amiable of moods, all present settled in a comfortable and convivially informal languor, Pat looked around his cabin, his mind absorbing the entirely restored comfortable ambience and the genial satisfaction of all present, himself included, before his gaze settled on Simon. His mind continued its cogitations even as Freeman cleared the table. 'Simon, I have given thought to your proposal to take aboard Mr Marston as your mate and as chaplain, and I would be pleased were you to send our invitation to the gentleman, if you will,' he proffered as the pudding emerged. Simon allowed himself a private smile, merely nodding by way of confirmation. 'Will you take a little of pot still with me, gentlemen?' asked Pat.

'Pot still?' queried Duncan, who had returned aboard.

'Whiskey, from the son of MacManus of Kilbeggan, in the fine County Westmeath. I have a bottle or two which Murphy ain't found. The glory of the world, so it is.'

'Och, certainly I will take a wee dram with ye,' Duncan replied with enthusiasm, heads nodding emphatically around the table.

'Mr Mower... *James*, perhaps you will grace us with a verse of your poetry?' suggested Pat in high good spirits.

'Why, yes sir. I have a new poem underway, the first stanza completed only yesterday... a return to sea and the parting with my wife prompting it.' Mower extracted a much creased paper from within his jacket,

'Amidst the rolling waves of oceans comes the lovely thought of you,
Through the soughing of the breezes and the sparkle of the dew,
In the shining light of morning and the blackness of the night,
Come wondrous recollections and dreams of past delight.'

'Magnificent, to be sure,' complimented a delighted Pat as all clapped, 'though a trifle short.' Would you care to scrape a little, Simon?'

'With all my heart, brother.'

'What do you care to play?'

'That is for you to choose.'

'Allow me to suggest our old favourite, *St Patrick's Day; Bacon and Greens* as we mariners refer to it, and then we shall play *the Rakes of Kerry*. I have a hankering for a reminder of the Emerald Isle; 'tis plainly far too long since I have gazed over the rolling green hills of Galway and the fields of Connemara, so it is.'

'An inspiring choice, without a doubt.'

'Capital. Have you seen my rosin?'

Friday 23rd May 1823   *Westminster, London*

On the day after the happy reunion with his officers, Pat and Duncan posted back to London, having arranged with the local carter in Truro to deliver all the remaining baggage packed by Sinéad to Falmouth on the morrow. The following morning the two friends presented themselves at the First Lord's private residence in Arlington Street. Mr Lowrey of the Foreign Office, George Canning's aide, was present to discuss all the political limitations associated with the arrangements for the expedition and to finalise the exact terms under which *Surprise* would be engaged and funded. The introductions were made without delay, the servant bidding them all to be seated around the large dining table when the discussion proper began. It continued for an hour, ranging over the most diverse aspects of the venture, including the readiness of *Surprise*, her victualling, the escort of Lord Byron, their intended port of arrival in Greece, contact with the

Greek authorities, communications with London and, eventually, the necessary secrecy of their arrangements.

Melville, anxious to wind up, rapped his spoon loud and vigorously on his cup to gain their attention. 'O'Connor,' said the First Lord, 'until such time as you are engaged in Greek service with a *proper* letter of marque from the provisional Greek government – not that such will count for much should ye be taken by a Turk, I venture – I am minded to suggest that *Surprise* ostensibly be engaged in hydrographical surveying. We have a first rate man in those parts: Smyth, *Mediterranean Smyth* as he is known at the Hydrographical Office, with *Adventure,* a sloop engaged in charting those waters.'

Pat merely nodded, the sophistry of the scheme not appealing to him in the slightest.

After a further half-hour of negotiation and discussion had passed, the First Lord summarised, 'Well, gentlemen, we are in consensus now. It is incumbent upon me to remark again upon the strict political limitations of our association with the provisional Greek government... that is to say... to say that no connection with His Majesty's Government will be admitted *in any circumstance.* I trust that is plain?' Nods all around the table and Melville resumed, 'The first task for *Surprise* is to escort Lord Byron, who has joined the Greek Committee and wishes to go to Greece himself, to Zante, and thence you are to establish contact with the Greek military authorities – such as they may be – with the intention of offering the assistance of *Surprise,* which must, note well O'Connor, be formally arranged. However, there is one matter of necessary precedence in this situation: the latest despatches from Constantinople speak of a new High Admiral appointed to the Turk fleet. His name is Khosref and he is seemingly held in high regard by the Sultan who accompanied the departure of his fleet, at least as far as the Dardanelles. Our sources acquainted with the Porte are minded that the fleet may make an attempt upon a landing on Candia, the island being riven by feuding between internal Greek factions. You are therefore to proceed *directly* to that region in order to assess Turk naval intentions and thence to report such to the Greek authorities, most preferably His Highness Prince Mavrocordato.' Melville paused to see if his instructions were understood. On Pat's nod he resumed, 'His Majesty's Government cannot become the recipient of any allegations of piracy from the Porte... and hence *Surprise* must become a Greek ship of war *only* after formal notarised request at the behest of the Greeks. Mr Lowrey will provide to you further instructions, as may be necessary from His Majesty's Government... in the strictest of secrecy and under cipher. He may deliver instructions of the first importance personally or via a representative known to yourself and to Lieutenant Macleod. In the first instance Mr Lowrey will provide the appropriate code books in order that the lieutenant may decipher any instructions that you may receive. You, Macleod, are also to write and return encoded reports of all political and military developments to the Admiralty. In that respect it is anticipated that you may seek to closely associate yourself with the highest of Greek political and naval authorities. A suitable translator will also be sent to assist you in that task. Their Lordships will further commit from the secret fund a sum sufficient, as we have discussed, for the maintenance of *Surprise* and her crew during the expedition. These funds will be paid to your account, O'Connor. It will be for Mr Lowrey to remit funds to you in specie or any other form of your choosing via His Majesty's Consul in Zante, as you will call for it. The value of any prizes taken will be deducted... *less forty per cent*... from the agreed subvention, which will leave an adequate sum for the payment of prize shares to the officers and crew. Should there be any capture by the Ottoman authorities of *Surprise*, gentlemen... *know you well* that their Lords and His Majesty's Government will disavow any knowledge of these arrangements, will plainly state that *Surprise* is *your private vessel* and, I suggest, O'Connor, that you will be festering in a Turk prison with no prospect of release and will probably be hanged... *or worse*,' Melville concluded on a dark and sobering note.

'My Lord, if you will, please to authorise a draft on my account,' said Pat quickly. 'There are many pressing calls for considerable funds, very large calls indeed, and I must have this immediately if I am to complete all our preparations and make my tide. There is not a moment to be lost.' Melville nodded to Lowrey.

'It leaves me, gentlemen, only to wish you well and good fortune,' said Melville with finality. 'I must away now to dinner with the Foreign Secretary, and so I bid you all farewell.'

Pat and Duncan left together, intending to overnight at the Feathers. Canning left accompanied by Lowrey, wishing them 'God speed.' 'A rum venture,' opined Pat, walking back along Pall Mall. 'I should scarcely have imagined it but a month ago. Am I not too old to be engaging in such capers?'

'Why, 'tis certainly unorthodox, brother, but ye are to consider that it has brought us - Simon, Pickering, Mower and all - back to sea, to our new home, our dear *Surprise*... a concentration of endeavours of which we have nae seen the like for many a year... and there is certainly something to be said for that.'

'I am very sensible of it,' replied Pat quietly.

Chapter Five

Must we but weep o'er days more blest?
Must we but blush? — Our fathers bled.
Earth! render back from out thy breast
A remnant of our Spartan dead!
Of the three hundred grant but three,
To make a new Thermopylae!

Sunday 1ˢᵗ June 1823   *Falmouth, Cornwall*

The rising dawn sun cast its weak light over sleepy Falmouth town, the air dry but chilly as Pat stepped up from the great cabin, shivering a little as he paced about on his quarterdeck. A thin mist arose about the ship from the warmer harbour waters. He drew a deep draught of the cold salt air into his lungs and gazed up at the rigging, masts, yards and sails, his keen eye finding no fault with any of the arrangements. He looked through his glass towards the town. There were fishermen and merchants on the Fish Strand Quay but barely a soul to be seen on the Custom House Quay. He stepped along the deck to the prow, nodding pleasantly to the three men on duty. Contentedly he paced back to his quarterdeck. Barton was one of the very few persons on deck as Pat gazed about, standing near the wheel and chewing his quid, only the three other crewmen forward being about so early. He was a constant reminder to all aboard of his late brother, a reminder that oft prompted Pat's recollections of his lost cox'n; even now, memories of those days ten long years ago still returned to his dreams.

'Good morning, Barton. Tell me, did you know your brother well in his last years?' asked Pat conversationally, still reflecting on his sleeping thoughts.

Barton, pleased to be asked, smiled weakly and nodded. 'Like my right hand knows my left, sir; I cannot say it any closer. Every possible leave we stayed together at our mother's house, our other brother, Robert, having been killed on *Irresistible* in the year 'twelve. Mother passed but a few months after he was gone: a broken heart, 'twas said.'

'He is, even now, mightily missed by his friends aboard too, Barton. A capital man he was, 'pon my word,' Pat left the subject there. 'Be so kind as to rouse the bosun to pipe the hands to breakfast.'

'Aye aye, sir.'

Back in his cabin, Pat passed a few minutes in pleasant solitude gazing through the lights, abstractedly watching a lugger coming in towards the Fish Strand. She was rolling in the smallest of swell, two score or more of frantic, swirling gulls behind her, their shrill squeals bringing his mind back to the day ahead. He sipped his strong black coffee whilst gathering his thoughts in preparation for *Surprise's* looming departure before shouting for his steward, 'Freeman! Bring more coffee, if you please, and perhaps some soft tack and kidneys too; butter as well.'

'Coffee's a'comin' d'reckly, massa, an' cook 'im relightin' galley now,' came Freeman's cheery reply from the coach.

Murphy too peered quickly round the door of the great cabin, looking crisper than his customary self so early in the morning - or at any time for that matter - thought Pat absently. His thoughts were interrupted by a still sleepy Simon coming into the cabin.

'Ah, Simon! Good morning; give you joy of our departure today. Will you take some coffee with me? So much to do. Sinéad and the family are expected at four bells, the mail coach at five bells and we will then be away directly on the tide.'

'And what o'clock would that be?' croaked Simon, his grasp of nautical horology quite failing him so early.

'Why, ain't I explained that to you no more than perhaps two hundred times?' quipped Pat, only half in jest and mercilessly joshing his old companion.

'I believe you may have had occasion to mention it, soul. You navigators are sadly given to jargon and a devotion to clocks and bells so very incomprehensible to those of us whose genius is more akin to the land-oriented kind. Pray, is there any coffee?'

he asked, yawning. At that moment Freeman returned with the pot, clutching too with obvious difficulty the soft tack and butter.

'Freeman, another plate for the Doctor... and ask the cook to double up the kidneys. If you will, please to send for Murphy,' said Pat in the mildest of voice, determined that nothing at all was to dampen his pleasure on this bright day of departure.

'Well, there ain't no bleedin' peace on this barky,' muttered Murphy almost inaudibly and only to himself - or so he thought as he shuffled into the cabin.

'Murphy! Top your boom there, you scoundrel, and you are to lay out my best coat and breeches athwart my cot when Freeman has served breakfast... and nicely pressed, mind,' shouted Pat to a sour-looking Murphy who was departing in haste.

The early morning passed swiftly, the mist clearing, a brightening sun rising to warm the quays, the myriad of gulls still calling, orbiting the later returned fishing boats awaiting their turn to tie up at the Fish Strand Quay with their pilchard catches. With the high tide bringing plentiful depth of water, *Surprise* had been towed so as to be nearer the more spacious Custom House Quay where the families of the crew had gathered to witness her departure; her best bower and a kedge anchor now held her position near two cables off the quay. The crew in their entirety were passing to and from the ship and the quay, all the ship's boats employed for this purpose, the men making their final farewells to family, friends and numerous other interested onlookers, a growing multitude of them gathering as the clock marched on. At the foretop the Blue Peter flapped vigorously, and at ten o'clock – four bells in the forenoon watch – the coach arrived with Sinéad and the twins. Pat, now in his best captain's attire, had previously stepped ashore to await and greet his family, who now came aboard *Surprise* in the boat. The ship's final preparations were left to Macleod, Pickering and Mower, the latter two sharing their time between their own families on the quay and their duties aboard, gently hustling along crew members dallying with their own kin whilst awaiting the mail and minding the tide. The crew had also made an extra effort for such an important event: their own best clothing, having no uniforms as such, had been washed, starched and pressed. Their pigtails were all replaited, as they sought as much as their captain did to look their very best on departure. The Wesleyans stood prominent amongst all, still garbed in red attire.

Pat had returned aboard to his quarterdeck; he contemplated the late arrival of the awaited mail coach. He was mindful with the very mildest of anxiety of the imminent ebbing of the tide. 'This is cutting it pretty fine, Mr Macleod; we will strike the Blue Peter.'

Sinéad and the twins were all standing on Pat's quarterdeck too and in a high state of excitement as the final preparations for departure proceeded all around them. Pat had no time to pass with them, his attention was all for his ship. 'Mr Macleod, the bosun is to send the topmen aloft,' he ordered, adding to himself, 'The mail coach is hellfire late.' He was hardly conscious now of his family's presence as his professional routine pressed in upon him, but he beamed in every direction, his own spirits never higher. Five bells came closer. The officers having called all the men aboard only the arrival of the mail coach was still awaited. The quayside families continued to wave and shout excitedly to their husbands and sons, more than a few tears being shed by many of the wives and sweethearts. The crew busied themselves with the very final preparations, still shouting last farewells and waving to the excited, assembled throng when they could. Only the barge with eight rowers now still waited at the quay for the mail.

As the minutes ticked away, from the Custom House Quay came the distant clippety-clop sound of hooves and the distinct clatter of metal wheels on the cobbles. The mail coach approached the quay, brought to a halt amidst the excited throng. Two figures stepped out: the first a rather short man in His Majesty's most elegant uniform, the second plainly a civilian. 'By God, 'tis William Codrington!' shouted Pat with delight.

'And my colleague, Michael Marston! To be sure, we have the blessing this day,' exclaimed Simon, great pleasure in his voice.

Pat shouted through his speaking tube to the quayside barge crew. 'Barton, bring those gentlemen aboard with their dunnage. Swiftly now, there is not a moment to be lost!' He turned to the master and murmured 'Mr Prosser, stand by.'

Within five minutes, Codrington and Marston had scrambled aboard, two of the barge crew passing up the arrivals' baggage and all following swiftly behind them. Pat waved his hat briefly to the two men before turning to his steward. 'Murphy, my compliments to Mr Codrington and Mr Marston, and will you kindly take their dunnage below.'

The high tide had passed near two hours ago and the ebb was about to succeed slack water. Before *Surprise* could begin to swing on her best bower - her bow still faced east towards the Carrick Roads, a kedge anchor keeping her station - Pat had decided that she would sail as soon as the ebb commenced; the gentle westerly breeze and lee-tide would greatly facilitate her leaving. All along the Custom House Quay the crowd, sensing the imminence of *Surprise's* departure, cheered loud and shouted vigorously, tears and joy all a-jumble. The crew, those that could spare a moment, furiously waved their scarves and shouted vigorously back, and exuberant loud whistling was heard from atop all the yards.

Pat was immensely pleased himself and minded not a jot this joyous breach of the customary, orderly routine of leaving port. The crew, many more hands in comparison with her departure from Plymouth Dock, made light work of all their tasks: the kedge was brought in, tops'ls unfurled, yards braced, the best bower swiftly catted and slowly *Surprise* shifted away from her anchorage, a very happy Pat content to leave her control to Duncan and the master.

Surprise moved off, the distance between the quay and the ship swiftly increasing. Slowly she gathered momentum, the wind acting upon her tops'ls, the ship now being driven across the inner harbour in the strengthening ebb current. Gradually, *Surprise* picked up a little more speed, but still the families ashore could be heard shouting fading farewells from the quay.

After a further ten minutes *Surprise* cleared the inner harbour and shifted into the Carrick Roads. Pat turned to the master and his second lieutenant, 'Mr Pickering, please take command if you will.' This was said to Pickering as a convention and courtesy, but mostly for the ears of Mr Prosser, in the knowledge that no sailor knew the harbour and Roads better than the master, a native of Falmouth. 'Please excuse me, my dear,' Pat smiled as he spoke to his wife. 'Mr Macleod, Doctor Ferguson and I are going into the cabin to greet our late arrivals.' Sinéad nodded, content to remain on the quarterdeck with the twins, quite fascinated by the spectacle of *Surprise's* departure. Pat was quite out of his depth as to how to manage his son and daughter, hurtling with great excitement around his province, the quarterdeck. To Simon, Pat muttered, with some little exasperation, 'Anyone might think we were aboard the Margate hoy.'

Simon said nothing, simply smiled. Pat was more than a little relieved to go below, prompted by Simon's earlier and gentle suggestion that it was not a day to stand on the strictest of shipboard custom and etiquette. They came down together into the great cabin, the new arrivals already seated and sipping tea, Freeman hovering near the door.

'William Codrington, joy be with you; 'pon my word it is good to see you again. Mr Marston, how well you look, sir. Welcome aboard. Freeman! Rouse out two bottles of the best madeira, if you please; the seventy-five,' said Pat pleasantly.

When Freeman had returned and was pouring the wine, all in the cabin had settled round Pat's table. Codrington explained that he had been away visiting relatives in the North Country, avoiding certain gentlemen of whom he declined to speak further, and had only very recently received Pat's letter. He had rushed immediately to Falmouth upon receipt of it, pausing only to don his uniform and pack the most meagre of baggage. Further necessities could be bought at their first port of call, and yes he would be honoured to shift to *Eleanor*, as Pat suggested, most honoured and pleased to do so. Codrington hurried on, explaining that his finances were in an assuredly temporary state of dysfunction, but he was in no doubt that a successful voyage would restore his treasury and his standing. Pat had not anticipated all his officer invitees would become available in response to his invitations and so, the appointment of a fourth lieutenant for *Surprise* being somewhat superfluous, the surplus of officers had been satisfactorily resolved by Codrington shifting to *Eleanor* where Pat was very pleased to have him in command.

Michael Marston had heard from his parishioners in his Cornish benefice of Pat O'Connor's planned return to sea two weeks previously. An educated, intelligent man, the past four years he had found increasingly tedious as parish parson to his tiny and generally unlearned congregation. His subsequent letter to Simon in Plymouth had enquired of the prospects for employment of any kind. It had reached Simon at precisely the moment that he had realised the necessity for a surgeon's mate, Pat more conventionally considering first of his need for sailors. In anticipation of the possibility that he could be called away from the ship, Simon had deemed it wholly prudent to engage a surgeon's mate. Hence Marston's letter was opportune. Upon Simon's affirmative reply, Marston had leapt at the opportunity to volunteer his services. Marston was a proficient surgeon's mate who had assisted Simon through a particularly bloody battle aftermath with serious casualties requiring immediate surgery during one of his voyages aboard *Tenedos*, because of which Simon was assured of his competency. The fact that Marston was also a knowledgeable naturalist further weighed significantly in Simon's considerations, finding on occasions that the company of nautical men could verge some way towards the tedious, Pat and Duncan being exceptions. Marston could also play the violin, albeit he had not been the most accomplished of musicians when last aboard *Tenedos*.

Pat looked out though his cabin lights, gazed at the white wake at the stern of the ship; *Surprise* was well out into Falmouth Bay, experiencing the customary chops of the Channel, sailing in a strong wind under all sail, white horses everywhere over a vigorous grey swell, spray spicules sweeping through the air and splashing on the glass. *Eleanor*, under the command of Reeve, trailed a mile astern. A few minutes of reflection and he turned away to return to his table, to his officers. Duncan, Pickering and Mower had left the master in charge on the quarterdeck and had come into the great cabin at Pat's invitation to greet their former shipmate, Codrington.

It was a strict convention within the Royal Navy that no one spoke at the captain's table unless in reply to the captain. In this instance the tradition had seemingly gone by the board as Pat's four lieutenants and two surgeons happily engaged in an animated babble of mutual reminiscences and experiences since their last meeting. He did not mind in the slightest since he was as interested as they all were in hearing their stories and was particularly delighted that all three former lieutenants had accepted his invitation. Of Marston he was not so sure, but it was inconceivable that anything could shake his pleasure in this particular day. After half an hour and Freeman having coughed at least three times at the door, and having brought in after the captain's nod two large pots of coffee, Pat rapped the table with his knuckles to call them to attention. 'Gentlemen, I am very much obliged to you all for accepting my invitation to join me, to serve aboard *Surprise*. Freeman, please pour the coffee. Only a very few days ago I had a fine crew and but one officer, and here we are today, three more former comrades with me once more, together with our old friend and surgeon Doctor Ferguson... Simon, here.' He patted his friend's arm affectionately, '... and Mr Marston too.' Pat could not quite bring himself to think of Marston as *Michael*, to consider him in the same close informality as he thought of Simon, cordiality between the two in the past never having progressed that far.

Simon, in quite flagrant breach of convention but in the knowledge that the new officers knew precious little detail of the voyage, its purpose or the obscured drivers of it, interrupted Pat in his momentary pause and his informality, 'Be so kind as to outline your clearer view of our voyage, sir.'

'Thank you, Doctor,' Pat, taking his cue, reverted to a customary minimum of protocol. 'I must tell you, gentlemen, that

I am no longer a serving Royal Navy captain; I have resigned the service.' There was an audible sharp intake of breath around the table. 'I have accepted the invitation of the provisional Greek government to advise and assist their formative navy on its methods to counter the Turk in the current struggle for Greek independence. Gentlemen, upon our arrival in the Ionians, *Surprise* will commence operating under a Greek letter of marque. *Eleanor*, however, will at all times retain her status as an English ship, sailing as a private vessel and thereby enjoying protection from Turk interference. She may be very useful to us with that safeguard and capacity should we need to separate our activities. As you know, I am accompanied by my family, who will become resident in Zante, and so on this first day aboard I must attend to them.' Pat looked around the table, 'Gentlemen, you will forgive me if I leave further explanations until the morrow when I hope you will all give me the pleasure of dining in the cabin... when we can speak further of these matters,' Pat concluded.

There was a murmur of further pleasantries before the officers shuffled out to settle in to their accommodation in the gunroom and to reacquaint themselves with the crew.

'Murphy, my wife will take my cot; please rig another in the cabin for myself; the twins will berth in the spare officers' cabins. Be so good as to shift their dunnage down there, afore supper if you will... thankee.'

Murphy, only too pleased to be asked on matters of this nature, indeed in the most polite manner, even thanked by his captain, being mindful of Pat's imminent dinner busied away in some haste.

Pat returned to his quarterdeck where Sinéad and the twins were still evidently enjoying the novelty and vivid sense of adventure. The weather was particularly clement, the sun near its zenith, and the wind, a gentle westerly, propelled *Surprise,* close-hauled but with her clean hull, at a steady six to seven knots. She had passed the Manacles at noon, making good progress.

By supper time and Lizard Point far off to starboard, Pat sat down at his table to eat with Sinéad and the twins. The youngsters were plainly excited at the adventure they had embarked upon and had busied themselves all day speaking with many members of the crew, engineering encounters with them, asking many and varied questions about *Surprise*, their past voyages and the crew's past experiences with their father. To all enquiries they received only the most glowing of positive answers, all mention of blood-curdling events or setbacks being most diligently expunged in the telling. Sinéad, more soberly, investigated the domestic arrangements for the voyage and queried all on the prospects for the weather: not that anyone could vouch anything more than generalities and platitudes. After supper, before leaving the table, Sinéad pressed Pat for his views on the potential dangers of the expedition but could glean near nothing about that, and so she ultimately contented herself with the short term prospect of the voyage to Greece – via Mahon, via Genoa and via anywhere else that wind and weather might take *Surprise* – as Pat laboured to explain the vagaries and vicarious nature of weather at sea.

As the twins, finally exhausted, went off to their berths below, Pat settled Sinéad within his cot. He decided on a little time for quiet reflection on his quarterdeck, the late spring evenings being pleasantly warm. It was these tranquil last hours of the day, the sun having set and dusk fading into the near total blackness of the approaching night that Pat, being a passionate astronomer, particularly enjoyed. At home, he had a telescope established in his own observatory. Aboard, he had a powerful glass which doubled for his military and astronomical purposes. The ship's activity was now subdued, supper having concluded, and on deck there remained very few of the crew. It had been a relaxing watch for them, the wind having being steady and westerly since sunrise, though veering north-westerly as the day progressed, and no tacking had been necessary during the day. Pat, Mower, the master, Barton and two helmsmen were the only ones present on the quarterdeck. Pat gazed back over her stern, her wake still visible for miles behind her with its trail of sparkling silver phosphoresence, her course so straight, unbending: two points west of south. He looked up at her yards, all braced to catch the prevailing north-westerly; since late afternoon so constant in its strength and direction, the helmsmen with little challenge to maintain her course with hardly any leeway. He slowly paced the length of his ship, enjoying the quietude of the moment, *Surprise* pitching very gently in the exceptional tranquility of the Channel sea state and with only the slowest and smallest of roll, near unnoticeable to any seasoned mariner. A few minutes passed before he stood on the forepeak; he swept the southern sky through his glass, the brightest of the stars already visible; the constants of *Vega*, *Cygnus* and *Altair* were shining brightly, the planet *Saturn* faintly emerging. Ten more minutes passed, Pat gazing at the night sky in all its emerging splendour until, with a deep sigh of satisfaction, he retraced his steps and regained his quarterdeck.

'A prime day, Mr Mower, Mr Prosser, Barton; I bid you good night, gentlemen, lads,' remarked a very contented Pat, pacing slowly past the wheel.

'Proper, sir, none better,' replied Prosser in his slow Cornish intonation.

'Good night, sir,' from Barton and the helmsmen.

Below in the gunroom, the officers were engaged in vigorous debate about aspects of the voyage that loomed large in their minds, principal amongst which was their captain's resignation. Simon, with possession of many if not all of the answers, could not freely comment and politely demurred from doing so when pressed, claiming scant knowledge. A strange look from Marston, peering out of his cot where he remained prone and in some little discomfort, the sea sickness claiming him after such a long absence from sea, rather suggested that he believed Simon to know more than he was prepared to let on.

Monday 2ⁿᵈ June 1823   *Bay of Biscay*

The Bay of Biscay weather was pleasantly clement, exhibiting none of the violent horrors that the crew had experienced on many a prior occasion. *Surprise* sailed on steadily at a comfortable five knots, the air temperature rising slowly as she made southing. From the gun deck came the sound of clicking hammers as the crew, a dozen men sitting about, chipped away at the round shot that had been brought up from the damp stowage of the hold where they had gathered a patina of rust. After smoothing with the chisel, the men oiled them with slush begged from the galley, it being a valuable perquisite of the cook. On the forepeak three men were polishing one of Pat's two personal chasers, *Lucifer*, all its old brown paint now gone and its bronze restored to a lustrous shine.

At his customary dinnertime Pat sat at his table in the great cabin with his officers: Duncan Macleod, Tom Pickering, James Mower and William Codrington all present. William Reeve, being master's mate in rank but for so long in Pat's service, and entrusted latterly with *Eleanor,* was also in attendance, Mr Prosser skippering *Eleanor* in *Surprise's* wake. All were in a high state of anticipation and curiosity. Finally there was Simon, seated alongside Pat and savouring the remnants of his coffee. Michael Marston, still indisposed by sea sickness, remained in his cot in the gunroom.

'How does Marston fare, Simon? I gather he is laid up, indisposed, the sea-sickness. Will we put him ashore at The Groyne?' This was said with a smile and a wink, Simon well aware of Pat having no prediliction for the clergy aboard his ships.

'Certainly not. He is merely incommoded at present, a temporary state; the rhythmical motion of this vessel it is - after years ashore on firmer standing. He sends his compliments. A low diet will answer, and he may return to his duty on the morrow.'

'I am gratified to hear it.'

After a most cordial dinner of the first quality, fresh provisions being in plentiful supply so soon into the voyage, and a pleasant hour spent in the most delightful of reminiscences, Pat caught the air of restrained anticipation and so began the briefing. 'Gentlemen, we are bound for Genoa for provisioning, beforehand touching at the Rock for fresh water and calling briefly at Port Mahon. Thereafter we sail for the Ionians where we will engage in surveying the Ionian waters until such time as we make contact with representatives of the provisional Greek government and so formally enter their service as a letter-of-marque. However, in the first instance we are tasked with a swift passage to the regions of Candia to ascertain the whereabouts of the Turk fleet, that we may report such to the Admiralty.' Blank faces all round, nothing said and Pat resumed, 'Mrs O'Connor, my son and daughter, Mrs Macleod and Mr Macleod's daughter will remain in residence at Zante whilst we are engaged in that task. Only when we have our official Greek commission will we become a combatant ship, and then we will be officially entitled to any Turk prizes we may capture. Note, gentlemen, we do not serve in any official capacity on behalf of His Majesty's Government... and therefore none of us may legally continue with our service rank, and so all must resign. The First Lord has, so you all will know, pledged to restore all of us to our former rank and seniority when we have completed our service for Greece, but note also... this particular aspect is to remain confidential, known only to those at this table and may not be communicated to anyone else. I trust you will remember of this.'

There was a general murmur of affirmative response from everyone present, all mulling over questions that had come to mind, but in the more formal ambience prevailing now that they were at sea all observed the long familiar protocol of the captain's table, withholding questions and comment until asked directly.

Pat continued his briefing, 'The Greeks have precious few ships with which to fight the Turks bringing reinforcements and stores to their troops in Greece. Two years ago the island of Chios was sacked and thousands of Greeks taken from that place as slaves. The Greek islands of Psara, Hydra and Spetses provide the only Greek warships, and these are generally armed merchantmen only, no regular warships being available to them. Their crews insist on payment in advance and will not sail without it. Most of the shipowners will not hazard their vessels against Turk warships - they will only fight *merchantmen*. There are, however, brave Greeks, Admirals Miaoulis and Canaris being principal amongst them, who will fight the Turk warships with what little they have to command. The Greeks have become adept at using fireship tactics to make up for their lack of numbers and ordnance.' Pat paused to look about him, 'New Greek warships *have* been ordered, notably two heavy frigates and six steamships, yet none are expected to arrive for some time, years even. Until then, gentlemen, *Surprise* will be the sole purpose-built warship fighting in the Greek cause. Our adversaries are many whilst the Turk frigates may substantially exceed our size and ordnance; we will therefore choose our engagements with the utmost care... and flee before great odds so as to fight another day. Mr Macleod has, in these past few weeks, studied the political and military situation. Mr Macleod, will you comment please?'

Duncan followed on, 'There is near civil war amongst the Greeks. Koloktronis is chief in the Morea, Odysseus in the East and Mavrocordato 'tween the twae. Messalonghi is under siege, Athens is in the hands of the Turk and the provisional Greek government resides in Nauplia in the north-east of the Morea. Och, the situation, gentlemen, is bleak indeed for the Greeks. It is to be hoped that the Turk resupply by sea can be hindered, so weakening their forces in Greece, until the Greeks can act resolutely as one, their infighting ceases and ultimately their wee state becomes more firmly established and with greater political support. If and when this occurs, gentlemen, it might be hoped that significant pressure might then be brought to bear on the Porte.'

'Thank you, Mr Macleod. Let us for Heaven's sake return to our humble level of honest mariners and our own honest intentions else we may run foul of politics, the politics of foreigners even, and that is the end of all comfortable talk. As can be seen, the Greeks are in a proper lather; a greater dog's breakfast can hardly be imagined, and it is we who are to pull their chestnuts out of the frying pan.'

Tuesday 3rd June 1823   *Bay of Biscay*

It was the morning of the third day out of Falmouth and Marston was feeling sufficiently recovered to consider taking some solid food for the first time. 'I am most thankful for your ministrations, dear colleague,' he said to Simon. 'Never did I think I would suffer so... and after so many prior voyages at sea.'

'A few days aboard will answer tolerably well. Allow me to offer you a trifle of this burgoo, Michael. Eat it whilst it remains hot. Here is a glass of the most excellent and medicinal madeira to follow. Then we will take a turn on deck.'

The fresh sea breeze and warm morning sunlight both being so reviving, Marston had recovered some colour after a few hours and so was able to walk unaccompanied, to go on deck. He stood on the lee side, grateful for the fresh air, leaning on the bulwark and gazing at the Spanish coast.

'Mr Marston! I hope I see you well, sir,' shouted Pat, looking forward from his quarterdeck and seeking an opportunity to extend some hospitality and cordiality to his chaplain. 'What do you say to a pot of tea with the Doctor and I?'

'With great pleasure, sir,' said Marston weakly.

After a few minutes they descended to the great cabin, Pat shouting for his steward, 'Freeman! D'ye hear me? Bear a hand there: bring some vittles for my guest... some eggs and bacon, a fresh pot of tea too. Send the word to the cook. Mr Marston, pray sit down, sir, you do not look well.'

It was a statement which struck fear, great fear into Marston. For an instant the fleeting thought that he might be set ashore flashed through his mind. 'Oh no, sir! It was only a passing malady, quite transient and perfectly abated now. Dr Ferguson assures me that the remedy is sea air, plentiful sea air... as much as possible; being aboard ship and far from land the surest of cures.'

Pat smiled, 'I hope you will give me the pleasure of joining the Doctor and myself for supper this evening, after which we will practice a little scraping; you *did* bring your instrument?'

'Why, sir, thank you, thank you; indeed, it would give me great pleasure to accept your kind invitation... and yes, I have my violin, I am very pleased to say,' Marston smiled broadly, the invitation so significant, so welcome, and his face for the first time shifting from the mask of strain.

Freeman soon returned with a steaming dish. 'Here,' said Pat, 'there is nothing like bacon and eggs to revive the body. Eat up, you look fair clemmed.' After Marston had left the cabin, suitably revived and considerably reinvigorated, all the bacon and eggs heartily consumed, Pat remained with Simon. 'What do you say to a fresh beefsteak... with beans... for dinner later... and perhaps we will enjoy a second pot of tea until then?'

'With all my heart, and conceivably might there be onions too? I venture the suggestion in the medical context. They are an excellent antiscorbutic, as you doubtless collect.' Simon laughed as the recollection of such banter came back to him from their former voyages together.

'Freeman! Show a leg, rouse out another pot of tea!' shouted Pat, perfectly aware that Freeman's ear would be hovering close behind the door, likely alongside Murphy's.

'That was an exceedingly cordial gesture, if my memory does not fail me. The more so as I collect you did not favour my colleague's playing when he was last aboard?' remarked Simon.

'I am so happy, old friend, being at sea once again... with a prime crew, fine officers to a man... with Sinéad here, the swabs happy and the Bay behaving herself; Marston's playing, bad or worse, is of no consequence. A toast, if you will,' said Pat, raising his glass, 'To our venture and may no new thing arise!'

'Our venture and may no new thing arise!' echoed Simon.

In the early evening after supper Pat, Duncan and Simon were astonished by Marston's playing. They started with the old Royal Navy favourite, *Bacon and Greens,* and shifted to *Corelli*, Marston's violin bringing a pleasing high end sharpness to the pair of Pat's 'cello and Simon's viola, greatly contributing to their enjoyment of the melodic sound of the *Concerto Grosso Adagio Opus 6 No. 8*, Simon's particular pleasure. The evening's ensemble, even allowing for Duncan's sometimes indifferent improvisations with the whistle, excelled everything previously heard in the great cabin, so much so that they were all greatly delighted and expressed volubly the most flowing of compliments at the end. 'Mr Marston, may I praise you most heartily on your violin,' said Pat, much to his own surprise.

'I am much obliged, Captain O'Connor, deeply obliged; thank you sir,' Marston replied, a little overwhelmed by the warmth of his inauguration to the cabin social scene.

'I give you joy of your nautical parish. Pray tell, sir, how did you impr ... *achieve* such an excellent talent since last aboard our barky?' asked Pat, still incredulous at the very substantial improvement.

'The melancholia, sir, long winters with dark evenings; then too the dwindling congregations in my benefice: my parishioners struggling to make ends meet, their long hard days working to earn a living - the cost of bread now so very high - and Sundays tending their vegetable plot... those that had one after the enclosures that is. Great poverty abounded in my parish.' Marston sighed, 'For a while I took to drinking the local cider... it started at harvest festivals, from flagons left as my gift... until I decided one day to stop before things got out of hand. To cheer myself, I took to my violin, practising every day, and sometimes I would have a visitor, accomplished in the strings, who would encourage me until I mastered all the sheets I had. Then I gave solo concerts in the church and my parishioners trickled back, but their numbers were still so few, many so poor and gone to the workhouse, husbands even selling their wives for lack of even a shilling. That, sir, is why the news of your voyage was so welcome to me, and I am here with the blessing of my good wife, Mary, to seek a new purpose, a re-invigoration.'

The latter comment struck a most sympathetic chord with Pat, and being a landowner himself, albeit in a small way, and an Irish Member of the House, he understood full well the implications of the accelerating agricultural changes, post-war, particularly the enclosures. Worst of all was the very high taxation regime imposed on corn imports and the peasants' staple, bread - consequently so costly. He commiserated wholeheartedly with Marston, 'Ah, the enclosures, the Corn Laws, the interest on bonds now reduced to a trifling three and a half percent whilst tax has risen to thirty-four shillings a quarter on corn. Boney is long gone yet income tax is still at two shillings in the pound... *two shillings!* How is an honest man to feed his family? 'Tis a pretty kettle of fish when bread is so dear. Mr Marston, I have so much enjoyed myself this evening; I thank you again for your company. Might I enquire if you would favour us with your playing after supper each evening... for an hour or so perhaps... as we cross the Bay?'

The captain's transformation was quite incredible to Simon who in past times had come to accept that Pat could not bring himself to favour the chaplain, even in his capacity as assistant surgeon.

'Why, sir, I thank you most kindly. I will look forward to tomorrow with particular enthusiasm,' Marston replied, as much taken aback as was Simon by his captain's gracious compliments and his invitation, his face shining with pleasure.

Murphy was less overwhelmed, as he complained to his sometime assistant, Old Jim Lamb, whilst helping Freeman and clearing the dishes back to the galley. 'Well, there be another of 'em now, all caterwaulin'; four of 'em, dinnin' away. 'Tis enough to drive a man to the captain's liquor store.'

'Would you be meaning *more often*, Murphy?' asked Barton, who was also Old Jim Lamb's cousin and consequently privy to certain shipboard practices, overhearing Murphy as he was helping himself to cocoa off the galley stove.

By Corunna the quartet had become well established, before Cape St. Vincent Sinéad had returned from keeping the twins company in the sick bay after supper to attend the playing, by Cadiz the ship's officers were invited to join them for toad in a hole and to enjoy the increasing ambience of informal bonhomie in the cabin after supper as the quartet played.

'God help us,' said Murphy, taking advantage of the absence of all officers from the quarterdeck, all being in the cabin, and chatting to Anderton, one of the helmsmen. 'What a screechin' awful yowlin' they do make, to be sure; 'tis a din worse than the bar o' the King's Head in Galway Town of a Saturday night.'

Surprise had come into Rosia Bay at Gibraltar in the late afternoon of the previous day. In the brightness of the following morning, Pat and his officers and most of the crew had gone ashore, Pat to show Sinéad and the twins his old haunts. Simon and Marston had left to climb the Rock and to observe the wildlife, Reeve and Barton remaining aboard with a few hands to supervise the loading of fresh water.

Marston, by now fully recovered from his seasickness, his morale restored substantially by his welcome and playing popularity in the cabin, exuded goodwill for all things including O'Connor, the officers and the crew. Duncan, Pickering and Mower he had become accustomed to many years previously, and all had extended a friendly welcome to him upon his return. Codrington and Reeve were also very amiable with him, and unsurprisingly he contrasted the lonely times in his small rural parish with the companionship aboard ship, in which he delighted. Ships fare, whilst plain for the most part, was plentiful and invariably accompanied by wine which, although varying from indifferent to excellent, was not the norm at his Cornish home, and a full plate with a glass of wine always present contrasted so very favourably with his recent hard times.

Upon gasping their way up the final yards to the summit of the Rock, Simon and Marston collapsed for respite, sweating profusely and gulping the last of the water from their flasks. As their breathing recovered they sat enjoying the magnificent views, content to recount fond recollections of their last time at Gibraltar when they had also climbed the Rock to observe the vultures, storks and eagles, all of which were still present and plainly visible. They sat basking in the hot sun, not a single cloud in sight, and when fully relaxed from their exertions supped from a brace of red wine bottles which Simon had brought along, reclining and eating plentiful cheese sandwiches, munching on crunchy red onions purchased that morning and cracking Gibraltar walnuts - a great favourite of Simon's. An inquisitive group of monkeys were watching closely from ten yards away. 'Marston, art happy? I am considering of a particular matter.'

'Pray tell, Ferguson; we have known one another long enough to speak our thoughts without giving offence.'

'Listen, will I tell you something? You know that O'Connor has resigned the service?' said Simon, 'This venture not being one in which His Majesty's officers can lawfully serve.'

'I am not unaware of this... this development,' said Marston cautiously. 'The officers speak of it in the gunroom... and there is a singular want of privacy for such discussions in that place... as you know full well. I am minded that the captain must be mortally cast down by such a change, the service being his life, even his very being?'

'To be sure, he did not choose this course lightly. It came about only after several years ashore and his dissatisfaction with their Lordships keeping him cooling his heels on the beach whilst all around him the fleet was shrinking. It has been a tolerably good decision on his part, I find. I do not collect seeing him happier than these past weeks. May I say, as you have now so fortuitously engaged with him in a social capacity, joining our scraping at supper, O'Connor could not be described as a philosopher, being something of a plain speaker in his honest tarpaulin way. You should mind where any dialogue might lead us, in particular you would be well advised never to let the term *privateer*... or even worse - *pirate! - God forbid*... cross your lips, and though one must never become the prisoner of words we must content ourselves with the term *letter-of-marque* should the subject of our capacity in Greek service ever arise. I collect we may have spoken of such afore, though these matters of mere procedure, of protocol I find oft slip the more − will I say − *philosophical* mind.'

'Is the nature of the privateer somewhat discreditable? I would be sure of my understanding in such a delicate matter.'

'Of course the privateer fights for what O'Connor and his colleague officers would consider as the basest of motives: solely for gain, for profit; purely mercenary are his interests.'

'And prizes hold no interest for him? I collect great joy abounding when prizes were taken in the past, the captain being particularly pleased; surely so?'

131

'That is plainly undeniable, Michael. Yet the captain would consider the two to be wholly different. The taking of prizes in His Majesty's service bestows a legitimacy which is morally absent from the perspective... from the thinking of the privateer.'

'Why, there is a distinction of course; no one would deny it.'

'Conceivably, your role will become of the utmost significance for our venture, and it would be a particularly unwelcome development were anything to arise so as to bring even the slightest of rift between you and O'Connor.'

'Never be so concerned, dear colleague; after years of shivering in Cornish winters, no fuel to be had save the odd windfall along the lanes, nothing of note ever occurring in my daily routine, no person of any education with whom to enjoy any meaningful discourse, this is most certainly the life I aspire to: interesting companionship and good commons. Be assured I will never cross him; no, such is inconceivable. You may be certain of that.' Marston nodded as he spoke, in emphasis of his understanding, whilst both stared intently at the whirling vultures overhead, entirely distracting Simon. His point made, Marston looked about him, his interest returning to the fauna, before loudly exclaiming, 'Over there, apes! Why, the rascals have seized our sandwiches!'

Wednesday 25th June 1823   *Western Mediterranean*

The wind was blowing a very favourable, gentle southerly as *Surprise* neared Port Mahon in the early afternoon, greatly facilitating her entrance to the harbour, a long and winding passage, no great width available and hence safe access so dependent upon the wind direction. Slowly she slipped past Fort Marlborough to larboard and Cape Mola to starboard, shearwaters flying in a multitude about them as they passed by with her courses furled, coming up next past the Lazaretto Fortress to starboard, sailing on reefed topsails alone, keeping to the north side of the channel, passing Cuckold's Reach, gliding through the narrow passage to the north side of the hospital island of Sant Felip Fort and approaching the Town Quay. The northern side of the great reach of water was devoid of buildings for the most part and presented a dry and brown landscape covered with the scrub oak native to the island, contrasting so starkly with the cultivation amidst the scattered buildings set back from the harbour. Orange groves covered with white blossom stepped back up the hillsides overlooking the town, the wind gusts bringing occasional scintillas of their scent, alternating with wild jasmine, wafting towards all on deck. *Surprise,* her topsails now double-reefed, slowed to a near stop as she turned hard to larboard with the last of her momentum just as she came abeam the Town Quay, no other ships being tied up. The southerly wind now pressed upon her at the bow, her topsails backed and she came quickly to a stop, letting go her small bower. The cable veered, *Surprise* drifted back slightly to leeward to set her anchor fifty yards off the Pigalle Steps. Long known in the Service as the Pigtail Steps, they led directly up to the top of the town. It was a place which the Surprises had visited many times before and was well known to them all. The whole crew were now on deck, many of them gazing at a port which they had, for the most part, lived in for four years until the year 'two when Minorca had been handed back to Spain after the Treaty of Amiens. Even since then the harbour had continued to be used as the Royal Navy base in the western Mediterranean. Pat and Simon on the quarterdeck looked hard for familiarities and changes, not many of the latter being evident.

'Why, 'tis been a long time since we first tied up here; it seems a lifetime ago,' sighed Pat with just the barest hint of melancholy in his voice. 'It ain't changed at all, save that I see no brigs or frigates, not a one here.'

'It is as if we were never away. A glorious place it is, no doubt.'

'Happy times here they were.'

'To be sure, that thought is never far from my mind these days, brother. I oft so dearly wish that Agnes could be here to share these peaceful days with us.' said Simon very quietly, and Pat did not hear him.

'Mr Pickering, be so good as to roster leave ashore for the crew; we will be here two nights. The Doctor, Mr Macleod and I will be ashore for both of them. Pray take command of the barky, if you will. Gentlemen, a walk up the steps and a pint of sherry in Jeraldo's Coffee House for old time's sake... on our way to the Royal, I fancy. Are you with me?'

'Aye, for sure,' said Duncan.

'I will be very happy, dear soul,' Simon replied wistfully, thinking of his prior, penurious days during numerous visits to Mahon for many a year after he had first met Pat.

Walking up the steps was something akin to a homecoming for all of them. Pat's mind wandered fondly to a discrete dalliance with a lady in Mahon before he had married, with the wife of one of the based squadron's officers, a liaison perhaps suspected but never coming into the open, the said officer losing his ship and his life in battle at sea a year later. He also fondly remembered a near romantic encounter with the wife of the landlord of the Royal, the lovely Marisol; near only because of the impromptu and perhaps timely arrival of Duncan who took a disapproving view, almost bringing them to an occasion of honour with seconds in attendance; the inevitably bloody conclusion fortunately averted by an engagement at sea in which Pat was wounded; the passage of time during his healing, Simon's care and intervention, and Duncan's solicitude for him smoothing the rift between them.

Though it was some years since Pat had been in Mahon he felt immediately at his ease; indeed, he was acknowledged still by brief but friendly greetings from several near-forgotten, nodding acquaintances as he walked along, few officers ever having brought so many prizes into the harbour. He might even now be a welcome guest in many respectable houses of the town.

The appeal of the sherry at Jeraldo's was a nostalgic pull, but the Royal beckoned more strongly, certainly for Duncan, as that was where his daughter Brodie and wife Kathleen were accommodated; and so they resolved to pass by Jeraldo's and bear directly for the Royal, aware that Kathleen and Brodie, not knowing precisely when *Surprise* would arrive in Mahon, might not actually be there. Kathleen had written to Duncan before they left Falmouth, advising of her love of the island, never previously having left the British Isles, and she was usually engaged in roving far over the interior by horseback, always accompanied by Brodie.

They strolled into the Royal by the familiar back way, through the little courtyard of orange trees, greeting a pair of English mastiffs, Duncan throwing two old walnut halves found in the depths of his pocket before the dogs would rise to greet them, slavering and panting in the heat of the early afternoon. Of Brodie and Kathleen there was no sign, but Marisol was still there: a little greyer, a little plumper, but still the same excitable and enthusiastic person that Pat was never likely to forget. 'Capitano Pat!' she shrieked, rushing to throw her arms around Pat's neck, to his evident joy as he swept her clean off her feet in the friendliest of embraces, Marisol squealing with undisguised pleasure.

It was becoming a little late in comparison with their customary dinner time aboard *Surprise* and so, after profuse greetings, several fondly remembered Royal staples were ordered including a hearty beefsteak pudding, a solomongundy and almond cakes to finish; all was washed down with refreshing bottles of a very palatable local beer – English beer sadly no longer to be had – and followed by generous brandies accompanied by a large pot of strong coffee, Marisol remembering well their affinity for it.

Later in the afternoon the tiring effects of the food, the several beers and brandies, together with the deep heat of the Mediterranean sun combined to dictate a siesta, as was the local custom. The three friends slumbered comfortably in deep chairs within the draught and shade of the inside of the Royal. They were awakened as the afternoon began to cool by an excited babble from the kitchen, Marisol in voluble exchanges with undetermined female voices. Within minutes an excited Brodie burst through the drape separating the kitchen from the public room, running across to greet her father as he rose from his chair.

'Och, my wee bairn, 'tis so wonderful to see ye, indeed it is,' said a delighted Duncan as he seized her up from the floor and they hugged. He bestowed a gentler kiss on both cheeks for

Kathleen, as is the Mediterranean custom, husband and wife settling into animated conversation, the reunion so pleasurable.

Another old Tenedos, Patrick Coghlan, now the ladies' escort, stood mute but smiling behind them before replying to Pat's greeting of 'I see Mr Macleod has dragged you from the Boora bog, Coghlan!' with his gruff reply 'Aye sorr, thankee.'

Friday 27th June 1823   *Mahon, Balearics*

Surprise slipped out of Mahon harbour with the aid of a benevolent north-westerly, greatly aiding her passage along the several miles of channel from her mooring near the quay, past the Lazaretto and out into the open waters; her courses, topsails and topgallants together giving her a steady seven knots as she set up for Genoa.

The previous day had been spent in shifting the little baggage of Kathleen, Brodie and Coghlan aboard *Surprise,* followed by their long delayed visit to Jeraldo's. It had changed not one jot since their very first drink there together, of cocoa, more than twenty years previously, many pints of sherry having been shared there since. The day had ended with a celebratory farewell supper at the Royal, Marisol in tearful embrace with Pat at the end, a little to his embarrassment, Sinéad being present but not caring to ask about Pat's old times in that dimension, recollecting a suspected brief dalliance by Pat with a young lady in Halifax, Nova Scotia during the war.

Despite the emotive farewells of the previous evening the mood aboard *Surprise* was buoyant. It was sustained all day through to a voluble and amiable supper in the great cabin, Marston and all the officers being introduced to Mrs Macleod and Brodie, the crew welcoming back their old shipmate, Coghlan.

Accommodation aboard *Surprise* was now becoming full, and so the officers had kindly shifted around their tiny cabin berths off the gunroom so as to make space for all the guests; the twins and Brodie adopted the larboard berths, Duncan shifting temporarily to Pat's cabin; Pickering, Mower, Prosser and Marston took the starboard cubicle berths, Codrington and Reeve serving aboard *Eleanor*. A little more space was afforded to the ladies because the captain had not engaged a clerk, and neither were there any midshipmen.

As the days of the voyage passed, the quartet of Pat, Duncan, Simon and Marston, playing after supper time, had already become something of a routine and an event that all four greatly looked forward to. Sinéad, now joined by Kathleen, was nearly always in the great cabin during their playing, and the lieutenants too were usually in attendance. Marston, in contrast to his diffident playing during earlier voyages, was now almost approaching virtuoso. His playing had, over recent weeks, inspired both Pat and Simon to strive harder to follow him. At other times the playing was so relaxed that they ventured enthusiastically and unprompted into surprising variations. Even Murphy by now was lingering close outside the cabin door, always helping Freeman serve the toad in a hole and had ceased grumbling at the much increased cleaning afterwards – except when with his mate Old Jim Lamb, for even Murphy had his position and reputation to consider of.

Sunday 29th June 1823   *Western Mediterranean*

The evening being pleasantly warm and the four musicians having been playing with great exuberance, Pat had left the great cabin door open through to the gun deck so as to capture a draught of air to cool the cabin. Sinéad and Kathleen being with the twins and Brodie in the gunroom, the quartet had been playing with great enjoyment for more than an hour, uninterrupted only when Marston paused with a broken string. Whilst he changed it Pat and Simon decided upon a brief recuperation.

'Might I suggest we take a turn on deck to take a draught of the cooling evening air?' suggested Simon, Pat readily agreeable. They stood up, left the cabin and stepped up the companionway to the quarterdeck.

Surprise was heeled over slightly to starboard and making, Pat judged, a steady six knots or thereabouts. With no tacking having been required for some hours there had been a pleasing lack of interruption of noise and activity to disturb a certain engrossment in their playing. On deck there was only the noise of the bow wave slapping along the hull and the faintest sound of wind soughing through the creaking rigging. The sun having set just half an hour previously, the early evening being fine and there being no cloud at all, the navigator in Pat gazed up high over the starboard bulwark at the readily recognisable orange glow of the emerging two brightest of the stars, hundreds more twinkling about them.

'Look there over the starboard side – *the starboard side.* Ain't that a prime sight? Are we ever blessed with any finer? Have you ever beheld such wonders?'

Simon stared out, quite unable to fathom precisely what Pat referred to, nothing being visible in the darkness. 'Quite splendid,' he ventured cautiously.

'Look up - *there* - so much to see. Do we have any greater splendours? Look there, our friends *Arcturus* and *Vega,'* Pat pointed high into the southern sky.

'Yes, brother, so I had understood. And, one may say, so very significant for you mariners, I believe.'

As Pat's eyes, after the bright illumination in the great cabin, became further accustomed to the gloaming and shifted from the stars he turned and looked for'ard beyond the mainmast. He could now make out and was astonished that it seemed as if the entire crew – rough and ready jack tars for the most part that they were – were sitting silently along the waist gangways, backs against the bulwarks, all evidently having been listening to the music of the quartet and patiently awaiting more. As Pat paused to take this in, he turned as if to speak to Simon, when a ragged ripple of applause broke out, growing steadily until all on deck were clapping, stamping and whistling loudly.

Chapter Six

What, silent still? and silent all?
Ah! No; — the voices of the dead
Sound like a distant torrent's fall,
And answer, 'Let one living head,
But one arise, — we come, we come!'
'Tis but the living who are dumb.

Monday 30th June 1823   *Gulf of Genoa*

The westerly *Ponente* blew *Surprise* steadily across the remaining leagues from Mahon towards Genoa. In the gunroom and on the lower deck, as proximity to Greece increased, discussion became rife over the mission. The old hands were wholly unconcerned about the nature of the enemy and the odds against *Surprise*, knowing little of the military balance between the parties. The officers were a little more knowledgeable of the Turk naval resources and those of their Egyptian vassal, specifically the French training of that particular fleet, albeit they were less familiar with the politics of the Greek revolution. Despite the uncertainties, all on board remained confident in the judgement and capabilities of their captain. Murphy in particular found himself very much more in demand with the crew, most of whom were aware that he had his ear to the captain's door and might therefore have gleaned a good grasp of the mission and its objectives. Yet, for all his persistent efforts, Murphy had not been able to eavesdrop with any degree of success as Pat had been circumspect with his briefings.

Surprise was no longer officially a Royal Navy warship, albeit she was still, in secrecy, *His Majesty's Hired Vessel Surprise*. Nor was she yet actually engaged with the anticipated Greek letter of marque but floating on a sea of rather less certain arrangements, at least until she had arrived in Greek waters and was able to formally engage with the provisional government there. Because of this multiplicity of uncertainties, discussion of the mission within the great cabin was limited in the extreme, nothing of substance crossing the table in Murphy's presence; indeed, there was little that Pat knew himself pending further orders which he understood would be delivered by messenger at some later date.

Notwithstanding the unofficial or indeterminate status of the voyage from Falmouth to Greece, Pat was in high good spirits. It was more than simply a return to sea, more even than the satisfaction of being once again aboard a frigate and with his long cherished aspiration for a crack crew achieved – for assuredly that was what he now had, bar the absence of any marines. No, for the first time in his long and successful sea-going career he felt not the immediacy of seeking out an engagement with the enemy, had no longer to keep one eye ready for an approaching vessel bearing Admiralty instructions and so he had discovered a deeper inner satisfaction, a calming self confidence, almost a renewal of purpose. All of which made him feel quite at ease with himself and the world, to the extent that he even began to feel at ease with Michael Marston who was now an assured evening visitor to the great cabin, accompanying Pat, Duncan and Simon in their musical relaxations, an addition to the trio that Pat, to his own surprise and satisfaction, increasingly welcomed.

'What do you say to another pot of coffee, Simon?' Pat prompted as they finished eating breakfast.

'With great pleasure, my dear,' Simon replied, adding presciently 'I give you joy of your present contentment. Long may it endure.'

'Freeman! Another pot of coffee, if you will; light along and fetch a bottle of the best madeira and see if there is anything left of the Sunday cake.' Pat paused for a few moments and looked closely at his friend of many years before responding to Simon's comment. 'I cannot recollect in all our voyages this exceptional feeling of self-quietude.'

'I am entirely of your way of mind, brother,' murmured Simon.

The gentle sea state for most of the voyage, the clement weather and the contentment that this had brought about, growing with the increasing distance from Falmouth, had created an atmosphere almost of tranquillity for all aboard *Surprise*. No longer, as far as the crew were aware, was she a Royal Navy ship, and hence the customary Articles of War were no longer read on Sundays, plus there were the families of both Pat and Duncan present. All these changes from regular routine had, quite unexpectedly, brought about great efficiency and sharpness in the crew in a way that Pat had never previously experienced: an attention to every detail in the daily routine of *their* ship, for that is how *Surprise* was perceived. The officers never found occasion to pick up on any defects of the crew, for remarkably there were none. The regular evening playing of the string quartet had considerably enhanced this pleasant ambience, and the musicians had since several days shifted to playing on the gun deck on warm and dry evenings as appreciation of their music had become near universal amongst the crew. Morale was therefore exceptional and not a soul had reported sick since the start of the voyage.

'Freeman! Freeman! Break out a case of the Haut Brion, the one with the long cork, the 'eighty-nine, in readiness for dinner and see how it is coming along with my cook,' shouted Pat, sitting on the chest against the stern windows, finishing his coffee whilst discussing the powder and shot stores with Pickering and considering his position generally, noon fast approaching. 'Why, Simon, ain't you shifting your old clo's and shaving for dinner?'

'Must I? I shaved only yesterday... or perhaps the day before.'

'I could never introduce you in polite company in those slops. Murphy remarked this very morning that in Falmouth we have cast away old sails, veterans of the Horn and battle, in finer fettle.'

'I am aghast, brother. You oft say that it matters not one jot at sea, that we may wear anything at hand which serves our comfort, and neither is it necessary for our vestments to be pressed nor washed particularly often... more than once a month, will we say.'

'It is Sinéad's day. The ladies will be present and doubtless in all their splendid finery. You would not care to disappoint them, would you? Perhaps clean clothes might suit?'

'Why, there is only a trifle of fat lingering on the breeks from that memorable sauce with the crubeens and trubs of last week; I forget the day; with such excellent tatties too... the fat is scarcely bothersome. I will be there presently.'

'Not in them old rags you won't, sorr,' hissed Murphy, beside himself, seething, and who could not refrain from comment.

Pat blinked as he heard the uninvited, the unexpected interjection. He seized his moment to press his friend, 'Doubtless, Simon, you will wish to present yourself before the ladies in fresh garb... and you will favour me most deeply by changing your clothes. Your sleeves resemble those of our young *Tenedos* snotties. This is surely a day on which our every effort will be remarked upon, our vestments particularly, and you would not wish to be laughed at when we are at the table.'

'I am a modest sort, clothes do not greatly signify in my mind.'

'For the love of God, cast away those scabrous slops if you will! The ladies may believe that you have stepped out of your store without so much as a candle and fallen into the stove's coal.'

'I see you will not be swayed. Oh, very well.'

'Clothes cover a multitude of sins, Doctor; particularly so as we get older, as you of all will know, and naked we have but little influence,' volunteered Pickering, bringing a bemused stare from his captain and a scowl from Simon.

It was Sinéad's birthday and Pat had invited all his officers to a celebratory dinner, to join his and Duncan's family. Afterwards he intended to give them what small extent of briefing that he was able. It was therefore an expectant gathering that took its place at the table in the great cabin. All officers were in formal uniform, albeit without Royal Navy insignia, and there being no marines on board each was attended behind their chair by stewards in smart blue jackets with brightened brass buttons and white gloves, near all of the men with gold earrings; all as keen as the officers to glean what might fall from their captain's lips for eagerly receptive crewmates. Before that the meal was to be eaten, to be enjoyed, the birthday celebrated. The captain's cook had been tasked with the provision of something a little above the norm. Pat's private stocks had been severely diminished for the occasion, and his cook, Wilkins, had quite excelled himself. After the customary glass or two of madeira, very popular with the ladies, Freeman and Murphy, Old Jim Lamb helping, brought out the food on the captain's best silver plate. They began serving dishes of freshly caught tuna, prepared as floured thick steaks and served with pureed peas and white sauce. In that expectant instant before anyone began to eat and as all looked over towards Pat, he raised his glass, rapped the table with his knife and, turning slightly to take in his wife to his right, Simon at her other side, he announced, 'Ladies and Gentlemen, a toast, if you will. To my dear wife, to Sinéad: a most happy and joyous birthday!'

'To Sinéad!' shouted by all. 'Happy birthday!' echoed around the cabin.

To Pat's left sat Kathleen; to her left Duncan was flanked by his daughter, Brodie. Michael Marston was at Sinéad's other side beyond Simon. On the opposite side of the table the twins were seated amongst Pat's officers: Tom Pickering, James Mower, William Codrington and William Reeve. Only the master, Mr Prosser, was absent, in command of *Eleanor* sailing independently for the approach to Genoa. Barton alone remained on the quarterdeck with the helmsmen.

'Mr Reeve, the bottle stands by you,' cried Pat, perceiving his most junior officer to be a little daunted by the very full gathering. With the family members present and the occasion being one of celebration the customary formality of dinner at the captain's table, of speaking only in response to the captain was quickly abandoned and a vigorous hubbub, the most amicable of conversation, ebbed and flowed around the cabin. Freeman and the stewards replenished the plate with more tuna steaks, eagerly consumed by the officers. Then followed fresh roast pork - one of Jemmy Ducks' number having been killed that same morning - served with crisp crackling and sage and onion stuffing with a brown onion sauce, carrots, shallots and mushrooms, all taken up in Port Mahon. The shipboard millers had not yet got to the supplies, the myriad of cats at Plymouth Dock having decimated their numbers, and the solitary, retained ship's cat, a most amiable cream tabby, was successfully keeping their numbers in check since.

'Brodie, my dear, allow me to cut you a little more pork,' Pat smiled to her, perceiving that she remained nervous throughout the gathering. At least until her covertly consumed wine, from a glass frequently refreshed from the bottle standing in Duncan's place, brought about a relaxation, when she began to converse with a little more animation with William Reeve. The twins were delighted to be attended by Pat's lieutenants, to be regaled with tales of *Tenedos's* experiences in the deepest and farthest oceans, all events of severe personal setback and bloodthirsty battle being most diligently expunged.

Sinéad in particular passed a most enjoyable time and commented, her pleasure so very evident, on how much she had been enjoying the voyage, 'The crew seem to be in the finest of form, Pat, and such a pleasant band of men too.'

'To be sure,' said Murphy, letting slip a plate which crashed to the table to cover his comment, but raising smiles from the two nearby stewards who heard it and Codrington who pretended not to have.

'Mr Mower... *James*; would you care to read us a poem, your most recent perhaps?' asked Pat.

'Why yes, I have it here, sir. 'Tis written for my wife, but will serve for all our wives... and today, with your permission, most particularly for Mrs O'Connor.' Mower clutched a wafer of paper taken from his inside pocket. The table quieted as he began, his softly spoken voice bringing complete silence to the great cabin,

'Amidst the rolling waves of oceans comes the lovely thought of you,
Through the soughing of the breezes and the sparkle of the dew,
In the shining light of morning and the blackness of the night,
Come wondrous recollections and dreams of past delight,
In the horror of bitter struggle when my heart is gripped with fear,
When my soul seems lost in darkness, blind and frantic; you are near,
Giving faith and courage to carry me o'er the steepe roaring sea,
In the bleakest of moments you shine bright in my memory,
Bringing rays of sunshine, my tired hopes restored anew,
I cast aside the darkness and cherish the lovely thought of you.'

The contemplative silence around the table remained, all present looking to Sinéad, until she spoke, 'Why, Mr Mower, that is the most beautiful poem I think I have ever heard. I thank you kindly.'

Loud applause erupted from all. 'Thankee, James; a most prodigious talent, genius, nothing less. I congratulate you,' said Pat amiably as the applause ended.

'Artistic creativity prospers well in the nautical mind! Congratulations, Mr Mower. Capital wine, sir, if I may say,' said Tom Pickering.

'Thankee; 'tis a particular favourite of mine, a Romanée-Conti, a burgundy of the year 'seventeen. Another glass with you,' replied Pat, swiftly sweeping off the table a bargeman which had crawled out of a biscuit before Sinéad might see it, stamping it flat on the deck.

'If you insist, sir; nothing serves dinner like good wine,' Pickering replied, smiling broadly at his host.

With the ladies and girls being present, Wilkins had suggested and Pat had readily agreed to conclude the meal with a huge jam Roly-Poly, now brought out and presented to the table by Freeman, a generous portion of it having been put by in the galley for the later enjoyment of the stewards. This sweet pudding was immensely enjoyed by the two girls, in fact by all, and none escaped the plate's return to the galley. When the meal had concluded, with little marchpane cakes – Murphy having pressed the cook to make them, ostensibly at Pat's personal request but in reality the desire originating solely in himself, marchpane being his particular favourite – the ladies and youngsters retired from the great cabin so that Pat could present what scant briefing he felt able to provide to his officers.

'What are millers, Mr Murphy?' asked Pat's daughter in a whisper as they were escorted out.

'Well, they are the very smallest of the ship's complement, Miss Caitlin,' replied Murphy, stretching his tiny reserves of tact to the extreme.

'Gentlemen,' the families had departed and Pat commenced his briefing. 'It may be some small puzzle to you that we are sailing to Greece but will arrive in Genoa tomorrow. Many reports of the war have come back from the events in Greece to governments and unofficial bodies throughout Europe, from diplomatic missions and non-accredited persons. A Greek committee has been established in London - as in so many other capitals - and emissaries despatched to discover the true nature of the situation in Greece. One such emissary has but recently returned, we are reliably informed, to Genoa, and we are to consult with this individual so as to ascertain as much as possible afore we arrive in some weeks time in the Ionian Isles to commence our service for Greece.

Pat paused to refer to his notes. 'Freeman! Freeman!' he shouted. As the happy black visage of Freeman peered round the door near immediately, Pat declared, 'After such a fine dinner - my compliments to my cook - I find I am in need of a brandy; light along with the bottle... and bring coffee too, if you will.'

Pat returned to his briefing. 'Gentlemen, we are but one fifth rate to face the combined Turk and Egyptian fleets, of which there be several first rates which we cannot expect to profitably encounter. Yet for the most part their fleet will be split into smaller flotillas throughout the islands. These will be engaged upon transporting stores to their forces widely distributed in the Morea as well as in western Greece. Our mission is to disrupt their commerce, their resupply; to encourage the Greek fleet as much as we can, to discourage the Turk; to bring hope to the Greek peoples throughout the mainland and the islands whilst

146

better organisation and greater resources can be assembled... and a new and modern Greek fleet is raised and trained. There are plentiful stories in high places of loans to be raised for Greece, of new frigates and steamships to be built and purchased, but these will not be here this year... nor indeed *next* year. Yet the war must be sustained with but what little is available until they arrive. We have *Surprise*... and she has beaten many a Frenchman and others. We have a crack crew... and the Turks do not: they being served in large part by slaves, including Greeks. We can go where we please... and appear out of the night to strike hard and disappear, to re-appear where we will, to strike fear into the heart of the Turk. That is our mission, gentlemen. I will entertain your questions, if you will.'

At that timely moment, Freeman sidled in with the brandy and coffee, having dashed the ready boiling water on to the freshly ground beans the instant after Pat's request, 'Coffee here, massa.'

'Sir, may I ask whether we will be serving alongside the Greek admirals or sailing independently?' asked Tom Pickering.

'A very good point, Mr Pickering; I incline to the independent approach, not least as I expect *Surprise* will be considerably faster than the Greek ships, but perhaps on some occasions we will be acting in concert with them.'

'Where will *Surprise* be based, sir?' came from James Mower.

'Afore we begin our active service we will leave Sinéad, Kathleen and the children on Zante, it being a British Possession where they will be quite safe from the Turk. We will be guided by what we find when we arrive there.'

'Speaking without the least authority and with unsurpassed ignorance of all matters naval, may I enquire how long we anticipate voyaging against the Turk... and are we ourselves assured of resupply, Captain O'Connor?' piped up Michael Marston rather unexpectedly and with a deal more confidence than ever hitherto demonstrated in the captain's presence, perhaps since becoming a more frequent visitor to the great cabin.

'We will be roving far and wide throughout the Aegean, Mr Marston, and roundabout the Morea. Resupplying in part from our captures, at least in powder and shot, consuming our shipboard stores until such time as there arises the need for a more plentiful re-provisioning and perhaps a refitting, when we will return to England,' Pat explained, in truth with rather more thinking aloud than he cared to admit.

'Who will pay us for our prizes, sir?' came possibly the most prescient question of all from William Reeve.

'Well, Mr Reeve, I expect that they will be condemned by some Greek prize court and sold, the monies to be held for our account. The specific arrangements we will have to see when we arrive in Greece,' replied Pat with greater confidence than he felt. More questions of lesser significance were posed but as it became clear that he had no precise answers at this very preliminary stage in the venture it was with some relief to him that the questions did not persist much longer. Eventually, Pat brought his officers attention to his final point with a rap on the table. He raised his voice slightly, 'Gentlemen, there is one point of the utmost importance which I will explain. Sailing alone we are very likely to encounter more than one Turk vessel; in such circumstances we will be hard pressed to fight them all, and so flight may be our sensible course. However, it will be of the very first importance for our survival - and will serve us well - were we able to fight both sides of the ship at the same time, keeping our distance so that we cannot be boarded. By that I mean fighting with complete crews for both sides and none of the running to and fro of the men in the customary way. Fighting both sides of the ship and firing all guns, were we to find ourselves between two Turks, will give us the best prospect of surviving and of winning... by all accounts the Turk not being more than an averagely competent gunner. That objective, gentlemen, is where will direct our training. We will exercise the great guns each day as we approach Greek waters... and damn the cost of the powder. I have some concept of appropriate tactics to fight the Turk, as I will explain when we are ready to exercise our guns. One last thing, gentlemen; as we have no jollies aboard, and so no sharpshooters to send aloft in any engagement, we must find our best dozen marksmen from the crew. There will certainly be poachers and the like familiar with a musket. Mr Mower, you are to talk with the older hands and see whom you may find.' The conclusion came with a degree of relief, and Pat held up his hand to stay any questions on his gunnery strategy before adding by way of confirmation of the end of the meeting, 'That will be all; thank you, gentlemen.'

After the officers and Marston had left, the families being still on deck, only Simon remained as Pat asked, 'What do you say to a glass of Sillery?'

'Well, if you insist. I do not like to sound inquisitive... you seem a whit uncertain... if I might venture a trifling observation.'

Pat thought for a moment before he answered. 'I suppose it is no use asking your opinion about the standing of the Greek government and any Admiralty Court that they may possess, and the likelihood of an equitable distribution from any prizes we may take? Young Reeve was, as all saw, quick off the mark there on this prime question; he hit the hammer square on the head... doubtless by now it will be a talking point all about the ship.'

'None whatsoever, my dear. I am no friend of speculation, and my opinion of that would be as valuable as yours on the prospects for a cure for the yellow jack.' Simon had replied to his friend's pessimistic question, rhetorically asked in absence of expectation of any helpful answer, as helpfully as he could. Perceiving a worry on Pat's brow, he continued, 'In so far as the officers and crew will be wondering about the prospects for prizes, for that is sure to be the case... as sure as Hestia's oath, you may care to collect that they consider Captain O'Connor exhibits the wisdom of Solomon in all matters nautical, and any indication from yourself on this matter or any other will surely remain unchallenged on this vessel; there is no doubt of that.'

Pat seemed to find this helpful, 'Well, there is something in what you say, and Solomon was - by all accounts - a sensible cove. Thank you. I believe I will take a turn on deck.' Deep in thought he left the cabin and had stepped only a few paces along the gun deck when an indistinct noise caught his attention. From for'ard, from beyond the scores of Monday's shirts hung to dry on lines strung across the deck came the sound of singing. He slowly paced down the deck to hear more, his ear and curiosity intrigued. Beyond the foremast the singing became quite clear, the sound coming from an unfamiliar form of stringed instrument,

'So fare ye well, sweet Donegal, our lasses and families all
I'm leaving that fair land, for the great oceans us do call,
It breaks my heart for us to part, where I spent many happy days.
Far away from friends and relations dear I'm bound for Amerikay.

And above all the skies of the port was the blue sky,
and I heard the birds singing for the dawning of the day
but there was no work from this town forthcoming,
just sympathy numbing the going away.'

Pat espied his Third, Mower, sitting for'ard near the galley with three of the crew: Beer, Knightley and Maclean. Their singing ceased as he approached. He wondered briefly whether there was any convention which might permit or preclude an officer playing accompanied by his crew, but dismissed the thought as he reached the quartet. 'A most pleasing song, Mr Mower, but pray tell me: what is that curious instrument? Is that six strings I see? Is that not a trifle ambitious? 'Pon my word we mere mortals struggle to scrape with but four strings.'

'There is no bow, sir; 'tis customary to pick at the strings with fingers.'

'Well, I never; a rum device it is, though it is certainly melodic, for sure.'

'It is Spanish in origin, sir. I took it up to set my poems to music, growing tired of the plain words. I bought it in London a few years ago after listening to a Catalan player, Fernando Sor.'

'A Catalan, you say? Our players will be keen to hear the story, no doubt.'

'Near my last half-pay guinea it cost, but when I heard its tone, so warm, I was lost.'

'Mellow it is, indeed. Your guinea was well spent, there is no doubt. We will look forward to hearing your fine playing and your singing in the cabin, Mr Mower. Beer, Knightley, Maclean... good night to you all.'

'Good night, sir,' echoed the reply. As Pat strode away, the singing resuming to the gentle sound of the Spanish strings.

'And I wish I was in Falmouth town and seated on the grass,
And by my side a bottle of wine, and on my knee a lass,
I'd call for liquor of the best, and I'd pay afore I go,
And I'd hold my Sally in my arms, with a lingering kiss so slow.'

Pat's evening was spent very pleasantly with Sinéad who joined him on the quarterdeck until the evening air cooled when they removed to the great cabin, sitting near the stern windows and enjoying private reminiscences of their years together. Duncan and Simon had considerately shifted to their berths in the gunroom. The twins, with Brodie, were being entertained by Kathleen, though they had last been seen pursuing Pat's cook for more marchpane and roly-poly; fruitlessly, Murphy long having removed the first, and his mates having consumed the second.

'You lead a very happy crew, husband; that is sure, even to my inexpert eye in these matters. And, if I am not wide of the mark, you are yourself most splendidly pleased to be here, to return again to voyaging in *Surprise* now, and in Doctor Ferguson's and Duncan's company too. Will *we* be happy again upon our return to Claddaghduff would you think?' asked Sinéad, her voice wavering.

Pat gazed into his wife's moistening eyes with deep benevolence. 'Be not concerned for that in the slightest, Sinéad my love. I have been at sea since I was much younger even than the twins; I have lived my life always in the company of sailors, fortunately with the very best of companions in Duncan and Simon. Indeed, Simon has saved my life you know, when I was shot in a cutting out party – did I never mention that to you... *perhaps not*. We have seen many a successful cruise in the dear *Tenedos*, success that has been the founding of our home and farm, a place which I very much look forward to coming home to, to be with you there... and I dare say I will not be at sea for many more years, my love, afore I am laid up... *in ordinary,* as we sailors say. Until then, in the few more years I have at sea, it is my dearest wish to see them out in command of a proper fighting ship such as *Surprise,* and since we have long since seen off Boney then there will be but few ventures in which we can profitably engage. All of us aboard do hope that this is one such venture. Nor do I say *profitably* wholly in the mercenary sense, far from it; there are few men in this crew who *need* to serve again at sea, many of them having taken very substantial prize monies to their homes in Falmouth in the years of the French wars. No, I find a sense of contentment in this crew, a satisfaction founded on returning to our home at sea, for that is how we all feel about *Surprise.* Though usually we have no wives here nor any of our children, we share the companionship of those that have served with us for many years; we are together, officers and men. All are here not for the prizes... though none would ever admit that; no, we are here because this is where we have all spent the greater part of our lives, and we are comfortable in the traditions of the ship and the service, each man secure in the steady routines of the day – unchanging routines – as sure as the sun will rise in the morning, and that is pleasing to us all. So you see, my love, we are fortunate, all of us, we have two homes, but we all begin to see that we will serve in our shipboard home only for a very few more years... and that is really why we are here, all of us to a man enjoying the time we have left aboard, in our *dear Surprise.* We are content also in that we know – *we know* – that we will be coming to our other home, our home ashore, to our beloved wives, to our children... and in a near time which will be with us almost afore we know it. Is that a satisfactory answer to your question, my love?' Pat concluded, observing Sinéad's tear-filled eyes with great concern and seizing his wife, now overcome, into his arms in a crushing embrace.

'Oh my darling, I love you so much,' was all that Sinéad could whisper in reply, blinking rapidly as the tears now flowed in great streams down her cheeks.

During the next day, the final day of *Surprise's* voyage to Genoa, the weather and sea state remained as tranquil as all those that had preceded it. As the warmth of the day faded with the sun sinking into the horizon of the western sky, leaving behind a splendid residual sunset, *Surprise* passed the western mole and La Lanterna to larboard and entered the harbour of Genoa under topsails alone, slowing as they were backed and coming gently to a stop, letting slip her anchor three cables off the quay.

Wednesday 2nd July 1823   *Port of Genoa*

After breakfast, the crew lowered all *Surprise's* boats, her proximity to the Old Pier greatly facilitating the taking on board of water and other provisions. With an unknown departure date, Lord Byron's specific plans not being known to either Pat or Duncan, the near quayside anchorage was considerably more convenient for going ashore, Pat anticipating much use of his barge.

'Duncan, pray tell, what news of our task to escort Lord Byron?' Pat asked after *Surprise* had been tied up and they, with Simon, were enjoying tea and second breakfast in the great cabin. 'We will need to acquaint ourselves with his Lordship's intentions. Do you know anything of his plans, his travel plans particularly?'

Duncan looked up from his bacon and eggs, 'Lord Byron travelled previously in the eastern Mediterranean in the company of his longstanding friend, Hobhouse, now a luminary of the Greek Committee. I have a letter of introduction from Hobhouse, given to me by Lowrey afore we left London, and I will send this to Byron's residence today. In a day or twae I imagine we will call upon his Lordship.'

'Until then, might I suggest that we take a day to see this magnificent city?' Simon interjected, sensing a rare moment of leisure at hand, wiping the grease from his chin onto his sleeve. 'It is a tolerably significant city for you mariners. By all reports one Christopher Columbus originated here, a mariner you may be familiar with. Those of us of the faith, of a more devout persuasion, will I say, are visiting the basilica of San Lorenzo - Saint Lawrence in the English parlance. Duncan, Brodie and Kathleen are with me, Sinéad and the twins too.'

'Murphy! Pass the word for Barton!' Pat shouted. 'Why, perhaps I will join you. I would not wish to appear singular.' He smiled, bowing to his friend's arrangements in pleasant accord.

Pat's cox'n entered within moments and touched his forehead. 'Barton, be so good as to deliver a letter ashore for Mr Macleod. He will give you the letter directly. You may require a local guide.' Pat had by now established that Barton was of a similar, reliable ilk to his much lamented, deceased brother and had begun to pass small tasks of some significance to him. At that moment Sinéad and Kathleen entered the great cabin in some small state of excitement with the prospect of going ashore and the appeal of an escape from the close accommodation of *Surprise*. The near total absence of personal privacy was beginning to grate after the month's voyage. The youngsters too, the novelty of shipboard life fading, were beginning to evidence some youthful truculence and impatience with the shipboard routine.

'Will you be long, Duncan?' asked Kathleen.

'Not at all, my dear, just a wee few minutes and I will be with ye. We will all be with ye. Pat is minded to accompany us, with Simon.'

'We will await you all on deck,' shouted Sinéad in high good spirits as the ladies left the great cabin.

'I will find the introductory letter for Barton, it is in my sea-chest, and briefly scribe an accompanying note; I will be with ye directly,' said Duncan.

'I will also be ready presently,' declared Simon.

'I suppose you could shave and change later,' Pat volunteered, a comment wholly disregarded by his friend.

The visit to the cathedral was a resounding success, the ladies and the youngsters being overwhelmed by the grandeur and scale of the edifice and its environs. Never before had they seen a city of such historic substance. Their walking tour continued for some hours, taking in the splendour of the palaces of the Strada Nuova before the long walk the length of the harbour to visit La Lanterna, the ancient lighthouse. In the late afternoon the long day of walking had quite tired them out, and so the youngsters were considerably more subdued walking back to *Surprise*, which was a relief to Pat.

After supper Murphy entered the cabin clutching a letter which he presented to Duncan. 'Pat, 'tis a reply from Lord Byron. His Lordship has invited us to attend him on Friday.'

Friday 4ᵗʰ July 1823   *Albaro, Genoa*

After dinner, Pat, Duncan, Simon, Sinéad and Kathleen set off to stroll the near three miles to Byron's home, guided by Barton, walking up, down and through narrow streets that only gradually widened as they walked further from the port and higher up the hill of Albaro until, pausing for a brief measure of relief from their exertions, they enjoyed a commanding view over the harbour and the city. They gazed at the splendid panorama of the bay before resuming their climb, eventually coming with some relief to the Villa Saluzzo as they began to tire in the enduring heat of the late afternoon, all perspiring freely.

The maid ushered them in and served welcome jugs of punch. After a few minutes, which were most gratefully appreciated for recovery from their exertions, Lord Byron entered the drawing room and nodded towards his visitors. He walked with a limp on account of his club foot. He was a tall man in his mid thirties but looked older, youth having faded from his face, some spark having been lost; his curly auburn hair was now streaked with grey, his thin moustache near white. Yet he nevertheless retained an impression of energy, of quick interest; his large, luminous blue eyes exuded a sense of restlessness. Byron was accompanied by a man with long black hair, bushy sideboards and an aquiline nose; dressed in, or so the ladies thought, rather untidy clothing that seemed to have seen better days – an observation which never occurred to Simon.

Pat made the introductions. 'I am Captain Patrick O'Connor. Thank you for your invitation, my Lord. May I present my wife Sinéad; my first lieutenant, Duncan Macleod and his wife Kathleen; and my surgeon, Dr Simon Ferguson.'

Lord Byron appeared to be in fine good humour and seemed genuinely pleased to receive his visitors. 'Your servant, sirs, ladies. We are favoured today and it pleasures me exceedingly to present my visitor, Signor Niccolò Paganini, the celebrated Italian composer and violinist, a son of Genoa. He is residing here at his mother's home to recuperate from recent illness. He has called upon me to discuss my poem, *Childe Harold's Pilgrimage*. He has but a token grasp of English and converses only in Italian and French.'

Paganini bowed to the ladies and shook hands with the gentlemen. Simon scrutinised him professionally: he did not look well, an undefined air of malaise about him, but then again he had treated sailors that looked far, far worse. 'Un grand plaisir, monsieur, enchanté,' said Simon with some passion and a reverential nod of his head, being acquainted with Paganini's music, if not his playing.

Lord Byron continued, 'Before Signor Paganini leaves very shortly we are to enjoy the playing of his most recent solo piece. Please to follow me if you will.' Byron led the party to the music room where Paganini took up his violin and, without any preamble at all, began to play. In the five minutes that followed, the most animated playing by a standing Paganini, with unsurpassed and wonderfully dextrous fingering and bowing, his violin seemingly coming to life in his hands, was utterly, blissfully exceptional to the ears of Pat - a greatly talented cellist - and Simon, a considerably accomplished musician with the viola. The flowing skill of Paganini was of an overwhelming virtuosity, unparalleled in anything that any of them had ever heard before, the most vibrant long notes held in the air for an age, others intensely resonating beyond that which Pat and Simon thought possible. The flowing continuity of the bow, his wrists flexing and shifting at astonishing speed, was simply beyond belief, the sublime music and his playing of it infinitely gratifying in its utter perfection. At the end they were in a state almost of shock at what they had heard before clapping from Sinéad and Kathleen jolted them from stunned silence to vigorous applause.

'Caprice vingt-quatre,' Paganini said simply before bowing to his tiny audience.

'My dear sir,' said Simon (in French), 'that was uncommon magnificent. We have never heard the like. We are both of us keen scrapers, indeed we are, yet we could never aspire to such wonders, never in life. Overwhelmed... we thank you most kindly, sir.'

'Merci, merci,' was all that a stunned Pat could utter before turning to Simon to suggest that, 'he should invite Signor Paganini to dine aboard *Surprise,* and perhaps he could bring his violin,' adding as an afterthought, 'Signor Paganini's schedule in Genoa permitting.' To Pat's deep satisfaction Simon's reiteration of his invitation was accepted with evident pleasure, Paganini adding something along the lines of "seeking Doctor Ferguson's opinion", but it was beyond Pat's pidgin French to follow.

After Paganini's departure the ladies remained in the music room, enjoying punch whilst the gentlemen shifted to the drawing room. 'My Lord,' Pat began, 'I have but recently become acquainted with the nascent developments in the Ottoman Greek provinces, coincident with my resignation from His Majesty's service. Lieutenant Macleod and I attended the London Greek Committee some few weeks ago, and having heard of your intended participation as an emissary of the Committee perhaps we may be of some small service?' Pat ended his rather brief and vague explanation, not wishing to dwell on the background to his particular circumstances, and he awaited Byron's response.

'My dear O'Connor... that is most kind,' Byron smiled. 'However, my banker has located and I have already engaged a ship, *Hercules*, Captain Scott, to convey my party from Genoa to Zante, perhaps in some few days time. It is generally held that the Turks are preparing a large expedition for the suppression of the rising. I am fully disposed to assist the Greek cause and with every means at my disposal, hence my departure to offer my personal assistance. I now await only correspondence from Blaquiere, an emissary of the Committee who is already in the Morea, before we depart.'

Pat hesitated in thought very briefly before concluding the meeting, 'Well, sir, I am delighted that our aspirations are therefore similar... we are sailing to seek the Turk fleet, which doubtless is a constituent of the expedition you refer to. Allow me to congratulate you on your admirable intentions, and we wish you success in your noble endeavours.' With that they took their leave.

The next few days were passed in taking onboard those few stores which had been omitted in the hectic provisioning of *Surprise* in Plymouth and Falmouth, the crew shifting everything about to the satisfaction of Simon's assistant, Michael Marston, he being of an exceedingly tidy disposition. In respect of the sick bay he was striving with an evident desire to please his master, to ensure every medication was readily at hand. The atmosphere onboard *Surprise* generally was relaxed, the crew having cleaned every conceivable part of the ship, all revelling still in their homecoming as they saw it, even to the extent that they had stripped the aged and peeling black paint from all the cannon during the voyage and then rubbed them down to the iron before repainting layer upon layer afresh until the guns looked as if they had left the manufactory that day, their new black paint gleaming pristine in the bright sun. They had also repainted the chequerboard sides of the ship with a precision that impressed every inspection, Pat insisting on the crew painting the Nelson yellow bands along the hull. All aboard concurred that it was a magnificent idea, the few Trafalgar veterans in particular being highly gratified. The officers had barely any need to direct the ship's activities, the crew being volunteers to a man, confident in their assured prospects under Pat's command for substantial prizes.

The ladies, Brodie and the twins were for the most part ashore in Genoa each day and even most evenings, enjoying the temperate early summer of the northern Mediterranean latitude, there being little for them to do aboard. They had hardly any domestic duties, Murphy being very jealous of and robustly resisting any attempted incursion into his personal province of care for Pat and Simon's accommodation and laundry – albeit it could have been argued that a little further help might have been justifiable in Simon's case.

During the morning that Pat was to dine in the gunroom with his officers, word was received that Paganini was to come aboard to join them. To the astonishment and pleasure of the hands, the man delivering the message was a familiar face, a former comrade who had served with many of them long years ago in the Mediterranean. Giobatta Repetto was a native of Genoa, retired from sea service and now - still active in his late sixties - he delivered letters around the town for important personages including Byron and Paganini.

Pat was sure he had met the man and invited him into the cabin. 'We have met before, I collect; yet I cannot fathom your name.'

'Repetto sir, if you please,' the greying, old man touched his forehead.

'Ah... Repetto, yes, it comes back to me... it must be seven years or more since we were shipmates. I collect you was with us when we sank *Iskander* and captured *Half Moon*... larboard watch, *Hurricane* gunner - am I right? It was back in the year 'sixteen... so it was. It is pleasing to see you again. You look in fine fettle, if I may say so,' said Pat, smiling, 'Are you keeping well?'

'Splendidamente, Comandante,' Repetto bowed, smiling broadly and deeply pleased that he had been remembered. He stood in silence, in awe and with transparent delight, being once again in his esteemed former captain's presence. He was pressed by Pat, with whom he soon commenced bantering about past voyages, to enjoy a glass or two in the cabin whilst Simon read the letter he brought in case of any reply being necessary. The subject of the letter revealed, Repetto declared that he was also a keen and proficient chef, and willing to help in the preparation of local Ligurian and Genoese specialities. Without further ado he was speedily introduced to Pat's cook.

Later Paganini was welcomed aboard with the utmost cordiality, and the much awaited dinner meandered through Repetto's simply stunning three courses; he had served them well: *zemin de ceci,* a chick-pea soup; followed by *pansoti* pasta with spinach and walnut sauce; finally cod stockfish cooked with potatoes, raisins and pine nuts in a tomato sauce. The food was a great success; the Genoese cuisine, unfamiliar as it was to the Surprises and the ladies - who marvelled at it - was relished by all in the most convivial of ambience. Several hours passed by in the most cordial of dialogue and banter, Simon translating from Paganini's French to English for Pat's officers who were being very welcoming to their most distinguished visitor ever. Paganini ate sparingly and seemingly with a little difficulty, but he complimented effusively the food and the wine, though drinking little. Late afternoon slipped pleasantly into early evening with a graceful acceptance by Paganini of Pat's invitation 'to play for a short while, perhaps his *Caprice vingt-quatre*?' adding 'on deck to the assembled crew.'

With surprising alacrity, some considerable bottles having been consumed during the feast, Mower and Codrington fetched the chairs from Pat's cabin out on to the gun deck, the stewards bringing more from the gunroom. The officers and the ladies settled to listen to the maestro; the crew too were gathered about the gun deck in anticipation, alerted by the stewards, quite a press of them attending, an ambience of joviality abounding. The men had already enjoyed their supper and grog, and with little to do as the day slipped away the impromptu prospect of music was very welcome to them indeed. They settled, sitting about the fore part of the deck, the hubbub of conversation dying in anticipation. Paganini did not disappoint, launching into Pat's particular request and playing with consummate passion and skill, his bow flowing with an elasticity which Pat, Simon and Marston could only marvel at, his fingers shifting to positions that they simply could not comprehend how he attained them. His music consumed all those listening to it, touching hearts and minds, its unrivalled and exquisite excellence registering even with the least musically inclined old tars, the sounds reaching deep beyond their ears and striking chords within their souls such that all other thoughts were wholly eclipsed, and they gazed in wonder and utter silence as Paganini played the piece until, with a final flourish of his bow, it reached its unwanted end. The conclusion of this, the most magical playing that all had ever heard in their lives, was followed by raucous, uninhibited appreciation from all the ship's company.

'That,' said Paganini - radiating with satisfaction - to his hosts after a bow to his audience, 'is how it plays in paradise.'

Pat, recovering from his absolute concentration in the music, complimented Paganini profusely, 'Very finely played, sir; the beauty of the world, so it was.' The sun was beginning to sink towards the horizon but the evening remained comfortably warm. Pat inclined towards and whispered to Simon, 'Will I ask him? That is to say, would you think he might play with us? We will never have the chance again.'

Simon simply smiled, his lingering contentment clutched firm as if to ensure its memory and precluding any contemplation of Pat's question. A deeply pleased and now somewhat emboldened Pat ventured to ask Paganini, 'Perhaps Signor Paganini would consent to playing just a very little more... and accompanied by the ship's musicians?' He was delighted when his request was accepted. 'Murphy! Barton! Rouse out our instruments from the great cabin, quickly now, there is no time to be lost.'

'Well, they be here already a'waitin' your say so, sorr,' Murphy pronounced with a smile of self-satisfaction, Pat's 'cello under his arm and carrying the violin; Old Jim Lamb held the viola and bows. With their instruments, the trio of Pat, Simon and Marston took their places alongside Paganini. They began, slowly at first as all adapted to their fellows, with Corelli's *Christmas Concerto*, followed by a magnificent rendition of one of Pat's particular favourites, Boccherini's cheerful *La Musica Notturna Delle Strade Di Madrid* - to Pat's mind a piece ideally suited to the collective shipboard temperament. It was a near twenty minutes of the most sublime playing by Paganini on first violin and sheer bliss for the accompanying trio. It was with the utmost satisfaction and shared congratulations that the piece came to its end. Vigorous applause followed from all the enrapt crew, young and old, *Surprise's* grizzled veterans realising that they were in the presence of genius. Simon and Marston rose as one, embraced, slapping their mutual backs while the ladies smiled and clapped until their hands were sore.

'Och, that was the most glorious piece of the world,' said Duncan.

As the applause died down and the quartet took their bow, Barton and Evans - a popular Welshman living in Falmouth and a tolerably fine tenor - quickly stepped up in front of the players and turned to the crew. Barton furiously waved the applause and chatter to silence.

'What's afoot?' a puzzled Pat muttered.

From Evan's deep booming voice came the stirring first verse of *Heart of Oak*,

> *'Come, cheer up, my lads, 'tis to glory we steer,*
> *To add something more to this wonderful year;*
> *To honour we call you, as freemen not slaves,*
> *For who are so free as the sons of the waves?'*

With only the slightest of pause the happy and delighted crew, more than two hundred of them now on deck, by way of their own thanks and appreciation scrambled swiftly to their feet and without hesitation joined the chorus of the song, the Royal Navy's traditional anthem, singing with great gusto and enthusiasm.

> *'Heart of oak are our ships, jolly tars are our men*
> *We always are ready; steady, boys, steady!*
> *We'll fight and we'll conquer again and again.'*

At the end of the song an animated and impressed Paganini clapped his hands and turned to Simon. 'Bravo! Bravo! Nous avons trouvé un petit coin de paradis ce soir.'

Pat, who had expected nothing like this, such a deeply pleasing and spontaneous gesture from the crew, beamed with evident delight, speechless. The crew continued to cheer Paganini with great shouts of 'Hurrah! Hurrah!' At the conclusion of this revelry, Paganini and Simon with Marston retired to the great cabin in close discussion. Pat thanked the

crew profusely for their impromptu singing, 'Barton, Evans...
thank you kindly; well done, well done indeed. Barton, please
thank the lads for a most generous gesture, most kind indeed,
thankee. Mr Mower, an extra issue of grog to the crew, if you
will.' He returned in high good humour to the gunroom with his
officers, the ladies retiring to settle the girls and Fergal in their
cots below.

In the cabin, Simon and Marston conversed with Paganini.
He had sought a consultation with Simon when they had met at
Byron's house. They conversed in French which fortunately
neither Freeman nor Murphy, both listening behind the cabin
door, were able to understand. To put Paganini more at his ease
Marston assured him that Simon had an Edinburgh medical
degree, had studied Paré and had been consulted by no less a
dignitary than the First Lord, Melville; and it was widely
understood that he had also been considered as a candidate for
Physician of the Fleet, though Simon had discretely demurred. A
clearly less anxious Paganini described his symptoms and
treatment, 'I have been ill since January. I consulted Dr Borda of
Pavia during June following weight loss and severe coughing up
of sputum. Dr Borda has prescribed opium for my severe
laryngeal cough and mercury for hidden syphilitic infection. I
take the blue pill.'

Simon responded cautiously, 'Sir, your account does not
suggest any fatal issue, and we are unable to differ with your
own physician and his diagnosis, he being presumably more
acquainted with your medical history than we. Yet, in candour, I
must caution you against excessive and prolonged treatment with
mercury, for such will most surely lead to undoubted
deterioration of the physical state of the larynx and the gums, and
to loss of teeth and general ill health; the consequences of the
mercury will be far, far worse than the mere possibility of the
emergence of hidden syphilitic infection. Mercury is generally
recognised as effective principally in the early, *the very early*
stage of syphilitic infection... as we see so often aboard ship. As
the finest musician it has ever been my pleasure and great good
fortune to hear, I must also caution you that the accumulation of

mercury over some considerable time will lead to tremors in the hands. Surely you, the master of the most exquisite violin I have ever heard, would wish at all costs to avoid that?' Simon's voice and mind filled with infinite sadness, regretting bitterly that he could offer no more optimistic a prognosis to this unequalled musical genius.

Paganini sighed, his disappointment was so evident in his face. 'Dr Ferguson, Mr Marston, I am obliged to you both for your ministrations and professional advice, for which I thank you most sincerely.'

All shook hands, the two surgeons lingering in the last moments with their visitor, as if to save the moment, to preserve the memory of their encounter. Shortly afterwards Paganini departed, leaving behind an exquisite musical memory to be treasured by scores of men for the rest of their days.

'Was your consultation of any service to our guest, Simon?' asked Pat.

'Oh, I could not possibly say. Certainly, Marston and I passed some time contemplating on the efficacies of familiar processes.' Simon paused, unwilling to add anything of a confidence. Seeing Pat's frown, a self-evident concern for the esteemed patient, he continued after a moment, 'We may consider further of our interest in mercury, which in some instances will prove disappointing.'

'Yes, he is of little use for navigation, though assuredly of astronomical interest.'

'So I have always understood, but what I meant was the metallic element of mercury, brother. It is used in the blue pill.'

'Oh, I beg pardon. As to our guest's playing, we will never hear finer, never in life; of that I am sure.'

Chapter Seven

In vain — in vain: strike other chords;
Fill high the cup with Samian wine!
Leave battles to the Turkish hordes,
And shed the blood of Scio's vine!
Hark! rising to the ignoble call —
How answers each bold Bacchanal

Tuesday 15th July 1823   Thyrrhenian Sea, bound for Leghorn

Becalmed in Genoa for several days and no contact having been established with the anticipated emissary from the Ionians or the Morea, nor having received any further instructions from Lowrey or Melville, Pat was anxious not to lose more time idling in port. Such inactivity was wont to lead the crew into predictably regrettable diversions. *Surprise* and *Eleanor* therefore now left harbour, preceding *Hercules*. The wind, having risen little above a breeze since dawn, had further dropped to a near calm as two bells were rung. Pat had not left his quarterdeck since rising, the south-westerly *Libeccio* making for a very slow departure from the harbour and something of a laborious task, frequent tacking a necessity to make any progress at all until they were well past the entrance and La Lanterna left far astern.

'Precious little wind, sir,' said Pickering.

'Indeed; though look to those high clouds, shifting along sprightly. I think we may see a blow tonight; 'til then let us put the fire hoses on the sails and we may see another half knot.'

'Aye aye, sir; engines to wet the sails. Mr Prosser, if you please.'

By mid-morning the frigate hardly raised a wake with every stitch of canvas set - including royals - and her studdingsails boomed out. Pat retired to the cabin for a late breakfast. 'Freeman! Look alive there! Rouse out my cook and see what can be found in the line of bacon, eggs and plenty of soft tack.'

This came as no surprise to Murphy, waiting alongside Freeman and accustomed as he was to his captain's preferences after so many years. 'Well, 'tis all been a'waitin' these two hours past, to be sure. 'Tis all ruined,' he muttered as Freeman scuttled away to the galley.

By the time Pat had eaten his solitary breakfast, the ruination of which he had scarcely noticed, and returned to his quarterdeck the wind had freshened considerably. *Surprise* was now making respectable progress on a broad reach, well heeled to larboard, the necessity for tacking now long gone; huge showers of spray were flying and the wind beginning to whistle loudly in the rigging, the stuns'ls and royals long since taken off her, the royal and topgallant yards struck down and the topgallant masts housed on deck. Duncan Macleod, Tom Pickering and James Mower all stood by on the quarterdeck. 'What a change. I think you are proven right, sir. Not long afore we see the storm,' said Pickering.

Pat gazed about him, assessing the weather and contemplating the sails, 'Mr Pickering, signal *Eleanor* to proceed independently to Leghorn. I smell very bad weather coming... and she may not keep station with us. Mr Mower, heave the line.'

The line indicated a not unexpected acceleration to a swift nine knots, according with Pat's growing uneasiness as he surveyed the sky to the west, voluminous dark grey clouds having now near blotted out the sun. The temperature had also fallen noticeably and the storm winds were upon them. The ladies had long since retired from deck to the gunroom. 'Mr Macleod, we will double-reef her courses. We will brace in the upper yards just a very little and we will have the fore-staysail set with double sheets.'

'Aye aye, sir,' Duncan reiterated the orders to the men.

Another hour passed and the storm winds strengthened further. 'Mr Macleod, we will take down the jib and flying jib.'

'A considerable change since this morning, for sure,' said Simon, who had joined the officers on the quarterdeck.

'I do so love a blow, but with the ladies and children aboard we will treat her tenderly,' shouted Pat.

Pat's appreciation of a blow was not something with which Simon personally accorded, despite his now long years as his seafaring companion. The rising violence of the waves had for the past hour sent spray flying across the waist of the ship, and the few crew of the duty watch that still remained on deck had donned oilskins and awaited the next order to further reduce sail. Pat was now certain of his suspicions and turned to Simon, 'It is coming on to blow very hard indeed. If the wind much strengthens and if it becomes uncomfortable we may have to lay to.'

'What? What did you say - *if* it becomes uncomfortable?' Simon shouted into the wind, clutching his still unbuttoned coat, heavy rain soaking him and the deck rearing up beneath him before sinking as fast into the trough of the steep swell, the rapid and contrary motions most unsettling. 'Just how uncomfortable would we have to be? It is very disagreeable up here! 'Tis a dreich day! I am fair drookit. I do not wish to sound discontented, but will this infernal tempest last long, would you think?'

'Why, of that there is no telling. One day, perhaps two or three if we are unlucky.' At that moment, as *Surprise* rose from the trough, she was struck full by the wind and rolled violently until her lee gunwhale was near subsumed within the furious wake streaming along her side, the unexpected ferocity of the lurch throwing Simon to the deck.

'You had best go below,' said Pat, hauling him to his feet. 'Look to the ladies. Ask cook for a hot meal without delay, we may extinguish the galley presently. Mind now, clap on, one hand for yourself and one for the ship,' Pat shouted, his words near drowned out by the wind, wild and constantly shrieking through the rigging. Tons of cold, grey water in vast torrents of spray traversed the quarterdeck and the gun deck was awash more often than not, clearing only as the bow reared up before crashing down into the next trough, the cycle repeating itself interminably, hour after exhausting hour. The sky had darkened considerably and the light was more akin to an evening dusk than late afternoon.

'An uncomfortable night ahead, sir,' said Pickering.

At six bells of the afternoon watch Pat made his next declaration. 'Mr Macleod, this sea will have our hide if we keep our sails. 'Tis time to take them in. I think we will pipe all hands on deck.'

'Aye aye, sir,' Duncan nodded. Prosser, listening in, seemed very relieved to hear the order and bustled away to rouse his men, almost all of whom had been below for some hours, few remaining on the exposed deck as the sea flooded it frequently as *Surprise* rolled and pitched violently. The order passed along, the men came tumbling up from below in great haste, assembling on the foc'sle and on the quarterdeck aft the waist, all staring about them, assessing the sea state and the commensurate sails, looking back to the quarterdeck for instruction.

'Mr Macleod, send the men aloft; double-reef all tops'ls and take in her courses,' ordered Pat, Duncan standing alongside him. The crew hastily scrambled to do so as the first lieutenant bellowed out the order. 'Mr Prosser, luff up!' shouted Pat. 'Bring her to the wind, let her lie, nothing off, handsomely now.'

'Aye aye, sir, luff and lie, nothing to leeward; Barton, steady so.'

The rain, heavy for several hours, became heavier, fiercer and so thick that for all on the quarterdeck it seemed to merge with the fury of the sea. Huge black rollers swept all about them as far as the eye could see and the most violent of wave tops were perpetually breaking all over the deck, the water never clearing from the lee scuppers before the next wave crashed over them. The fury of the wind about them and the crashing all around of the tremendous seas made hearing difficult and orders near impossible to communicate, yet the wind was noticeably still increasing, as was the height of the rollers, white water breaking off their crests, torrents of spray whipping away within the wind's wild fury. *Surprise* was both pitching and rolling, lateral stability now solely afforded by her double-reefed tops'ls and fore-staysail. The afternoon had slipped away into an uncomfortable evening and the light was nearly gone under the press of black cloud and sheeting heavy rain, the wind screaming aloft in the halyards; *Surprise* could do no more than lie-to. Yet for all this press of extreme seas and weather, four men now being necessary to hold the wheel, Pat remained unperturbed; indeed, his officers still alongside of him on the quarterdeck believed that he was actually enjoying himself, for he was too. Precious few others shared the feeling; all on deck were soaked to the skin, all below thoroughly uncomfortable. No hot food had been served since the crew ate dinner at midday and no hot drinks were available, the galley fire having been extinguished as a safety measure. Little light now permeated the gloom below deck and the severe rolling and pitching made even those with the strongest of stomachs nauseous. The ladies and children were badly sick, retching so violently that Simon was called to attend, and he administered a particularly strong dose of laudanum. Marston too had succumbed to sea sickness and was of no use. At four bells the first dog watchmen disappeared gratefully below for respite and to eat hard tack with grog.

'The carpenter reports several seams working, sir. Eighteen inches in the well,' reported Mower, Pat receiving the report with unconcern.

'Chain pumps, Mr Mower, if you please.' By five bells of the first watch and the sky being inky black, Pat retired below to check on the ladies, leaving Mower in command on deck. Duncan had already retired to rest, the sea state and wind having been slowly diminishing for some hours: the reefed tops'ls and fore-staysail had sustained her throughout the violence. The severe rolling of earlier hours had subsumed to something less uncomfortable and the ladies and twins were all lying in their gunroom cots in a semi-sleeping state, their discomfort having been eased by Simon's laudanum. Brodie alone was sitting up, quite unconcerned, talking in Gaelic to a somewhat discomfited Patrick Coghlan. 'How are you, little one?' asked Pat, smiling encouragingly.

'Quite well, sir; thank you kindly,' said Brodie in obvious good cheer, most pleased to be able to assist Simon tending the sick and distressed.

'The worst is past, my dear,' soothed Pat.

All through the long night the wind continued to decline and at six bells of the middle watch the men were able to take the reefs out of her tops'ls, which greatly further aided her stability and progress. It was close on dawn before the storm finally blew itself out, the sea state declined and the gale dropped to a tolerable blow when the hatches' battened tarpaulins were removed. The galley fire was relit, to the deep satisfaction of the crew, and hot food and drink was once again served. *Surprise* shook out her courses to give a respectable spread of canvas once more and she resumed her voyage.

To Pat's great satisfaction Freeman appeared in the cabin with tea and a hot breakfast, and with too the welcome news, 'Ladies feelin' very better, takin' tea, massa.'

A very tired Pat, for he had not retired all night, was much relieved to hear it, 'Pass the word for Mr Pickering.'

As Pickering entered the cabin, Pat asked, 'Tom, is there any sight of *Eleanor* or *Hercules*?'

'None, sir.'

'Well, keep us set firmly for Leghorn, we will doubtless meet them there. Mr Macleod is resting and I will sleep now for a few hours. You have command.'

Eleanor, a most weatherly sailor, had preceded their arrival at Leghorn, but of *Hercules* there was no sign. It was a full three days before she arrived. Captain Scott had returned in the storm to Genoa, the horses having become unsettled, kicking out their stalls in the hold.

Tuesday 22nd July 1823   *Leghorn*

Little time was needed by *Surprise* in Leghorn other than that necessary to take on water, to revictual the supply of a few fresh comestibles and to repair the slight storm damage. *Eleanor* had suffered no discernible damage at all and *Surprise* required only the most minor attention. Captain Scott, having rectified in Genoa the damage wrought by the panicked horses, had no need to dwell in Leghorn at all. Nevertheless it was Lord Byron's intention that *Hercules* would stay for a likely two more days before departing, during which he would seek news from the Morea and Greece generally. Hence *Surprise* and *Eleanor* left without *Hercules*, Pat mindful of Melville's urgent reconnaissance task. Whilst in Leghorn, Byron had kindly communicated to Pat that it was now his intention to land in Cephalonia rather than in Zante, upon the advice of his passenger, Hamilton-Browne, a knowledgeable Hellenic sympathiser and a friend of the Zante governor.

'Cephalonia, Zante... 'tis all one for us, Duncan,' Pat remarked with some acerbity whilst playing chess with his First after supper.

'Whining will serve no purpose,' muttered Simon, his head not shifting from his book.

Duncan did not look up from contemplation of his long planned knight's move, merely riposting, 'I think ye are in a wee difficulty. Does the game begin to tire ye, at all? There, my friend - checkmate!'

As greater southing was gained Simon and Marston were keenly anticipating passing by Etna and more particularly Stromboli, both men in great hopes of witnessing a spectacular eruption. 'With the blessing, it is to be hoped that we will witness fire atop one or the other of them,' said Simon in the dispensary one morning after breakfast.

'Has Captain O'Connor some worry with which he is pre-occupied, colleague? I have received no invitation to the cabin these past two days. Am I in his disfavour, in breach of some nautical protocol or convention of which I know not?' ventured Marston a little anxiously when they had finished up the dressings.

'Not at all, dear colleague; be not concerned, the captain's mind is a military one. Such souls have a predisposition towards order, regularity and convention in all affairs. I fear he finds this venture a trifle unorthodox, and with no channel of communication being apparent to him - an expected envoy never appearing in Genoa - the further distance we are from home the greater his discomfort. Doubtless matters will take their course.'

Pat had completed his breakfast in Sinéad's company, and after she had left to join Kathleen, Brodie and the twins he hailed his servant. 'Murphy! Pass the word for my officers.'

His lieutenants, Simon and Marston accompanying, appeared and they all sat at Pat's table. 'Gentlemen, we are but one small frigate... and expected to engage the Turk whenever we can. Most likely we may encounter more than one of their warships. They have several seventy-fours - *which I certainly do not intend to engage* - and many frigates, a deal of them more modern than our *Surprise*. I have been considering of this and my plan to fight with best prospects for success... for flight too. Indeed, as my plan assumes that we will likely be outnumbered, it will be necessary to maintain all possible speed at all times... and such will best be preserved by strictly avoiding course changes and any manoeuvring... which would usually reduce our speed.' Pat paused to assess the attentiveness of his officers, all of whom were wholly fascinated. 'In action we will fire the foc's'le long nines...'

'The long nines... sir?' whispered Marston.

Pat turned towards his surgeons in explanation, 'That is our *bow chasers*... during our approach from astern of our enemy... in the hope of damaging masts or rigging so as to degrade their speed and steering. As we close, the carronades will open with shot only, no grape or canister. For three rounds their fire will be directed low, near the waterline of our enemy. Even at the range I intend *Surprise* to open her fire from, no closer than four hundred yards, the smashers will assuredly penetrate the enemy hull and may - with the blessing -start their sinking. After three rounds - as we get closer - the carronades will switch to shot with grape too, the better to cut their rigging. The long guns will open double-loaded with shot and with grape, seeking to tear their rigging. For their second round they will switch to canister replacing grape so as to smash their guns and kill their men. I have no intentions of slugging it out... and so if it don't look like they will strike their colours then we will be away at all possible speed.' Pat observed the affirmatory nods from his officers. 'To repeat myself for clarity, gentlemen... depending on our enemy -

brig or frigate - we will make a direct approach to close to two cables; we will *ne'er mind manoeuvres and go straight at 'em*... as Nelson advocated.'

The lieutenants all looked doubtful, Pat could plainly see their glum faces. It may have been advocated by Nelson in the great heyday of fleet battles but it was a high risk tactic that could be very costly: the approaching attacker could be battered by its prey, possibly even raked, bow to stern, particularly in the final one thousand yards of closing which was the maximum effective range of ship's guns. The attacker could not reply except with bow chasers, and so the tactic had been abandoned long before the end of the French war.

It was Marston that interrupted again, 'I am no sailor, sir, but what will your enemy do with his great guns while *Surprise* strives so to reach him? I beg your pardon, sir, doubtless you have considered of this.'

Pat looked about the cabin before he continued, 'Yes, gentlemen, I see your concern, but we may expect that the Turk is not yet as expert as the French and the Americans became. Thus it will be necessary to retain the weather gauge throughout our approach, to preserve all possible speed... and to swiftly change our own course if the Turk comes round. One final point, gentlemen; we will not extinguish the galley fire in action.'

This comment drew sharp intakes of breath from the lieutenants but Pat pressed on, 'I intend to fire red hot shot... and with reduced charges so that the ball will lodge within the target and will not penetrate through both sides of her hull. The consequent fire will give the Turk something more to struggle with. Of course, we may only be able to heat a very few shots in our galley. Mr Mower, you will discuss this with cook and the gunner. We shall practice heating and firing red hot shot in our great guns.' With this Pat concluded his briefing, his lieutenants' initial doubts being only partially dispelled, but to some extent replaced with a keen interest to find out if the aggressive, innovative tactics and the increased gun crew capabilities afforded by hot shot could be developed successfully.

After divisions Pat announced an exercise would be carried out, explaining to his experienced gun captains his intentions of fighting the ship from both sides, all the crew listening with manifest interest. '...fighting that is with gun crews serving the great guns on both sides concurrently – *at the same time, Dalby!*' He glared at Clumsy Dalby, who plainly was seeking some clarity as to his role and muttering to his gun captain, Old Pennington. 'Mr Pickering will command the larboard battery and Mr Mower the starboard. Mr Boswell... Master Gunner... you will favour me by commanding the carronades on the quarterdeck.'

'Yes, your honour, sir,' grinned Boswell, delighted by his captain's instruction.

'Lads, we may find ourselves in situations where the odds are very much against us. We are but one small frigate... though all of us would vouch the very best of frigates, WOULD YE SAY?'

There was a barrage of affirmation from all present, as if anyone could doubt it, before Pat resumed, 'We must fight fast... and fire from both sides. Fast! That is three broadsides within five minutes. If we can do that there is not a frigate that can stand against us. CAN YE DO IT?'

Huge roars of confirmation erupted, subsiding as Pat raised his hat. 'Lads, we have not been at sea aboard the like of our dear *Surprise* for four years or more. Doubtless 'twill take time to recover our past form. We start today. Look lively lads... and God speed!'

The crew became instantly alert; the spectacle and occasion of firing the guns was always exhilarating, but firing both sides together was a rarely experienced tactic, the crews by convention and training switching from one side to the other. As their larboard gun was reloaded they trained and fired their starboard one and vice versa. Would there be enough men to fire both sides together and still achieve three broadsides per side, all within five minutes, Pat's minimum competency standard, as they all knew well? Would depleting the sailing crew to furnish more gunners diminish the ship's speed of manoeuvrability, a critical function in battle, as they all fully understood? The loss of such manoeuvrability could well bring the potential for catastrophe, which some, including Pat, had experienced personally when *Java*, critically unable to steer, had struck to *Constitution* in the year 'twelve. For this first exercise, no shot would be loaded and wasted, no targets set afloat; it would be simply running out the guns and firing the powder, with extra wads rammed as shot. They would see what timing could be achieved firing three rounds. Pat had no intention of keeping the new and old gunners wholly separate, a division which would slow the firing rate from many of the guns, and so every experienced crew had been diluted with new men, most with at least some experience of firing the guns. Most men in a man-of-war had had occasion to do so at some time in their career; even the cooks were retired gunners in many cases, but the new men had been drafted from their customary stations, standing by to make sail and course changes as required, to bring the frigate closer to its enemy or away as the battle dictated, thus the experienced crews all found themselves with a new crew member or two whom the captains invariably instructed to 'Keep out of the way! Jump when I says so! And be ready to heave that gun in and out as fast as fast can be! As if your very life depended on it – as it surely will! D'ye hear me?'

'We will ripple the firing, bow to stern, to spare her timbers,' declared Pat to his lieutenants. 'Stand by on my command.'

There was not a living soul below decks as the exercise was prepared, save for the powder crews in the fore and aft magazines. The ladies and girls – although it had been firmly suggested by both Pat and Duncan that they retire below to the gunroom – could not hold their curiosity in check and they stood on the quarterdeck in keen anticipation, never having seen the guns firing. The bulwarks forward of the great cabin were also taken down. Pat gazed down from his quarterdeck, reflecting that it had been over five years since *Tenedos* had fired her great guns in anger, even longer for *Surprise*. Five years of near total inactivity and four or even more years in many cases since any of the crew had even run out a gun, let alone fired one. What would happen? The gun captains - every one of them as keen as mustard to actually open fire - shouted encouragement to their men 'Attend! Look alive! Stand ready!'

The carronade captains and crews were less happy. It was only with severe cajoling that the lieutenants had switched gun captains and experienced gunners from long guns. Not one had volunteered for the short carronades, considered ugly by most gunners. And who would expect them to transfer willingly, for they were attached to their own guns, all of which were fondly named – aptly as far as their crews were concerned – with such striking names as *The Nailer, Axeman, Dutch Sam, Hell's Mouth* and *Hurricane*. Long years before, Pat had found the nearest thing to a mutiny aboard *Tenedos* when some gunners had been switched to the carronades, and only personal intervention alongside his lieutenants had smoothed things over. He reflected that it was no longer like the Royal Navy of Old Jarvie's day, but perhaps that was for the best; the morale on board *Surprise* was better than ever he had remarked before in all the ships he had previously served on. Perhaps it was just a reflection of the fact that every gun crew dearly wanted to show their best and they doubted that they could do so if relegated to a carronade, for that is how they saw things and who was to say that they were wrong. The carronades were close in smashers, short of range but absolutely deadly when they were close enough to be fired, firing a ball near twice as heavy as the guns. They could also fire canister, two hundred and fifty balls each of two ounces which could sweep an enemy deck clean if used at the opportune moment; they could fire grape, nine balls each of near four pounds which would tear sheets and rip away rigging and thence substantially degrade the enemy's speed and manoeuvrability with a single broadside. They were usually fought by a crew of four, now reduced to two so that Pat could implement his plan, spreading his experienced gun crews a little more thinly and fighting both sides of his ship concurrently.

If *Surprise* encountered two ships and found herself between them, and if both sides could be fought and deliver three broadsides in five minutes then *Surprise* would be the most deadly of adversaries. Of course there was *Surprise's* transitioning to the firing position to be carefully managed. A slow approach could expose her to repeated broadsides from two enemy ships, and depending on her relative speed she could be under sustained fire for up to fifteen or so very unpleasant minutes. Pat had considered this before deciding on his tactics, for they gave *Surprise* – if she did find herself in a position to fire her broadside from close in – a potentially decisive advantage: the near certainty of holing the enemy hull. Were they to clear the enemy decks with canister and grape then it would be so much the better to deter enemy boarding parties, very important with *Surprise* no longer carrying any marines.

Before commencing firing the decks had been wetted and sanded and the magazines protected with thick 'fearnought' screens over the hatches to prevent any danger from sparks. The more experienced crew had stripped to bare chests, had stuffed cotton waste in their ears and wound scarves about their heads to afford a little protection from the anticipated thunder. All stood by their guns clutching rammer, sponge and powder horn; the slow-matches having been replaced some years before in favour of the modern flintlocks. Pat had adopted this change with reluctance and still kept slow-matches lit alongside the guns by way of precaution against the flintlocks misfiring.

The great guns had all been aligned with one of several marks Pat had ordered to be painted on the deck whilst in Plymouth so that every gun's fire would converge on the target at differing ranges. It was an aid devised by Captain Broke of *Shannon* where Pat had first noted it. His tactical preparations for their mission lacked not the slightest detail: the magazine had been filled with best red, large grain powder, all guns had been fitted with spare breeching ropes in case of damage to the tackles – a gun recoiling with cut breeching rope or damaged tackles represented a substantial danger, the deck had been wetted and sanded to prevent slipping of barefooted men - straining with every sinew to haul the heavyweight guns through their ports, near each port stood a water bucket for the sponge - wetted each time before it was run into the barrel prior to loading the charge, aside the gun another bucket was filled with water for the crew to quench their thirst and slake the bitter taste of smoke, and gun captains all retained the lit slow-match within a third barrel to keep it dry in case of spray. Behind the gun captains stood the second and third lieutenants, pacing the deck; each overseeing one side, no midshipmen being aboard to share the task.

Pat and Duncan looked down from the quarterdeck. 'Mr Prosser, you will oblige me by hauling our wind three points... and keep her steady at six knots, no more,' declared Pat.

At last, after a final survey of his deck, he spoke to Simon, 'Be so good as to mark the time on your fine repeater, Doctor.' He turned to his wife, 'Sinéad, Kathleen, girls; be ready! We are about to commence firing.' He turned forward and shouted to his men, 'Cast loose your guns! Out tompions! Run out your guns!' Within moments there came a drumming, roaring noise as twenty-eight guns were pushed forward over the deck, the six quarterdeck carronades shifting more easily on their wheels within their constraining slides. 'Prime your guns!' Pat bellowed, and finally, 'From forward, a rolling fire ... FIRE!'

To the passengers on the quarterdeck the loud great crack of the guns – for they had never heard it before – and the spectacular jets of shooting red-orange flame were simply beyond anything they had ever experienced, and they shrank away in awe. The effect of the rippling barrage progressing down both sides of the ship and the firing coming closer overpowered them as they looked down from the quarterdeck. The noise was louder than the loudest thunderclap they had ever heard. The girls shrieked in excitement but the ladies cowered. After a few moments the carronades fired from behind them, a higher cracking sound in comparison with the deep boom of the long guns. Noxious black smoke enveloped all on the quarterdeck and Simon shouted to the ladies through the din, 'Come! Come below! Swiftly now! There is nothing here for you, as you can plainly see.' He shepherded them down to the gun deck and on down to the gunroom, the rolling thunder of the continuing barrage following them.

On the gun deck the forward crews, now glistening with sweat, were worming and sponging their guns, ramming in fresh cartridges and wads - though no shot - and re-priming the flashpans as fast as they could go. Newcomers were being cursed by their captains, communicating with gestures, nods and a rare shout. Two had fallen on the deck, squealing like stuck pigs, not shifting quickly enough as their guns had recoiled - leaping from the deck before crashing down on their wheels. The unfortunates had forgotten their captain's instructions to stand clear, and their legs had been struck by the gun trucks. Another new gunner was being berated for dropping the wormer as he leapt back in panic. Two captains were screaming at their powder monkeys for the cartridge. None of this escaped the immediate attention of the lieutenants. As the aftmost guns fired, the lieutenants waved their hats, ordering the forward ones to fire again. The noise was deafening, even below in the gunroom where the passengers trembled as the second broadside rippled aft, the shaking of the deck being only very slightly less violent than it had been on the quarterdeck. Smoke drifted down the companionway, and they coughed in the noxious air.

Amidst the frenetic activity, the thunderclaps and the bilious smoke from the guns firing, two men could be seen coming from the galley stove attired in heavy gloves and carrying a glowing red hot shot between them in steel pincers, moving towards larboard number seven gun, *Hurricane*, the nearest gun to the galley. *Hurricane* had already fired its first shot and was back inboard from its recoil, the barrel being swabbed before a fresh powder charge was loaded. The gun captain, Old Pennington, was coaxing his crew 'Faster, faster, you whoreson buggers. D'ye think the Turks will wait whilst you fumble about at the breech.' Their evident reluctance to load the red hot shot and their severe grumbling was only overcome by the confidence they had long placed in him; the marked reduced-charge bag was rammed down, followed by the wad, and then the ball was gingerly introduced by a nervous crew, a crew in great trepidation and plainly aghast. Loading red hot shot with just a wad separating it from its powder was surely asking for disaster; another wad followed and all was rammed tight, the man with the rammer fearing for his hands. The gun crew edged away from their captain, away from their gun, surreptitiously, a pace or two back from their customary stations, as far as they could decently shift. To their astonishment and very great relief no spontaneous detonation occurred. Old Pennington shouted to them, the gun was hauled forward by the crew, the lanyard pulled and the flintlock pan powder flashed through the vent to fire the charge and send the glowing ball out across the waves. No gun crew ever felt more relieved.

Some little time later, as the aftmost gun fired its third shot, Pat shouted, 'Avast firing!' and the guns fell silent. Simon had long since returned to the quarterdeck; he peered at his Breguet repeater in anticipation of Pat's only question, 'How long?'

Simon replied with an answer that he knew would dissatisfy Pat, 'Seven minutes forty seconds. Would that do tolerably well for our first time after all these years?' One glance at Pat's glum face confirmed his expectation that it would not, not by a long chalk.

'Draw and house the guns, if you please,' Pat, standing above the waist, shouted the command, which was echoed all down the gun deck by his lieutenants.

In the evening a glum Pat settled to his supper of toad in a hole with Duncan and Simon. The dish appeared to Simon to be more blackened than the norm, though Pat seemed not to notice. 'Pray tell, brother, what ails thee?' prompted Simon.

'Eh?' Pat looked up, frowning. 'We must fire faster. We will likely be outnumbered... and only the very fastest of firing will preserve us; 'tis clear that the crews are rusty, like a half-baked old hinge.' His dissatisfaction was pronounced in a very strident, gloomy voice.

To Pat's muddled metaphor Simon could only offer a sympathetic, 'Surely, dear, there is time enough to improve on today's tolerably promising start?'

'Sweat, Simon, saves blood. Very poor, it was. We will be sunk afore we fire our second at that rate.'

'I am concerned to hear it. But would you expect the finest horse, though in want of training, to win the King's Plate at the Curragh? Not even Patrick O'Connor... the optimist of all the world... could hold such a glorious hope, and 'tis little different.' Simon laughed.

'Optimist of all the world? That is coming it a trifle high.' The timbre of irritation was now plain in Pat's voice.

'Doubtless you have not forgotten your considerable expenditure in canal stock, in bank stock and latterly in South American bonds? Indeed, I collect there was even mention of gold mining. You are assuredly not frittering your capital away in such a venture, eh?'

'Gold, I assure you, was found in Wicklow in the year ninety-five... or was it ninety-six? The promoters, Mrs Webster, Mr Mills and Mr King, were introduced to me; they explained that the gold was in the granite, in the bedrock through which flowed the Ballinvalley River, and from which it was a mere simple task to pan for it in the water... where bountiful quantities awaited simple harvesting. Their colleague, Mr Sharp, showed me the nuggets found there... '

'And *sharp* would be right,' murmured Simon, Pat not listening, not detecting the *double-entendre*.

'... said that some early prospectors had cleared thousands, declared that my farm sat on the very same granite... and doubtless it was only the want of financing of explorations that had precluded the discovery of gold in Claddaghduff itself. Sure, I have a little capital now in the Gannoughs, in the very smallest of mine on the hill there. Investments... *investments* they are, and 'tis a bull market at present, though there is never a certainty in them. There is no sure investment, as all men of commerce will know. There is but little return in leaving precious funds in Consols and Navy five per cents when prices are rising again.'

'I dare say there is not. I do not set myself up as an authority on investments... I rub along,' declared Simon, 'My father's bequest was so very small, and hence my penurious nature would never permit of such follies. Nor could I tell a bull from a bear, save they were standing alongside of me.' Simon laughed loud. 'Doubtless I have been too long immersed in the medical world and that of the naturalist!' Simon laughed again.

'You would surely never say I was rich? I have but scarcely a dozen acres; three quarters are bog and the remainder provide but the smallest of potato crop, and that only in a good year – it has failed these past two years – and 'tis only the accumulation of prize monies that has kept us from the workhouse; my half-pay could never feed even the wife and wains.'

'For God's love, it seems to me that if the boggies will believe our beloved Jesus did raise Lazarus from the dead then 'tis not remarkable that unscrupulous sharps will always find plenty of blunties to gull. Gold, Pat? Gold? In Ireland? I am amazed! Do you leave your precious sense in the cabin when you step ashore?'

'John Darcy did assure me there is gold in Galway, in Mayo too, on Inishturk island it has been found. Many a day have I fished near that place... and the prospects for this promising enterprise have been scrutinised by the most sagacious of advisers.'

'I fancy salacious might answer better than sagacious.'

'Salacious, of course. I knew there was something not quite Bristol-fashion there. Salacious, a prime word; I dare say that is with an L?'

'An impecunious man should never indulge in speculation, brother, nor a wise one, even when he can afford it.'

'''Tis investment, not speculation. Can ye not see that?' Pat spoke now in a raised voice.

'Far be it for me to affirm anything about investment. Folk have the strangest notions of what is sound and what is more akin to the throw of the dice.'

'I merely seek a sound home for my precious small capital, as you know well,' Pat replied, his tone growing more irritable.

'There is no call to grow chuff, ' Simon retorted.

'You would have me laid by the lee again,' Pat's vexation and voice deflated; he knew he could not best Simon - save in matters nautical, where his friend had scarcely the sense of the greenest midshipman.

Simon heard the resignation and amiably proposed, 'What do you say to us scraping a little? A cheering ceilidh tune or two... and perhaps a bottle of your admirable port? Is that trifle of toad in a hole in the dish spare perhaps?'

A suggestion of a little playing customarily brought Pat round to his sociable side. He passed the little silver dish. 'Yes, yes, of course we will; 'tis just that my mind had shifted from the pleasure of being back on board after these past four years to thinking how best we would be fighting the ship once more. Murphy! Murphy! A bottle of my best port, if you will... the seventy-five... and no breakages, d'ye hear me?' Pat sighed, 'Of course we have time to improve, and so we will, without sparing the powder. Yes, here you are, I have quite lost my appetite.'

Friday 25th July 1823   *off Sicily*

Stromboli to starboard as *Surprise* approached the Messina Strait at the top of the day presented none of the keenly hoped for signs of eruption and Etna, once through the Strait, displayed only a very little smoke, the somnolence of both being a great disappointment to all on board. Simon customarily passed much time every day on the quarterdeck with Marston, the two of them watching keenly for birdlife. He sometimes also tried his hand at painting watercolours in Duncan's expert company, accomplished artist that his friend was. Despite spring being a far more favourable time to see large scale northbound migration, late July still presented opportunities to see some birds returning early to their African wintering grounds.

'Look there, quickly! Over there! Surely that is a Montague harrier, *Circus pygargus*?' shouted Marston, waving his arm.

'No, colleague, I believe it is a fine example of Eleonora's falcon, the bearded vulture, *Falco eleonorae*,' Simon replied, peering intently through Pat's best Dollond five-lens achromatic telescope. It had been loaned solely to Marston with the strictest of instructions as to its care, Pat not wishing to see it in Simon's hands where it had been near lost on several occasions.

The birdwatching was necessarily abandoned after dinner as the great guns exercise was resumed every day as *Surprise* sailed east, holding her course for the Ionians, the times for firing three shots from both sides steadily reducing until Pat pronounced himself satisfied only when this was achieved once again in his self-imposed maximum five minutes. By then, they anticipated arriving in Ionian waters the next day.

In the evening a great concern came upon all aboard as Duncan's wife, Kathleen, became unwell. For several days and nights she had suffered a return of the mild symptoms of her former illness, suffering night sweats and struggling to cough up a glutinous white phlegm. It was exceedingly painful for Simon to see, even more so to diagnose it as likely to be consumption; and it brought back the most heartbreaking memories of his deceased wife who had long been afflicted by it before she died. A believer in the recuperative qualities of fresh air, he ordered a cot made up for her on the quarterdeck, and he sat with her all night to the exclusion of all other activities, Sinéad attending, whilst Duncan was relieved of all duties by Pat and sat with them, both men striving to maintain a cheerful, encouraging demeanour in front of the ladies whilst privately harbouring the most desperate of fears and anxieties.

Saturday 26th July 1823   *Ionian Sea*

The first faint glow of morning twilight, and Pat called Simon and Duncan across to the stern rail. 'How is she?' he asked with a feeling of immense trepidation. Duncan, in his distress could find no words; he merely nodded.

Simon spoke up, 'She has not been best served in her accommodations. The small cabins are incommodious even for those of us who are well... *and a trifle short*... but the dear soul has been suffering for some days, and she has feigned that all was well when asked. I regret to say it is not.' Grave anxiety visible on the faces of both his close friends, Simon resumed, 'However, I am minded that given blessed recuperation from the tiring motions of this vessel... and a lengthy spell of taking the airs... with the most benevolent of diets...' He paused as if to check himself before making his pledge, '... then she will make a recovery. I am minded the dis... *her illness* is not advanced; she exhibits the mildest of symptoms, and we may - with the blessing - *confidently* anticipate a goodly degree of recovery. Of course I cannot vouch that it will be a complete one, for such knowledge as we physicians have of this drea... *this matter* is far from complete.' He stared closely at fearful faces. 'Duncan... my dear friend... I will attend her until she recovers.'

Duncan, gratitude mixing with fear, still could not speak; his breathing was coming fast and unconcealed tears were constantly wiped away on his sleeve as he strived for an equilibrium.

Pat, his arm upon Duncan's shoulder, reached his decision, 'Gentlemen, we will touch at Cephalonia this day to put Kathleen ashore... with Sinéad and the children... before we go on to our mission.'

Shortly after dawn the heights of Cephalonia came into view from the tops. *Surprise* continued her steady, easterly course all morning until she eventually turned north to enter the great bay of Argostoli in the early afternoon, making frequent short boards against an adverse but weak summer north-easterly *Gregale* before heaving to and letting go her anchor in seventy-five feet of water in the Roads, a little outside the harbour proper; Pat had not the slightest wish to encounter officialdom in the short spell of *Surprise's* visit, possessing no official papers.

'Simon, you will stay with Kathleen... that is my order,' declared Pat emphatically. 'I have no intentions of any engagement; it is a reconnaisance only that we are engaged upon. I anticipate no action.' Simon simply nodded, preoccupied with his patient.

Without the slightest delay, a breathless Kathleen was lowered with the utmost care into the barge, Simon and Duncan accompanying her for the short pull to the quay, Duncan fretting, Pat's bargemen taking no more than ten minutes, whence Kathleen was carried gently up the steps, Sinéad and the youngsters following.

It was after dinner, in the late afternoon when *Eleanor* appeared, anchoring a cable away from *Surprise*. Codrington crossed to *Surprise* by barge on Pat's signal.

In the great cabin, as the hot and breezy day shifted to the relative stillness of early evening, warmth still plentiful, the gun port lids being hauled up to capture what cooling breeze might still be had, Pat briefed his officers; an anxious and plainly fretting Duncan had returned. 'Gentlemen, we are arrived in Greek waters. Politically however, we are in Ionian waters. That is to say the United Islands of... principally Corfu, Cephalonia and Zante... with four lesser ones: Lefkas, Kythira, Ithaka and Paxos. Together they are a British protectorate, quite independent of Greece and free of any Turk suzerainty. No Turk ship will venture here. The Governor, Maitland, has placed the islands in a state of quarantine from mainland Greece. No one can cross to them without incarceration on account of the plague so prevalent on the mainland. At present we are flying English colours and perfectly welcome. When *Surprise* hoists Greek colours we may expect that to change. For that reason we shall take every possible sounding afore we change our flag. Mr Codrington, *Eleanor* will at all times maintain her English status, and so may come and go as she pleases save for any contact with mainland Greece. I anticipate that we will be formally in Greek service afore many more days have passed. Make your personal preparations, such that they may be. We are departing without the slightest delay for Candia, to find the Turk fleet.' With no more than another half-hour elapsing as her anchors were hauled up, catted and fished, *Surprise* departed the anchorage to disappear into the gloaming.

Chapter Eight

Trust not for freedom to the Franks —
They have a king who buys and sells;
In native swords, and native ranks,
The only hope of courage dwells;
But Turkish force, and Latin fraud,
Would break your shield, however broad

Monday 28th July 1823   *aboard Surprise, off Candia*

The dawn had been quite exceptional, spectacular even, a glowing red orb rising above the haze and throwing a pink blanket over a sea quite devoid of any ripple, slowly turning orange and finally yellow whilst burning through the few wispy cloud remnants lingering over the clearing mountain extremities of Candia off the larboard bow, the summit of Mount Ida prominent. With barely the slightest zephyr of wind to disturb the flaccid sails, the temperature being already hot and the deep blue sky promising much greater warmth to come later, and with no respite of a cooling breeze in prospect all aboard anticipated another smouldering day. *Surprise* had sailed southbound at all speed, pushed for thirty-six hours by a benevolent north-westerly *Maestro* since leaving Argostoli, but since then the ship had been fighting to make only the slowest of progress, tacking frequently to make headway against a strong summer southerly coming from the far North African shore, and she barely moved. The sound of creaking rigging was the solitary noise breaking the rare silence, with only the exception of an occasional bird call. Even so early in the day the windsails, rigged to provide a little relief to those below, could do nothing against the heat. Overnight, *Surprise* had glided with infinite slowness and across the calmest of flat seas towards Candia, royals hoisted up and stuns'ls all boomed out, but these made no difference, the frigate arriving within distant sight of the island's peaks shortly after the dawn and scarcely closing since then.

The ship's bell, rung by Clumsy Dalby – who had seized the role with alacrity and who struck the bell with unequalled vigour – tolled eight bells. *Surprise's* officers stood on the quarterdeck, Duncan bravely standing his duties with them, all anxiously sweeping the horizon in every direction with their glasses, the crew on watch washing the decks: wholly unnecessarily they thought, having done it every day for as long as anyone could remember, and scarcely a speck of anything necessitating cleaning could be found on them. The crew laboured with a sense of expectancy, an awareness of events about to happen, felt an omnipresent foreboding, a keenly felt anticipation. Of what they knew not, but every one of them had picked up the discreet signals, the frequent conferences of Pat's officers, their alertness with their glasses and their urgings to the topmen to stay vigilant.

'How far off Candia are we would you think, Mr Prosser?' asked Pat.

'To pass Cape Vouxa, perhaps another four leagues, sir.'

'What does the line signify, Mr Mower?'

'Barely half of one knot, sir; we may as well be anchored.'

'Very well; Mr Pickering, let us pipe the hands to breakfast while we are becalmed.' Pat descended the steps to the gun deck. 'Ah, Mr Marston, there you are; will you take a bite with me? I think there is still some bacon - *if it ain't gone off* - and maybe some sausage.' They entered the cabin together, Pat calling to his steward, 'Freeman, a fresh pot of tea, bacon if we have it, and sausages, eggs, soft tack; and enough for Mr Marston too.'

Murphy was also present, keenly aware of the sense of anticipation pervading the ship, and he hastened as quickly as he could to the galley with Freeman to fetch Pat's breakfast so as to ensure no time was lost and his ear was returned as close to Pat's door as he dared without precipitating admonishment from his captain, who was, fortunately for both of them, long inured to Murphy's foibles and irritating shortcomings.

Pat stared as unobtrusively as he could at Marston, wondering whether he had decided well in leaving Simon behind. 'Should we sight any Turks, Mr Marston, you may yet find some wet work below. I pray we do not... with Dr Ferguson remaining on Cephalonia to care for Kathleen,' Pat said, adding, 'Please take a seat, I doubt that Freeman will be long.'

'How was Mr Macleod's wife, sir, when we departed Argostoli?'

'Oh, tolerably comfortable and no more in danger; he did assure me of that... though the prior days were as anxious as any we both ever found at sea. Her illness was thankfully not severe, so said Doctor Ferguson. Indeed, Kathleen remonstrated with me from her bed to depart when I declared that I would wait another day afore sailing. She quieted herself after accepting my promise to depart directly only if she would accept that Dr Ferguson remained to care for her.' Pat paused to reflect, another matter pressing on his mind. 'Oddly, we have seen ne'er a one of the Greek fleet, which Mavrocordato's agent in Argostoli assured me was bound for Candia too. There is no relying on your foreigner, Mr Marston... and this Greek enterprise is a damned fine pickle of fish.'

Marston did not dare to correct his captain's metaphorical muddle, and just at that moment Freeman returned with their breakfast: a huge pan of sausages, highly spiced and peppered so as to disguise their advancing term and doubtful flavour; and eggs, coffee, with plentiful toasted soft tack baked fresh by Wilkins - a rare treat and offered as if in compensation for the ageing sausages. He brought too one of the few remaining pots of Falmouth marmalade, though the butter, beyond rancid at the end, was long gone. Freeman set it all on the cabin table, bowed his head and withdrew to return to his station outside Pat's door. Pat nodded his appreciation of Freeman's endeavours but then peered at the sausage, sniffing, as if seeking to verify or assuage his doubts over the desirability of Wilkin's efforts. 'Allow me to help you to a little of this sausage,' he murmured in a rather cautious, subdued voice. He continued quickly as if to preclude any objection, 'I fancy Dr Ferguson will doubtless be following us in *Eleanor* by now. Reeve is a prodigious fine master of her, and with Codrington to spell him there will be no speedier vessel on God's ocean - if you will forgive my reference to our Lord?' Pat added hastily.

'No matter, sir, I imagine our Lord would wholly concur with your opinion,' Marston replied, smiling. 'Is the Greek cause now precarious in Candia, sir?'

Pat looked up from scooping eggs on to his guest's plate. 'Sadly, it seems so. The Porte has sent its Egyptian vassal's army to subdue the Greek rebellion... and it is feared that Candia is their first port of call. The Hydriot commander, Tombazes, has struggled unsuccessfully against internal fighting amongst the Greeks for some time. It seems that the Greek fleet has other matters to deal with, for we are here alone, but with this absence of wind neither *Surprise* nor any other ship, Greek or Turk, is likely to fetch Candia. Tombazes's men - we hear they are fighting in Lautro - may soon find themselves sorely pressed, if they are not already,' Pat opined gloomily, adding, 'We may yet have to employ sweeps.'

'Where is Loutro, sir? My knowledge of the geography of these parts is weak.'

'Oh, it is near Sfakia, on the south-west coast of the island; the province of some or other Greek band of brigands.'

'What could have happened to the Greek fleet, sir?'

'Without doubt they have a difficult task. The Turk is unfettered to arrive at any part of their coast and all their islands, to sack and plunder any of the Greek port towns. Perhaps they are already engaged in evacuation elsewhere? Perhaps their admirals have received reports of the Turk fleet movements and sent their ships away to find them? Perhaps the crews have again refused to sail for want of pay? Certainly they have fine admirals in Miaoulis, Canaris and others, and they do not lack for bravery. In the year 'twenty-two at Chios they defeated a Turk fleet much larger than their own with the deployment of fireships, the Turks being terrified of them. Even the Turk admiral was killed in the engagement... after running his ship aground to seek an escape from the *bourlotas* - as the Greeks term them. No, 'tis far from sure who will win this war, but the advantage must still lie with the Greeks, for it is they who are defending their homes and their families. If only they would agree a consensus of government and military command, for the want of such is the Turk's greatest weapon, and we will be here for many a year yet until the Greeks can speak with one voice, of that I have no doubt. That is unless our lads develop the Greek approach, for want of pay.' Pat laughed out loud with great mirth at this thought. Marston smiled, pleased to see his captain in good spirits. The prior years of naval inactivity with its inherent uncertainties and then the sudden thrusting upon him of a command in the service of a rebellion had taken a degree of toll upon him he thought. Now, as a first mission of some importance was developing, the becalmed state of *Surprise* was plainly unhelpful. Would Patrick O'Connor be up to the emerging danger and challenge before him? Marston put the question aside, recollections of past times quashing his concerns. A sociable near hour passed until breakfast was finished; Pat looked to his companion, 'Come, let us go up and see what we are about.'

The studdingsails and royals had made little difference, *Surprise* was sailing, near drifting, with every stitch of canvas she possessed aloft and made barely a knot. Three more dreary hours passed and Pat had long returned to the shade of his cabin, when from the tops an excited shout was heard; indistinct but clearly audible as the cabin doors through to the gun deck remained open to catch the tiniest scrap of cooling breeze, but the words remained unrecognisable nevertheless. He let fall his cutlery on his plate and, abandoning his barely half-eaten second breakfast, hastened up the steps to his quarterdeck.

'Mr Pickering, what's afoot?' he asked. 'Ships? Where away?'

Pickering indicated to larboard, towards the east, into the still lingering haze, 'Over there, sir. The topman thinks he sighted a ship, perhaps two... hull-down on the horizon... but I see nothing.'

Pat stared hard into his glass; the sun had climbed away in the past half-hour, the haze thickened and it no longer hurt his eyes to stare carefully for long, tense minutes before he finally exclaimed, 'There! Four points off the bow. Look hard, Mr Pickering, they come and go. Damn that haze. Mr Mower, we will beat to quarters.'

'Clear for action, Mr Prosser,' Mower ordered the master.

Prosser shouted down to the deck, 'Beat to quarters.' *Surprise* having no marines aboard, the task was carried out by Clumsy Dalby.

Pat remained all the time peering into his glass, declaring at last, 'I see no sails.... no sails. Why, they must be galleys, sails still furled. Turks! That is why we could not see them! Galleys for all love! I would never have thought it. Why, I ain't seen one for twenty years, and that in Venice. Have you ever seen such a vessel, Mr Mower? Well done that look out! Half an hour more and they would never have been sighted with the Candia headlands behind them. Who saw them?'

'Young Pennington, sir,' declared Duncan.

'By God, that fellow has the very best of eyes,' said Pat. 'There's a guinea in my purse for him... a capital hand... well done Pennington!' He lowered the telescope, cleaned it with the briefest of wipes with his handkerchief before peering again through the indistinct, early morning haze, a thin wispy mist rising from the warmer waters into the colder air. 'With no wind we will be sore pressed... they are capital vessels for manoeuvring.' Several more minutes passed; all the time Pat continued to gaze through his glass at the approaching galleys. Finally he spoke, very quietly as if he did not wish his words to carry, 'Mr Macleod, we may shortly find ourselves in some difficulty. No wind to shift or turn, no means of training our guns to bear if they come for'ard or astern of *Surprise* - save for our chasers. As galleys their bow and stern guns can fire only fore and aft. Most likely they have twenty-four- or even thirty-two-pound guns, which will far outrange our own... and they can row into any position to their advantage. They can stand off all day and beat us to a pulp. However, need teaches a plan. We must confuse them as best we may. We will hoist a Turk pennant and below it a yellow jack.'

'Would that be entirely regular, sir?' came the unexpected interjection from Marston, looking on aghast, his question spoken with the most anxious of voice, eyebrows being raised by all on deck within earshot.

The interruption was such a gross breach of protocol that Pat himself was entirely taken aback, his mind solely focussed on the imminent threat from the galleys. He simply stared at Marston without expression for a bare few moments, his look becoming very cold, before turning back to his first. 'Mr Macleod, I want the Turks to see no one on deck. Every gunner is to crouch behind the ports and not to show even the top of their head around them. Send a man to the heads, to lie there as if dead. Set everything aloft all ahoo, our royals and tops'ls all a'fluttering - and her courses too - everything all loose and flapping. We will look like Bedlam. Mr Mower, leave the gun port lids down but unshackled; prime the flashpans; send half a dozen shot to be heated in the galley stove... and run it hot so we - and Johny Turk - see no smoke. We will let them come close, our deception will reel 'em in. Remember, Mr Mower, be sure to tell the captains of those two guns a'side firing red hot shot to load only reduced charges. It will serve us well if their balls do not break out of the Turk hulls, and so the better to start fires burning inside. Mr Pickering, remind all other captains - of the eighteens that is - to fire low; they will break scores more of splinters as they strike - and so better to kill their men. We will load both shot and canister, hundreds of iron balls from fourteen guns will quickly disable the rowers. For the carronades, Mr Boswell, load shot only and aim low, so that they may smash holes in their hull... perhaps below their waterline. We shall clear our quarterdeck from Turk sight.' Pat now turned to his cox'n, 'Barton, put the strongest twelve lads we have in my barge and eight more into the cutter. You are to command them both from the barge. Make fast the boats to *Surprise* at her bow with short lines, thirty yards only, no more. Stay behind *Surprise,* close by her hull at the starboard beam so the barge and cutter will not be seen by the Turks... and Barton,' Pat spoke gravely to his cox'n, 'it will be for you and your lads to haul her round by the bow when we signal, so that we may fire our guns; 'tis our only chance.'

'Aye aye, sir, twenty men into the boats, hide and haul her round on your signal,' Barton repeated his instructions and hastened away to gather his men.

As the boats, filled with the chosen men, were being tied to *Surprise's* bow, Pat looked back at the galleys, still far distant but clearly approaching. 'Mr Marston,' he said quietly to his immediate companion, 'You may care to make your preparations below.'

Marston appeared quite unprepared for Pat's prompt at that moment, the responsibility of ship's surgeon now thrust upon him and the prospect of an engagement looming large. 'Those galleys, sir, will it be necessary to engage them? Perhaps flight would better serve our cause if we are to reach Candia and without hindrance to our purpose in that place?' The helmsmen and the master near the wheel exchanged shocked glances.

Pat's reply was infused with only the mildest of indignation. 'Do not think me a warmonger, Mr Marston, a death-or-glory merchant. I assure you, I had rather see a brace of fine ships burnt and sunk than lose a single man of my crew killed or wounded. We have no wind, no means of flight. Those galleys will soon be upon us... before we know it, and to fight presents our only prospect for salvation.'

'Sir, pray forgive my doubtless ill-considered notion, but can we not fly His Majesty's colours as *His Majesty's Hired Vessel Surprise*...' Marston pressed, a little nervously, '... and would they not then pass us by?'

Pat looked again at his assistant surgeon and chaplain with mild astonishment and not least a modicum of irritation, and he replied with as much impassivity and formality as he could find, 'Why certainly we could, Mr Marston... until they asked for such Admiralty papers as His Majesty's ships all possess - of which we have none! Since we have not received our Greek letter of marque either, we would be treated as pirates, and to be taken without any flag flying would likely condemn us to be hanged. No, we must run or fight. As we have no wind we cannot run, and so we must fight. We can fight only as a Greek or strike our colours as a Greek. We may hope that the Turks may not yet know of any frigate in Greek service, and that small thing may yet set things in our favour.' The latter point was said more confidently than Pat felt.

Marston, now realising from Pat's tone of gentle rebuke that he had overstepped the mark, anxiously sought to make amends, 'I have expressed myself badly, sir; plainly I am not to teach you your trade; I beg you will forgive my impertinence and please accept my apologies, if you will.'

'Oh, I think we may overlook it this once, Mr Marston,' Pat relented, smiling, bearing no ill will towards his chaplain, his respect for Marston undiminished. 'Mr Macleod, all sails loose to a bowline. We will likely need to shift away quickly and at best speed. There will be no time to make sail. All canvas flapping will doubtless aid our deception.'

'Aye aye, sir.'

'Mr Mower,' said Pat, 'Prepare our marksmen. They are to stay out of sight, and on my mark to climb into the tops to fire down on the Turk officers only, *officers only;* make that plain to them, and were they to clear the Turk quarterdeck then gun captains next, but only *after* they have swept the galley quarterdecks clear. Each man is to carry two muskets, ready to fire, with powder and shot for six reloads. I doubt this business will last longer.'

'Very good, sir; we have ten men to send aloft with some competency with the musket.'

'Keep them all close below the bulwark 'til I shout,' Pat reiterated. 'Mr Pickering, all hands to keep silent as the Turks near; pass the word.'

An anxious hour slipped by with infinite slowness until the nearing galleys became clearly visible without a glass. On *Surprise* not a soul could be seen, neither about the gun ports nor on the quarterdeck where Pat and his companions crouched low out of sight. He turned to Marston, alongside him, and whispered 'God between us and all harm.' The chaplain only stared.

All of Jemmy Ducks' brood had been taken below and at the heads a very convincingly dead seaman lay over the prow. Barton and his men were waiting patiently, tied alongside in the boats. Pat, lying on his chest on the deck, peered through his glass through a gun port wedged just ajar, scrutinising the approaching Turks.

'Mr Marston...' whispered Duncan, Marston lingering still on the quarterdeck and looking very dismayed, '... will ye go below, sir? Ye may be needed in the cockpit presently. Afore ye know the shot and splinters will be a'flying about.'

'The wind is freshening, sir,' said Pickering quietly as the loosened topsails began to flap vigorously, the southerly wind picking up.

'Aye, Mr Pickering, that may yet be our saviour,' Pat replied, adding, 'They are diverging now, the first heading to come at our bow and the second to hold back, near on the line of our stern, as would I were I their captain. Doubtless they intend to position so as to rake us, one after the other. They are half a mile away now, no more. Our guns are all double-shotted?'

'Yes sir.'

'We will hold our fire for short range when our shot will smash straight through both sides, even double-shotted and with canister too.' More tense minutes passed. The only noises that could be heard were the loosened sails rattling their lines and the creak of timbers, *Surprise* rocking with the most gentle of motion. The crouching crew held their silence, anxiously awaiting their orders.

From the nearest Turk galley, closing from ahead of *Surprise*, came a hail. Her oars were raised, and the galley, a mere hundred yards or so away, began to slow perceptibly. From the Turk the shouts came louder and more frequently. The second galley was some hundred yards or so behind her companion, but coasting to position herself at *Surprise's* stern, losing way as she too slowed, her oars raised. The moment was eerily quiet, merely the slap of wave against hull breaking near total silence as the vessels converged. Time, to Pat's mind, seemed to be standing still. He looked again at his watch, mentally noting the time. Never before had the closing seconds to an engagement ever passed so slowly.

A very few tense minutes more and Pat judged the critical moment had arrived; he leaped to his feet to shout his orders, 'Note down the time, Mr Pickering, and give the order to our boats - to row as if all our lives depend on it, for they surely do!'

Pickering leaned over the side and bellowed to the men below in the boats, 'ROW, LADS! PULL FOR ALL YE ARE WORTH!'

'Mr Prosser, strike the Turk flag and the yellow jack; hoist Greek colours. Swiftly, gentlemen, to your guns, if you will,' this to Pickering and Mower. As they hastened to the companionway Pat rushed forward to look down over the waist rail to his gunners on the gun deck below. 'NOW LADS!' he shouted through his speaking trumpet, 'HAUL THOSE GUNS OUT! SWIFTLY NOW!'

The change aboard *Surprise* was instant: up sprang sixty men on the quarterdeck and gun port lids were hauled up. On the gun deck a hundred more hastened to run out their guns. The eighteens on each side began to be hauled out; at each gun six men were heaving and sweating to haul the two tons weight until the barrel protruded far through its port. At the two guns held back their crews waited. From the galley came four men carrying two red hot shot in tongs which they hurriedly loaded into the two remaining guns, numbers seven and nine, *Hurricane* and *Delilah*, on the larboard side. The unfamiliar Greek flag, blue stripes bold on white, fluttered lively at the mizzen gaff in the strengthening wind, as if with its own vitality. No one aboard *Surprise* had time to notice or consider the strange flag. The startled Turk galley had also sprung into life and her men had resumed rowing. Urgent shouting of orders and whips cracking could plainly be heard by all on *Surprise* before the galley's bow guns spoke with a fearsome thunder, blasting roundshot and flames from their barrels. Great clouds of bilious smoke thrust out, enveloping the gap between *Surprise* and the galley, near off her bow, the two vessels just a mere fifty yards apart. Fortunately, the galley shot flew high, making a sound like tearing silk in passing twelve feet or more over *Surprise's* quarterdeck.

'Greek slave gunners amongst the galley crew perhaps sighting their country's flag at *Surprise's* mast and firing high?' was the thought that struck Pat. The swell too was noticeably increased in the past hour, and the galley's bow alternatively rose and fell as she approached. He pondered on this as he looked about the sails and rigging. Little damage was evident on *Surprise* save for some holes and tears in her main course and foresail – which had not been furled as they would normally be in an engagement, they being left loosely hung as part of Pat's deception – and a section of rigging had been torn away. *Surprise's* marksmen were sent hurrying up the shrouds, their burden of two muskets being no weight at all in their haste. He leaned far over the side and shouted loud encouragement, 'HAUL HARD, LADS!' to the men in the barge and the cutter, the twelve and the eight, who were now pulling frantically, as they had never pulled before, and gradually, in agonisingly slow progress, *Surprise* began to come round by her bow.

'HOLD FIRE! HOLD FIRE! NOT YET! NOT YET!' shouted Pat over the rail and down to his officers and gunners. Pickering and Mower, standing just below the boat stations forward of the quarterdeck, repeated his orders. A further long minute passed, Pat near biting through his tongue, looking about and behind him, studying the approaching second galley with some anxiety for a long, long ten seconds, a lifetime in such desperate moments. From aloft on *Surprise* a ragged musket fire was opened upon the Turk quarterdeck and several figures on it fell down, stricken.

'The Turks will be reloading, sir,' remarked Prosser unnecessarily, he being more than a little nervous, adding, 'The second galley nears our stern quarter.' *Surprise* had now been hauled further round, and although no more than a little way past half way to parallel with the forward galley all her guns could just be brought to bear, their shouting captains having driven their sweating crews to haul the gun carriages round to their very limit.

'FIRE! FIRE!' shouted Pat with all his voice, waving his hat, and the ear-shattering crescendo of noise was near instantly reached as all of *Surprise's* larboard battery opened fire almost simultaneously, great flashes of red-orange fire and dirty, grey smoke belching out from the guns and the smashers, two red hot shot amongst the missiles, the deck shaking violently and the masts quivering. *Surprise's* crew had not missed, could not possibly miss, the distance now no more than forty yards. Along the galley side, from the shot strikes great gaping holes could be seen by Pat and all his larboard crew, many of her oars being smashed and many more missing; much of her bulwark was battered clean away, her bow guns thrown aside by shot strikes. From the thousands of canister shot projectiles the effects at such short range were horrifying: dead and dying men lay strewn across her deck, not an officer could be identified and no shouting of any further orders could be heard amidst the carnage aboard her.

On *Surprise* the gun crews had no time to stare; amidst the shouts of 'Hurrah! Hurrah!' the most frantic reloading was taking place and the frenetic activity on the decks was spurred by the orders and curses of the gun captains, the powder monkeys rushing as fast as they could shift to bring fresh charges. All along the larboard side the guns were being wormed, sponged, charges and wads rammed home, shot and now grape reloaded, and guns run out as fast as any crew had ever managed to do so before. With *Surprise* turning as the desperate rowers hauled her round, the second galley was near directly off *Surprise's* stern, still one hundred yards off and none of *Surprise's* ready starboard guns could yet bear on her. The barge and cutter crews were still rowing frantically, not yet tiring, Barton's shouts of encouragement hardly audible. Few could still hear with any clarity, the noise of the guns drowning out all else. *Surprise* was coming round further each minute by the head yet it did not look to Pat as if *Surprise* could fire before the second Turk fired, and so all attention remained on the first galley, clearly stricken very badly and aflame too, black smoke rising from amidships. She was plainly shearing off, some semblance of command restored, and a very desultory rowing could be seen at her beam. *Surprise,* larboard guns swiftly reloaded, fired again, delivering another fiery series of hammer blows on the first galley, and this time firing grape too. The missiles inflicted the severest carnage on the galley crew, still reeling from the roundshot and canister of the first broadside. It looked as if the deck had been swept clean.

Barely a man was left standing or sitting, scores lay dead athwart her deck and on her benches; dozens of corpses had already been thrown into the water. The first galley was clearly in great distress, presented little danger and so could be relegated from Pat's attention. He turned away to consider the second, less than sixty yards or so astern, and her guns, he thought, bar a miracle could not possibly miss *Surprise*.

'LIE DOWN, LADS! LIE DOWN!' screamed Pat, 'FLAT AS YOU CAN! LIE DOWN!' and, convention abandoned, he threw himself on to his chest on the quarterdeck. Instantly, BOOM, BOOM thundered as the second galley fired. The near shots, so close, did not miss their target. The sound of the explosions was heard just fractionally before the balls smashed through the stern of the ship, the lights of the great cabin not the least impedance, the shots flying through the coach and rising, tearing across *Surprise's* deck midships, cutting rigging and rising to rip through foremast sails. Pat's command to his men to throw themselves down to the deck had probably saved at least several of their lives. He turned his head and looked about him whilst still prone, seeing anxious faces staring back towards him from the quarterdeck gunners. Within minutes the galley's guns roared again. Again the shot entered *Surprise* below them, striking and smashing through planking, breaking the companionway and its steps from the quarterdeck to the gun deck into kindling, having entered again through the great cabin, shattering much of the remaining glass panes in its windows. One shot smashed into the capstan and the second struck one of the guns amidships before ricocheting off into the heavens.

'UP LADS! UP NOW!' shouted Pat, leaping to his feet. 'Mr Pickering...' he leaned over the rail and shouted down to the gun deck, '... send the larbowlins to haul tight the tops'ls, the courses and to brace every yard all a-tanto, topgallants and all. We will need to catch every breath of wind if we are to survive this day.'

'Aye aye, sir; larbowlins to make all sail.'

On *Surprise's* gun deck, as the men of the larboard gun crews swarmed to their task, the starboard gun crews waited anxiously for the command to fire. Double red hot shot had been loaded in those two nearest the ship's galley, *Pure Poison* and *Old Nick*. On the barge and the cutter the crews were tiring, drenched in their own sweat, breathing heavily and strength near gone. Yet still they valiantly pulled at their oars, but very feebly now. Fortunately, their efforts were no longer necessary as the second galley was now near abeam *Surprise*, to starboard, but backing her oars frantically. The first, to larboard, had plainly had enough, had broken off any intent of further action; command had been restored to her and the few remaining unwounded oarsmen were plainly striving to shift her away from *Surprise* as best they could. *Surprise*'s starboard gun crews now had the second galley in their sights, a bare forty yards off her quarter. A few shots still rang out from the tops as the last of the marksmen's powder and shot was fired, seeking officer victims aboard the second galley, although the still-billowing smoke much obscured any targets.

Pat looked about him, seeing many a gun captain's enquiring face staring towards him, and in that same moment he observed with a near overwhelming surge of grateful relief – which welled up from deep within him, suppressing momentarily his anxiety – that there seemed fortunately few casualties. He raised his arm and, sensing the roll of the ship being at the precise position to unleash the cannonade, in an instant brought it sweeping down, his cap in hand, with a concurrent shout of 'FIRE!' to his starboard crews, his shout echoed by Pickering and Mower 'FIRE!' All guns, it seemed, exploded together instantly, with a cacophony of deafening, roaring, thunderous sound, the deck pulsating and the masts shivering violently under the great strain: vast long fiery flames belched out, the guns sending their deadly missiles on their way, for *Surprise* too at this short range could not possibly miss.

Frantically the crews rushed to reload their guns, the anxious captains urging their sweating men to haste amidst more shouts of 'Hurrah!' The powder boys were running amidst the frenetic activity of guns recoiling and men heaving them out again to bring their fresh charges from below, shot together with grape being rammed into the barrels. As each gun was run out it was fired again without delay or any order being given, and a second ragged barrage erupted again from *Surprise's* starboard side, hurling more death and destruction at the galley.

Thick, sulphurous smoke enveloped all on deck in its bitter, choking maw. In moments, as it began to clear, blown off to larboard by the still freshening wind, all aboard *Surprise* could see that the galley was utterly destroyed. Its larboard side was near crushed along its length by the heavy blows from the great guns, the carronades in particular firing a very heavy ball and doing frightful damage. Barely a solitary intact oar remained and a huge list was now remarked upon. Of the galley's boats, wheel, capstan and binnacle there was no trace left; her mainmast had been shot away, its sail half in and half out of the water; alongside it floated great swathes of timber jetsam, many wounded and dying men visible all about it; smoke rose from the galley midships as the embedded, red hot shot did its work.

On the galley, all was in chaos: dead men were strewn about her deck, oarsmen struggled to rise from their positions, a very few men at her ends were striving still to ready their guns; shouts of command could still be heard from determined officers, urging shocked and stricken men to action. At that moment *Surprise* fired again, the third volley not nearly concurrent as each gun crew reloaded and fired as soon as the grapeshot could be rammed into the muzzle and the gun run out again through its port. At a bare thirty yards distance the carnage on the galley was immense: the shocked survivors of the first and second discharges were swept away as if by a hurricane. The devastation wreaked by the shrieking hail of grape left not a single man standing or sitting, bodies upon mangled bodies lay prostrate all over her deck, blood ran in small streams across the deck and out from the scuppers. Shrill, screaming wails of agony could plainly be heard from men who would never be whole again.

Pat averted his gaze from the galley, the ghastly, gory business being done. The horror unleashed from his guns had removed all danger to *Surprise* with just five broadsides. He shouted, 'CEASE FIRE! CEASE FIRE! ALL HANDS TO THE BRACES!' He called down to his second, 'Mr Pickering, recover our lads from the boats. Swiftly now, afore the galleys turn about; we are still vulnerable to an enterprising captain, and one against two; though I doubt they have still any spirit for a fight. Mr Prosser, luff up and touch her; south as best you can.'

'Aye aye, sir; are they finished, would you think?'

'Were I their captain I would be hastening towards land at best speed, so as to beach and save what may. Let us capitalise on this freshening wind and be away as quick as we can,' ordered Pat, huge tremors of relief shaking his body. His thoughts were mixed: anxious feelings of caution tempering the momentary jubilation he felt at a near miraculous victory, for assuredly that it was.

The Turks would not fight again and might not even make any beach let alone reach home, the damage they had suffered being so extreme. The attention of all aboard *Surprise* now turned to gaining as much speed as she could achieve in the stiffening breeze, for it was still no more than that. Course and topsail yards were braced at their extremes to harvest what they could and studdingsails were rigged again on their booms. The Greek flag still streamed vigorously at the mizzen. The barge and cutter crews had been recovered, utterly exhausted and dripping, so little strength left that they were barely able to clamber up the ship's side, the boats left in tow, bobbing far astern on lengthened ropes. All the rowers collapsed on the deck, the ship's boys bringing them water which all gulped gratefully, pint after welcome pint, speech quite beyond them.

'WELL DONE, LADS! WELL DONE!' Pat found a moment for a grateful shout of praise and a wave of his hat from his quarterdeck before returning to gaze on the galleys, for they were now three hundred yards or more astern of *Surprise*, not moving in the water and more smoke visibly rising from both of them. Pickering and Mower had now joined him on the quarterdeck. Of Duncan, who had shifted below to the gun deck at the beginning of the battle at Pat's bequest to help his other lieutenants - *Surprise* having no midshipmen - there was no sign. 'Mr Mower, go below and ask Mr Marston of our casualties, if you will,' he said softly through dry lips, great fatigue now clearly evident in his face and sweat having streaked the black powder smoke particles engrained in every pore of his skin; a bloody gash was evident above his eye and blood was running copiously down the side of his face.

'Aye aye, sir,' Mower replied wearily, tension releasing as the adrenalin rush subsided and exhaustion set in.

'Water, massa?' asked Freeman, emerging, proffering a cloth and the ladle from a bucket he was carrying.

'Thankee Freeman, thankee... obliged,' was all a grateful Pat could say, gulping greedily, the water gushing from the ladle into and out of his parched mouth as he swallowed the warm pints, pausing to spit to wash away the foul and acrid flavour of the gunsmoke whilst an anxious Murphy strived to mop the blood from his face even as Pat waved him away.

The shattered galleys were still watched closely until they had been left some five hundred yards in *Surprise's* wake, a very weary crew settling to recover from their exertions, the ship's boys bringing water buckets along the deck to quench the thirst of the crew, for the sun had yet to reach its zenith and the air temperature was measured already at eighty-seven degrees on the Fahrenheit scale.

'I think they will have their hands full for some hours or more, Tom,' Pat said to Pickering, relief now awash in his voice and formality slipping away. Mower had returned to the quarterdeck. 'How many men have we lost, James? God, how I wish the Doctor was here with us.'

Mower wiped smoke from his eyes and sweat from his brow, and with the barest smile of relief reported, 'I am pleased to say, sir, that we have suffered no deaths, though Mr Macleod has been knocked down. He is below, unconscious; Mr Marston is tending him. Ten more men are being treated; eight with splinters, two of them severe. One of the new gunners has a crushed foot, as he did not move swiftly enough when his gun recoiled. The last has a severe burn on his leg from the red hot shot; I know not yet how it came about,' Mower concluded.

'A cheap victory,' said Pickering, adding, 'Here, sir; take my scarf, for you are bleeding well from above your eye.'

'Yes, indeed it was, Tom; thankee; 'tis but a scratch. I thought we surely would be dished that time. I find I care little for the taste of this victory. Perhaps I find I am becoming old?' said Pat, wiping a renewed small stream of blood away from the side of his face.

'And only twenty minutes since the first galley opened upon us,' Mower added.

Pat looked his Third squarely in the face for a few moments, as if collecting his thoughts from far away before replying very quietly, 'Would anyone wish such horror to last longer, James? I collect that *Chesapeake* struck to *Shannon* after just fifteen minutes, only eleven of them firing. I was there... and that was a bloody affair, Captain Broke severely wounded and poor Lawrence of *Chesapeake* losing his life. No, twenty minutes is plenty enough for me. Such bloody butchery; I venture the Turks have lost scores of men... and most likely many Greeks amongst them... galley slaves, poor souls. Now they know there is a frigate in Greek service... and our next engagement will afford us no surprise.'

One of the aft companionways being smashed to pieces by a ball strike and the other obstructed by the debris, Pat walked forward to the foc'sle and descended the steps to the gun deck. He paced aft very slowly amongst his weary gunners and crew, looking at each of them as he passed by, staring about him and assessing the damage, exchanging a word here and there, passing many a compliment and asking of many an old shipmate until he returned to the point amidships where his men could congregate about him and hear his words. He halted and the animated discussions amongst the crew faded slowly as all became aware he waited to speak. The furore and hubbub had now ceased, and the slap of the bow wave along the hull was again audible, *Surprise's* speed increasing with strengthening wind. The sound of cut shrouds slapping against halliards, against yards and masts intermittently interrupted his words to his men, spoken with great pride as he stood amongst them. 'Well done, lads. Well done, every one of you. A bloody business, but never better gun handling did I ever see on *Tenedos* in all our actions, and you have my compliments and my best thanks.' There was a growl of appreciation from scores of voices before Pat continued, 'Lads, we cannot tarry here to take prizes, nor to sink those galleys, for we have no standing with any flag, neither Royal Navy nor Greek. Let us eat now, rest awhile afore we clean guns and ship, but remain vigilant, for the Turk has many more ships and we are but one. Mr Tizard, it seems that you have much work to do,' said Pat wearily, waving to the smashed planking and the quarterdeck steps.

'D'reckly, sir,' replied the carpenter cheerfully.

Pat continued his tour, stepping down to the lower deck where a very busy Marston laboured amongst the injured, helped by three assistants including Mrs Boswell, the gunner's wife: one of the few women permitted to sail with them by long convention.

Fortunately, the generous dispensing of laudanum had quieted the agonies of the four most badly wounded seamen: one with a foot quite crushed by the recoiling gun carriage of *Hell's Mouth*, amputation being at the forefront of Marston's deliberations but inexperience and doubt staying his hand, and a second who had taken a deep splinter right through his thigh, fortunately missing all the major blood vessels. It was a large splinter which Marston had struggled to remove, and he had succeeded only with the man strapped to the gunroom table with two assistants to hold his struggles and one to quieten his screams, the injured man biting down on a block held in his mouth to safeguard his tongue as the splinter was drawn back and out in two agonising minutes.

The third casualty had taken a significant splinter into his chest, penetrating his lung, and his life expectancy was now short, draining away like the red froth bubbling from his mouth and nose, Marston finding the wound far beyond his limited competency to treat. The fourth, a man burned by the red hot shot, William Currie, had also been given plentiful laudanum and now slept a deep sleep, his pain temporarily suppressed for some hours whilst his brother sat by him. Six others were awake and talking amongst themselves, their smaller and less critical splinter wounds all cleaned and dressed by Marston. All would, bar any infection, recover completely.

'How... how is it, Mr Marston?' asked Pat anxiously, his concern very evident in his voice, low and wavering.

Marston looked up, wiping the sweat from his brow with the back of his bloody hand before replying to his captain, quietly but with confidence and conviction in his voice. 'Sir, I believe I may answer for all but one of these men. I am very fearful for Symes here, who I am not competent to treat. I doubt that even the finest surgeon could preserve him. I shall keep him as comfortable as can be until he is gone. He will be with God this day. He has an hour, perhaps two; no more.'

Pat stooped down to the cot and looked at his stricken shipmate, anxiety plain in Pat's face. He stared for some moments at the unconscious Symes whose breathing was greatly laboured; gently he took his hand and he whispered, 'Ye are not alone, Symes. Your shipmates are here, with ye. All are hereabouts.' No reaction from Symes, and Pat remained, unmoving, quite distressed and staring intently at his shipmate as if willing something, *anything* ... but quite what Pat did not know. He sighed.

Marston, determined to return his own attentions to his patients, interrupted Pat's gaze and silent thoughts after a long minute, 'Mason should recover, given time. It will be some weeks at least, perhaps months afore he will be fit and about on the leg that took the splinter. Edwards here may lose his foot, but I will defer to Doctor Ferguson on that and keep him tolerably comfortable until then. The six men over there will be fit within a few weeks,' he concluded, waving his hand towards the more fortunate half a dozen of the wounded.

'How is Mr Macleod? Where is he?'

'Freeman and Old Jim Lamb have taken him to his cot. His head was struck hard, a splinter most likely; fortunately its force was surely spent when it struck him for there is no wound, save a scratch or two and a bruise. He is unconscious, a great swelling on his head. Freeman remains with him, attending, should he awake.'

'When will he recover?' Pat asked nervously.

'Sir, I can saw, cut, stitch and dress wounds, but his injury is far beyond my paltry skills. Our Lord may preserve him, but I can do nothing. Rest is the only remedy. We must leave him be, sir; silence will be beneficial... and we... we will pray for him.'

'Thank you, Mr Marston,' murmured Pat, looking back at Symes, his relief at so small a butcher's bill tempered by the impending loss of one of his crew. Symes was a long-serving Tenedos and a Wesleyan elder too, if Pat's memory served him; and Duncan's critical status pressed hard upon him.

'I must see that wound above your eye,' said Marston.

'Oh, 'tis nothing, a scratch.'

'That's as may be, but an inch lower and you would have required Nelson's patch. I will attend you later.'

'Thank you, Mr Marston... *Michael*,' Pat repeated his thanks very quietly and left Marston to his ministrations. He walked aft to Macleod's cot and looked at his unconscious friend for some minutes, nodded to Freeman and then walked slowly and disconsolately back the length of the lower deck, to and up the for'ard steps, looking again in assessment at the treated casualties. He paced aft once more along the gun deck, nodding to his men in passing; the after-battle exhaustion, the onrushing severe debilitation of his energy which came every time with the release of tension, and the great shock too of finding his friend so dangerously wounded, all left him unable to speak with any of them. He nodded to several enquiring faces staring at him as he passed by, his thinking frozen, and he scarcely noticed the blood oozing all down the side of his face.

Back in the great cabin a very tired Pat sat alone at his table, deeply unhappy, his head in his cupped hands, his chair amidst hundreds of glass shards scattered all over the deck from his shattered cabin lights, perhaps half remaining intact. The adrenalin rush of the battle was near gone and exhaustion was draining his every fibre as its successor. Gratefully, he sipped a large tot of fiery Greek brandy accompanied by strong black coffee, freshly brewed by his cook. He was reflecting on the engagement and the casualties when Murphy entered, together with his chum, Old Jim Lamb, another long-serving veteran of *Tenedos*'s many voyages and these days still serving as cook's assistant and Murphy's dogsbody.

'Well, Jim here will clean up the cabin, sorr, an' I'll fetch your dinner d'reckly. Will I take a look at that scratch on your 'ead, sorr? 'Tis still all a'bleedin' o'er your collar?' asked Murphy, concerned.

Pat slowly raised his head, his reply very quiet, the tone of despond plain in his voice, 'Oh! Thankee, Murphy, a wet cloth will serve; 'tis nothing... and dinner will be welcome, I am fair clemmed. Would you ask Mr Pickering and Mr Mower if they would care to join me? Pass the word for the carpenter. Perhaps Mr Tizard could board over some of these broken panes later?'

Murphy was gone when Pat looked up again, but within, it seemed, bare moments his officers had joined him and Freeman had returned with a large pot of lobscouse, bowls and all, Old Jim Lamb clutching two bottles of claret and glasses. Murphy fussed about his captain, wiping the still flowing blood from his forehead and the side of his face, and would have pressed on to clean the shirt with Pat in it had he not waved him off with a softly murmured, 'Thankee Murphy, thankee Jim,' as Lamb was affectionately addressed by all aboard, the captain included. 'Gentlemen, we shall not stand on ceremony this day. Please, allow me to help you to this food whilst 'tis still hot,' said a very muted Pat, as he ladled out generous bowls and pushed them to his officers, realising in that moment that he was very hungry and had eaten nothing since leaving his breakfast uneaten. Mower poured the wine, and for a few minutes all three said nothing but ate hungrily, the lobscouse soon devoured, yet the wine remainder still lingered in the bottle.

When they had finished eating none spoke; all looked to the others as if seeking to avoid any inappropriate comment as Murphy busied about them, collecting the bowls. Pat looked up to his steward as Murphy's hand hovered about the bottle; he could not shake from his mind the sight of Duncan lying unconscious in his cot. 'Murphy, will you kindly take the cold ham and a jug of ale, and set it alongside Mr Macleod? Mr

Marston will be busy for many an hour, and I would not care for Mr Macleod to come round in the night with thirst and no drink nor any bite at hand.'

'Well, sorr; I will be taking turn and turn about with Freeman, sitting with Mr Macleod until he does,' Murphy replied, no trace of the curmudgeon in his voice.

'Thankee, Murphy... thankee kindly,' whispered Pat, nodding gratefully to his steward.

It was Mower who spoke first, seeking to lift the gloomy ambience in the cabin and in breach of the custom that the officers did not speak except to reply to their captain. 'A bloody business, sir; there must have been scores and scores of dead and wounded on the second galley from the close firing, and after our grape I could not see a soul sitting or standing on her deck.'

Pickering too had sensed the mood, and seeking to lift his captain's spirits added his own observation, 'The first galley took a pounding too. I doubt either will see the Golden Horn again.'

Pat looked up at his officers for a few moments and settled his glass on the table. He licked away the blood from his lips, trickling still from the gash above his eye, and his quietly spoken words seemed to struggle from afar, a long way back, pulled from deep down in his memory, 'At Trafalgar, I collect when *Colossus* took *Swiftsure*... the Frenchie that is... I was serving on her as Third in those days... we had inflicted near five hundred casualties in her crew of seven hundred and her sides ran red. It was said that *Victory's* first broadside, fired at Villeneuve's flagship, *Bucentaure*, inflicted four hundred casualties and smashed or shifted twenty guns on her decks. It is assuredly a bloody business we are engaged in, gentlemen. We may take small comfort from the thought that the Greek cause is just... and our few casualties.' He took a draught from his glass and, no one else caring to speak further, he resumed, his voice revealing his sorrow, his fatigue. 'We will lose another old shipmate this day. Poor John Symes. For many a year he made his way, with me... with us... I think since the year 'six. I collect he was with us, alongside of me when we captured *Half Moon*, seven long years ago or more. To be sure, our lease on this life is short.'

'What now for our mission, sir?' asked Pickering.

'We're done with that,' replied Pat. 'If the Turk fleet was here I doubt they would patrol with two ancient galleys. No, it's back to Cephalonia for us, to Doctor Ferguson at all speed.'

Tuesday 29th July 1823   *aboard Surprise, off NW Candia*

After breakfast the crew mustered to divisions. They gathered on the gun deck, so many that some stood as far forward as the galley, the majority standing fore and aft of the mainmast. The seaman with the lung splinter, Symes, had fought hard for his life and lingered, but he had died shortly after midnight. Pat and his officers shifted down to the gun deck as the crew assembled. The topmen remained aloft, ever alert, and the only other men not present were the men at the helm and the injured, who remained below. The Wesleyans, four score or more of them, had turned out in their best white attire, washed and starched. Every man was adorned with a purple scarf, their customary colour for funerals, in due deference and respect to their deceased comrade, Symes having been one of their number. At six bells of the forenoon watch the temperature had risen steadily to a baking hot eighty-five degrees but the still strong south-westerly wind did little to cool the assembled crew. Marston waited to begin the service. Behind him stood all the officers, hats removed, looking silently forward at the gathered crew, the Wesleyans prominent at the front. With a sharp tap of a fid on the repaired capstan, Mr Prosser captured the hands' attention and the assembly came to order.

Pat stared at his men for some moments in silent contemplation, his gaze roving across them, picking out near faces he long remembered from his earliest commands; nearly all he could see were old *Tenedos* hands. The crew quietened as all became aware he was waiting to speak. He was, of course, oft acquainted with death and funerals at sea, but the first such in many years struck hard at his mind's equilibrium and it was some minutes, the crew holding their silence, not a single whisper uttered, before he was able to begin, the bleak significance of the moment weighing heavy in his thoughts. He removed his hat, tucked it under his arm and began, 'Lads, we are gathered this day to respect our old shipmate, John Symes, who has sadly lost the number of his mess. Long-serving with us these many years on our dear *Tenedos* and now *Surprise,* 'tis assuredly a loss to us all.' There was a general murmur of accord in the briefest of pauses before Pat continued, finding difficulty with his words, 'Our friend, John Symes, has crossed the bar for the final time, but let us remember him today and long in our future.' He looked about him again for a few moments, as if seeking guidance in this, the most painful of his duties, and then he resumed, speaking slowly and softly, 'I have asked Mr Marston to speak a few words... afore we bury our shipmate.'

Pat stepped back, to the side of the smashed companionway, and Marston stepped forward to the makeshift lectern. The chaplain began to speak, a little slowly at first yet with the assurance of deep conviction, his words firm, steady, unwavering, 'I am mindful of a prior eulogy, a very famous one by Pericles at the end of a previous Greek war, long past. I could never do better than to borrow just a few words of that most magnificent speech, so famous in Greek history.' Marston paused for a few moments to gaze upon his audience, all silent, all reflecting on their past acquaintanceship with their lost shipmate. From all about them, from the air and from *Surprise* herself the customary sounds of their sea-going routine, of gulls calling, of the bow wave slapping on the hull, of the creaking rigging, all pressed on them with particular clarity as Marston took a deep breath and resumed, 'Pericles said this: *In doing good we are unlike others; we make our friends by conferring not by receiving favours. Such a man may benefit his country or his cause whatever the obscurity of his condition. On the battlefield their feet stand fast in the confidence of freedom, and in a frank and fearless spirit, and in an instant, at the height of their fortune, they passed away from the scene, not of their fear, but of their glory.*' Marston paused again to look up, sweeping his gaze across the gathering: all remained mute and quite still. In the reverential silence he continued, *'The value of such a spirit is not to be expressed in words, but in foreign lands there dwells also an unwritten memorial of them, graven not on stone, but in the hearts of men. Make them your examples, and esteeming courage to be freedom and freedom to be happiness, do not weigh too nicely the perils of war.* We bid our farewell to our comrade, our friend, our brother... John Symes... rest in peace.'

Marston's short reading found favour with all his listeners, grave nods and murmurs of "Hear him" signalling their accord with the deep sentiments expressed in Pericles' eulogy. Marston took another deep breath, looked about him again and resumed speaking. 'We will conclude this sad day with but a fragment of Psalm one hundred and seven... *They that go down to the sea in ships... and occupy their business in great waters; These men see the works of the Lord... and his wonders in the deep.*' As Marston finally concluded and raised his head to gaze at his audience Pat looked to the four sombre Wesleyans holding the bier on which John Symes lay, bound in his hammock, two eighteen-pound shot at his feet, and at Pat's sad and silent nod they tilted the bier through the open gun port and John Symes slid overboard to his watery grave.

Thursday 31st July 1823   *approaching Argostoli*

In the last flickering moments of the fading light in the dusk, little wind also remaining, *Surprise* slowly came about in the approach channel into Argostoli, no Greek flag in evidence on *Surprise* on this occasion, Pat being mindful of the necessity for diplomatic conventions not to be breached, as would be the case were the Ionian government to be made officially aware of her real duties in Greek service. Whether the government was now actually aware at all of her duties, officially or otherwise, he knew not, but the hastily repaired battle damage along her sides could not be concealed from even the most inexpert eye, particularly the smashed windows of the great cabin. Although the carpenter had done his best to patch the worst of the splintered planking along the gun deck (fortunately no shot had penetrated *Surprise's* hull below the waterline) and had replaced, after a fashion, the disintegrated companionway steps to the quarterdeck, lacking suitable materials and with so little time available much of the repairs could at best only be described as jury-rigged.

'We will lay a little farther off from the harbour this time, Mr Pickering, and perhaps a kedge might keep her damaged stern lying away from prying eyes on the shore?' Pat suggested to his second lieutenant as the crew prepared to drop anchor, *Surprise* moored a little over three-quarters of a mile off from the quay.

'Aye aye, sir.' Within a few minutes Pickering reported, 'The lads are lowering the cutter now to get you quickly ashore.' As *Surprise* steadied on her anchor Pat clambered down into the cutter, helped aboard by Barton who had stowed Pat's small bag under the prow. Marston remained aboard ship to tend the wounded and Codrington joined Pat as companion for the short ride to their accommodation outside the town, a tiny house which had been offered and rented for the shortest of term in the village of Metaxata. The row for the most discreet landing place at the far end of the harbour quay was swiftly accomplished. *Eleanor* was tied up alongside the quay, but of her crew only a watchman could be seen. It being past 11 p.m. the port office was closed, and so there was no customs agent at hand to delay them. The horses were rapidly procured from Pat's agent at the fringe of the town and in the cool of the very late evening they made light of the familiar road at a steady pace, slowed only by Codrington, he being unaccustomed to horses and so most uncomfortably served by his poor riding proficiency. At midnight they reached the house, candles now burning and visible through the windows. The horses were tethered at the trough, and without any ado, Pat, anxious to see his wife and to enquire of Kathleen's health, swept through the door and into the small living room. To his very great relief Sinéad sat talking to Kathleen and Simon, all of whom leapt to their feet with great pleasure to greet the arrivals. Pat, much pleased, noted Kathleen's substantial improvement. Without ceremony he swept his wife into his arms and stood hugging Sinéad tightly for several minutes, their private exchanges whispered between them after initial exclamations of mutual joy. It fell to Codrington to greet Simon, Kathleen hastening to the kitchen to procure refreshment for the arrivals.

'Is that coffee I smell? By God that is welcome,' said Pat. Sinéad was now free of his embrace, the two of them seated opposite Simon and Codrington, Sinéad tightly clutching Pat's hand.

'Here it is and there is brandy too, warmed bread, olives and local cheese,' said Kathleen, placing all on the small adjacent table.

'Thankee kindly, my dear,' said Pat, consumed with happiness. 'I am greatly thankful to see you much recovered.'

'No small thanks to Doctor Ferguson here... and my beloved sister's attentions.'

With Kathleen now near completely recovered from her illness, the most unsettled man present was Simon, plainly greatly fretting about his absence from *Surprise*, away without him, his fears rising on his close scrutiny of Pat's healing head wound, small as it was. 'Pat, what is that fresh wound I see, by your eye?' Simon interrupted with acute concern in his voice, his anxiety rising at the sight of Pat's injury. 'What has happened?' Suspicions of conflict flickered immediately into his mind. 'Pray be good enough to tell me of your voyage, brother.' In his anxiety Simon was wholly forgetting the presence of the ladies, waiting only until after Pat had gulped a great draught of his coffee. 'I have languished anxiously in this place since your departure, my proper place being aboard our dear *Surprise*.' He spoke with a discomforting feeling of premonition, 'Did you engage in any conflict, pray tell; and were any of our crew stricken? Am I needed now aboard?'

'Perhaps the ladies might wish to retire?' Pat volunteered cautiously, though his suggestion was completely ignored by both. Accepting that, he recounted his story. 'Even afore we reached Candia we were assailed by two Turk galleys; though we saw 'em off with little but a few of our spars knocked away and some broken windows in the cabin.' A long pause, Pat concerned for the ladies, 'Symes was killed by a splinter into his lung...' A sharp intake of breath from all listening, 'Sadly, there was nothing that Marston could do for him. Mason too, took a tolerably sizeable splinter in his upper leg... which Marston took out with some difficulty; it will be some months afore he can reach the tops again. Then there is Edwards, one of the new gunners; his foot was crushed by *Hell's Mouth*... he did not mind the recoil.' Squeals from the ladies. 'He is in some pain, though Marston did not care to amputate the foot and awaits your opinion. Another of our gunners, Old Tom Currie's younger brother, William, is mightily burned on his leg from hot shot... Marston can keep him comfortable only with plentiful laudanum. Half a dozen others have lesser splinter wounds... but doubtless they will recover within a week or two.'

'Dear Lord, I was not there in their need,' Simon gasped.

Pat, unsure of how to put it, Kathleen being present, had kept mention of Macleod to the last. With great trepidation he returned to his story. 'Duncan was struck down by a splinter, a blow to the head, and he ain't woken up since; Marston is caring for him.' With that dreadful finale Pat concluded his grim list.

Kathleen screamed, rose from her chair, dropping her cup and stood stock still. Sinéad gasped and rushed to embrace her sister. After a few moments the two ladies turned to stare at Pat. They looked horrified but said nothing, the shock so great, even as Simon sprang to his feet. 'Hell and death. If only I had accompanied you. I will be away directly... at all speed for the ship... I must attend to help Marston.'

'I am sure the morrow will serve,' Pat suggested, 'Marston is a competent doctor and is with him.'

'I need not tell you, brother, that there are occasions when one may fairly state that there is not a moment to be lost. I am away.'

'I will ride with you,' Kathleen declared, and strong-willed woman that she was would brook no protest, asserting that her recovery was complete, no one - including Simon - caring to contradict her.

'Take our horses. They are outside, and though not fresh will not mind another hour. William Reeve on *Eleanor* will take you across in the cutter. I will return in the morning,' said Pat, realising any further effort to dissuade Kathleen and his friend from leaving until the morning would be fruitless, realising too that Sinéad would never release him until many more hours had passed.

Friday 1st August 1823   *aboard Surprise, Argostoli*

Late morning brought Pat, somewhat restored in spirit, back aboard *Surprise* to check on his wounded crew members. A bruised Codrington could not agreeably contemplate the immediate return ride to Argostoli and so remained at the house in Metaxata, intending to walk back in the cool of the evening. Brodie and the twins had left the house together, earlier in the morning to walk to the port. Looking about him, Pat noted agreeably that repairs were underway to the planking, several of his crew busy painting over previously damaged and repaired timbers. Before lingering further to inspect his ship he went below to visit his severely wounded shipmates; all had now been accommodated in the tiny cabins off the gunroom, previously occupied by Sinéad, Kathleen and Marston on the voyage out from Falmouth, the lesser wounded having been discharged for light duties. There was no sign of his surgeons and so he looked in first to Duncan's cabin. Brodie was sitting at the side of his cot on a small stool, gripping his hand, the evidence of plentiful tears streaked down her face. She looked up as Pat entered, her face so very pale. In answer to Pat's unasked question she shook her head, all the while her wide, liquid green eyes seeming to bore into his face, questioning, imploring, her physical stillness at odds with the frantic racing of her thoughts, the deep, deep pain pressing, tearing through her mind.

'Courage, child... he is in the best of care. Dr Ferguson will set him to rights. Where is your mother, lamb? Where are the Doctor and Marston?'

'Mother has stepped out for a moment. The doctors have both been here, sharing the watch over father all night, looking too to their other patients... and they retired but an hour ago.'

'I will return in a minute or two, my dear. Will I send Murphy with some tea, with a sandwich perhaps?'

Brodie shook her head, could say no more and turned back to her father. Pat moved along to look in at the next cabin.

'How goes it with your brother?' he asked of Tom Currie.

'Mending slowly sir, thankee. He has taken some burgoo today, and the Doctor has given him laudanum against the pain, so he is a'sleepin' still.'

"'Tis the ramrod for him next time. No more hot shot for him,' Pat joked weakly.

'Aye sir, that's sure,' smiled Currie, pleased with his captain's interest for his brother.

'Mason, how goes it?' asked Pat of the patient in the next cabin.

'Toppin', sir; stitched up better'n the wife's sewin', thankee,' came the cheerful response from Mason.

'Good man. Ye'll soon be back to my barge crew,' Pat replied encouragingly. The last patient was Edwards with his crushed left foot. Happily no infection had set in although the foot was swollen to the monstrous size of twice normal and was deep blue, black and yellow in colour. 'Ye won't be at the Maypole next year, Edwards,' smiled Pat to the obviously pained sailor.

To his credit, Edwards returned a sickly grin, and in a laudanum-slurred voice answered his captain anxiously, 'Will I keep the foot, sir? To be sure, I won't be any use in the riggin' if 'tis gone.' To which Pat could only reply, 'If anyone will heal it, Edwards, it is Doctor Ferguson, of that you can be sure.'

After Edwards pained 'Thankee, sir,' Pat headed to the great cabin, intending to speak with Simon and Marston. 'Murphy! Murphy there! Ask the Doctor and Mr Marston to step into the cabin at their convenience.'

Within a few minutes the surgeons entered, both looking extremely tired. Murphy, needing no bidding, brought in a great pot of steaming coffee and withdrew from the cabin. In Pat's absence overnight, Murphy with Old Jim Lamb had removed the last of the shattered glass and timber shards whilst the carpenter had boarded over many of the gaping holes, the window remnants; and the cabin, though much darker, was no longer so exposed to the elements.

'How are the wounded, Simon?'

'All are tolerably comfortable. No small thanks to my colleague here who has served them as well as ever I could.'

'How is Duncan?' Pat asked anxiously.

'He is still unconscious. The blow to his head must have been very great; the swelling is receding but slowly. It would not be erroneous to believe he may not come round for some time. I have known such cases to last many days, weeks even. You are to consider that generally such injuries do heal in time, though we must pray that his intellectuals are not impaired.'

'Will Edwards keep his foot?' asked Pat when all were seated.

'With the blessing, we have some small hope of that. Thank the Lord there is no infection - no smell of the gangrene - and no cut vessels, it seems. When the swelling recedes the prospect will be plainer to see though in any event I cannot see him ever running again, for the damage to bone must be so very severe. He may retain a club foot, with luck. 'Tis Marston to thank for that, the foot cleaned and set as neat as ever it could be, as are the splinter cases. No better a job could I have done.'

Pat turned to Marston and spoke slowly whilst nodding as if in confirmation, 'Mr Marston ... *Michael*, you have my most particular thanks for your excellent service helping those men. For sure they are in good heart because of it.'

Marston's heart swelled and his eyes watered; never before had Pat referred to him in company as Michael. This was recognition as a friend and comrade of the very first order, and his pleasure ran deep. It was all he could do to reply with the briefest of words, 'Thank you sir. It was no more than any other man of medicine would do.'

Pat would have none of this and spoke further, deep conviction in his voice, 'No, that is not true. I am informed that you have barely slept these five days past, never leaving your patients and tending to them as they have recovered; ministering too with words of support and comfort all these days and nights. They... and I... are surely in your debt. There is no doubt of that.'

'Thank you, sir,' was all that Marston, quite overcome by his captain's thanks, could manage to mumble.

'Most excellent work, Michael; I could not do better. Neither could I have saved Symes, for his wound was so very severe,' Simon added, which was some small comfort to his friend.

Murphy entered the cabin to announce, 'Well, the dinner is in half an hour,' adding, 'There is plenty enough sea pie for three, sorr, fresh tunny it is.'

Pat, when such thoughts occurred to him – which was very infrequently – marvelled at Murphy's efforts to manage the minor details of his life. The implied invitation to the two medical men, who were generally held in the very highest esteem by the crew - Mr Marston now having joined those Olympian heights of crew respect after his treatment of their wounded comrades – could never have been respectfully delivered by anyone else aboard other than Murphy. 'Thankee, Murphy. Sea pie for three it is, in half an hour... and a bottle or two of the best wine in my stores, *if you will*,' Pat bellowed after his steward who, despite the boldness of his suggestion, had departed in haste before any unwelcome rejoinder could come from his captain. 'I trust you will tarry for dinner, gentlemen?' asked Pat to observe the proprieties, the answer assured.

Within mere moments, Murphy hastened back into the cabin, excited and quite breathless. Without ceremony or invitation he gabbled out his message. 'Mr Macleod, sorr... Mr Macleod... he's a... a...'

All shot up from the table, fearing the worst, Pat shouting at his steward, 'Calm yourself, Murphy. Mr Macleod, what of him? Spit it out man!'

'Well, he's a stirrin', maybe a'comin' round, sorr.' Murphy was near shoved aside as Pat and his surgeons pushed round him and out the cabin door, hastening to the companionway and below to the gunroom, to Duncan's tiny cabin berth, the illumination so poor after the light of the great cabin that they could barely see the pale face, the lips quavering; nor hear the murmurings which were so indistinct, his eyes still closed. A very nervous Freeman stood outside the door, his customary cheer quite absent. Kathleen was now seated alongside Duncan's cot, holding a cloth with which she had been wiping Duncan's brow. Brodie stood in the corner, silent, openly weeping, tears in profusion visibly soaking the handkerchief she clutched.

'Stand aside, Pat,' ordered Simon, stooping to listen closely to the barely audible words and to feel the pulse: steady, constant, unwavering, a little stronger; his breathing near normal once again. 'Duncan, you are awakening, tell?' the words were laden with relief.

'Aye, these past few minutes,' came back the very faintest of whisper. 'A glass of water would be the grandest thing.'

Pat's own sigh of relief was audible to all. He stooped and seized Duncan's hand, but did not speak as Simon resumed. 'Listen, brother, do not speak further or call out; rest, do not agitate yourself. Freeman is here with the water and will attend you until you can sit up. You have had a very severe knock on the head and must stay here some days more.'

But Duncan had already slipped back into sleep. Pat stared at him for a few moments before turning his gaze to Simon, his questions unsaid, his face saying all, extreme relief combined with concern.

'He will do well, with the blessing. Time and rest will serve him now,' Simon opined, nodding, his quiet words bringing a tidal wave of release to all pressed into the tiny space, the palpable fear and tension diminishing.

With great relief they exited to return to the cabin, leaving Kathleen and Freeman hovering near Duncan, she gently wiping his brow and face, the steward very quietly resuming his low singing of an African song as they left.

Seated once again around the table they sipped sweet Greek white wine, Santorin Vino Santo, Pat's original cellar so very substantially diminished, and nibbled on stale Captains' Thins brought by Murphy until he served the sea pie within a quarter hour. 'What of you, in our absence, Simon?' asked Pat, 'I am pleased to see Kathleen now so well.' His relief at Duncan's recovery was still very evident in his voice, low, wavering.

Simon set down his cup and replied in the gravest of voices, his tone strong in emphasis of his disapproval. 'My ministrations to Kathleen were comforting only and not strictly necessary. As I thought it would be, Kathleen was mending not long after you departed - the beneficial effects of land, plentiful fresh air and good comestibles. I beg of you, I must never be left behind again. My place is on this ship, alongside of all who sail in her.'

'On that, dear friend, you have my solemn word,' pledged Pat.

In the still lingering warmth of the evening Pat arrived home and sat with Sinéad on their terrace, high on the south-western flank of the island's premier peak, their small supper slowly consumed with few words said. He sipped his brandy and held hands with Sinéad as he contemplated the southward vista of the gently descending terrain of small farmsteads, irregularly shaped fields and green copses leading down to the coast, the heady scent of rampant honeysuckle so prevalent in the air, the constant chirrup of cicadas the only sound in the tranquillity of the moment. He gazed across the calm, still waters of the channel between Cephalonia and the low gentle hills of Zante to the south in the distance; the light was beginning to fail but it was still possible to look upon a hazy view of the far hills of the Morea, still just visible in the soft, near-dusk light to the far left before Mount Aenos blocked out any nearer view of the mainland. 'Will I tell you about poor Duncan?' he asked, gently breaking the contemplative quietude of the past hour.

'How is he?'

'He is mending. He has awakened for a moment or two before settling again to sleep. Simon and Kathleen are tending him. He will be well, with the blessing. I hope I may speak with him in the morning.'

'Thank God and Saint Patrick,' said Sinéad and then fell back into silence.

A half-hour passed before Pat spoke again, 'I am much set back by Kathleen's illness... and I noted Simon's shock in recognising her condition, her particular sickness... He has served her very well.' Another minute elapsed before Pat resumed, 'I am mortally cast down to see Duncan wounded so. The poor man insisted that he would serve... *with his wife in* Simon*'s attentions*, and then... to be struck down so. He is the unluckiest soul... and what will I make of it. We have all - Simon, Duncan and myself - served our turn... yet here we are again... amidst blood and damnable death - *excuse me my dear.*'

Sinéad turned to gaze at her husband, the tears in her eyes beginning to stream down her cheeks, 'My love, these thoughts are natural to all of us. Patrick O'Connor is getting older and perhaps becoming more like us *ordinary* mortals. Would you wish us all to return to Claddaghduff? Perhaps it is time to enjoy retirement there. No one would deny you have earned it.' Sinéad was now sobbing profusely and struggled to add, 'We have no longer any want of money; you have no need to fight any more battles.'

Pat embraced his wife gently. 'Here, take my cloth,' he offered, wiping the tears from his wife's face.

An hour went by: darkness had descended outside and the flickering light of the candles reflected off the windows. Pat continued to sit close to his wife, holding her hand.

'Give me hope Pat... hold me... please. I cannot endure much longer. Promise me we will leave these struggles... poor Duncan... poor Kathleen.' Sinéad was still crying loudly and now shaking uncontrollably. Pat pulled her gently into his embrace.

A long and pensive pause followed as Pat considered his wife's pleas. Finally, some few minutes later whilst still holding her tightly about him, he answered her, 'Sinéad, my love... I am sensible of your sound thoughts... and that is where we will set our course. Yet I am now here... with many all about me, old comrades and new; we are - all of us - engaged in Greek service. Before too much longer... we *will* return to Connemara together... though afore that we will finish this undertaking in the service of Greece. We shall see this task through to its bitter end. After that it is my hearth and horse for me... at home in peaceful Claddaghduff. No more voyages, neither for King nor foreigner, no more battles, no more deaths. I have seen plenty enough. Thank you for your kind words. Be assured we will enjoy retirement together... afore all of our time has slipped by.'

Chapter Nine

Fill high the bowl with Samian wine!
Our virgins dance beneath the shade —
I see their glorious black eyes shine;
But gazing on each glowing maid,
My own the burning tear-drop laves,
To think such breasts must suckle slaves

Saturday 2nd August 1823   *Argostoli, Cephalonia*

In their finest dress attire of starched and pressed white dungarees, blue smocks, black hats, neckerchiefs and with the most carefully plaited of pigtails, Pat's barge crew, Barton in command, rowed him dry across to the quay of Argostoli accompanied by Simon, Pickering, Mower and Codrington. The captain of the port was standing on the quay as they tied up, a frigate being a most rare arrival in Argostoli. He was a native Cephalonian and an affable man, welcoming Pat's party and introducing himself with neither airs nor formality, 'Teodosio Cazzaitti, at your service, gentlemen.'

After introductions had been completed Cazzaiti readily opined his belief in the imminent arrival of the Greek fleet and his anticipation of its destruction of the Turk.

Pat did not think fit to disabuse him of his optimism, 'Captain Cazzaitti, please to introduce us to the Resident.'

The port captain explained in heavily accented and imperfect English, 'Colonel Napier away... he with General Adam, with Admiral Moore, gone see Turk Pasha. You see secretary, he is here.'

'Very well, Captain Cazzaitti, the secretary will serve. Please, if you will, lead on,' said a resigned Pat.

Cazzaiti was pleased to escort Pat's party to the Resident's house, a short walk away albeit tiring in the blistering heat – though it was only a little after nine in the morning. A servant met them at the door, bidding them wait whilst summoning the maid. After a short while, Pat growing irritable in the intense humidity, the maid brought them to the office of the Resident's secretary.

Captain Kennedy, a most amiable man, seemed genuinely pleased to greet them, his voice resonating with natural warmth and with the most gentle of Ulster inflections. 'Good morning to you, Gentlemen. John Kennedy, captain of Royal Engineers and secretary to Colonel Napier. The Colonel is away presently, likely for a few more days.'

Pat's impatience drained away in a moment, presented with this hospitable aide. After he had introduced himself and his officers Kennedy replied, 'Your servant, Captain. Gentlemen, may I offer you tea? Punch perhaps?'

The temperature had been rising steadily since breakfast and it was now hotter than Pat could recollect it ever being, even hotter than his days in the West Indies. 'Thank you, Captain Kennedy, punch would be most welcome.' Pat was now sweating heavily in his best dress uniform of a particularly heavy cloth, pressed to perfection that morning by Murphy. It was now bereft of any Royal Navy insignia save for the Nile medal in his buttonhole, a paucity of official status which Kennedy could scarcely miss.

Kennedy smiled, 'The maid makes a particularly fine punch with green tea... and we may even have a little Trieste ice left in store which we receive with tolerable frequency from Corfu.' As Pat and his officers were seated in the secretary's office the maid promptly returned and served the iced punch. Kennedy continued, 'The Resident will return within a very few days, Captain O'Connor, and will no doubt be pleased to receive you. Until then may I enquire as to the purpose of your visit? We have received no prior notification of your arrival in the Islands, official or otherwise.'

With no change of expression Pat looked carefully at Simon on the opposite side of the table who, almost imperceptibly, shook his head, just once. It was enough of a signal for Pat who replied cautiously, recalling a now distant briefing from the First

Lord. 'Captain Kennedy, *Surprise* is not a Royal Navy vessel as such. Rather she is chartered to engage in hydrographical surveying in the waters of His Majesty's Protectorate. We are here to provide our assistance to Captain Smyth, *HMS Adventure*, whose fine surveys are much appreciated by their Lordships at the Admiralty. Their Lordships are minded that in the present - will I say - *delicate* political circumstances a survey vessel of some military standing might well be more respected by any belligerents she may encounter in the course of her task.'

Simon was most impressed with Pat's credible polish added to Melville's strategem. Pat, though no academic, was remarkably quick of thought when pressed in such circumstances, a particularly valuable talent when engaged in and considering of his immediate military options. Pat's lieutenants assumed blank faces.

Whether or not *Surprise's* self-evident damage had been reported to him and whether Kennedy believed or doubted Pat's story his face did not register either way and his reply was noncommital, albeit in a tone that suggested he was a little sceptical, 'I *see*, Captain O'Connor. No doubt Colonel Napier will be pleased to discuss that with you on his return. In the meantime, if I may be of any assistance to you and your assignation please do not hesitate to ask of me.'

After the customary pleasantries of leave-taking Pat and his officers returned to *Surprise,* Pat and Simon to take their supper together and to discuss matters further. Later, Duncan somewhat recovered, Pat visited his cabin and chatted with him in his sickbed, recounting the visit to Kennedy and the declared intentions of surveying. 'What else was I to say, Duncan?' Pat asked of his friend.

'An admirable answer it was, sure, and one which will endure tolerably well until such time as we secure our letter of marque. If ye collect our briefing from Lowrey in London... in a wee few days I am to meet with his promised contact here in Argostoli, who will make himself known to me... and who will have the most recent information on the political and military situation in the Morea and in Greece generally. Until then we might seek some larger and longer term accommodation for the ladies... and assume the task of surveying... whatever that may involve. I have nae doubt that ye will make a credible fist of it for the benefit of any onlookers, for there will surely be Turk agents in this place.' With that, the exertion proving greatly taxing for Duncan, Pat determined to let him be, much to Kathleen's relief; and he fell asleep within moments.

Sunday 3rd August 1823   *Argostoli, Cephalonia*

It was during Pat's second breakfast with Simon that Mower reported *Hercules* entering the bay and proceeding slowly towards them, her courses reefed and approaching the outer anchorage of Argostoli's port.

'Pat, listen will ye now?' said Duncan who had insisted upon joining them for an hour in the cabin. 'I say this advisedly... might I suggest that we maintain just a wee dialogue with Lord Byron for the moment, only that which is necessary; and perhaps it should be conducted solely through myself until at least such time as we have secured our Greek letter of marque. I widnae care to see any association between ye and such a well known Hellenist to be remarked upon, particularly when ye are here officially for hydrographical purposes? Would there be any more of those tolerably flavoursome kidneys left in that pan?'

'You are truly more suited to these... these engagements under false colours than ever I will be, Duncan, being just a simple jack tar. Do we, I wonder, ever profit by them?' Pat mused.

'Och, to be sure it would all be much simpler were such trickery and deceit never necessary, my friend.'

'You may consider of this,' Simon interjected, 'Would the Greeks ever have taken Troy without the deception of the wooden horse?'

'Such sharp practice... that is scarcely my line of country, Simon,' said Pat.

'Forgive me if I am in error, brother, but I do collect our dear *Tenedos* hoisting certain colours on occasion, colours which were never strictly in his Majesty's gift?' Simon failed to conceal his mirth, laughing out loud at his jibe, which did raise a smile from his captain and a little weak laughter from Duncan, the first in many days, both Pat and Simon very pleased to hear it.

Tuesday 5th August 1823   *Argostoli, Cephalonia*

Colonel Napier came aboard *Surprise* at eight bells of the morning watch, being sighted beforehand by Barton as the Resident was being rowed out from the quay. He was accompanied by Kennedy. Barton alerted Tom Pickering who entered the cabin as Pat was finishing his first breakfast, Duncan recovering well enough to be sitting longer with him.

'Sir, we have a visitor approaching the ship. Possibly the Resident as he is accompanied by Kennedy.'

'Very well; I shall come on deck directly. Murphy, light along and ask the Doctor to join me in the cabin in ten minutes. And Murphy, ensure that he is shaved and clothed respectably for our visitors,' said Pat pleasantly. 'Duncan, I must visit my closet, and then I will speak with Simon. Tom, please to welcome our guests on deck, if you will.' Pat stepped in to the quarter-gallery.

'Of course, sir.'

'Napier,' said the visitor simply, introducing himself as he climbed aboard up the accommodation ladder and on to the deck, hand outstretched towards Pickering, Kennedy following.

'Lieutenant Pickering, sir, at your service. Please to step into the cabin. I will tell you that our First Lieutenant is there, recuperating after... after a fall, sir; he remains weak and is unable to rise.'

Napier nodded and strode behind Pickering into the cabin, proffering his hand to the invalid without ceremony, 'Napier; how do you do Lieutenant?'

'Lieutenant Duncan Macleod. my pleasure, sir. I am a wee tait indisposed, as ye can see,' Duncan replied, shaking his hand. 'Captain O'Connor invites ye to please sit at the table, he will be here in a moment.'

Freeman, familiar with Pat's expectations, appeared unbidden after a peremptory knock, setting glasses and cups on the table. He whispered to Duncan, 'Doctor coming, massa; he no find wig.'

'Are you associated with the other vessel recently arrived, *Hercules*, Lieutenant Macleod... with Lord Byron aboard?' Napier came straight to the point.

Just at that moment, Duncan's reply hanging in the air, Pat entered the cabin with Simon, having just caught the question. Simon stood quite resplendent, Duncan thought, in clean pressed clothes and freshly shaven, his wig newly-powdered atop his head; a rare sight indeed. 'Colonel, will I present Captain Patrick O'Connor and our surgeon, my particular friend, Doctor Simon Ferguson.'

'Your servant, sir,' said Simon with a slightly theatrical bow.

'Good morning to you both and a grand morning it is, to be sure,' said Pat, shaking hands with Napier and Kennedy, looking keenly towards the guests. He was speaking with his usually indistinguishable Irish lilt very much to the fore, Duncan noticed, a little puzzled. Pat continued quickly, leaving no opportunity for anyone to interject. 'To be sure, 'tis a pleasure and a very great honour to meet one of Ireland's most illustrious sons...'

'Most kind, Captain, but I am hardly that...'

'... a veteran of the Peninsula and of the 1812, and a staff officer to His Lordship, Wellington, to boot. Did you know that, Lieutenant Macleod?' Pat quite nimbly diverted all thoughts from Napier's unanswered question but left unsaid the other thought on his mind: 'and cousin to Lord Edward Fitzgerald, leader of the United Irishmen and the Rising.' It was a subject Pat was particularly keen to avoid, being a former sympathiser of the brotherhood in his enthusiastic, younger days. Pat continued, brooking no interruption and smiling as he turned to Kennedy, adding, 'Captain Kennedy, you are of the Donegal Kennedy's, I venture?'

'Why, yes indeed, a Donegal man I am, Captain O'Connor. Are you familiar with the county?' replied Kennedy.

'Most certainly I am, sir; the glory of the world, so it is. I once hooked a prodigious fine salmon at the leap in Ballyshannon and I have played 'cello in the Donegal style with Hugh Doherty in Glencolmcille – I visited in the year Boney was sent to Elba. My colleagues and I are particularly fond of our music and often tend towards the traditional rather than the classical. Perhaps you would like to attend our playing? We have a fine quartet aboard; that is myself with my officers and our assistant surgeon, Michael Marston - who exhibits a particular talent with the violin. Excuse me Colonel, Captain, I blather on inexcusably. Would you care for tea, a glass of madeira perhaps?'

Pat paused only for long enough to draw breath, but Napier interrupted. 'Thank you Captain O'Connor,' he said, a little taken aback by Pat's verbosity. 'Doctor Ferguson, are you, perchance, acquainted with our Emerald Isle?'

'I am familiar with the sweet County Clare, having once visited the Burren... a wondrous place for fritillaries you know, the water beetle too, very rare. 'Twas a splendid few months I was there afore I reluctantly bade farewell to return to my position in Plymouth Dock.'

Fortunately just at that moment Freeman entered bearing a tray of madeira and tea. Duncan could bear his captain's rambling diversion no longer and, seizing his moment, interjected, 'Thankee Freeman; well done. Colonel, Lord Melville has requested us to assist Captain Smyth, *HMS Adventure*, in his hydrographical surveying of the Ionian waters and thereabouts... with particular interest in the Corfu Channel. His Majesty's Government is particularly keen to help the economies of the United Islands prosper, given the Turk blockade of the Morea and the merchants of Corfu wishing to stimulate their olive oil sales, greatly depleted since the end of the war with Boney... and likewise the local currant producers, their trade also being much down.'

If Napier and Kennedy were astonished by Pat's blathering and Duncan's subsequent efforts at a plausible explanation for *Surprise* – a warship of some significance - appearing in this emerging place of congregation for foreign supporters of Greek independence, ostensibly to facilitate further the growing principal commerce of the Islands of which they were perfectly aware, by additional hydrographical surveying they gave no sign; both their faces remained blank, as if weighing the truth of Duncan's remarkable statement.

'Colonel, there is one matter in which I might beg your assistance,' said Pat, 'My family and Lieutenant Macleod's seek accommodation ashore, their present lodgings suited only for a very few weeks and *Surprise* being oft away. Can you suggest some suitable place of abode for them within, shall we say, no more than an hour of the port and suited to a horse and carriage?'

'Of course I will assist. If I may, I offer the assistance of my brother, Charles. He is here on the island and perfectly acquainted with suitable locations,' Napier volunteered.

After finishing the madeira and tea Napier stood to leave, bidding farewell and adding pleasantly, 'If we may render any service, however small... Captain Kennedy and I would be delighted to accept your offer to hear your ship's musicians. Captain O'Connor; perhaps you and your officers might join us for dinner in the Residence at your convenience? We must away now to *Hercules* to attend His Lordship. I bid you all good day, gentlemen,' Napier concluded and departed with Kennedy.

'Duncan, you are indeed a dissimulator of the very first order. That was a tolerably entertaining story, olive oil and currants indeed! How did you conceive of that?' asked Pat, puzzled and intrigued.

'Och, I know nothing of such things, but Codrington joined us yesterday for dinner in the gunroom, and we discussed *Eleanor*. She is in need of a deal of new canvas now; ye collect she was nae refitted when *Surprise* was in Plymouth Dock and 'tis four years since she was last out of the water. Codrington was explaining over the very finest of plum duffs for pudding – with fresh raisins which came aboard only yesterday morning – that his family had some interests with a Venice merchant, one customarily buying the olive oil of Corfu and the currants of Cephalonia and Zante, all near unobtainable for him 'til the Turk blockade of the Morea removed the mainland competition from the market. So, ye see, 'twas nae the fanciful story ye thought it to be,' Duncan concluded with just the slightest note of triumph.

'My compliments, brother,' said Simon, 'that was a capital invention. Would there be any of that plum pudding left? Tea leaves the strongest of cravings for just a very little morsel of something sweet.'

Pat smiled, 'I venture *Surprise* has a greater prospect of sinking a seventy-four than our duff had of surviving Murphy's return to the galley.'

Thursday 21ˢᵗ August 1823   *Argostoli, Cephalonia*

Near three weeks had elapsed since *Surprise's* arrival and no contact had been received from the provisional Greek government, although Duncan did expect to hear news from Lowrey in due course. A larger house in the village of Metaxata had been found for the O'Connor and Macleod families for a longer term, the short distance of some five miles from the port presenting no great inconvenience for travel to and fro. The house belonged to a relative of Captain Cazzaitti who had immediately offered to assist their search for accommodation. It offered a fine view of Zante to the south with a distant glimpse of the Morea far beyond. The ladies were very pleased with the location and threw themselves enthusiastically into arranging their accommodation as they wished it to be. Patrick Coghlan with some half a dozen of *Surprise's* crew – principally those hands who had served in Pat's Claddaghduff household – was tasked with cleaning the house and the fresh painting of its walls, all without the slightest delay being brooked by the ladies.

Simon had accompanied Pat and a much recovered Duncan to inspect the new house. 'Here we be, Simon; 'tis a plain, honest abode, but wide is the door of a little cottage,' pronounced a delighted Pat.

'Little is what I behold, Pat, and there are many of us. Would there be a room for me? There is a veritable cornucopia of intriguing plants and diverse avians about this place which are not familiar to me. There is always a want of time to study such fascinations when we are engaged in your briny world, plants and birds alike all absent... save for the gull.'

'Why, of course there is. Eight bedrooms there be, though in some, small as they are, I would not care to swing the cat out of the bag.'

Pat felt obliged to stay and assist in the establishment of the family abode for several days, Duncan recuperating there; a handful of Surprises helped out with the moving of all the baggage from the ship. Such enforced domesticity increasingly grated with Pat as he considered the lack of progress with the mission proper until, to his delight, the morning arrival of Surprises from the port brought welcome news. He spoke to his wife immediately breakfast had been consumed, 'Sinéad, my dear, Duncan awaits a most important letter from London... and the packet from Corfu is expected today.' No response, Pat announced, 'We will be away directly for the port.' Shortly afterwards Pat and Duncan departed for Argostoli, carefully riding two locally purchased, fine Thessalians at a snail's pace, it being a gentle hour for the horses, Duncan carefully favoured in his recovery and Pat mindful of the extreme heat. To their great surprise a most familiar old acquaintance awaited them on the quay, sitting outside the port captain's office in the shade.

'Abel Jason, so it is! How it pleases me to see ye again!' exclaimed Duncan, vigorously shaking the hand of his old shipmate and friend, *Tenedos's* former purser.

'I am very happy to see you, Mr Jason,' declared Pat, pressing his hand until Jason near winced.

'It is most pleasing to see you both again, Captain, Lieutenant,' replied Jason, extricating his sore hand from Pat's excruciating, steely grip. After the customary cordialities, enjoyed by all, he apprised them of his own mission. 'I am arrived today from Corfu, having taken a packet there from Falmouth in great haste at the bidding of Mr Lowrey, and herewith is a letter from him,' he declared.

'Pat, perhaps we should repair aboard the ship ; here is nae the place to discuss any letter, nor indeed to decipher it. Doubtless it will be encoded.'

'Let us go aboard, directly, out of this damn furnace; perhaps we will find a cold bottle of Sillery,' said Pat, irritable since reflecting on his abrupt departure from his wife, his whole body seemingly bathed in sweat.

Once returned to the great cabin and settled, sipping pleasantly cool champagne fetched from the lower hold by Freeman, he being sent to tell Pat's cook that Jason would join them for dinner, Duncan asked of his old friend, 'Pray, Abel, we hope we see ye well... and will ye tell us of your activities these past four years.'

'I am in perfectly good health, thank you.'

'Heartily pleased,' said Pat with evident pleasure.

Jason resumed, 'After our return from the South Atlantic my cousin pressed me to assist him in the further development of the family estates, an occupation of which I had long begun to tire, and so the letter I received from Mr Lowrey enquiring as to my interest in rendering him some assistance was manna indeed; I hastened to London, and that is how I am here.'

Duncan looked across to Pat, 'Will ye excuse us, sir; it may take some wee time to extract Lowrey's message from his letter, it no doubt being in his code?'

'Why of course. Stay here in the cabin, if you will. I shall be on my quarterdeck. Please to shout for Freeman should you require further refreshment.'

Jason brought Lowrey's letter from his inside breast pocket and pressed it on to the table whilst Duncan, Murphy assisting, shifted the table itself towards the stern windows where the sunlight could aid their deciphering. 'It is in the D3 code with one shift I see,' Duncan pronounced after a few minutes. 'One moment, I shall find my key.' He went down to his cabin to search his dunnage, re-emerging after a quarter hour. Near another hour passed. 'It has been some considerable time since I last engaged with this task, dear Abel, and I find some difficulty with all these combinations, however the message has emerged in principle, and we will bring this to Captain O'Connor's interest with nae delay,' Duncan remarked, sending Freeman to find the captain.

Pat appeared after a very few minutes with something akin to worry across his latterly unperturbed face as he looked at Duncan's grave expression. 'Freeman, we will take coffee now, if you please, and see if cook can find any of those marchpane biscuits.'

Though Freeman was gone, Murphy loitered still by the door. Duncan, well acquainted with the steward's tendencies, whispered, 'Pat, 'tis clear from those parts of this letter which are satisfactorily decoded that the situation in Greece is far worse than we had thought. Internecine strife abounds throughout the provinces... and the government in Nauplia, since January, carries nae sway either in the Morea or elsewhere. So much so that the letter of marque for *Surprise,* promised by Secretary of State Mavrocordato, cannae safely be brought to us here with the Turk embargo on all marine traffic throughout these waters associated with the United Islands - save for His Majesty's ships. The letter will therefore be brought and entrusted to the Greek government's representative in the western provinces, in Messalonghi, where we are to collect it... however, the town has been besieged by the Turk fleet under Khosref since late in July.'

Freeman returned, looking downcast, 'Ain't no biscuits left, massa. Cook bakin' more. Here be coffee, fresh now. Anythin' else, massa?'

'No, Freeman. Biscuits when ready will be most welcome, thankee,' said Pat, pre-occupied with his contemplation of the letter's contents and having no intention of enlightening Murphy's self-evident curiosity, he lingering still near the door. 'I dare say there will be some significant Turk ships 'tween Cephalonia and the mainland. We know little of the lagoon and shallows afore Messalonghi, and with no pilot available to us it would be a passage with some hazard. No, we cannot take *Surprise* there. No doubt her arrival would be remarked in Constantinople within a week and Corfu in just a day or two when King Tom... *Maitland* would throw us out of this place directly.' Pat pronounced his assessment rather gloomily before continuing, 'A way must be found to collect the letter of marque when we know it has arrived in Messalonghi. We surely must not act again without it, for such would be plain piracy... and if taken we would all be hung from the yard, and rightly so. We will send *Eleanor* if necessary to fetch the letter. She can slip over in some fog, and being so much shallower in draught she will better cross the bar and navigate the lagoon approach to the town. Without a local navigator or the finest of charts we could not hazard *Surprise* on such a venture.' A plan began to form in his mind, 'As we are here supposedly assisting Captain Smyth in hydrographical surveying, it would not go remarked were we to ask of him his charts for that place. Until we possess the letter we will offer our assistance to Smyth and see what can be done.'

Sunday 31st August 1823   *Argostoli, Cephalonia*

After breakfast, church and divisions had concluded, Pat, Simon and Duncan together with Marston, Jason, Sinéad and Kathleen went ashore in the barge to join Napier and Kennedy for dinner, the musicians taking their instruments. Pickering and Mower accompanied them, Mower desperately keen to meet his poet idol, Byron.

Napier, with his colleague Kennedy, welcomed them all most warmly to the Residence. Lord Byron, having already arrived, greeted them in the friendliest of manner, Mower being rendered tongue-tied as he shook hands with the great man. 'I am, sir, a devoted admirer of your most excellent works,' whispered Mower, in complete awe.

'Thank you kindly, Mower. Are you a poet yourself?' Byron asked in an encouraging tone.

'Why, yes, sir; indeed, I am.'

'Then I hope that we may find occasion to read your own works together...' offered Byron smiling, '... here in this most pleasant and tranquil place; none finer for any bard could there be. Perhaps we will both enjoy the creation of further works? I will await you. Please call at your convenience.'

'Thank you, sir; it is my most precious hope that I may do so.'

Byron introduced his companion, Count Gamba, who had accompanied him from Genoa. It was a most affable gathering at the Colonel's table, several bottles of a superb Amontillado enjoyed by all as they sat waiting to dine. The chef had excelled himself, serving a most excellent selection of grilled fish, accompanied by a local retsina, followed by sofrito – albeit his Lordship demurred in favour of cheese – served with a magnificent burgundy, and then baklava puddled in honey; finally, there was copious local brandy and the strongest of Greek coffee to conclude, a finale wholly to the taste of Pat, Simon and Duncan.

It was with tremendous satisfaction that Pat thanked the Resident. 'A capital dinner, Colonel Napier; we must see how *Surprise* can thank you. If only we were still a commissioned vessel, I think we would assuredly press your cook,' he joked in the cordial ambience of after dinner contentment.

'Most assuredly, sir, I have not eaten as well since leaving London,' added Jason.

'And what are your activities and intentions here in Cephalonia, Mr Jason? We are already accompanied by probably the most well known Hellenist of all, here beside me in his Lordship,' Napier said, smiling towards Byron whilst seizing his opportunity for a prescient question, which alerted them all to some caution. 'Would you be another, at all?'

'My dear Colonel, my sympathies lie wholly with the Greeks, of that I make no secret, but I am here merely as linguistic assistant to Captain O'Connor. I have some proficiency in the Greek and Turk languages - which may conceivably be called upon should *Surprise* encounter any of the ships of either side in the current strife. I am come from Corfu on account of attending to pressing family affairs before my Admiralty letter of appointment was delivered to me. It was too late for me to reach Falmouth ere *Surprise* left. Tell, Colonel, how do you anticipate matters developing in this conflict... and how are you affected here in the Islands?' With this question Jason smoothly switched the interest of the ensemble.

For Colonel Napier, a distinguished veteran of the Peninsula and the Hundred Days, such questions held no fear as all looked to his answer. 'My dear Mr Jason, as an officer of the Crown and being subordinate to Sir Thomas Maitland, my duty lies in maintaining the avowed neutrality of the United Islands. Sir Thomas, who may fairly be called a rough old despot, is very strict on that and will brook no infractions of our neutrality, as is rightly so, and my own personal opinions must be subordinate to that. I must tell you all that Sir Thomas insists on a policy of strict quarantine for anyone coming to these islands from the Greek mainland where disease and pestilence is rife. We will brook no traffic at all with Greece.'

Lord Byron interjected, 'It is sure that Maitland's neutrality prevails, even here, for I can find no means to cash my bills of exchange. Both Cariddi and Corgialegno, the richest proprietors and merchants in the island, have refused me... which is a considerable inconvenience.'

'Virtue never has been as respectable as money,' remarked Pickering.

Pickering's comment did not distract Napier, who was assuredly aware that Byron's pro-Hellenic sympathies would not find favour with Maitland, and he continued, 'As a military man it is obvious that the Greeks lack a great deal. Professional officers and a standing army are woefully absent. Their struggles are contingent on little more than militias, who are in reality brigades of bandits, fighting amongst themselves more often than against the Turk. They have no artillery, no cavalry, no training regime, no commissary... and they feed off their impoverished fellow countrymen. Our sources report that the German Legion survivors in Nauplia are starving and subsist only on tortoises!' There was a laugh from all present, several minded that perhaps salt pork was not so bad after all. A smiling Napier resumed, 'Such is perhaps not wholly unpalatable to you mariners, accustomed as you are to eating the turtle, but plainly it evidences the woeful lack of money and any kind of proper administration. The Greeks have very few of warships, but no one would doubt their courage, and if that alone can deliver them then delivered they assuredly will be. They have two particular admirals: the Psariote, Canaris; and the Hydriote, Miaoulis. Both have fought the most successful actions against the Turks. Yet for all that, their fleet lies inactive, their crews in want of money, and so the Turk, Khosref, blockades Messalonghi in impunity with his squadron of fifteen of sail whilst twenty-thousand Ottoman troops besiege it by land. The Greeks have several generals: in the east, Odysseus; in the Morea, Kolokotrones. Everywhere there abound innumerable politicians, all squabbling amongst themselves, the prominent one being Secretary of State Mavrocordato, who I believe has now fled to Hydra under threat from Kolokotrones.'

At this news, most probably throwing their plans into disarray, Duncan glanced quickly at Pat who had similarly taken it in and who now seemed sunk in thought.

Napier continued, 'Should the Greeks succeed in uniting their forces by land and securing stronger warships, then they have a prospect of victory. Until then they will always be suppressed - if not controlled - by the Turk who by virtue of his fleet can place his brigades anywhere throughout the Greek communities in any of the Ottoman provinces. Any seasoned general would relish the task of bringing the disparate Greek forces to a concerted direction, but that seems unlikely to come about on account of their political chaos. They have plentiful foreign volunteers... adventurers and dreamers for the most part... and ill-equipped to meet the full force of even the most lamentable Turk brigade. Yet any capable admiral with but a modicum of sound warships might well intercede with great success in choking off Turk resupply... as, gentlemen, there is certainly no Turk Nelson.'

At this, as if prompted, there was a polite but subdued laugh from around the table before Lord Byron interjected, 'Colonel Napier, surely that is too pessimistic? Greek heroes, as worthy as any of their predecessors of antiquity, are dying every day, most recently the brave Marco Botzari; and the honourable aspiration for freedom surely beats as firmly in Greek hearts as it did in Napoleon's subject peoples. Even that man... one of arguably military genius... *as is said by some*,' - a few frowns around the table - '... could not hold the tide of freedom at bay; and so are these adventurers, whom you state are so ineffective, not providing a beacon, illuminating the path to follow for the peoples of Greece to throw off the Turk yoke?'

'Very admirably put, my Lord,' said Napier, 'but it cannot be denied that Bonaparte was beaten only by the most experienced and substantial forces of the Alliance, on land and by sea, and only after very many years of costly struggle - and even then it was a near run thing. No, it would not do to underestimate the Greek difficulties, nor the time it may take them. Yet, were I pressed to conjecture, I would have to favour the Greeks.'

Neither Pat nor Duncan wished to pursue the subject of the discussion and so they politely refrained from comment. A little further time passed before it became apparent to all that no confluence of opinions would be established between Napier the soldier and Byron the poet. It was therefore a moment of some relief when the maid announced the return of the ladies when Pat brought the military debate to a timely end, 'Colonel, might we perhaps conclude your most excellent dinner with a piece or two from Corelli ere it becomes time to depart?'

'A most admirable suggestion, Captain O'Connor,' Napier replied, beaming jovially at Pat. 'Captain Kennedy and I have been keenly awaiting your concert. We hear so little of the classics here in Cephalonia. Please to continue.'

'If your Lordship pleases,' Pat looked towards Lord Byron, 'My colleague, Michael Marston, will precede our Corelli with his version of a most magnificent piece we encountered first in his Lordship's home in Genoa, where it was played by the finest musician it has ever been my good fortune to hear. He will play Signor Paganini's *Caprice Vingt-quatre*, though with Dr Ferguson's viola rather than the violin; we find it adds a pleasing warmth to the piece.'

'Most happy, O'Connor,' Byron replied, 'Please to begin.'

Whilst Marston could not achieve the exquisite perfection of Paganini, his own playing was close to virtuoso, and at the conclusion the small gathering was deeply impressed, thanking him with robust clapping, Duncan, Simon and Pat included. It was then for the quartet to play on for another twenty minutes or so of Corelli, Duncan contributing his own gentle and subtle additions with his whistle, before the convivial occasion came to its end.

Napier and Kennedy were delighted, applauding with gusto as the musicians finished. The Colonel stood, as if in timely summation of the event, and spoke with boundless gratitude, 'Gentlemen, so very invigorating; I congratulate you all most profusely. Sadly, there is so little opportunity here for us to enjoy such stirring musical talents. I beg you, please accept my... *our* invitation to dine with us again... and allow us, if you will, another blessed moment in which to hear such prodigious fine musicians.'

'Most kind, Colonel, and thankee for your hospitality on behalf of all of us,' Pat replied, delighted to establish such good prospects for future dialogue. 'I regret we must now away to our abode, sir, my officers to the ship.'

As they prepared to depart, Lord Byron, being kindly solicitous to the ladies, enquired of them their contentment with life aboard ship, he himself still being accommodated on *Hercules*.

'Thank you for your interest, my Lord', Sinéad replied; 'We have shifted from *Surprise* and now reside in a little house in Metaxata on a warm south slope. It is a most pleasant village where we enjoy the vista towards Zante.'

'Perhaps that place would suit my own modest needs, for I must very soon quit the ship. I collect that the Colonel's brother may indeed have suggested it,' Byron remarked.

The Colonel thanked them again for their playing, smiling and shaking hands with them all as they left the house and bidding farewell as Captain Kennedy escorted them out to the street. The afternoon was passing into early evening as Pat, Duncan and their families, Simon with them, set off in contented, jovial spirits to stroll back to their new home ashore, Mower and Pickering to return to the ship.

'The prospects of securing our Greek commission are receding like the tide, Duncan. Will we leave for Hydra, would you think?' asked Pat an hour later as they sat with Simon in their easy chairs on the terrace in the approaching dusk, the whirring sound of cicadas all around them, the air still warm and scented with pungent honeysuckle and the gentler, more subtle wild rosemary.

'In this uncertainty of political stability I fear such a move might serve only to prematurely disclose our intentions, and would secure little were we to find Mavrocordato absent from Hydra. The close preservation of our intentions for the moment must best serve our interests. Better to send *Eleanor* to Hydra - with Jason perhaps - to find out what is afoot. 'Til then we will persevere with sailing up and down the coast.'

Simon interjected, 'Indeed, 'tis a pleasant enough prospect, though I marvel that such repetitive contemplation of your watery realm holds such evident interest for you mariners. Is there a shard of that toad in a hole left at all?'

'Surveying, Simon, for us mariners is a most engaging pastime; the understanding of our realm is of prime importance. You are to consider that his Majesty has lost many more ships to rocks and reefs in poorly charted waters than ever struck to Boney's fleet. But I see you jest. *Adventure* and Smyth will be here afore long and then we shall meet a surveyor of the very first order. Until then we are in accord, *Eleanor* with Jason will be sent to Hydra tomorrow to see the lie of the land. Freeman! Ah, there you are. The Doctor has set his fancy on another of your admirable toad in a hole rations, if you will; thankee kindly... and perhaps we will share another claret!' Pat shouted to Murphy, even ashore never far from earshot.

Wednesday 17ᵗʰ September 1823   *Argostoli, Cephalonia*

It was more than two weeks before Captain Smyth and *Adventure* eventually arrived in Argostoli to revictual and to take on fresh water, having spent some weeks off the west coast of the Ionian Islands in assessing modifications to charts made some years previously; the west coast being reckoned generally free of Turk warships and the Greek pirates who still abounded throughout those waters despite the risks from Ottoman patrols enforcing the blockade.

'William Smyth, sir, at your service, Captain O'Connor,' said Smyth, proffering his hand as he stepped upon *Surprise's* deck. *Adventure*, with her shallower draught, had tied up to the quay that afternoon, Captain Smyth replying to *Surprise's* near immediate signal of invitation.

Being keen to establish a cordial dialogue with the undoubted expert of Mediterranean hydrography, Pat and his officers shifted towards the cooler great cabin, Smyth delighted to be in the presence of one of the Royal Navy's most famous naval officers. 'May we offer you a little refreshment, Captain Smyth; perhaps a glass of wine with you, sir?' Pat prompted hospitably as they settled around the table.

'I would not suppose, Captain O'Connor, that you might have a cold bottle of sack?' enquired Smyth.

'Freeman!' shouted Pat, who was through the door before he had uttered the second syllable. 'Check the stocks and see if we have any sack. I collect we may have a few bottles left of the Manzanilla.' It was on such occasions that Freeman excelled, having taken aboard a very few days beforehand a small supply of ice from the Corfu packet, well wrapped in stout hessian within wooden boxes now deposited low in the ship, melting slowly at the extremities, and from which Freeman was able to chip out just a very little on each occasion to further chill the cooled bottles as they came aboard from the net.

Around the table and in good humour, all enjoyed hearing Pat exchanging recollections with Smyth of their earlier times in Ionian waters, albeit Pat was also pondering how best to make his intended request for the charts he sought. Freeman returned with two bottles of the Manzanilla and six glasses. Pat was impressed by his steward's success and all were most happily pleased by the chilled sack. 'Well done, Freeman; a colder glass I ne'er had when we were off the Horn... and tolerably welcome in this heat. Thankee, Freeman. Captain Smyth, we are engaged by the First Lord to offer our assistance with your surveying of the Ionian and neighbouring waters... *should you have need of it.*'

Pat paused momentarily to assess Smyth's reception of his ruse. No response other than a cautious nod, he pressed on, 'Lord

Melville is most anxious that the charts of the waters 'twixt the United Islands and the mainland be as accurate as can possibly be, so as to avoid in the current troubled times any conceivable charge of territorial infraction by the Turk authorities... however unlikely that might be. Their Lordships have sent our ship, though she be only a fifth rate, on account of the very troubled situation with the Greek risings in the Morea and western Greece, anticipating that she may go to waters where any prudent captain would well baulk at any prospective challenge to his ship from the Turk authorities. *Surprise* – well, her predecessor that is – was, as you are aware, from former times a ship known well in these parts. I have been particularly charged by Lord Melville to survey again the waters at the approaches to the Gulf of Patras...'

'My own survey of those waters is particularly detailed, sir,' Smyth could hold his tongue no longer.

Pat nodded and resumed in apologetic tone, 'I have no doubt, sir, that any such further survey will find no distinction from your own most commendable charts from the year 'thirteen, excellent as they are. I have always used them myself and ne'er found fault, but when their Lordships request we find it is our unfortunate and thankless lot to obey. Captain Smyth, might I enquire, sir, if you could possibly provide to us - on loan of course - your most recent charts of that particular area? With any additions you may have personally annotated... including the region of the lagoon of Messalonghi. Should we find ourselves disoriented in, say, the most extreme instance of fog or of storm, no pilot being available to us, such charts would be of quite inestimable value,' Pat concluded with his principal objective, his important question credibly asked as best he could put it.

Smyth, graciously and having taken no offence at their Lordships ostensible request, replied without hesitation, 'Of course, Captain O'Connor. I have indeed my own charts with many a marking that never was printed by the Admiralty... and I will be most pleased to loan them to you. If I may have them returned at your conclusion I would be in your debt, sir.'

'And I in yours, Captain Smyth; thank you kindly,' Pat replied, finding Smyth something of a kindred spirit and having himself plotted a useful chart or two during his voyages. He added, 'As a most proficient hydrographer, it is to be presumed that you have an interest too in our celestial aids. Jupiter is prominent these past few nights, and I have an excellent Dollond glass. Would you care to join me aboard this evening for supper and celestial gazing? We are surely blessed here with these wondrous clear skies.'

Smyth was noticeably pleased by Pat's invitation, swiftly according with it, 'Most kind, Captain O'Connor. I shall return after six bells of the last dog watch. It is a particular interest of mine since visiting Piazzi and his observatory in Palermo, and I will greatly look forward to our evening.'

'And I too, sir,' replied Pat, smiling warmly as he shook hands with the departing Smyth.

Saturday 15th November 1823   *Metaxata, Cephalonia*

Considerable time had passed aboard *Surprise* surveying the Ionian waters with still no news having being received from the provisional Greek government. *Eleanor* had returned from Hydra several weeks previously. Codrington had been unable to provide any further information. Jason remained absent, having failed to meet with Mavrocordato, and had stayed on Hydra, lingering in the hope of doing so. *Eleanor* had subsequently been sent again to recover him.

Surprise having recently returned to Argostoli, Pat and Duncan were staying with their families in the Metaxata house, which the ladies had put into admirable order. After supper the two friends sat contentedly on the terrace contemplating the view towards Zante, two bottles of the finest quality robola finished.

'Will I tell ye of the recent news, brother?' said Duncan. 'Our neighbour Lord Byron has abandoned his plan to go to the seat of the provisional government at Tripolizza... his Philhellene colleagues, Hamilton Brown and Trelawny, having returned with news of further internecine strife. His Lordship had sent with them his personal letter urging an end to this fratricidal insanity... which is jeopardising the London Greek Committee's loan, and they returned bearing a letter from Mavrocordato seeking an interim loan from his Lordship himself in order that the wages of the Hydriot fleet could be paid, withoot which they wilnae sail to relieve Messalonghi.'

Pat set down his glass and turned to his friend, replying only after a long sigh, 'Dear Lord above! Had we conducted our affairs like this in the year 'fifteen, Boney would now be presiding in Westminster, His Majesty would doubtless be left languishing in the Marshalsea to rot and *Surprise* would be sailing under French colours. He sighed; his Lordship is plainly of a more benevolent mettle than us mere mortals. And what is he to do about it?'

'Admirable man that he is - were there more of his ilk - he has sent his emissary to Tripolizza affirming his personal commitment to providing a loan of four thousands sterling or the equivalent in dollars upon the arrival of the fleet, and he is now disposed to go directly to Messalonghi to assist the Greek defence there.'

'It is to be hoped that the fleet will bear with them our long awaited letter of marque,' said Pat with more hope than conviction, his dolorous face exhibiting the despairing pessimism he felt at that moment.

Chapter Ten

Place me on Sunium's marbled steep,
Where nothing, save the waves and I,
May hear our mutual murmurs sweep;
There, swan-like, let me sing and die:
A land of slaves shall ne'er be mine –
Dash down yon cup of Samian wine!

Saturday 22ⁿᵈ November 1823   *Metaxata, Cephalonia*

After breakfast Pat and Duncan with Simon, who had joined them early that morning from the ship, strolled through the village to visit Lord Byron in the hope that perhaps his Lordship, who was most presciently receptive to the political winds blowing from the Morea and who received many letters from his several emissaries throughout much of Greece might be able to apprise them of the current circumstances generally and Mavrocordato's specific situation, his location particularly.

On the first floor of his apartment the poet was gazing from his window as the maid showed them in. 'O'Connor, Macleod, Ferguson, how pleasing to see you all. Look here, I do so enjoy this vista,' declared Byron, looking tired but smiling. He turned again to the window, 'I was admiring it only last night, my daughter only latterly recovered from sickness, and I have myself been sleeping ill. The calm, though cool serenity of a beautiful and transparent moonlight showing the islands, the mountains, the sea... with a distant outline of the Morea traced between the double azure of the waves and skies. These sights, of such beauty, have quieted me enough to be able to write. Look, Zante is there to the south... and in the far distance one can glimpse the hills of the Morea. Here in my modest home, in this blessed landscape and amongst these simple people... I have found tranquillity such that has eluded me for too many of these past years. Do you not find it acts upon you in that way?' Byron turned again to his visitors, 'Excuse me, may I offer you tea?'

Simon was plainly moved by the poet's eloquent words, and before Pat could answer he replied softly, 'I am no philosopher, sir, but I find that too often our hearts are oppressed by our minds, and sadly our mind can be oppressed by our heart. When we are fortunate to find that neither is the case we oft know not how to embrace the absence of anguish and but slowly do we come to rejoice. I give you joy, sir, if that is where you find yourself. Leave that place only with the utmost reluctance. Speaking as a medical man, these thoughts are beyond our gift... but of their recuperative benevolence one may not praise them too highly.'

Byron had listened patiently to Simon and continued to look at him as if contemplating the sense, the merit of his words. He stepped towards Simon, grasped Simon's hand between his own and murmured, 'Thank you kindly for your words, Ferguson; none finer could come from any poet's lips. Would that we had more time together to enjoy such discourse.'

'Sir, I am gratified by your kind words.'

After a few pensive moments, Byron still firmly gripping Simon's hand, each of them silently contemplating the other, Pat intervened, 'Beg pardon, my Lord, by that do you mean... that is to say... is your Lordship leaving this place?'

'My dear O'Connor,' Byron replied, breaking as if reluctantly from his thoughts and his grasp of Simon's hand, 'I have recently received a letter from Secretary of State Mavrocordato, whom I pressed to state the intentions of the Greek government so as to assist the formulation of my own plans. He reports that President Conduriottis has himself paid the first month's pay for the fleet in Hydra, which is to sail shortly in anticipation that I shall loan their continuing costs. I am minded to do so... and I shall reply urging Mavrocordato to come to Messalonghi, to show himself there, the better to demonstrate some restoration of political unity. I am now resolved to go to that place and assist their efforts. I will go first to Zante to cash my bills. Messrs Barff and Hancock there have offered to do so... and on the most generous of terms. It will surely be a loss to leave this place, but sitting here I can do little for Greece.' Byron sighed, his weary voice reflecting his feelings of dismay with Greek disunity. The maid returned with tea and announced a further visitor: Colonel Napier had arrived. 'Pray, do come in, Colonel,' shouted Byron with a friendly inflexion.

Napier entered the small room and the maid busied about to serve all with tea. 'Good day, my Lord. I have called first upon Captain O'Connor... to be told he was here. Captain O'Connor, as I left Argostoli your schooner was approaching the quay. I am sent by the Governor, the packet recently arrived from Corfu, to determine and report the further interests of yourself and Lord Byron... Maitland lamenting that I tell him nothing at all.' The reference to Sir Thomas was spoken with a knowing smile on Napier's face.

It was Byron who replied, 'Napier, we have known each other for some months... and I will say a respect akin to a friendship has arisen between us in that time. So I will tell you in honesty, I am quitting this tranquil place where I have been pleased to find a home, which I shall sorely miss, and I am going to Messalonghi in some few weeks time. I will presume upon our friendship and ask that you retain that confidence until I have left. I wish, Colonel, that you might accompany me. I am sure that no more admirable leader of military men could the Greeks aspire to secure. I will gladly write you a letter of introduction to the London Committee to that effect.'

'You are too kind, my Lord,' Napier replied. 'In the first matter, my report to the Governor must be sent by the December packet to Corfu, but I understand that Maitland is not well and has gone to Malta, and so it may be some time before he receives my letter... and by then you will have departed Cephalonia. In the second matter I cannot comment, but I thank you for your sentiment. Captain O'Connor, in frankness, sir, may I presume that surveying is not perhaps the sole interest you have in and about these islands?'

The question produced only a pregnant silence for a few moments before Pat replied after evident deliberation, 'Colonel, *Surprise* has completed her work on the *west* coasts of the islands of Cephalonia and Zante... but there remains interest to the *east*.'

It was the most circumspect reply, with everything left unsaid, which Napier could hardly fail to notice, though he did not press further before Pat resumed, 'We must be away, gentlemen, *Eleanor* having returned.' Pat, Simon and Duncan left after cordial but swift farewells.

The news from Jason when they reached *Eleanor* at the quay in the early afternoon was deeply significant. 'Finally I was received by Mavrocordato, he being for some weeks reluctant to confide in me, and he was also... perhaps... uncertain of the intentions of the combined fleet. It consists of nine Hydriot and five Spezziot brigs. Quite small for the most part and hardly armed at all in comparison with the guns of *Surprise*. How they will fare against Turk vessels of some size is far outside my province, yet they are intending to sail at the end of the month. Mavrocordato himself will accompany them; not in any official capacity but as a volunteer, he being no longer in office. They will sail to Messalonghi, and their intention is to break the Turk blockade.'

After the shortest of pauses Pat replied, his officers all with him in *Eleanor's* small cabin, 'Thank you, Mr Jason; that is news of the very first importance. Gentlemen... Doctor Ferguson, Lieutenant Macleod and I will return to Metaxata this evening to make our arrangements. We will convene on the morrow at eight bells of the morning watch. Our plans will be revealed after we have mustered to divisions. Mr Mower, please to replenish *Surprise's* water. Mr Pickering, provisions for thirty days. Mr Codrington, the same for *Eleanor*. Mr Reeve, my barge is to be ready at the quay tomorrow at seven bells, if you please. I bid you all good day.'

The ride back to Metaxata was a little more urgent than usual, the heat of the day slightly cooler than in prior weeks, despite which it was a hot and perspiring Pat who dismounted outside the house. 'I shall be mightily pleased, Simon, to be astride my quarterdeck once again... in the fresh sea air, salt wind in my face. I tire of many more days astride this horse, willing that he is, on this damned inferno of an island. Praise be we are hauling up our anchor tomorrow... though when we might see our long awaited letter of marque the Lord only knows.'

'In the plainest of speaking, I fear you have been eating rather better here these past months and tending again to obesity, brother. Salt horse and ship's biscuit will serve you well until you can shed at least thirty pounds,' replied Simon, disregarding his friend's personal feelings entirely. 'Will I prescribe a daily purgative to assist you?' The comment was wholly ignored by Pat, and they drifted into a contemplative silence for the remainder of the ride.

At supper, shared with their families, Pat announced to their considerable dismay that *Surprise* and *Eleanor* would depart next morning and be away for some weeks. *Eleanor* would return to apprise them of their circumstances were *Surprise* unable to do so, for such seemed possible once the Governor became aware of any participation by *Surprise* in the conflict, when the strict Ionian neutrality policy would preclude her returning to the Islands without fear of seizure or even forfeiture, the United Islands authorities having no knowledge of her covert appointment.

Wednesday 10th December   *near Ithaca*

The ship's bell had just rung six times in the morning watch. The weather, hazy but dry, promised a fine day or so Pat thought as he contemplated yet another uneventful day: nothing of note had happened in the two weeks since *Surprise* had left Argostoli. He picked at his first breakfast. *Surprise* was a few miles off the east coast of Ithaca with a light and following north-westerly wind. 'Another week of cruising up and down this channel, Ithaca to Zante, Zante to Ithaca, ne'er any ship to be seen and I venture the crew may soon be minded to press us to join the enemy; the only vessel we have seen was that Greek mistico running the blockade yesterday. Much more of this to'ing and fro'ing and we shall ground on our own beef bones ere we ever see so much as a Turk... and no commission yet in hand neither. We are blighted by delay, infernal delay. I am sorely hipped,' an irritable Pat grumbled.

'What news from the captain of the mistico, brother? Ye hailed and spoke with him, I collect,' asked Duncan, reaching for the bacon dish; Pat, unusually, had not consumed much.

'Very rum developments if he can be believed. The captain said that he hailed from Hydra. The Albanian besiegers of Messalonghi have marched away... fearing to starve in the winter, no doubt. The Turk fleet has retired to beyond Patras and sits under the guns of the Little Dardanelles, hence the mistico running in daylight. The Greek fleet has plainly sailed, but the mistico is faster by perhaps a knot or two and will sail at all speed at night, accustomed as they are to running the blockade. The captain said the fleet was but an hour or two behind him as he passed Modon. I think I shall go on deck.' With that he took his Dolland glass and stepped up to his quarterdeck.

A half hour passed and the masthead lookout shouted, 'Sail ho! Two points off the larboard bow.'

Training his glass, Pat, his instincts sparked by the report, could see a brig followed closely by several more sail, too indistinct as yet to clearly make out, the morning mist persevering. 'Mr Pickering, maintain this course until we close and can see who is there. They are beating close-hauled into this north-westerly. It will surely be slow progress. Stand by to come about in good time, and then we will keep a parallel course,' added Pat, keen interest having replaced his prior lassitude.

The next half hour passed inexorably slowly in growing anticipation as *Surprise* closed on the approaching ships, Pat studying them closely with his glass. Puffs of smoke erupted from the leading ship and cannon fire could be heard. 'A Turk brig, I fancy. Pursued by four or five Greeks; brigs too, but smaller. Her captain is handling his ship well.' Pat murmured his commentary aloud, watching frequent course changes as the quarry sought to use her longer range guns to disable or rake her pursuers. 'Mr Macleod, we will wear ship,' Pat declared, reaching his decision. 'Bring her about and maintain our distance at two miles from them, not a cable less.'

The first lieutenant reiterated Pat's order and the crew with supreme efficacy brought *Surprise* gracefully on to her near reversed course. She, like the combatants, now required frequent tacking to make the slowest of progress into the wind. The Turk ship and her pursuers gradually approached as *Surprise* still sought to recover speed.

'Mr Macleod, we shall clear for action,' ordered Pat.

The sound of Clumsy Dalby's drum brought every member of the gun crews running to their stations, all gun ports opening. With the thunderous rumble of the carriages across the deck, their frenzied crews heaving with all their strength and sweating with their exertions, the long guns were swiftly run out on both sides of the ship and the men stood ready, a great sense of expectation prevailing.

'The Turk is being harried at every tack by two or three Greek brigs and her escape must be doubtful. Her captain is surely weighing his prospects at this very moment,' said Pat quietly to no one in particular but heard by all on his quarterdeck, Marston and Simon too, they having stepped up to see what was afoot.

The nearest Greek was on a converging course with *Surprise* and the distance closing quite rapidly, she having separated from the chasing pack. She was now no more than one mile off *Surprise's* starboard beam but presented no danger to the frigate, it being within *Surprise's* far more considerable fire power and range to maul or destroy the Greek brig before she could even engage.

'Steady, Mr Macleod, he wishes to see who we are; let us steer two points to leeward and do so without haste,' ordered Pat.

The Greek was now a mere half mile abeam of *Surprise*. Perhaps content with the identification of her as an English ship – her unauthorised colours flying prominently in the stiff wind – she turned away towards her compatriots, a mile or more ahead.

'Maintain course, Mr Prosser. Mr Macleod, I think we will see what is about over there,' said Pat, beginning to wonder where the end of this chase might lie. The Greeks lay between the Turk and the approach to Patras. The Turk was cut off with no prospect now of escape: she plainly could not outrun her Greek pursuers. The sound of cannon fire became louder, more frequent, more vigorous as *Surprise* gained slightly on the protracted skirmish.

'Set topgallants, Mr Macleod.' Pat stared with professional fascination through his glass. 'Look, the fox pursued by the hunt, I fancy, and no bolt hole available. The Turk is in a dreadful dilemma, quite damaged. Her trysail is shot away and her boom spar shattered. Look, she is steering for Ithaca now. I doubt that she will make the turn into the bay for the port afore the hounds close for the kill.' *Surprise* had closed a little and the action was no more than a mile ahead. 'The Turk is plainly finished now; she has turned away to leeward with no sea-room available to her. Her captain must be intent on beaching her to save sinking or capture.'

Another half hour passed. 'The Turk captain is a most determined fellow. Look, the brig has struck the rocks. The Greeks are standing off now and lowering boats... 'tis a flagrant breach of Ionian neutrality and doubtless there will be the devil to pay for someone. Mr Pickering, we will come about and approach no closer; stand down the gunners. Mr Prosser, set course for Messalonghi, if you will. I am set fair for my second breakfast; will you join me, Mr Macleod?' asked Pat.

'Certainly, sir, I would like it of all things, and I have a sure craving for a pot of tea this past hour. Would it be wise to approach Messalonghi in *Surprise* rather than in *Eleanor*, d'ye suppose?'

Pat wasted no time in thought, 'Whether or no, we are going. We have wasted far too much time, seen precious few Turks and I venture it will be as well to find Mavrocordato ere too many more weeks are gone.'

The tedium at the start of the day had now gone and the decisive Pat O'Connor of old was returning, Duncan thought. Some further hours elapsed with the crew remaining in a state of excitement, the officers scanning the horizon and Prosser bringing *Surprise* close to the approach to Messalonghi until he enquired of Pat, 'Shall we stand off, sir, and send our cutter to seek a pilot? I have not the least acquaintance with these shallows.'

'Never fear, Mr Prosser, I have Smyth's personal chart in the cabin; Barton shall fetch it, and we will be assured of safe passage. Smyth is a perfectionist you know,' declared Pat bouyantly.

Within the hour *Surprise* had threaded her way over the bar, through the outer islands and cast her anchor inside the lagoon, a mile or so off Messalonghi town. Pat was swiftly aboard his barge, and his immaculately dressed bargemen rowed him through the gentle chop to the distant shore. Some two hours later the Greek fleet followed them in, *Surprise* being surrounded by a dozen or more small brigs, no hostility in evidence. A tumultuous reception, which seemed to consist of the whole population of the town, had gathered to welcome their fleet. Firearms were discharging and even the odd cannon could be heard above the good-natured demonstration of the newly relieved residents. The besieging Ottoman army had departed some two weeks previously and now resupply by sea was once again at hand. The port captain, once he was eventually found, declared that there was no quarantine, unlike the Ionian Islands; no papers would be required, and Pat's crew were at liberty to come ashore – indeed would be welcomed, for assuredly there would be festivities and celebrations until the dawn.

'I think that we shall remain aboard *Surprise* until the morrow,' Pat declared after short consideration. 'It would not do to be here, the crew ashore and drunk, all kicking up Bob's a-dying were the Turks to return. No, we shall allow shore parties of no more than two score... but from tomorrow and for a few hours only. Let us return to *Surprise*.'

Supper was taken by the crew on deck, watching the distant lights and listening to the festivities of Messalonghi, every man wishing they were there, the celebrations continuing all night.

Thursday 11ᵗʰ December 1823   *Messalonghi Town*

It had been very late when Pat had finally turned in, and he was therefore most displeased to be roughly shaken awake shortly after first light by Duncan shouting directly into his ear, for that is how it seemed. 'Pat, wake up! Quickly now! Hurry, ye must

255

come on deck. Wake up! There is a great deal of commotion between the Greek ships. What it signifies we cannae tell.'

Throwing on his cape, Pat hastened up to the quarterdeck, Duncan trailing. 'Mr Pickering, what's afoot? Why am I shaken awake at this ungodly hour, pray tell?'

Pickering pointed towards the Greek ships. 'There seems to be some disturbance between the Greek brigs, sir. I think between the Hydriots and the Spezziots, even several have run out their guns and are hoisting anchors. Look there, sails unfurling now and the crew hauling on a kedge to swing her round. Will we beat to quarters?'

In an instant Pat decided, 'Yes, beat to quarters, but do not open our gun ports until we grasp what is happening here. We do not want any of the Greeks to see us as a threat. Murphy! Murphy, there!' Pat shouted down to Murphy, loitering below the steps to the quarterdeck and chattering to Old Pennington, all within Pat's earshot. 'Will we send down your hammock? Rouse up Freeman and ask him to bring coffee on deck!'

'Well, Jesus bejabers, the water ain't 'ot yet an' Freeman's bin grindin' the bleedin' beans this past half hour,' moaned Murphy, not loud enough for Pat to hear.

Pickering turned to Dalby, 'Dalby, beat to quarters.' The resonant beat swiftly brought bleary-eyed Surprises rushing up from below, slow-matches fetched lit from the galley, powder boys standing by their guns with reloads. Hammocks were hastily tied into the rigging with many loud curses from men who had but recently been watching the shore festivities before retiring late to their sleep.

'My glass, Murphy,' shouted Pat, grasping his coffee gratefully from his steward, Freeman not returned from the galley. He took a deep draught of a lukewarm, bitter liquid. 'Murphy!' he shouted to the fast receding steward, 'Did you find this vile stuff in the bilges? Toss it over the side and bring fresh.'

'Take my glass, sir,' proferred Pickering, 'Here.'

'Well, coffee first, rush, rush, glass next; to be sure, I'll be a'labourin' all bleedin' night afore long,' muttered Murphy, bearing away the coffee pot on its tray.

'Never fret when busy, Murphy, save it for when idle,' Pickering remarked as Murphy passed by.

'Thankee, Mr Pickering; an admirable notion indeed.' Pat peered through the glass with anxious curiosity. 'What on earth are they doing over there... anchors hauled up and sails unfurled with yards all ahoo? What do they know? Is there any news or sightings of Turk ships?'

'None, sir.'

Within a half hour there seemed a general awakening of all the Greek fleet; several had caught their wind, sails filling with a steady north-easterly off the land.

'Mr Codrington, you are to take *Eleanor* to the quay and see if you can determine what is happening. Mr Mower, take Mr Jason with you in my barge and approach one of those brigs still anchored. Hail and ask them for an explanation. Mr Macleod, let fall tops'ls and spanker, leave them slack; warp her bow round to the south and prepare to get underway.'

Murphy returned, holding out Pat's Magellan jacket. 'Well, put it on d'reckly, sorr,' he remonstrated, 'You'll catch your death.'

'Are we departing, sir? And what of our purpose here?' asked Duncan anxiously.

Pat had by now scrambled into his clothes, brought up by Murphy, ''Tis just a precaution. No ship has fired, though some have run out guns and are leaving so swiftly, sails and rigging all ahoo, that I wondered if they might even cut their cables, but no. It seemed for some minutes like hostilities were about to break out between the Hydriots and the Spezziots. Who is to know what is up? They are foreigners you know. Where is Mr Mower?'

'Over there, sir. He is aboard the near brig.'

Another half hour passed and the barge returned alongside, Mower and Jason swiftly scrambling aboard. Pat hastened towards them, anxious to ask their news. Mower revealed the startling story which Jason had gleaned from the captain of the Spezziot brig. 'It seems, sir, that the Hydriots captured a huge booty from the Turk which ran aground on Ithaca yesterday -

half a million of piastres. They have refused to share it with the Spezziots and are running away with the lot. The Spezziots are boiling with rage, as might be expected, hence guns being run out... though her captain said he doubted anyone would actually fire.'

'Such conduct cannot be considered amicable,' remarked an irritated Simon, who had appeared on the quarterdeck barely half dressed.

Pat looked up to the heavens and turned to his First, exasperation plain on his face, 'Tell me, lest I forget; these are the people we have come here to assist... running away with the prizes, with no fair distribution... readying to fire upon their brothers! What brings these people to such acts? Will we haul our cable and return to England directly with no more time wasted here? Stand down the crew, Mr Pickering. I shall take breakfast and then go ashore to see if there is anyone in charge of this house of Bedlam.'

With some exasperation and followed closely by Duncan, Pat stomped back into the cabin. Murphy was there before he arrived, and perceiving his ire announced in the meekest of tones, 'Well, Freeman has your breakfast ready, sorr.'

'Tell him to bring it in directly, Murphy; thankee,' replied Pat, tiredness returning to his voice.

Later in the town, the atmosphere remained highly charged; excitement at the fleet's arrival and their delivery from the Turk blockade was now mixed with consternation, the fleet having left in haste. Pat had gone ashore with a small landing party, and Codrington came striding briskly towards them along the quay, accompanied by Reeve and a Greek civilian, seemingly of some standing, he being surrounded by an entourage of a score or more civilians and militiamen, all cheerfully mingling with half a dozen Eleanors. A somewhat flustered Codrington brought the march to a halt in front of Pat. 'Captain O'Connor, sir. Will I introduce Mr - that is to say - *Prince* Mavrocordato?'

Pat could not have been more surprised had Nelson himself been introduced. The many months of waiting to meet this very man, weeks of surveying, more weeks of fruitless patrolling the

Ionian waters off the Greek coast, two successive days of beating to quarters and now the man was here himself, standing in front of Pat and Duncan. He was at first glance an unimpressive man in his early thirties with unkempt long black hair, a huge drooping moustache, slightly short, a little overweight and with thick lensed spectacles, though his companions exhibited considerable reverence towards his person.

'Your Maj... your Highness. It is an honour to make your acquaintance at long last,' Pat extemporised, much taken aback by such an unexpected development and inwardly floundering.

Duncan interjected to save his captain's embarrassment, 'Prince Mavrocordato... sir... Lieutenant Duncan Macleod at your service. I believe we have some business of a confidential nature to discuss. Will ye join Captain O'Connor and myself aboard our vessel, *Surprise*, so that we may engage with some confidence of privacy?'

'Captain O'Connor, Lieutenant Macleod, I would be honoured to visit your ship. Let us do so without delay,' replied Mavrocordato with a sigh. He gave instructions to his cohorts and turned back to face Pat, 'Captain O'Connor, would that I could have arrived in this place sooner. Alas, the wheels of Greek politics do not turn smoothly,' he sighed again, 'and the consequences are sometimes quite brutal... as perhaps you saw this morning. Let us away to our business before we are overtaken by other necessities... please, lead on.'

'Barton, help his Highness into the barge... and row dry back to the ship,' said Pat. His barge crew had mingled with the Eleanors, seeking further explanation of this evidently important Greek about to come aboard. A half hour later and back in the great cabin, coffee having been served and a brace of bottles of cooled Amontillado consumed - which his Highness seemed to favour -Freeman was sent away to seek something better than biscuit to offer their guest. Pat remained unsure of how to begin, and being no diplomat struggled to find a start, 'Your Highness, it is an honour to welcome you aboard His Maj... that is to say aboard our dear *Surprise*. We have passed the summer in these waters gaining but little understanding of the current political situation. You will readily understand therefore that we are most pleased that we now meet with you.'

'Captain O'Connor, the honour is all mine, sir. It is a very great pleasure to meet such a renowned naval officer. My aides have provided to me the most interesting of information, the quite exceptional account of your prior service in our waters and an account of your sinking of the Turk ship *Iskande*r. It is an exemplary record, doubtless of no equal.' Pat nodded politely and simply stared.

A slow but most cordial hour of pleasantries elapsed until Duncan could discern that Pat's reserves of patience and diplomacy, limited as they were even at the best of times, were being sorely tested. He brought matters to a head, 'If ye will permit me... your Highness will collect that Captain O'Connor and his ship arrived here in the Islands since some months past... and we remain anxious to assist your struggle for liberation... yet lacking any commission we are unable to engage withoot the most serious consequences. Indeed, a charge of piracy might well be levelled against us, were we to do so. Does your Highness possess the letter of marque that we understand has been prepared for our arrival?'

Mavrocordato peered genially over a pair of half-spectacles. 'Of course, Lieutenant Macleod; the letter is here with me, signed since some months by President Mavromichalis and by myself as Secretary of State, though it is an office I no longer hold.' Reaching inside his jacket the Prince removed and handed over the long awaited document to Pat, who grasped it eagerly; it was the long awaited key to their endeavours, an entirely legal start now possible. Mavrocordato continued, 'Perhaps you could study that at your convenience, sir, and if it proves acceptable then the Hellenic Republic will be pleased to consider that you are in her service. Sadly, as I am no longer Secretary of State and am come here only in the capacity of a simple volunteer, no changes can be made to the terms. However, the President has consulted closely with one of your compatriot officers in our service, one Captain Hastings, in preparing the letter. He therefore trusts that you will find it acceptable. My aide,

Monsieur Léli, will come to you in Cephalonia. He will tell you of our priorities and communications when you return there. Captain O'Connor, I must now go ashore else doubtless some other burden will accost us. Thank you for your interest in serving Greece, gentlemen; we are assuredly poor of funds but do not lack for appreciation of our friends.'

Pat gingerly placed the precious letter inside his table drawer, shook hands with the Prince and replied cautiously, 'Doubtless the letter will serve, your Highness. It is an honour to commence our service for your country.' Pat paused for a moment before resuming, 'My First here, Lieutenant Macleod, is particularly tasked by our Admiralty with facilitating communication between this ship and your naval colleagues. In the first instance, it is proposed by their Lordships that he shall pass some time with you to gain a familiarity with your procedures.'

'That will serve us well, Captain O'Connor. The Hellenic Republic is obliged to you.' They shook hands.

'My crew will set you both ashore. Good day, sir.'

Duncan hastened away for his sea chest as Pat escorted Mavrocordato to the ladder for the barge. Returning to his quarterdeck after they had disembarked – Duncan with time for only the briefest of farewells to his fellow officers before he departed – Pat stood there, sadness returning to his mind as he contemplated prior occasions when he had seen off one or the other of Duncan or Simon, but the feelings of loss and anxiety never relented. His attention was restored by Tom Pickering standing in front of him, enquiring of his intentions as the men at the helm looked across, patient enquiry written all over their faces. Pat pondered their new status: should he now hoist a Greek flag? Should he make any announcement? Instead, he simply murmured to Pickering, 'Take us out of this place, Mr Pickering. We will return to Argostoli. Keep a sharp watch for any ships, Turk or Greek.'

'Can you still see them, Mr Pickering?' asked Pat, rubbing his eyes.

'Aye sir, the mistico appears to be going ahead of the bombard, but 'tis now difficult to be sure with the light failing.'

'Let us pray this wind remains a favourable westerly,' Pat opined, straining his eye into his glass, searching for the two vessels, now near three miles distant and disappearing into the oncoming colder darkness of the night, it being near 10 p.m. 'Let us pray too that the Turk fleet stays at Patras Roads, for that is where it is said to be from our reports obtained in Zante. It is to be hoped that both vessels reach Messalonghi without interception and without any help from us. I would wish that the Turks did not yet know we had come to the aid of the Greeks, and so I prefer not to be sighted with them. That is why we shall keep our distance from the bombard and the mistico.'

'What are the Doctor and Mr Jason to do, sir, in their company?' enquired Pickering.

'Mr Jason is to translate... he speaks the Greek and the Turk; should his Lordship be accosted by either side. The Doctor is to aid Count Gamba similarly. Though he speaks nothing of either the Greek or the Turk, he will support the Count with his story that they are bound for Calamos. That is, should they be waylaid. Let us hope that will not be the case. We will shadow them, principally his Lordship, and interpose *Surprise* between them and any Turk that comes along seeking to stop them. That is, if we can stay in sight of them during the night. They are showing no lights whilst running the blockade,' said Pat, explaining his strategy, 'Will you double the watch men?'

'Aye aye, sir, that we will,' replied Pickering.

Just at that moment Freeman appeared. Since *Surprise* had left Falmouth he had assumed a right to tread Pat's quarterdeck, at least as long as he professed to be bearing any message or refreshment, a presumption that Pat had not thought fit to disabuse him of, the formalities of the whole voyage having become somewhat less than that which the strictest Royal Navy captain might have mandated. 'Stirabout he spoilt, massa, gone cold. You want fresh?'

It was a welcome reminder to Pat that he had quite forgotten his customary supper in the activity of the departure from Zante, plus the near sleepless crossing from Cephalonia having been made the night before, and Simon, his usual companion for supper, also having transferred to the bombard. In the close following of the two vessels for five or so hours since leaving Zante he had not shifted from his quarterdeck. 'Thankee Freeman, I will come to the cabin shortly. Supper will be most welcome... I am amazing short set. Mr Pickering, would you care to take some supper with me? Ask Mr Mower if he will join us too. Freeman, supper for three if you will... and look out a bottle of port from my stores; a bottle of the da Silva of the year 'fifteen would serve admirably,' said Pat pleasantly, continuing half in thought and half in speech to his lieutenant, 'Now there is an enterprising man. I met him in London one year, I collect it was in Black's... Bruno da Silva, would you know? He also had a letter of marque to arm his ship so as to more safely bring his wine to London. He kindly gave me a case of his port wine. I have always bought his wine since and ne'er opened a spoiled bottle. Come, let us go to the cabin; all this talk reminds me it is time to eat. Mr Prosser, you have the barky.'

Tuesday 30th December 1823, 5 a.m.   *aboard the bombard*

Simon and Gamba had remained on deck whilst the mistico, which was now lost from their sight, had been in close accompaniment. They had lingered for hours until going below to seek sleep as 3 a.m. approached and the wind freshened to a much colder northerly, progress near stopped. Now returned to near the wheel, Simon spoke to the captain, his voice carrying his worrying uncertainty in his words, 'Would it be uncivil, sir, to ask of your intentions, your expectations of our landfall?'

'Can we ask the wind of its intentions, Doctor Ferguson? I know not. These are difficult waters for the navigator... shoals and rocks all about us,' replied Captain Valsamarchi cautiously. He had declined to continue at best speed in the darkest hours despite the danger from Turk patrols, being concerned for the shallows, preferring to mark time and await first light. So after a cold supper of black bread and cheese with thin red wine, Simon and Gamba had sought uncomfortable sleep for two hours on a huddle of blankets of doubtful provenance. At five o'clock, in the first lightening of the emerging dawn and some small degree of better visibility welcomed by the captain, they had stirred, the motion of the vessel changing and awakening them as it gained speed. Simon gazed, shivering, at the grey and choppy waves, the wind now having shifted round to the customary north-easterly *Gregale* of those island waters.

'Pray tell, Captain; are we far now from Messalonghi?' asked Simon.

'We are approaching the Scrofes, the small islands and rocks outlying the lagoon. In several hours we will be in the anchorage some way off the town. The water will become very shallow soon for all the remaining distance from here to the town. Great care of navigation is now our foremost priority,' Valsamarchi replied, his cautious reservations plain in his voice as well as in his words.

5a.m. aboard the mistico

'Will you take tea with me, Jason?' Lord Byron asked. The two men had enjoyed the most cordial of conversation since losing sight of the bombard around midnight, the two crews having continued firing pistols and carbines for another half hour or so in a fruitless effort to maintain contact. The captain had shortened sail so that the following bombard, lagging a mile or more astern, might keep up with the faster mistico.

'That would be most welcome your Lordship, WAIT!' Jason exclaimed. 'Look there, look, over there, do you see it? A ship, larger than the bombard, I venture... just there.'

'Keep silent and do nothing,' ordered the captain, appearing beside them, great anxiety plain in his voice. 'It is a Turk frigate and he will be near alongside in a few minutes. We cannot escape him. Our only hope is to pretend we have not seen him for as long as that is credible... and hope we reach the shallows where he cannot follow. Keep silent if you value your life... and pray to your God.'

With a sinking feeling Jason could not take his gaze from the approaching frigate. Indeed the eyes of all were focused upon it, the mistico's crew urging every last half knot of speed from their vessel as they contemplated two very different destinies: which one would occur would be made plain in the next few minutes. The Turk frigate was plainly bent on their interception and fast approaching, sailing large, wind astern of her, a creaming bow-froth plainly visible as she swiftly closed.

5 a.m. aboard Surprise

'Sails ahoy! D'reckly off the starboard bow,' hailed the watchman atop the foremast.

Pat, astride his quarterdeck once more, peered long into his glass before shouting, 'Mr Mower, beat to quarters.' Pat bellowed his commands to all around him, the crew hastening up to the yards with alacrity, the alarm and urgency clear to all in his voice. 'Mr Mower, open gun ports and run out the guns! All crews to stand by their guns. We will leave our English jack flying for now, but prepare to hoist the Greek flag on my command.'

'What do you see, sir?' asked Tom Pickering.

'It is a Turk frigate, I venture, and closing on the mistico, perhaps a league between them,' Pat announced, looking again for a few minutes through his glass. 'The mistico will surely be struggling against this northerly, as are we to close on her. We cannot reach the mistico afore the Turk hauls alongside of her and takes them, but, God speed, we may yet distract him – if he has seen us. He is on a beam reach, a league and a half from us if he is a yard and barely one from the mistico, though he will be sailing with some southing too. It will take us three parts of an hour to close on him,' said Pat, the urgency diminishing in his voice as he had now calculated the likely time before any action could commence.

'Pray earnestly to your God, gentlemen, and keep still your silence,' reiterated the captain with a degree of despair. All aboard could no longer ignore the hailing from several crew on the quarterdeck of the Turk frigate, which had swiftly crossed their bow a bare fifty yards ahead, firing a gun to reinforce her command. The frigate had now turned and was running down the mistico's larboard side, perhaps only fifty yards away, the two vessels moving in opposite directions, angry faces visible on the Turk deck, as all aboard the mistico could not fail to notice. The Turk guns were run out and at such close range, were the frigate to fire, obliteration of the small mistico and all on board her could not fail to be the result.

'I do not understand why he is passing by close-hauled under full canvas with no notice of us,' said the captain to Jason. 'Perhaps he thinks us simply the stupid crew of a stinking fishing boat; we are not dissimilar in size and rig.' After a few more minutes he added, 'We are too close now to the rocks for him to come about, I pray we may be saved. Thank God... thank God.' The captain was breathing more easily, his relief so evident in his voice. The frigate had by now cleared their stern, though she loomed large still with her bulk and presence so close to them.

'Captain, will you now put us close into those rocks so he cannot possibly reach us again?' asked Lord Byron with the utmost concern in his voice. 'Never fear for any damage to your vessel for I shall guarantee you any necessary repairs.'

From the deep sigh of relief from the captain, no bidding or any guarantee was necessary at all; no slackening of sail or speed was made, but the little mistico seemed now so close to its destruction from a different means as the shallows were upon them. The captain, knowing the waters intimately and with a sure touch, ordered a swift series of course corrections to bring the vessel through between two islets and to safety from both the frigate and the rocks. 'We can go no further, the wind being so much against us now,' he declared. 'If the Turk so wishes, he may yet launch boats to capture us, and we can do nothing. We have but a very few sidearms and to use them would be folly, ensuring our certain execution after capture. We must await a change in the wind to continue to Messalonghi or we may beat for hours into this wind and sail for Dragomestre where we can at least take to the land and away from any Turk pursuit. What is your preference, sir?'

On this sobering note, Jason and Byron paused but briefly to consider their fate before Byron declared, 'To Dragomestre, Captain. We must not be apprehended. Let us proceed as best we may to that place.'

'Yes, my Lord,' nodded the captain, his own relief so evident.

5:30 a.m. aboard Surprise

'The Turk has seen us, Mr Pickering, and he has left the mistico alone. He is coming towards us with a full spread of canvas and at best speed. Another twenty minutes and we shall see his mettle,' said Pat, staring intently through his glass. Within the minute he added, 'No, he is slowing. I venture the light is good enough for him to see our colours, and I doubt that he would wish to challenge an English frigate, even as we are in their claimed territorial waters and off the through channel for the United Islands. I fancy the Turk will be no trouble. He is turning away... yes, he is going about and so does not fancy engaging with us.'

6:30 a.m. aboard the bombard

'Look, a sail over there, approaching off the starboard beam,' the captain announced, a little more buoyantly, to Gamba and Simon as they peered with straining eyes into the rising but low sun, just barely above the horizon. 'We are still some twelve miles out from Messalonghi... but the Turk fleet is said to be beyond Patras at Lepanto.... and I believe it will be a Greek warship sent out to ensure that the whereabouts of the Turks remain known. We are hoisting the United Ionian Islands flag. The topman reports he also saw another, a smaller vessel - perhaps our mistico - beyond the Scrofes islets some two leagues ahead.'

'May I borrow your glass, Captain?' asked Simon, being far less sure than the confident Greek captain. 'Thank you,' he added, taking the proffered glass, and after peering intently for a few moments he enquired mildly, 'Would I be correct, Captain, in thinking that a red pennant might signify a Turk?'

At which comment Captain Valsamarchi brusquely snatched back his glass and looked hard at the approaching ship, a frigate as could plainly now be seen and flying a Turk red flag at her mizzen. 'Hell and damnation!' he shouted - or the Greek equivalent, for that is how it sounded to Simon, no translation being necessary. The captain and his crew were stunned, in some disbelief that this was happening to them. The Turk fleet was supposedly shut in at Patras or even beyond the forts of the narrows, the Little Dardanelles as they were called, and at that moment they began to despair. Within what seemed like moments the frigate approached, turning swiftly into the wind to lose way and came near alongside.

'They are hailing us now,' said Gamba to Simon, gazing at him with the utmost attention and deep concern, 'What should we do?'

'Might I suggest, sir, that were you to have any papers of a confidential nature – confidential that is in the matter of his Lordship's intentions in the Morea and for Greece generally – aboard this vessel, that they would be better for his Lordship's and indeed our own interests and prospects were they consigned over the side... and with the benefit of a large leaden weight?' Simon replied in a measured tone.

'Of course, of course, I will do so immediately,' said a greatly agitated Gamba, and he rushed off in great anxiety to his berth to retrieve them.

'What can I say?' asked the captain of Simon. 'God help us! They will surely ask why we, flying an Ionian flag, are so far away from the Islands channel. What conceivable explanation have I to offer? We will be taken as blockade runners and likely put to death.'

Gamba now having returned and the revealing documents being clutched by his frightened servant on that side of the bombard which was opposite the Turk frigate, he whispered to Simon, 'My servant shall throw our papers - they are weighted - into the sea should any boat put off from the frigate.'

Just at that moment the Turk ship lowered a small boat. The servant panicked and threw everything into the water where all sank immediately from sight.

'My dear Gamba, do you have anything else of a conceivably incriminating nature?' asked Simon as the Turk boat drew alongside. The Greek captain was summoned into it without any of the pleasantries as are customary between navigators.

'Nothing,' replied Gamba with some relief.

'Then I will join the captain and go aboard the Turk vessel. We are merely en route for Calamo and have lost our way in the night,' said Simon with some measure of sang froid.

At that moment there was shouting from the Turk frigate and some pointing of hands to the south-west. All looked about, towards far and approaching sails in the direction of Zante. Simon could not be sure at this distance, no longer having the benefit of Captain Valsamarchi's glass, but he wondered if it could be *Surprise*, possibly with her consort, *Eleanor*, coming to their aid. The Turks were obviously becoming nervous, the shouting from their quarterdeck ever more shrill and strident. Simon hastened with alacrity to scramble down the net to join Captain Valsamarchi in the barge, and its crew rowed hastily across to the frigate. The Turk captain was shouting to his first officer, now taking charge on the bombard, to bring her behind the frigate and follow its lead. Within a few minutes both vessels were underway, heading north-east towards the Straits, beating slowly into the wind.

7 a.m.   aboard Surprise

'It is the bombard... alongside the same Turk frigate,' said Pat, his spirits sinking, the realisation that the bombard was captured hitting him particularly hard. He continued to peer through his glass, the morning light still weak, visibility poor. 'They are getting underway, towards Patras; the bombard is captured... and

Simon too. Mr Pickering, send to *Eleanor,* "follow *Surprise* closely, bombard and Turk together".'

Just then there was a shout from the foremast topman, 'Sails Ho! Two point off the starboard bow... six ships... seven.'

Pat swept his glass to the north-east, pausing to study the horizon for long moments before lowering his glass. 'By Jove, 'tis a whole fleet of ships,' he exclaimed, looking again through his glass as if to confirm what he knew he had seen, 'and plentiful frigates amongst them. It cannot be the Greeks. It is the Turks come out from their anchorage at Patras. I think we must leave the bombard to the Turk. Plainly we cannot prevail against such numbers. We must turn away.' This was declared in a tone of deep resignation. 'Well, that surely signifies our departure, gentlemen,' he added. 'Signal again to *Eleanor* "follow closely". Mr Pickering, Helm up! Let her go off! We will go west and away, back to Cephalonia. Home, gentlemen; we can do no more here this day and must await another time afore we try again for Messalonghi.' Pat ordered their turn away with considerable disappointment in his voice, tiredness creeping in after a second night of very little sleep.

7 a.m. aboard the Turk frigate

Simon sat alongside Captain Valsamarchi on the planks of the Turk deck, surrounded by towering, deeply hostile Turk sailors, angry faces prevalent. A frightened Captain Valsamarchi whispered to Simon, 'The Turk captain feared the mistico was a fireship and so left her alone when they espied an approaching ship of war behind it, coming so as to take off its crew when it became ablaze, and then we appeared and they became concerned that we too were another fireship, set to grapple with and consume them.'

'Are we in extreme peril?' asked Simon nervously.

Valsamarchi nodded towards a most ferocious Turk, speaking loudly with his captain who was holding his drawn sword and staring closely at them. 'There, that big fellow, he may be the second officer; he is urging the captain to cut off our heads and throw us over the side, and then to sink our vessel.'

'Oh, dear God,' exclaimed Simon, fearing the worst as the Turk captain stridently shouted something to the crew.

A great babble of vehement exchanges now took place amongst the Turk captain and his officers, Simon growing ever more anxious by each passing minute. Though he could understand only the barest smattering of the Turk language, the exchanges were so fast and furious that nothing could he comprehend, and so he looked with great anxiety to Valsamarchi for translation. The Turk captain, thankfully, appeared to be gaining control of the argument, his officers subsiding yet staring menacingly at their captives. Valsamarchi strained to hear whilst gazing unblinkingly at the Turk captain.

'Put them in irons,' bellowed the captain.

Valsamarchi translated for a very frightened Simon's benefit, adding in a whisper and with great uncertainty, 'The captain seems familiar to me.'

The captain himself had shown no such sign of recognition and shouted his question at them, asking if they were bound for Messalonghi. By now Simon and Valsamarchi were closely surrounded by a deeply hostile, gabbling crew, two of them clutching chains and close enough for Simon to smell their foetid breath, even to see a plethora of rotting teeth and to observe the hostility in their unwashed faces.

'Be not afraid,' advised Valsamarchi.

A bewildered Simon thought it advice of very doubtful validity for rarely had he been in such a perilous predicament, one which seemingly offered only the immediate prospect of chained confinement; perhaps even death was now close at hand. 'Your advice is doubtless kindly meant, sir, though you will understand why I find myself hesitant to accept it,' he whispered, fearful as another four Turk seamen approached closer with rattling chains, every one glaring viciously at them.

The next development was utterly astonishing to Simon: his companion stood up, the Turk seamen halting in their intentions, as taken aback as was Simon. Valsamarchi gulped, rose unsteadily to his full height, the Turks pausing, and then he addressed the Turk captain in a loud and confident voice, 'Will

Captain Zachiriá kill the man who saved his life, the man who saved his brother's life, who saved his crew from shipwreck in the Black Sea?'

The Turk captain started with indignation: that one of his miserable captives should address him was impudent in the extreme! He swivelled swiftly towards them and stared at Valsamarchi, intense curiosity now in his eyes, peering closely at Valsamarchi's face for some moments but saying nothing. Slowly a long minute passed before uncertainty flickered across the face of the Turk captain, and then in an instant a change of demeanour came about, anger giving way to curiosity, concern even. He stepped closer, no more than inches away from Valsamarchi, and said in the most fluent Greek, 'What? That cannot be. Is it you, Spiro?' The Turk captain dropped his still unsheathed sword to the deck, raised both his arms in the air and, without further hesitation, seized and embraced Valsamarchi tightly, as if meeting a returning brother – one long deemed lost, holding him close as if to prevent any second separation, for clearly that is how he felt. His demeanour displayed huge happiness, astonishment and joy, all of which was showing on his face, quite unconcealed; and then he stepped back a pace, grasped and shook Valsamarchi's hand vigorously for several minutes more, seemingly lost for words, both of them now smiling widely at each other. The crew, all tension relieved, relaxed immediately; indeed, they too, once the captain's story was understood, embraced his evident happiness, and the chains were removed from sight, all hostility ceased with this most unexpected turn of events. A very welcome turn, thought Simon, relief flooding through his every fibre. He marvelled at this swift reversal of fortune and stood staring at Valsamarchi and Zachiriá in a state of complete disbelief.

'Come Spiro, with your companion to my cabin. We shall have soup and coffee together, my friend,' declared Captain Zachiriá, his attitude so positively reversed from the frightening moments of their first minutes aboard the frigate. 'Captain Zachiriá, at your service sir,' he nodded to Simon when they were in the cabin.

'Please introduce me and thank the Captain for his attention, Captain Valsamarchi, if you will,' Simon replied, savouring every sip of the proffered Turkish coffee as if it were his last, but grateful relief now near superseded by a degree of restored normality in his voice.

For near an hour Valsamarchi and Zachiriá exchanged reminiscences of the intervening fifteen years since they had last met in extreme circumstances - so Simon gathered - before their conversation turned to recent times and their present situation. Zachiriá explained his particular fear of fireships, having been captain of the Turk admiral's flagship that had been engulfed by a Greek fireship at Chios in the previous year, and swimming from the burning ship to save his life, but the Admiral, Kara Ali Pasha, had lost his when struck by a falling, burning spar. A further hour passed as Valsamarchi and Zachiriá continued to reminisce, Simon content to allow his anxieties to further subside as he enjoyed the Turkish coffee, and then it was time for Zachiriá to return to his duties.

'We are to be taken to see the Admiral later. Zachiriá will vouch for us,' Valsamarchi explained. After Zachiriá had left them and returned to his deck, Valsamarchi concluded his scarcely credible story of how, at some risk to himself and his crew, he had rescued Captain Zachiriá, his brother and his crew from their sinking vessel some fifteen years beforehand. So long ago that mutual recognition had dimmed but had not, fortunately, been totally extinguished.

4 p.m. aboard the bombard at Patras

Under the close scrutiny of its captors the bombard had reached Patras, letting go her anchor alongside the Turk frigate amidst a Turk fleet of fourteen ships. The captain's barge came alongside the bombard and Gamba crossed to the frigate, summoned by Captain Zachiriá. On boarding he was greeted by a somewhat more relieved looking Captain Valsamarchi, waiting with Simon. Valsamarchi repeated his explanation of the recent turn of events for Gamba's benefit. Gamba listened without interruption until the end of Valsamarchi's story and he offered only, ''Tis strange but true, for truth is always strange, stranger than fiction. Verse fourteen of his Lordship's poem *Don Juan*, did you know?'

'Count Gamba,' Captain Zachiriá spoke sternly, 'your captain, Spiro Valsamarchi, has confessed that it is your intention to reach Messalonghi in contravention of the blockade. What say you?' This was translated by an Italian, Captain Francesco, in the service of the Turks as pilot at Patras.

'That is most certainly not the case, Captain. We are bound for Calamos and merely became lost in the dark of the night,' replied Gamba valiantly, glaring coldly at Francesco. 'What Valsamarchi has to say is of no worth whatsoever, for I have chartered his vessel for Calamos, as his papers will vouch, and therefore I must remonstrate against our detention and that of our vessel,'

Simon then interposed, shrewdly observing more than an intermediary's interest on the part of Francesco - perhaps a pecuniary one; perhaps too he was anticipating a goodly share of the prize, as the eight thousand dollars aboard the bombard had doubtless been discovered. He spoke very seriously, surprising himself with his calmness, 'Captain, respectfully... as one seafaring man to another and as personal physician to Lord Melville, His Majesty's First Lord of the Royal Navy, I appeal to your undoubted goodwill as a fellow navigator and to your considered observance of the appropriate diplomatic formalities. Our continued detention will not sit well with his Majesty's ministers at the Court of St. James's. It will no doubt bring the severest remonstrations to the Sublime Porte from his Majesty's ambassador in Constantinople. Will you care to consider of that?' Simon concluded, studying Zachiriá's reaction closely.

Captain Zachiriá was by no means an unintelligent man and the potentially dangerous implications for himself of his arrest of the vessel he readily perceived. He peered closely at Simon as if in assessment of this unkempt, unimpressive man before him, and his face broke into a great slow smile. 'Captain Valsamarchi's story was no doubt motivated by fear, Doctor Ferguson. By the grace of God and his Prophet Mahomet I have no doubt that the Admiral will release you and your vessel without delay.' This Zachiriá declared after but the briefest of thought – roundly sinking his interpreter's aspirations for a share of the booty, acceptance of that being visible to all in his countenance. Zachiriá continued, 'I am so sorry to detain you, and perhaps you would be so gracious as to complain to the Admiral of your capture at my hands, so far out beyond the Gulf, so far from the forts and many, many leagues beyond the line of blockade, for that will surely be well received on my return to Constantinople, the Greek warships being known to be in those waters. With God's grace and that of his Prophet Mahomet this recommendation will be worth a half million of piastres to me.'

'I will assuredly do so, Captain. Thank you kindly, sir,' replied Simon with great relief, contented by the success of his reference to his somewhat exaggerated credentials, as was Gamba who continued to glare at Francesco with deep hostility for the remaining time of the interview.

Captain Zachiriá continued affably, 'We must all be grateful to God and his Prophet this day, for they have granted me the opportunity to thank again the man that saved my life, Spiro Valsamarchi. He is a good man, and it pleases me that I can repay but a small portion of the debt I owe him. God in his benevolence has smiled upon us all this day.'

Simon permitted himself a wry smile and replied simply, 'I am of your way of thinking, Captain. All men have need of the Gods; and that, sir, is the opinion of a wiser man than us. Homer it was.'

The mood of the interview now being more cordial, Gamba picked up the bag he had brought across from the bombard. 'Captain, may I present you with my very modest gifts?' he said to Zachiriá, handing over a small cloth-wrapped bundle. 'Here are bottles of rum and porter, and a telescope. The latter may be of some use to you in your professional capacity as a seafarer and navigator.'

Zachiriá seemed genuinely pleased, particularly with the telescope, and after thanking Gamba he announced, 'Doctor Ferguson, Count Gamba... until tomorrow, when we shall meet the Grand Admiral, his Excellency the Pasha.'

Zachiriá shook their hands, and with that the interview was concluded, Simon and Gamba being escorted to the deck and taken by barge back to the bombard. When they were returned aboard and alone in Valsamarchi's cabin, Gamba seized Simon's hand and shook it with both his own, saying, 'A companion's words of persuasion are effective. That too is Homer, Doctor Ferguson. A most fine intervention; you have my thanks, sir. I am greatly in your debt.' His overwhelming feeling of relief was plain in his voice.

'Not at all, Gamba; though the Dear knows it is not a day I would care to repeat. Would there be any prospect of good coffee to be had on this vessel... and perhaps a tot of brandy? For medicinal purposes only; it will relax the fibres.'

'I will press Valsamarchi. Doubtless there will be brandy, perhaps coffee too.'

'And perhaps a final Homeric quote will serve us well this day?' Simon added, the tension within him near gone.

'By all means,' replied Gamba, curious.

'There is a time for many words and there is also a time for sleep,' said a deeply fatigued Simon.

Chapter Eleven

A king sat on the rocky brow
Which looks on sea-born Salamis;
And ships, by thousands, lay below,
And men in nations;---all were his!
He counted them at break of day---
And when the sun set, where were they?

Wednesday 31ˢᵗ December 1823   *Dragomestre port*

In the morning of the final day of the year, Lord Byron mused aloud about their predicament in a somewhat melancholy review, his words steeped in great sadness consequent to the loss of his friend. 'Jason, Gamba has been taken by the Turk frigate yesterday; that was plain to see. My horses are all lost and also some eight thousand dollars of mine all gone, but never mind, we have more left. We had a narrow escape last night, being so close under their stern... hailed even; and again this morning, the Turks perhaps searching further for us. But here we are, run away once more, with the sun and clearing weather, within a pretty little port; but whether the Turk may seek us again and send in their boats to seize us is another question, especially if we remain long here, since we are blocked out of Messalonghi by the direct entrance.'

Jason searched for some consolation. 'We are at least safe here from the Turks, my Lord. If necessary we can take to the hills and walk to Messalonghi should any of their vessels approach the port,' he offered, seeking to cheer Byron.

'No, such thoughts had occurred to me also. But the mountains are impassable... so the captain of the mistico has explained to me. So steep that land affords no road to reach Messalonghi; indeed, plentiful snow now abounds upon them and far below their summits... we see it here in the wind. There is too the matter of roaming brigands, Turk and Greek, twixt here and there. It is quite impossible, a desperate resort for us at best.

No, we must await Greek ships from Messalonghi to escort us ere we leave this place... and hope that they might arrive before any inquisitive Turks,' Lord Byron concluded a sobering assessment.

The Fort of the Morea, Patras

After hours of unsettled and anxious waiting Simon and Gamba were finally escorted to meet the Ottoman supreme commander and Governor of the Morea, Yusuf Pasha. The Pasha was lying on a sofa smoking a pipe and did not rise to greet them. With a wave of his hand he indicated to an adjacent sofa on which they were expected to be seated. Servants brought them strong Turkish coffee and pipes filled with mild but highly aromatic Turkish tobacco. As Simon enjoyed the coffee and Gamba smoked his pipe, the Pasha continued for several minutes to speak with his officers and counsellors seated around him before he turned to Gamba and Simon, when his minions' murmurings ebbed to silence. Smiling broadly he offered greetings – expressed in Turkish and translated into Greek by his secretary, Gamba translating into English for Simon's benefit - before asking them for an explanation of their incursion into the blockaded Greek waters.

Gamba reiterated his story as told to Zachiriá, adding his lamentations concerning the state of the Morea, 'Such turbulent times, Excellency; making the aspirations of the mere traveller utterly difficult. Bandits and brigands abound throughout the Greek provinces, particularly the Morea, and safety to be assured only within your Excellency's military oversight.' Gamba finished with a complaint about his capture by Zachiriá 'sailing brazenly alone and taking them so far beyond the line of blockade.' The Pasha, for the most part inscrutable and listening through his interpreter, nodded and appeared mollified with Gamba's additions, satisfied with his explanation and was seemingly pleased to hear of his captain's exploits.

After a brief pause the Pasha conversed again with his advisors before turning to Simon and asking, 'What does Sir Thomas Maitland think of the Greek brigands pursuing my corvette upon the rocks of neutral Ithaca and the slaughter of many of its crew including the captain, my nephew? What of the money lost which was onboard and which was to pay my troops? Will Maitland not seek revenge for such an outrage by those pirates?'

Slowly Simon stood up, the somewhat theatrical move allowing him a further few moments with which to formulate his reply. He addressed himself directly to the Pasha, speaking with conviction, 'My name is Ferguson, Excellency; physician to the First Lord, Lord Melville. Assuredly, Excellency, His Majesty's Governor, Sir Thomas Maitland...' Simon paused to let Gamba translate into Greek and the Pasha's secretary to translate into Turkish, '... deplores most strongly the incursion of the Greek pirate ships. Speaking personally and without the least authority... it seems likely that His Majesty, through the august offices of his Governor... will make recompense to your Excellency in due course.'

The Pasha nodded gravely, indicating his comprehension, seemingly satisfied with Simon's response, and declared, 'We will detain you no longer; your passports will be returned to you and you may continue your travels.' After an imperial wave of his hand in dismissal he turned again to his secretary to dictate his orders for their release. Gamba and Simon rose as one and thanked the Pasha, both offering a diplomatic bow before retiring from the room.

'My dear Doctor Ferguson,' said a very grateful Gamba when they were finally outside the Pasha's residence, 'you were most convincing in your statement, and well received it was too, but is such recompense likely to be forthcoming?'

'Oh, I have not the slightest idea, Gamba, yet it would not surprise me. The Governor, Maitland, is reputedly a man of the strictest demeanour and would doubtless have been outraged by the Greek incursion on his imperial coastal periphery. Such minds customarily tend towards rigour and rectitude. Some clever mechanism for recompense may likely emerge from it, given time. What do you say to a perambulation along the coast whilst we are here and awaiting our passports? The marshy nature of the landscape suggests we will find a goodly population of waders... and perhaps raptors too, I dare say.'

'By all means, Doctor Ferguson; I will bring a fowling piece, and I believe I still have a few bottles of porter,' Gamba replied, relief still evident in his voice.

Saturday 3rd January 1824   *Messalonghi*

Prince Mavrocordato was volubly grateful for the return of *Surprise*, the frigate having anchored that morning a mile off from Messalonghi in the nearest deep water anchorage. Some little way off were the five Spezziot brigs as had been there during *Surprise's* last visit, but of their crew very few were visible about their decks. Pat had gone ashore, rowed in his barge to the town, and they were seated in a small house in which Mavrocordato held court.

'Thank you most kindly for your valued escort of his Lordship from Cephalonia, Captain O'Connor. No doubt it was the appearance of your ship which drove off the Turk frigate, allowing Lord Byron to escape. I have word from my agents of the encounter. He is in Dragomestre, a small port along the coast to the north-west. I have sent a squadron of our gunboats and the brigantine *Leonidas* to fetch his lordship from that place. He will be quite safe in the waters behind the offshore islands. I have asked our fleet to go to sea to find the Turk fleet so that no similar and untoward event can recur. The Turk frigate with Dr Ferguson is gone to Patras. The English consul there, Mr Green, will doubtless make representations for his release. Come, I would speak with you about our situation in the Morea and also in Candia, where the assistance of your own frigate will now be so beneficial.'

'May I ask, sir, where is the rest of your fleet, the ships that captured the Turk brig on the shore of Ithaca?' asked Pat.

'Sadly, the Hydriots with their nine ships have gone home to Hydra, their month of pay from the government having run out and Lord Byron having declined to provide funds for further months to such mercenary crews. The five Spezziot crews are also ashore for want of pay. Lord Byron possesses of an understandable, if not wholly accurate perception of our mariners, I fear. Whilst it is true that they will not sail without pay in advance, such pay is certainly meagre, and they do not hesitate to place their lives at risk in the service of our embryonic state... though doubtless the prospect of prizes is not entirely absent from their considerations. The Pasha has already called upon the Ionian government for compensation for his loss of half a million of piastres; in turn the Ionian government has called upon ours, but there is nothing to be done. There is no money, and even were there money to be found doubtless it would never be paid over to the Turks. No, we are now indeed in bad grace with the Ionian government, and the money seized from the Pasha's brig all gone to Hydra. The Spezziot crews, when their Hydriot compatriots departed, left their five ships anchored out there and came ashore, refusing to continue to serve without further pay being received. My own interventions between them may have prevented a worse debacle, one which would have been to the lasting shame of all Greeks. I find I am now appointed head of the provincial government here and no longer am I a simple volunteer. Our resources remain meagre, our equipment but little, troops few and money nil. This is common knowledge and will certainly find your ear during your stay. I hope that you will not be so dismayed as to leave us too, Captain O'Connor?'

'Your Highness, we are presently well equipped and want for nothing other than direction,' Pat replied, more positively than he felt at that moment, the loss of Simon, for that is how it seemed, weighing heavy on his spirits. 'My jack tars waited for many months, a year or more for their pay when fighting Boney; a bare few months late is of little moment to them. Now that we have our letter of marque and can begin seeking Turk prizes our prospects will doubtless change for the better.'

'Thank you, that is most heartening. We await the arrival of Lord Byron, which will assuredly change our circumstances here in Messalonghi for the better, and I believe will be so very favourable for all of Greece.' Mavrocordato continued, 'However our situation in Candia is far from favourable, deteriorating in fact, and I have been asked by my government to convey to you the ever more urgent need for succour for our forces there, so very severely oppressed by the Turks. We are at our last throw on the island, men and arms dwindling. One more victory for Hussein Pasha there and we are done for. In the matter of interdiction of Turk resupply ships, your frigate could be most profitably engaged. Our commander in Candia is also a Hydriote, Manolis Tombazes, and he has but recently been sore pressed by plentiful Turk reinforcement. It is conceivable that in some very few weeks to come he may require to evacuate his remaining combatants from the island. In this too your ship will be invaluable. Will you therefore, Captain O'Connor, accept our direction for your service as guard ship here until our need becomes greater in Candia, when you will sail to help us there? It will give me grave concern to lose your frigate from here, where it may serve the protection of Messalonghi, our own fleet having left us and the Turk squadron still here in Patras, but the needs of our compatriots in Candia may become more urgent still.'

'We will replenish our water tomorrow, your Highness, and with that we may stand ready to depart on your order for Candia without delay. Are you able to gain any news of Doctor Ferguson and Count Gamba through your sources in Patras?' Pat asked, a little anxiously.

'My agents will bring news within a very few days, Captain. Of that you can be assured,' replied Mavrocordato as positively as he could put it.

Outside and once again at the quay, a disconsolate Pat stood in the pale winter sunlight, the warmth of the day ebbing with the onset of the early evening and a cooling easterly wind coming off the hills. The prospects for Simon, captured and helpless in the fiercely hostile midst of the plainly untrustworthy foreigners, filled his mind with a chilling dread. He contemplated his immediate plan, standing silently and looking rather distantly across to *Surprise,* moored a mile off in the lagoon, staring vacantly at nothing in particular, his small band of shipmates standing ready about him.

A few more minutes passed by, Pat still absorbed in his private deliberations, until he became aware of his men staring at him when his attention returned to them. 'Mr Pickering, we will allow a rota for crew leave ashore this evening. Not less than half the crew to remain aboard *Surprise* in case of any eventuality. Tomorrow after church we will water the ship, my barge to be used to carry our barrels to and fro. Barton, look about for a clean water supply. I believe I will return to the barky,' Pat concluded.

With half of his crew and officers ashore in Messalonghi, their leave reinforcing Pat's painful awareness of the absence of his close friend, it was all Freeman could do to try to bring some cheer to his captain's gloomy face by ensuring the very first quality of his toad in a hole for supper. He was accompanied by Murphy, bearing a bottle of the finest red that Pat had ever had in his stores, a Romanée-Conti burgundy of 1817, supplies of which in only the tiniest quantities had become available after the demise of Bonaparte. It was a bottle long previously secreted away by Murphy, who had wholly unfounded pretensions of wine knowledge but more real aspirations of usurping Freeman's role as butler, the bottle put by for no reason other than his vague and indiscernible feeling that some prime reason would come up. Murphy was sadly disappointed, the savoury aroma of the freshly cooked toad in a hole and the taste of the exceptional red being scarcely noticed, producing no more than a grunt from Pat who was seated at his table studying his Admiralty charts of the Aegean.

Murphy persevered, 'Well, sorr, now your supper will be a'ruined if it ain't eaten up hot.' This producing no response from Pat he added, 'Mr Marston is asking of you, and would you care to see him in the cabin this evening?' adding almost as an afterthought, 'sorr.'

The question broke Pat's train of thought. He seemed to welcome the disturbance of his morose mood and looked up, 'Why yes, thankee Murphy; please pass my compliments to Mr Marston, and if he should care for a little music I am at his service. Freeman, could you kindly bring extra toad in a hole and a glass for him? This is a prime wine, Murphy,' said Pat, noticing the bottle for the first time. 'I collect that you said we had none left. Was it in Gibraltar... or in Mahon?'

'Well, it was in the wrong case, in with the claret,' Murphy explained unconvincingly. 'The extra toad in a hole and glass will be here d'reckly... sorr.' Murphy hastened away before he could be asked further questions by his grumpy captain.

'Ah, Mr Marston, there you are, come in. Please, take a seat, over there near the window; we have still a little light. You have brought your violin... excellent.' Freeman bustled in and set down the glass and toad in a hole for Marston, Murphy hovering at his elbow with cutlery and napkin. 'Allow me to pour you a glass of this most excellent burgundy, perhaps near my last one. We are certainly favoured to enjoy it,' said Pat, his voice flat, toneless, even despairing

'Thank you, sir, most kind,' Marston was now extremely anxious, wondering if he might somehow stand in bad grace with his captain. He took a large gulp, 'An excellent wine. Never have I tasted better.' A sideways glance afforded him the impression that his captain, who was pacing slowly and repetitively up and down the cabin, was far from contented.

'Murphy there, we will have this bottle's fellow to follow, if you will.' Pat turned to look at his guest, and Marston could plainly see Pat's face betraying his unhappiness.

'Sir, should it be even the smallest concern, I feel sure that the sick bay presents no difficulties at all until such time as Doctor Ferguson returns,' offered Marston, perceiving that his captain looked greatly worried, depressed even. Pat remained silent.

'Well, this is the last one,' declared a bouyant Murphy, returning within a few minutes and triumphantly clutching the famous burgundy.

'Thankee, Murphy. Mr Marston, please, the toad in a hole is cooling. This surely is the very finest of wines. You will allow me to refill your glass,' Pat was striving to brighten, to observe the civilities. 'Now, what would you care to play, as we lack our viola?'

'Perhaps a little *Vivaldi* might bring some cheering warmth to our playing, sir? What do you say to the *Four Seasons*? I have oft heard it played in this cabin. *La Primavera*, if you will?'

'An excellent choice, Mr Marston; Dr Ferguson and I do enjoy playing that most wonderful first movement. Why 'tis not more popular these days is a mystery to us all.' With a determined effort to entertain his visitor, the toad in a hole and burgundy having been enjoyed by both of them, Pat set to with his 'cello, but he played diffidently for half an hour before setting it down on his knee and looking across towards Marston. His guest had winced at Pat's sometimes flat and occasionally shrill notes, had become uneasy, but held his tongue; no words were necessary: it was plain that Pat's heart was not in his playing. Marston had patiently held in check his observations of Pat's errors, his captain's gloomy mood so evident despite his best efforts to play and to entertain his visitor, and so the chaplain had doggedly persevered, he much wishing to cheer his captain, but all to no avail. Pat sat quite still, his 'cello on his lap, his face devoid of any expression, his indeterminate gaze void of any focus, his clenched fist slowly and repeatedly tapping on his chair leg.

'Captain O'Connor, it pains me that you may consider me to be presumptuous, yet I find my observations and leanings... that is to say my inclination in our Lord's service necessitates my enquiry. Pray tell, sir, if you are not equal to company... are you well?' asked Marston gently.

'There is no need like the lack of a friend,' whispered Pat with something akin to despair in his voice.

Marston became aware of a growing, perhaps necessary shift in his own position, from shipmate to chaplain. 'Perhaps, sir, I should leave you alone to your thoughts...' said Marston very quietly, '... or could I be of some small service to you at this hour of... of distress? I have some little experience in my capacity as a man of God in... in such difficult times. Pray forgive me if I presume too much.'

'Why, Mr Marston, I believe that you may.' Pat looked up and peered closely at his companion. He whispered his explanation, 'I am tolerably uncomfortable since Simon was taken by the Turks. We have served together since the year 'three, and I have loved that man as a brother for so long, more than twenty years, that I can scarcely believe what my life would be like were he never to play his viola again in this cabin. I have fought in many a battle, lost many a fellow crew member, yet never have I felt such a loss, no, let us say a *potential* loss so personally. Some months ago... you may collect... my new cox'n, Barton, joined us, and he reminded me so powerfully of our loss of his brother in the year 'thirteen. So many years have passed by since then yet he is oft still in my thoughts.'

Marston looked into his captain's troubled face for long moments before replying, summoning every vestige of the authority he considered vested within him by his calling into his voice, 'It is surely a great compliment to you, sir, that in all your years at sea and... and doubtless other men having been lost serving with you that you have retained your compassion for your fellow man. Your humanity is plainly preserved, as all can see, and no one could ask more than that. Though doubtless at such times it surely seems a heavy burden.'

'Scores, perhaps a hundred or more men have been lost on those vessels I have commanded, Mr Marston. It is indeed a burden I am oft reminded of. A sleepless night and some of them are there... in and out of my dreams. Old comrades such as Brannan Barton often... and others that are too many to remember; even many of their names I regret I cannot recall.'

'Sir, your mind is doubtless much disturbed by the thought of the possibility, *the mere possibility* that you may lose more men in this venture. You have gained many victories in His Majesty's service. No more celebrated captain ever commanded any English ship, even Nelson included – I doubt that anyone would dispute that – and thanks to you are we not so very much safer in our English homeland - Bonaparte's invasion never having departed? Do we not sleep safer in our beds, surely so?'

'I would never wish to boast away about my own service, Mr Marston, but there are times when I contemplate whether 'tis finally time to tie up for good, the end of my sea-going days, a life ashore. No more loyal and good men would I lose,' Pat stopped, the strain and distress so evident in his ashen face, and he looked to Marston.

It was the prospect of Simon being lost forever that had brought this despair pressing to the forefront of his captain's mind, Marston realised, and he replied softly but with firm conviction in his voice, 'Captain O'Connor, you are to consider that Doctor Ferguson has not been killed in conflict. He was not injured nor taken in the heat of battle. He is reportedly now in the custody of the most senior officials of the Turk regime in Patras, officials who will certainly accept their diplomatic responsibilities and the requests of British consular officials to see him. He will stand well with the protection of his British passport and the standing of his companion, Count Gamba. I think therefore, sir, that we may safely place our confidence for his well-being and ultimate return in diplomatic conventions.' Marston looked at a still silent Pat O'Connor and persevered, 'We may most assuredly also place our confidence in our Lord. Let us take comfort in the words of psalm thirty... *Weeping may endure for a night, but joy cometh in the morning.* Doubtless soon we will have news of Doctor Ferguson,' Marston concluded.

Pat looked up directly at Marston with an affinity he had never formerly felt for him and said quietly, 'I would never have countenanced a chaplain aboard any of my ships but for the persuasion of Doctor Ferguson. It is he that we both have to thank for you being here. I thank you most kindly, Mr Marston.' It was all that he felt able to say, but he rose to his feet, seized and shook Marston's hand with an iron grip, a further half minute passing and Pat still holding it firm. 'Thank you... you have been most kind... listening to the dreary woes of an old salt... I take comfort from what you have said. Please excuse me, I find my mind ails me; I believe I must retire. I bid you good night.'

Sunday 4ᵗʰ January 1824   *aboard Surprise, Messalonghi*

'Good morning, Murphy, Freeman,' said Pat in pleasant surprise, gazing at the silver tray as his breakfast was brought in by his stewards, the burden a plethora of fried bacon, eggs, mushrooms, tomatoes and toast. Murphy laid cutlery and napkins.

'Well, it is, to be sure, sorr,' said Murphy before Freeman could speak and noticing his captain's tone of approval, a change very much for the better in comparison with the prior evening.

'Pass the word for Mr Pickering and Mr Marston. I will inspect divisions at four bells and we will rig church for six bells,' Pat ordered, 'and Murphy, be so good as to check our stocks in case of any further bottles stored in the wrong cases.' This he added in the lightest of stern tones, the merest hint of a smile on his face.

'Aye aye, sorr, d'reckly,' replied Murphy, his spirits lifting as he felt the improvement in his captain's mood.

At divisions many a thick head was evident, the crew having enjoyed a very rare run ashore in the prior evening amidst the best that Messalonghi had to offer. Yet all were present, which was testimony enough to Pat that he had a prime crew, not a pressed man amongst them. He doubted that any of them would have been other than volunteers even were the press still to be a recruiting force. 'The Press,' he mused, 'where would his Majesty's fleet have been without it?' And yet on his own ships during the war he seldom employed pressed men. *Tenedos* in particular had long been known as a happy ship and its crew favoured with plentiful prizes; prizes which had substantially enriched those crew from Falmouth and indeed the town generally. 'Dalby, have you had a fall?' asked Pat, looking at a very swollen black eye and heavily bruised cheek. 'What have you to say for yourself?'

'Climbing back on deck, sir,' replied Clumsy Dalby, a fiction no one aboard believed, least of all Pat, knowing Dalby's temperament well of old. 'Hmmm,' said Pat, moving on.

'Mr Tizard, are you with us fully this morning?' asked Pat, the ship's carpenter favoured with his title as a non-commissioned officer as was his rightful due, but seemingly striving with some little difficulty to appear fully awake. Pat did not wait for his reply, but passed on to the crew of *Axeman,* all of whom seemed considerably worse for wear. 'Hartley, Johnston.

Do I see you both Bristol fashion this morning?' asked Pat pleasantly, although to everyone the answer could hardly be in the affirmative.

''Twas the ouzo brandy, sir; they said it should be drunk with plentiful water, but Barton said the water supply wasn't greatly clean... so we left it out,' explained an amiable but somewhat emboldened Hartley, obviously to all still suffering from the ouzo.

'I see,' said Pat, concealing his smile as best he could. 'Perhaps you need to see the Doc...' Pat's words tailed off as the recollection of Simon's absence returned to him.

Hartley, with surprising mental agility, quickly redeemed himself, replying with conviction, 'As soon as he is aboard, sir.'

It was a consoling belief that Pat clung to in his thoughts during the remainder of his inspection, much abbreviated due to the evident fatigue of his crew. 'Very good, Mr Pickering,' said Pat when he had finished although "very good" it would most certainly not have been described as by any of his peer captains during the French war. Pat had more important things on his mind, and their status as a letter-of-marque had slowly changed his perceptions of what was strictly *de rigeur* aboard *Surprise*. The long layoff since his command of *Tenedos* had, to his own reluctant admission, taken the edge off even his own demands of his crew, but not his expectations, his confidence in his men being diminished not one jot. 'Mr Marston, we will hold church a little earlier this morning if you will,' said Pat, the ship's bell striking five bells. *Surprise* held steady in the very mildest of swell, hardly a breath of wind evident, and the sails, left hanging in case of any urgent necessity to shift, hung loosely from the yards, but still the sharpest of eyes remained at the tops, gazing seawards. The morning was warming with the sun's progression towards noon and remained dry with not a cloud in sight except over the far peaks of the Morea to the south.

'Are you ready, Mr Marston?' prompted Pat, the crew assembled, a degree of disinterest visible on many a face.

'I am quite ready, sir.' Marston stepped forward to the sea-chest customarily used as the pulpit on the deck. He began the service with the reading of the Covenant prayer, '*Christ has many services to be done. Some are easy, others are difficult. Some bring honour, others bring reproach. Some are suitable to our natural inclinations and temporal interests, others are contrary to both. Yet the power to do all these things is given to us in Christ, who strengthens us. I am no longer my own but yours...*' Marston paused, a heavy spell of coughing from several men breaking his train of thought. A glare from Pat towards the offenders and the chaplain resumed, '*Put me to what you will, rank me with whom you will; put me to doing, put me to suffering; let me be employed for you or laid aside for you, exalted for you or brought low for you; let me be full, let me be empty, let me have all things, let me have nothing; I freely and wholeheartedly yield all things to your pleasure and disposal.*' He concluded by calling on the crew to join him in a hymn, thinking that perhaps the more jaded of them might be revived by the singing, but plainly this was not the case – as was evident by the many for whom song remained beyond their powers this morning after the prior evening's indulgences – and so he moved swiftly with no urging from Pat to the last piece of the service, his oration. His reference as he commenced to their missing shipmate, the Doctor, did bring about a resurgence of concentration and a shuffling of feet, the torpor sloughing off the grossly indulgent of the prior evening. It was a change that was particularly noticed by Pat, now listening intently to his chaplain. Marston swiftly moved on to his conclusion, one on which he had determined as most appropriate to his captain's mind after Pat's confiding in him of the prior evening, 'I will finish our service this morning with the very shortest of quotations, words from psalm one hundred and twenty-one... *I will lift up mine eyes unto the hills, from whence cometh my help. My help cometh from the Lord, which made heaven and earth...*' Marston paused again, annoyed, looking up from his bible as a widespread murmuring became evident within his audience.

Before Marston could utter a further word there came a loud shout from the lookout on the main mast, 'Ship ahoy, larboard beam.' Instantly all eyes stared directly out to sea.

'Murphy, quickly now, my glass!' shouted Pat.

'It is a small ship, sir, shifting very slowly against the north wind – well, the breeze – hardly any way on her at all, and it may take her some hours yet to get in,' said Pickering.

Murphy returned with the glass and Pat continued to study the approaching ship very carefully and for some minutes, it being barely visible amidst the haze and the sparkling light refractions over the water. Clarity improved steadily as she gained a mile in the next hour, all aboard *Surprise* gazing at her approach, Marston's service quite forgotten.

'My God, could it be? Could it be? It is the bombard, it is Gamba's bombard!' shouted Pat to Tom Pickering standing alongside him, and quite uncharacteristically slapping him on the back, great joy and excitement welling within him. 'Barton, go aloft! Quickly now, signal to her,' Pat ordered his cox'n.

'Aye aye, sir,' replied an excited Barton, the lingering effects of the prior night falling away in an instant, and he clambered up the ratlines at a speed never exceeded by the fastest of the young midshipmen of all Pat's prior commands. Another half hour passed but no reply came from the approaching ship in response to Barton's signals. Apart from the men aloft, all aboard *Surprise* were now leaning on the larboard hammock netting and staring intently at the distant vessel, still moving very slowly, tacking every twenty minutes or so to make any headway at all, but closing inexorably.

'I think we can be sure she is the bombard, sir,' said Pickering with growing conviction. The ship was now not more than two miles off and her hull form and sails becoming ever clearer. A great hubbub of excitement was growing amongst the crew on the deck, preparations for dinner quite forgotten, the cook indignant as he emerged from below but soon taken up in the suspense and anticipation, the dinner burning and remaining quite ignored by all as it ruined in the galley as a further hour passed. The bombard, for all were now sure that was what she was, was now barely a mile away and all could perceive two waving figures on her prow, identities still obscured. The effects of the haze were now considerably diminished, the sun higher and the late morning much warmer. Pat studied the ship with his glass, tears beginning to well from his eyes as it became clear that Simon was one of the two figures waving back vigorously.

''Tis he, the Doctor; Mr Pickering, Mr Marston, 'tis Simon... and Gamba, returned to us. Thank God... thank God, Mr Marston,' Pat pronounced, wiping his eyes on his shirt sleeve as unobtrusively as he could, thinking perhaps it was not good form for his crew to see their captain shedding tears. But all were looking away towards the bombard, cheering and waving frantically, shouting and laughing, pointing towards the returnee, joy endemic to all.

Another half hour and the bombard came near alongside *Surprise*; her anchor let go and her jollyboat was lowered. Simon, together with Gamba, was rowed across to *Surprise*, willing and jubilant hands swiftly hauling them up the accommodation ladder without ceremony, Pat standing close by. Royal Navy convention quite forgotten, the crew pressed forward to greet Simon, who staggered under the onslaught of much backslapping whilst edging slowly through the throng towards Pat, smiling at all and greeting many with a handshake. 'Good day, shipmates. I am most sensible of this prodigious fine welcome.'

Without any ado Pat embraced his friend in both arms, hugging him fiercely, finding himself quite unable to speak, and finding too that it was impossible to halt the tears of relief that streamed down his face, a flood-tide of joy, now quite unashamedly visible to all. The ensemble of Pat and Simon shuffled through the impromptu crew assembly with the aid of Pat's officers clearing a passage towards the cabin. Pickering and Marston led Gamba down to the gunroom, rightly perceiving that Pat would wish some time to speak with Simon alone. After several minutes of pushing through their jubilant throng of shipmates, Pat was able to close the great cabin door behind them, their ears ringing with the cheers of the crew behind them still. Not a one had taken the slightest notice of Mower's calls for 'Silence! Silence there!' half-hearted that they were. On deck, the ship's officers now swiftly brought to an end all pretence that the crew inspection was "very good" and a series of commands were barked out by Mower to the still excited crew, half going below for a belated and ruined dinner whilst the others were pressed to a myriad of ship housekeeping tasks which they minded not the least.

'Simon,' said Pat, seizing his friend's hand. That the single word was all that a moved Pat O'Connor could utter and that he was overwhelmed was plain for Simon to see.

'Pat, oh you are a good hearted soul. Stand firm, brother,' said Simon gently.

Pat had now recovered his composure, but still could find no words and simply stood there, gripping Simon's hand in a vice-like embrace, his strength overwhelming any intention Simon may have had to step back. A near minute more passed, Pat searching for the right words to greet his friend, until the status quo was broken by the voice of Murphy, insistent and whining in its usual tone but cheering and warming too by its very familiarity.

'Well, there is one last bottle been found o' that Roman burgundy, sorr, and will dinner now be convenient?'

'That exquisite elixir? The seventeen? Murphy, you are a fine fellow. That is exceedingly handsome in you,' remarked Simon.

'Yes, yes, Murphy, thankee,' croaked Pat, finding his voice at last. 'I rejoice to see you, Simon. You look quite famished. Come straight to my table; I have asked Wilkins to cook the best he has in his store, and a glass or two of good wine will answer the case.'

'And I am so pleased to see you again, Pat; for a moment after we were taken I thought my time had come. The Turk crew were as hostile as could be.'

They settled at Pat's table and Freeman arrived within a very few minutes with a steaming dish of swordfish soup and fresh baked bread – normally a rare delicacy, but the proximity to Argostoli affording Wilkins welcome scope - and flour - to practice his art.

'Please, Simon, eat up, you look fair clemmed.'

'Thank you, Pat; rations, though edible at best, have been short and infrequent these past days. At many a meal did I have a hankering for some morsel more nearly resembling food. Though perhaps we are too accustomed to our good fare in these recent times?'

Pat smiled, his customary good spirit returning, and he refilled their glasses. 'I collect the County Clare in that dreadful year 'seventeen. A visit to the Burren to see old acquaintances, no food to be found, nor a potato to be had anywhere... Mrs O'Rafferty's cow killed, nothing to feed it... and her son leaving the land for America, for Boston. Lord, we are well blessed these days, to be sure... though I do not need to tell you that. Here, we have nothing finer on this ship, drink the last bottle with me. I can think of no better occasion.'

Between mouthfuls of bread and spoonfuls of soup Simon recounted the story of his capture and subsequent release. A smiling Freeman brought a huge dish of stewed boar, cooked with plentiful bacon and mushrooms, and accompanied by a mound of steaming rice. Simon resumed his tale between gorging on the food. One incongruous but seemingly important recollection of Simon's which bemused Pat was his days before release studying the wading birds of the coastal marshes: herons, plovers, cormorants and many others being mentioned, and raptors too, including harriers, ospreys and eagles of several variants. It all passed over Pat; he merely nodded with pleasure, spoke but little and contented himself with refilling their glasses, his returned friend's presence giving him immense pleasure, and he called to Freeman for several more bottles as they enjoyed their reunion dinner together.

'We departed at 4 a.m.,' said Simon, 'unfavourable winds held us back until then, and even whilst we sailed they were scarcely less of an impediment. We had waited with a deal of anxiety for our passports as ships arrived from Cephalonia, fearing that Turk agents might speak with the Pasha of our intentions to go to Messalonghi and assist the Greeks; hence, fearing too that we might be detained further; but what news of Lord Byron and Abel Jason?'

'Safely hereabouts... along the coast, and they will be with us presently,' said Pat. 'Pray tell, have you considered further of the Turk fleet?'

Simon hesitated, the question not one for his personal province he thought, a little perplexed. 'Not as often as I might or perhaps should have done,' he replied cautiously.

'But what Turk ships did you see in their squadron whilst you were there? Did you count frigates, brigs and the like?' Pat raised his voice in emphasis.

'I did not. I am ashamed to say such enquiry was far from my mind, brother,' Simon replied. 'I dare say there were a score or more, all with several masts, guns aplenty and the associated plethora of sails and nautical accoutrements so familiar to you mariners. Mind, it was only a general impression; I do not commit myself to the precise number. As to what form of vessels they were, that I cannot say. Doubtless there were both frigates and brigs. Shall we say a half-dozen of each? Let us not split hairs for all love, Pat.'

'Simon, 'tis a matter of some interest for our prospects.'

'I dare say, but I never paid it any attention.'

'Can you remember of the number of vessels at least?'

'I should have to consider of it.'

'Pray do, if you will.'

'The Pasha asked me of the prospects for compensation from Maitland for the very considerable specie wrecked on his coast and stolen by the Greeks, and 'twas only the mention of Melville as my patron - that is to say in a medical capacity - which secured our release. That seems sure to me.'

'Lord, what a fellow you are,' Pat smiled cheerfully.

Tom Pickering looked in to announce that Gamba had gone ashore in the barge, and took the moment to shake Simon's hand again. Two pints of coffee followed their dinner until they simply sat back in the deep satisfaction of their mutual company.

It was Marston, a full hour and a half later, that eventually interrupted a quiet reverie that had turned to slumber, knocking persistently and admitting himself to find them both emerging from a semi-sleep state. 'Would the gentlemen wish to join me and play for the crew on deck this evening? Our playing has been requested,' he declared.

'What say you, Simon?' asked Pat.

'With infinite pleasure; after supper, if that is convenient for the operation of this vessel,' Simon replied with particular satisfaction, looking closely at his friend's wide smile.

'Brother... may the hinges of our friendship never grow rusty.'

Some hours later the trio, Pat and Simon now more awake, emerged on the quarterdeck; the crew were sitting patiently along the gangways and on the forecastle, conversing in little more than whispers. The wintry evening was fine and dry but the temperature was cooling noticeably, and all on deck were dressed for warmth. From far across the lagoon Messalonghi remained very visible; the lights from houses were now beginning to be seen as the dusk set in, reflecting as weak shimmering ripples on the flat, still water. The trio began with an old favourite, the third movement of Mozart's *third violin concerto*, the light and delicate playing accompanied by the crew tapping their heels on the deck, the music now almost as familiar to them as it was to the musicians. As the piece closed a general round of applause came from the crew and the musicians nodded their heads in appreciation. Then came music from Bach, Boccherini and Corelli, all received by increasing applause until they reached their finale, the wonderful solo *Caprice Twenty-Four* from Paganini, played by Marston. Although he could not approach the genius of Paganini, never did any of the assembly enjoy hearing a piece so much as they did that evening. It was a memorable occasion, the crew in great heart, the joyous satisfaction of all with Simon's return so obviously endemic. The music had been played far into the night with such heartfelt vibrancy and zest, and a memory of those moments would be cherished by all for the rest of their lives. At the end the crew clapped until their hands were sore and stamped their feet until the officers became concerned for the deck – unwarranted concern as almost all were barefoot. The trio looked at each other in deep satisfaction, then stood and took their bow before retiring to the cabin.

'A wonderful day, Simon,' whispered a very emotional Pat.

Monday 5ᵗʰ January 1824　　　　*aboard Surprise, Messalonghi*

In the early hours of the dawn, with thin shafts of light permeating the darkness from behind low cloud, Pat awoke and stepped briskly to his quarterdeck to look about at the sea state, the weather and to check for any sighting or report of any ships. Far visibility remained obscured by mists arising from the sea surface and *Surprise* rocked gently in the slight swell. Pat, bereft of anything save his shirt and breeches, shivered in the cold northerly wind. To his astonishment, anchored a bare fifty yards off from *Surprise*, was the mistico on which Lord Byron and Abel Jason had embarked in Cephalonia and later sailed from Zante. He spoke quietly with a descending watchman who declared that the mistico had arrived, according to their fellows previously atop, at six bells of the First watch, and that no one had thought that its arrival warranted waking their captain from his slumbers. The master, Mr Prosser, had been on duty when it arrived, declaring, 'The Captain needs more his rest than an awakening with news of a boat scarcely bigger than a fishing boat, even one on which Lord Byron might or might not be travelling.'

A growing number of Surprises gazed over towards the mistico. Little activity could be seen on her deck until at seven bells of the morning watch the mistico's boat sheered off from her side. It was bringing back Abel Jason to *Surprise*. By now many more of *Surprise's* crew had emerged on deck, including Simon, and whilst Jason's welcome could scarcely resemble that displayed for Simon, he was nevertheless very warmly greeted by all present as he stepped aboard, particularly Simon, before being hastened off to the cabin for breakfast with Pat, Simon and Tom Pickering.

As they settled at Pat's table, Jason began his account to an eager audience. 'We had remained three days in Dragomestre after our escape from the Turk frigate... until a Greek gunboat, sent by Mavrocordato from Messalonghi, arrived to take us there. However, his Lordship declined the offer and determined to reach Messalonghi free of obligation and in his own vessel, and so we set off again in the mistico. We later stranded on the Scrofes rocks, his Lordship urging his attendants into the water to push us off whilst the Greek crew did nothing but fluster and lament their ill fortune. Fletcher - his Lordship's valet - and three or four servants struggled valiantly and shamed the Greek crew into assistance until we were off. More Greek gunboats arrived the next morning, and in their company we have been beating all the way against the wind until we arrived yesterday evening, too late to navigate the shoals into Messalonghi, but we espied *Surprise* and tied up as near alongside her as we dared in the darkness.' Jason concluded his story but added as an afterthought, 'His Lordship is undaunted by his near capture and demise. He remains in good heart for this venture. I admire him greatly.'

'And rightly so! His Lordship is a pearl amongst a bed of thorns,' Pat opined. 'Are you acquainted with his Lordship's plans, Jason?'

'I believe that he is preparing even now to go ashore, leaving at about ten o'clock.'

'Well,' said Pat, 'we will postpone our own sailing for one day and accompany his Lordship ashore. His Lordship is deserving of our escort. Mr Pickering, prepare my barge and its crew, as best dressed as they can muster, if you will. The barge is to be priddied particularly well today... fit for a Lord; for a Lord it is we will be carrying.'

'Aye aye, sir,' said Pickering, nodding, a smile on his face.

At 10 a.m. Pat's barge came alongside the mistico, and Barton with great care assisted Lord Byron down the side and into the seat alongside Pat. Simon and Jason sat in the seat ahead of and facing them. The crew had plainly done their best: all of the old *Tenedos* hands had donned their old watchet-blue jackets - retrieved from the depths of their dunnage - which had never before been seen on *Surprise*, and they had buffed the brass buttons until they shone brightly. Others without jackets of their own had begged the loan of them from their shipmates. All were attired in clean, starched and pressed white duck trousers, in little shoes highly polished to gleaming black and wore low-crowned hats with the customary ribbon with the ship's name to the fore – run up by Whitaker, a mainmast hand who had been a tailor before being pressed in the year 'eleven. The barge crew's long pigtails had plainly all been combed out before being tidily replaited, and a better turned out barge crew Pat had never seen. 'Very creditable, lads, well done,' he said, filled with pleasure and reflecting that his crew did justice to the old saying: *You can always tell a ship by her boats*.

Byron himself was attired in a clean and freshly pressed red cloak, undoubtedly of military origin. He was wearing a golden metal helmet resembling something of ancient origin.

'Ancient Greek perhaps?' wondered Simon. He looked closely at Byron for a moment or two before speaking, Byron noticing his gaze. 'My Lord, I am but recently become an admirer, and speaking with the greatest presumption, a friend, for I hope that is how you may consider of me... and if you will forgive my remarks, your arrival in this place is of the very deepest significance. Might I say therefore... with infinite respect, that your cloak is most symbolically suited to your purpose this day, though perhaps the helmet less so? We may consider that the Greek need is for modern arms and such a helmet may strike the observer as a relic.'

Byron considered the comment for a few seconds before leaning forward to grasp Simon's hand and replying, 'Thank you, Ferguson; that is a most prescient thought. I venture you are too polite to say what you really meant... that I look like a buffoon. It would please me were you to keep the helmet as some small memento of my friendship for you too, for indeed that is my sincerest perception of you,' and with that he removed the helmet and placed it in the bottom of the barge.

'Welcome, my Lord,' said Pat warmly, marvelling at the spirit and generosity of the man, his humanity so evident, yet preserving a humility that oft escaped others elevated to such heights.

'Thank you, O'Connor,' Byron replied, taking and shaking Pat's hand, smiling all about him; to Pat's scrutinising eye, the barge crew all plainly feeling honoured to be there in his presence.

'Barge away, Mr Pickering... row dry, Barton!' ordered Pat.

The sun was now free of the south-eastern cloud and shining brightly as they rowed across the calm, still waters of the lagoon, the winter day warming as the morning had passed. Byron's arrival had been observed by the Greek ships anchored off the town, which fired their guns in salute as he passed by within Pat's barge. Word had also reached the town itself because the fortress began to echo the gunfire of the ships. Another twenty minutes steady rowing by the crew, none wishing to splash their most honoured passenger ever, and the barge pulled up on the beach of the town. Pat sprang ashore, helping Byron from the barge. Huge cheers broke out from the waiting crowd, which surged around the arrivals. Duncan, Pat was pleased to see, was standing alongside Mavrocordato, and although he had long claimed complete recovery from his head injury of the summer, the recuperative benefits of a month ashore in relative rest had served him well, Pat thought. Prince Mavrocordato in all his ceremonial finery, stepped forward to welcome Byron, grasping his hand as the rest of the barge crew scrambled to the beach, the crowd cheering still and the guns of the town continuing to fire their loud welcome in the background: fully a twenty-one gun salute.

GLOSSARY, for pressed shipmates

Bargeman................weevil (usually in the bread and biscuit)
Blunties ....Old Scots term for stupid fellows
Boggies....................Irish country folk
Bombard..................Mediterranean two-masted vessel, ketch
Bower......................bow anchor
Breeks......................Scots term for trousers or breeches
Bumbo....................'pirates' drink; rum, water, sugar, and nutmeg
Burgoo....................oatmeal porridge
Captains' Thins........Carr's water crackers, a "refined ship's biscuit"
Caudle....................thickened, sweetened alcoholic drink like eggnog
Clegs........................Scots term for large, biting flies
Crubeens..................boiled pig's feet
Dreich......................Old Scots for cold, wet, miserable weather
Drookit....................Scots term for drenched
Etesian....................strong, dry, summer, Aegean north winds
Felucca....................small sailing boat, one or two sails of lateen rig
Fencibles..................the Sea Fencibles, a naval 'home guard' militia
Flat..........................a person interested only in themself
Flux..........................inflammatory dysentery
Gomerel....................a stupid or foolish person
The Groyne..............La Coruña in north-west Spain
Hallion....................a scoundrel
Hoy..........................small (e.g. London-Margate passengers) vessel
Jollies......................Royal Marines
Kedgeree..................a dish of flaked fish, rice and eggs
Kentledge..................56lb ingots of pig iron for ship's ballast
Laudanum................a liquid opiate, used for medicinal purposes
Lobscouse................beef stew, north German in origin
Marchpane..............marzipan
Marshalsea..............19th century London debtors' prison
Mauk......................Scottish for maggot
Meltemi ....Greek and Turkish name for the Etesian
Millers....................shipboard rats
Mistico....................similar to the Felucca sailing vessel
Nibby......................ship's biscuit
Puling......................whining in self pity
Scrovies ....worthless, pressed men
Solomongundy........a stew of leftover meats
Snotties..................midshipmen
Stingo......................strong ale
Treacle-dowdy........a covered pudding of treacle and fruit

Trubs.........................truffles
Yellow jack...............Yellow fever (or flag signifying outbreak)

I hope that you have enjoyed reading this book in my series
"The continuing voyages of HMS Surprise".

You can find out more about my books by visiting my website:
https://alanlawrenceauthor.wordpress.com/

Alan Lawrence